Blue Sky Tomorrows

A Novel in the *Triorion* universe

By L.J.Hachmeister

Novels by L.J.Hachmeister

Triorion: The Series

Triorion: Awakening (Book One)
Triorion: Abomination (Book Two)
Triorion: Reborn, part I (Book Three)
Triorion: Reborn, part II (Book Four)

Triorion Universe

Blue Sky Tomorrows

Forthcoming

Shadowless – Outlier (Volume One)
Triorion: Nemesis (Book Five)
The Laws of Attraction
Corbyn Black: The Demon's Kiss

Short Stories/Anthologies

"The Gift," from *Triorion: The Series*
"Heart of the Dragon," from *Dragon Writers*
"Prisoner 141," from *Parallel Worlds – The Heroes Within*
"Soul Song," from *Unlocking the Magic: A Fantasy Anthology*
"The Waking of Jim Walker," from *Crash Philosophy*

This book is dedicated to Noelle and Yuko
for saving more than just this universe

"Be a rainbow in someone else's cloud."

— Maya Angelou

Blue Sky Tomorrows

Chapter 1

On Cam's tenth birthday, the skies turned black. He ran out of their apartment, forgetting the cardboard cutout of a birthday cake, and his sisters who did their best to assemble some kind of meal as his mother screamed for him to get back inside. He had to see, he had know what sent deep, bass vibrations that unsettled the flimsy walls and floors of his home, scrambled the digital interfaces on the sidewalk advertisements, and turned all the radio broadcasts into static.

Cam stopped halfway down the crumbling front stairs, his neck craned. Behemoth warships scored the Cerkan sky, blotting out the sun, casting a great shadow over the city. His entire body vibrated from the rumbling ships' engines.

Red insignia on the wings.

His heartrate doubled.

The United Starways Coalition.

As his mind wrapped around the galactic military's arrival, sirens cried out.

"Camzen, get inside!" his mother slurred, stumbling out of the door, brown bottle in hand. She tipped forward, catching herself on the iron railing. "It's not safe."

Cam ignored her. How did she know? Not safe was a single-bedroom, east-side apartment crammed with five people, and a mother who drank herself into oblivion each day. Or long winters with no heat and scavenging for food in back alleys and dumpsters. Not this. This was something else, a monstrosity, another world, bigger than his, colliding—

Kara burst through the front door, dodging their teetering mother, and ran to him.

"Hide," she said, grabbing his hand.

But Cam resisted, transfixed by the interstellar juggernauts and the swarms of fighters dropping from their open bellies.

"Cam!" Kara, ten years older and stronger than him, yanked him inside. "Help me with the others."

Dazed, he didn't realize what she asked him until she gathered up their entire lot—his drunk mother and two other sisters—and guided them down into the utility room in the basement.

No electricity flowed through the broken lightbulbs, but the lone, rectangular window, smeared with dirt and debris, let in enough light for him to make out the bulbous shapes of the water heaters and furnaces, and the silvery webs that connected them. He didn't like the damp smell, or the smoke residue from whatever maintenance person came down here under the guise of work.

"Keep Em and Sarh safe," she said, trying to comfort the four-year-old twins as they sobbed and clung to her leg. Prying them off, Cam led his little sisters over to the driest spot and sat them while Kara tended to their mother.

"It's those *chakking* leeches!" his mother slurred.

"Shhh, mama," Kara said, brushing back her peppered hair and guiding her down as she collapsed against one of the inert furnaces. "Everything will be alright."

Still clutching her bottle, the inebriated woman muttered another slew of expletives as her eyelids drooped shut. Kara took off her jacket and covered their mother, making sure to tuck in the sides.

The walls rattled, shaking the dust from the ceiling and unsettling the spiderwebs. Em and Sarh whimpered, hanging on to one another. Cam did his best, putting his arm around them, but they didn't calm to him the way they would have to Kara's solace.

Other families crowded inside as the steady thumping of gunfire and bombs drew closer. Still new to the complex, Cam didn't recognize half of the dirty-faced kids or the slow-moving adults Kara helped to find a place to sit or lie. Some of the younger adults approached Kara, talking to her in low whispers while everyone else cried or hid their faces.

He didn't like the congested smell of unwashed bodies in a cramped space, the way the old woman next to him coughed and hacked, or how the twins pushed his arm off, whispering to each other in their secret language. He especially didn't like his mother, oblivious to another attack by the USC, unable to do anything but lie there, head drooping, and snoring loudly for all the rest of the complex to see. He stared at her, wishing her to wake up, to see how he didn't cry anymore, and after five years of being fatherless—motherless—cold, hungry, tried, angry, afraid—he didn't need her anymore.

But he did need someone.

"You okay?" Kara asked, kneeling in front of him. Her brown eyes, much like his, searched for the answer he would not give her.

An explosion, this one closer than the one before it, shook the building, making the children and adults cry out.

Cam nodded.

"It's going to be okay."

When he didn't respond, she repeated herself, this time taking his hand. "It's going to be okay, sweet boy. I won't let anything happen to us."

She said it with such sincerity, such authority, that despite all that had happened, all that had been stamped into him by the street-slums, by terrorism and death, moved aside, allowing something he wouldn't let himself feel. Not unless Kara said it.

The lopsided-smile, the one that inevitably came with her ridiculous giggle, lightened her face. "Cam-cam, don't make me sing it."

He bit his lip, not wanting her to, and wanting her to at the same time.

"Alright then. *Rain drops a fallin' today*," she sang just above a whisper, "*washin' all our tears away. But the sun will come again, and take away our sorrows. Just hold out, my love—*"

She kissed his forehead.

"*—for blue sky tomorrows.*"

Blue sky tomorrows.

Her promise since their father was killed and their mother withdrew; since their entire world was ripped apart by the telepath wars.

"I got you," Kara said, pinching his side. He squirmed, but she only doubled her attack until he relented and met her gaze with a smile.

"How about we play our game?" she asked, settling into a cross-legged position.

"Now?"

"Why not?"

Cam pulled at the knots in his shredded shoe laces and shrugged.

"Okay," Kara said, closing her eyes and conjuring their imaginary pieces. "I've got four knights, one paladin, and a queen. You've got a mage and a hawk. Twenty by twenty board, elimination only."

"Come on!" Cam exclaimed. Not that she ever made their strategy games easy. Yes, his hawk wouldn't take any damage unless his mage got hit, but two against six much stronger opponents didn't seem fair.

"Okay, since it's your birthday—you get first move."

"Oh, gee, thanks."

"You're welcome."

Cam sighed, thinking through the moves. Kara loved making up games to play with him, from memorization to word play, but strategy games, especially this one which she insisted be played in their heads, always tripped him up. *But why is she making this one so hard?* Usually she gave him a chance.

Frustrated, he picked at the peeling rubber on his shoe. "It's impossible."

"No, think it through," Kara said, calm and intent.

I can't do it. He dug his fingernails into the worn bottoms of his shoes as the seconds ticked by. Every time he failed to think of the winning move, he felt like he failed her, embarrassed himself, falling short of whatever expectation she had for him.

Then it struck him. *She's a strategist, I'm not.*

She expected some kind of coordinated attack with his mage and his hawk to draw out her forces, surround them, and strike down her pieces in one swoop. He couldn't do that, or at least he couldn't see how. *But I can play her.*

"Hawk, b2 to g5."

She countered, bringing her knights to attack formation.

"Hawk to b2."

She followed, her queen protecting the rear.

10

"Hawk to f5."

Puzzled, she sent out her paladin, dividing her forces, leaving an opening that—if he were smarter—he might have been able to exploit.

"Hawk to h3."

"Are you thinking this through?" she asked, frustration in her voice as she diverted her attention to his mage.

He sent his mage on the run, letting his hawk continue in a random flight pattern.

After five minutes of his nonsensical moves, she crossed her arms and scowled. "For real, Cam?"

He continued on. "Mage to h3."

"You're just running away."

Another five minutes passed as she chased him around the board, bombs thumping away, shaking the dust from the ceiling.

"Alright, I'm calling it," Kara said, throwing up her arms.

"Great, I win."

"You didn't win—you ran away."

"You gave up. That's elimination, isn't it?"

Kara's expression went from frustration to amusement. "So that was your strategy?"

Cam diverted his eyes. "I'm not smart enough to beat you on the board. All I could do was stall and hope you got annoyed enough to quit."

"But you are smart," Kara said, leaning forward and tousling his hair. "You identified the real threat—me, not the game pieces. And you figured out your opponent's weakness."

"Pesky little brothers?"

"You got that right," she laughed. Taking one of his hands in both of hers, she whispered, "remember something for me, okay?"

"Huh?" he said, not understanding the sudden serious shift in her tone.

"This place. This war, this misery; it can bring out the worst in people, Cam-cam." She glanced over to their mother but returned her gaze with an extra squeeze of his hand. "I love you; there is love in your heart. Don't let anybody—anything—take that away, make you forget who you really are."

He tilted his head, confused, trying to understand what she meant.

"Kara."

A handsome man with blondish hair, blue eyes, and serious expression called to her from underneath the rectangular window. He stood there expectantly, canvas backpack slung over his shoulder, holding the one of the straps with a fingerless glove. Kara let go of Cam's hand, but gave him another pat on the head before joining the man.

Cam didn't like him. Something about his clothes didn't fit, even though they looked like any of the other rags and second-hand-shop attire the rest of them wore. Maybe it was his posture—perfectly erect, with muscular shoulders that filled out his soiled jacket. Or the way he looked at his sister, the directness of his focus, as he whispered whatever he didn't want overheard.

Standing on her tip-toes, Kara gazed out the dirty window, said a few words to the man, and then returned to Cam.

"Cam—the bombings have stopped. I'm going to go check if it's safe. Stay here."

"No," Cam said, scrambling to his feet as she followed the blonde man to the door. Not after what happened last time. There could be ground troops, drones, a second bombing run—

"Give me a second," Kara whispered to the man. Cam narrowed his eyes at him as he gave his sister the hand signal to make her exchange quick.

"Don't leave," Cam said, grabbing on to her jacket.

"I need to make sure it's safe."

"Let someone else go," he said, knowing the futility of his argument.

"Who?" she said, nodding at the handful of adults. Cam didn't look, not wanting to see their poor conditions, debilitated by disease, neglect, or malnutrition, especially their mother.

"Let someone else go," he insisted.

"But this is how I can help."

"Help who?"

"Anyone I can," she said, holding on to his grip.

"How?"

"Look at these people, Cam."

Cam glanced again over his shoulder, seeing their lowered gazes, shaking hands; hearing their whimpers and muffled sobs of the children.

"Maybe I can't win this war, but I can be brave for these people. Even the smallest gesture can mean so much, like checking for an all-clear." Kara nodded toward their mother, slumped over and mumbling into her bottle. "Without hope, there is no tomorrow."

Cam let her go.

Sliding down to a sitting position, Cam sat against the utility room door, waiting and listening for any sound to indicate Kara's return. The twins wandered back over to him, opening and closing their hands, asking for any remnant of food from his previous day's search. When he turned out his pockets, showing them nothing but lint and crumbs, they both curled up next to him, too exhausted to put up a fight.

"Those *chakking* leeches will kill us all!"

Cam made himself smaller, hoping that no one else would associate his mother's drunken exclamations against telepaths with his presence, or that of his sisters. But no one stirred, not even throwing so much as a casual glance her way.

"They killed him—they killed my Yashin," she sobbed, covering her eyes and shrinking into herself. "*Chakking* leeches. Death of this world. Death of this galaxy. Kill them all!"

"Pssst, Cam."

Colin, the boy from the floor above them, snuck over on his hands and knees to sit by him. Any other time, Cam would have distanced himself from their overly friendly neighbor, but at that moment, he welcomed any distraction to get his mind off of his raving mother and the mention of their dead father.

"You hungry?"

Cam looked around, careful that their interaction wouldn't be overheard. With the war between the United Starways Coalition and Cerka, his homeworld, in its third year, not many went to bed each night with a full belly, and any mention of food tested even the strongest bonds between people in a starving population.

Colin, a bright boy who would have excelled in school if it hadn't been blown away two years ago, understood the protocol just as well as Cam. Turning his back to the rest of the refugees, he

13

produced two blue mints from the flap of his ragged overalls. Something that, long ago, Cam would have taken out of a restaurant bowl in handfuls and tossed at his sisters on the hovercar ride home. Now, despite the dirtied plastic wrapping and age cracks splitting the blue discs, he salivated, anticipating the sweet treat that would tease his empty stomach.

"Where'd you get those?" Cam asked.

"That guy that was talking to your sister. He had more."

"Candy?"

"No, military rations."

Cam frowned. It didn't make sense. Military rations, as opposed to the less caloric, nutrient-deprived civilian rations handed out by the relief organizations, were hard to come by, even for the bigger street rubs and the organized gangs.

"Share?"

Cam accepted the candy, but put it in his pocket as Colin popped it in his mouth.

"What's wrong? You should eat it."

"I'll wait," he said, stomach gurgling as he thought about how he'd split it four ways. "Thanks."

Still turned away from the rest of the group, Colin rested his forehead against the faded brick wall, his cheeks sucked in as he savored the mint.

"Those *chakking* leeches," his mom babbled, smashing her bottle into one of the water heaters. Two older men tried to calm her as she flailed and cried. "Yashin...they killed my Yashin. Those leeches brought this war! They brought the USC!"

"I hate this place," Cam whispered, pulling his sisters in closer and looking away from his mother.

Colin chuckled. "Yeah, I'm getting out."

"No one gets out."

"My cousin on Neel got out. Took the Dominion entrance exam and got sent to the academy the next day. Pretty sweet deal I hear. And you get to kick some USC *assino*."

Cam didn't believe him for a second. The USC ships had been attacking Cerka for years, and despite years of dutifully paying tribute to the Sovereign, not a single Dominion ship came to lend aid to the dwindling planetary forces. And now that the USC brought their warships, their biggest interstellar vessels, it would only be a matter of days before what was left of the Cerkan government surrendered. The telepaths—the *leeches*—had won. They would be released from prisons, and granted back their citizenship, despite the threat they posed.

Still, he asked: "Where... where do you take the test?"

Colin twirled the messy dark hair that reached his shoulders, eyes glinting. "In a couple weeks we're supposed to meet at the old arcade. The CCWF is hosting at some secret place."

Concerned Citizens for World Freedom. The biggest anti-telepath movement on the planet, the group that his father pledged his life to after a leech stole his position at the factory. The one that convinced his mother that their father's death, a supposed critical sacrifice during the anti-telepath demonstrations, meant the freedom of Cerka.

"Don't go."

Colin frowned. "Why? It's safe."

Cam disagreed. Nothing about the hate group was safe. Still, he couldn't argue the desire to leave, to get out of the ruined city by any means possible.

"Look, my mom... she isn't doing so well," Colin said, looking over his shoulder at the shivering woman hugging her threadbare sweater to her skeletal frame. "If I don't join, then..."

He didn't have to say it. They all knew what happened to orphaned kids in a war-torn city.

Hiding his tears with a quick wipe of his sleeve, Colin brought his bare feet underneath him and offered Cam a quick piece of advice: "You should sign-up, Cam, before it fills up. Dunno when it'll happen again."

As Colin returned to his mother, Cam decided he couldn't wait any longer. *Gotta check on Kara.*

Sliding out from underneath the twins, he stood up and pressed his ear against the utility room door, listening for any warning signs. Stillness. Quiet. It almost unnerved him more than the bombs.

"Where you going? Camzen!" his mother cried. "Get back here!"

In one quick movement, Cam opened and shut the utility door behind him. He paused, holding his breath as he looked and listened.

15

No movement up the cement stairs that led to the apartment complex entrance; only the whistling of the winds between the boarded-up windows and the leaves skittering through the sparkling sea of shattered glass and broken fixtures from previous attacks.

Cam tip-toed up the stairs, mindful of the slightest movements. Afternoon light, dimmed by the starship blockade, filtered through the windows in dusty yellow beams. He followed the fresh footsteps through the debris and peeked out the front door.

The air stunk of bomb-discharge, making him cough and cover his nose with his sleeve. Eyes stinging, he gazed down the block, but the haze of brown smoke and poor light made it impossible to see more than a few houses down.

His better sensibilities questioned his actions: *Go back. It isn't safe.*

But he couldn't. Not after spotting the same treads in the dust-covered walkway leading out into the streets.

Where did Kara go? She was just supposed to check—not go out into the battle.

Keeping his eyes and ears peeled, Cam walked down the block, the apartment complex disappearing behind him. Gunfire and sirens sounded off in the distance.

It isn't over.

(Where is Kara?!)

Cam darted his eyes back and forth from bullet-pocked structures to collapsed rooftops. He didn't recognize anything. Up ahead, where the corner store, pawn shop, dingy old laundromat sat, he spotted a smoldering pile of rubble. Dark figures, bent into unrecognizable shapes, moaned underneath the fallen beams and walls.

Those are—

Bodies. People.

bloody—

Cam couldn't process it all. He wanted to look away, to run screaming back to the underground utility room, and curl up with his mother. But as he turned, his eye caught the same blonde-haired man he saw earlier kneeling next to his opened backpack, speaking into what looked like a rectangular communications unit. Next to him, a

16

young woman with pink-streaked hair hunched over a bloodied man, tending to his wounds.

Kara.

He did something stupid. Something against what all of his years of surviving in the war-torn city taught him.

"Kara!" he cried out, running out to her.

Don't alert the drones, the soldiers—it's not safe—go back—

Not without Kara.

"Kara!" he screamed again, trying to get her attention as the ground shook.

She whipped her head toward the sound of his voice, unable to find him as a thunderous boom reverberated all around them.

Losing his bearings in the commotion, Cam tripped, landing hard on his chest, knocking the wind from his lungs. Gasping for air, he rolled onto his back as black drones whizzed past.

Run—

As he scrambled to his feet, the first bomb dropped behind him, catapulting him forward and onto his side. Cam heard a snap just before pain lanced up his left arm and into his shoulder. Blood and bits of broken asphalt covered his tongue and lined his mouth, making him gag.

Kara—

Pushing himself up with his good arm, Cam caught a glimpse of the black-winged viper before the attack ship disappeared into the smoke.

"Cam!"

Kara.

Amidst the chaos, he saw her. Kara, his older sister, the only person who cared about him in the whole world, running toward him, arms outstretched as the dark skies fell.

Chapter 2

Cam stirred amongst a confusion of arguing voices.

"We can't take him, Niks."

Everything hurt, and opening his eyes made the world wobble and spin. He caught glimpses of two figures above him, both female, one with a partially shaved head and unusual orange-colored eyes. Shouting and gunfire echoed in the distance, making it hard to discern their words.

Where is my sister? he wanted to ask, though his words came out in a jumble.

"We can't…leave him."

The ground rumbled, and what felt like hot rain stung his face. Cam groaned and squirmed, but gentle hands held him down.

"…at max capacity… Niks… the vipers are headed..."

Something cool pressed against his aching left arm. At first, he jerked it away, but firm hands brought it back to a bent position, and the coolness returned.

A thunderclap boomed overhead. Screams and shouts filled the air.

"We have to go—now—"

The coolness ripped away, and the pain to his arm returned. Cam forced his eyes open to see what beast wailed in his ears, what sent reverberations through his chest. A transport ship the size of city block hovered a few meters off the ground, ramp descended for the armored USC soldiers to jump back aboard. Smoke and embers swirled through the air as the transport's glowing engines perturbed the ruined environment.

Cam coughed and brought his uninjured arm to shield his face and eyes as the transport ship tilted on its side, blasting him with heat and wind. Through his fingers, he spotted two soldiers hauling the body of a bloody, unconscious person up the ramp, carrying them by the feet and under their armpits.

Is that—?

A woman with pink-streaked hair.

"Kara," he rasped, struggling to his feet.

The ramp retracted as the soldiers and his sister disappeared into the gray belly of the ship, thrusters flaring.

"Kara!" Cam stumbled across the broken pavement, banging his shins against canted slabs and scraping his hands as he crawled and clawed his way toward the rising starship.

Missiles streaked across the sky. Cam screamed with all the breath left in his lungs as formation of vipers descended from the clouds.

"Run!"

A hand clamped down around his right wrist and yanked him away.

Cam tripped, but a pair of arms steadied him.

Colin.

"Come on!" he screamed, pulling on Cam to follow him as he picked his away across the street and down the alley connecting them to another row of fallen buildings. Colin wouldn't let up, even as Cam begged for him to stop.

"Kara—they have Kara!"

"We have to hide!"

The ground quaked as more bombs fell from the darkened skies and smoke pumped into the air. If not for Colin's strong grip, Cam wouldn't have kept his feet, not with the dizzying barrage of flashing lights and deafening sound.

Finally, after taking him down the subway tunnels, Colin let go. Cam collapsed against the green-tiled wall of a ticket booth heaving for breath as the steady *thump-thump* of bombs came down from above. The red emergency lights strung along the wall flickered, threatening to pitch them in full darkness.

"You okay?"

Cam didn't answer. Tears stung his eyes as he crossed his arms to hide his shaking hands.

"What happened to your arm?"

Cam looked down at the torn sleeve of his sweater. A reddened, raised area marked his forearm, but no obvious bone deformity. He remembered the sharp pain, hearing the snap—

The coolness, those voices…

Did someone repair it? It still ached, but—

No. That didn't matter. The smoke, dead bodies, the howling sirens, the USC transport, armored soldiers—

Kara.

"Hey…"

Cam finally regarded Colin. Blood stained his overalls, and a sizeable clotted gash cut across the side of his face. Still, he couldn't think of anything but the heavy, urgent feeling carving into his chest.

They took her. The USC took Kara.

Those rat-chakkers!

"I've got to go back," Cam said, using the wall to steady himself as he got to his feet.

Eyes glazing over, Colin shuffled back a few steps, then plopped down. "Everyone's gone, Cam."

At first, he didn't understand. Kara was still alive, he just had to find her—

Then, the inflection, the weight, of Colin's words sunk in.

Everyone. Gone.

Feeling light-headed, Cam sank back down. As waves of nausea washed over his stomach and up his throat, he tried to think of something good, something right in the world, as he imagined their apartment complex reduced to rubble, and all the residents—

Mom

Em, Sarh

—buried inside. He gripped his sore arm and brought his knees to his chest, remembering his sister's face, her sweet voice, the way she smiled as she sang their song of promise:

"…But the sun will come again, and take away our sorrows. Just hold out, my love, for blue sky tomorrows…"

"I can't," he whispered, shutting his eyes.

"Huh?"

"Nothing," Cam said, letting anger seep into his words to mask his tears.

"I'm scared, Cam," Colin whispered, his voice on the edge of breaking.

The emergency lights sputtered, then dimmed, as another series of bombs dropped not far from their location.

Cam clutched his knees to his chest and waited for the coming darkness.

***

Cam woke up in a crimson pool of light, panicked and confused by the windowless, dank surroundings. Then, as the pain of his injuries reasserted themselves, he spotted the subway signage dangling by a nail over the ticket booth and remembered his circumstances.

Black skies.

Kara leaving.

(They're gone.)

But before despair could settle into his bones, he clung to what he remembered: Kara, taken by the USC, injured and weak, but alive.

I have to get her back.

"Colin?" he said, voice echoing down the subway stairs and into the shadows. No sound, not even the thumping of bombs.

As he moved to get up, he noticed three dried pieces of fruit carefully arranged on a piece of flattened newspaper at his feet. Treasures in a decimated city where little food could be found.

Kara's voice sliced into his mind: *"...Even the smallest gesture can mean so much..."*

Colin. His stomach gurgled.

Why? Why would that stupid kid share his food with him—and then take off?

Cam took one of the dried pieces of fruit and placed it in his cheek, savoring the sweet, leathery taste as he stuffed the other two in his pants pocket.

He's probably searching for supplies, or scouting...

Either way, Cam figured he would come back, a smile on his face, enthusiastic about whatever he found in the wasteland. He'd want to stick together, to form a partnership—

No, he thought, urgency spurring him to his feet and back up the crumbling steps. The thought bothered him much more than he could understand, enough to dull the ache of his injuries and anxieties tightening his chest as he stepped onto the broken street.

21

He squinted, eyes adjusting to the yellow morning light muted by the haze as he surveyed the wreckage. The few buildings that survived stood gutted, with entire floors exposed or blown out. The USC warships, gone from their low station, left behind a new darkness. Black smoke chugged from the eastern fires, filling the sky, keeping the world in shadows.

Cerka, his homeworld, Calenthia, his city, gone. Kara, missing, the rest of his family dead.

As anger and despair churned in his gut, he thought of his mother, of the emptiness in her eyes, the waste of her body; the absence he felt in her since his father's death.

"Without hope, there is no tomorrow."

Cam turned his gaze to the horizon, stuffing down his fears with the promise he made to himself.

No tomorrows. Just today, and whatever he had to do to survive, to find Kara.

Eyes misting, he repeated to himself his own words, hardening himself to the consequences, as he reentered the city alone.

***

Fear and hunger distorted Cam's sense of time, bloating and elongating the hour, or reducing it into a haphazard blur of events. As he wandered the streets and back alleys in search of food and shelter in the cold Calenthian fall, one day bled into the next, and with the skies blackened, he mistook the hour.

His sister had grilled it in to him years ago: Always find shelter before the sun set. The night brought out the worst kinds of monsters—scouts, troops, street gangs, thieves, wild dogs. But with the smoke clouding the skies, and the few working streetlights shining like floating beacons in the brown haze, he lost track.

Pulling his sweater tighter around his shoulders, he scanned the city block from behind the safety of a fallen arch from a caved-in department store. Not a soul in sight; only the sound of a loose street banner flapping against some bricks. He should have waited, listened for longer than a few seconds, paid attention to the hairs prickling on the back of his neck. But an empty belly tore him away from his hiding spot, propelling him to the back of an abandoned corner market, where a tipped-over dumpster spilled into the alley.

The sour, mingling odors should have sickened him, but having not eaten in days, the sight of fruit peels and candy wrappers in a sea of mish-mashed garbage hinted at a meal, something, anything, to quiet his aching stomach.

Rummaging through the soggy detritus, Cam didn't notice the grouping shadows behind him, or the clicking of claws against the pavement. Not until a low growl shook him from his search.

On his hands and knees, Cam spun around, coming face-to-face with a pack of three dogs. He knew the kind; the mangy, nocturnal strays that banded together, roaming the streets just like him, in search of food and shelter. Except this time, he wasn't with his sister and her friends and had no means to defend himself.

The one closest to him with red eyes and dirty-gray fur bared a mouth punctuated with pointed teeth, growling and snarling as the two others, flanking on both sides, mirrored his aggression. Cam froze, not sure what to do. The savage hunger in their eyes, the brutal need that drove their cooperation, meant only one thing.

I'm going to die.

The certainty struck him, shaking the scream from his throat. He grabbed whatever squishy, soaked item came up in his hands and flung it at them. The dogs ducked and skirted out of the way, but his distraction didn't last long.

Running as fast as he could down the alley, Cam made it as far as the front of the corner store when the first jaw clamped down on his ankle. Pain exploded up his leg. He screamed and kicked, trying to free himself as the second and third dog lunged, tackling him to the ground.

Teeth came at him, biting down into his arm, the side of his head. Blood gushed down his face and into his eyes and mouth, garbling his cries. As he gasped for air, the world narrowed down into flashes yellow teeth, crushing weight, tearing bites.

—help me—
I'm so sorry
Kara, please—
(My sister.)

Anger, hot and wild, ignited his ravaged body. His hands, near one of the dogs' face, found the soft of his eyes and dug his nails in until he felt a pop and something warm and gooey slather his fingers. A yelp, then a whimper, and a skittering of feet followed.

With his right hand freed, he slammed his fist into the second dog, spitting the bloody contents of his mouth at his face, trying to blind him. The dog backed off for a second, enough for him to grab a broken brick and try hitting him again, this time cracking the dog's skull.

Primitive instincts electrified his focus, dulled his pain. The last dog released his leg, but went for his throat. Cam shot up his arm just in time, but the dog clamped down around his upper forearm, thrashing him about. Fear and panic unmoored his thoughts as flesh tore from bone.

Kara's face, her infectious smile, flashed through his mind.

"...just hold out, my love..."

I can't—

"...for blue sky tomorrows."

Light. Blinding, white. Light that couldn't have come from the overhead streetlamp. His attacker released him, the dogs whimpered, withdrew. As shouts and gunfire cracked overhead, two of the dogs scattered, back into the dark recesses of the fallen buildings.

Voices, from somewhere nearby, rose over his ragged breaths.

"No way he's still alive."

"He's street rub. 'Course he'll survive. *Goddich* savages."

"You alive, kid?"

The question, spoken in Common with a southern accent, didn't make sense. Cam lay on the ground, chest heaving, blood obscuring his vision.

I don't know.

The light bobbed up and down as footsteps crunched down on the broken asphalt. Someone knelt down close to him, nudged him on the side. Without thinking, he flung out his fist, but a gloved hand caught it.

"Still got some fight left in you, huh?"

A strong arm lifted him to his feet, held him up until he wiped the blood from his eyes and steadied himself on his one good foot.

Several soldiers and an officer wearing blue and black uniforms stared at him, guns pressed to their chest. Their faces, hardened and grizzled by a merciless war, gave no hint of compassion.

The Dominion Core!

No, not quite. These men wore the uniforms, but they looked patched together, poorly fit.

Then it dawned on him as the officer handed him a rusted multi-phase gun.

These are loyalists; the militant sect of the CCWF, out patrolling the streets. The ones that fought for their freedom by any means possible.

Any means.

(Father—)

"Finish the job, kid."

Cam didn't understand. Not until the officer pointed at the dog he blinded twitching and writhing on the ground.

The gun felt heavy and awkward in his hand, the rusted grip grating against his palm. He'd never fired a gun, though he'd had many pointed at him on house raids or family detainments.

"Go on. Before him or his friends come back and finish you."

The thought of another mauling chilled him. Everything—his arms, legs, his face—throbbed and screamed, and when he imagined what he looked like now, mangled and forever scarred, the tension spread out across chest, ratcheting his anger.

But as he raised the gun, the dog somehow got his feet underneath himself and stumbled forward. Cam sucked in a breath and held it.

The man wearing the officer's uniform, chewing on the end of an unlit cigarette, bent down and whispered in his ear. "Kill the enemy before he's got a chance to kill you."

The gun shook in his grip, but the weight felt good, terrible, ready to inflict the damage he couldn't do with his bare hands. Still, the dog—alone and injured, separated from its pack—no longer threatened him. It whimpered and whined, shaking its head, unable to navigate in the new darkness.

"Show us you're a soldier," the officer said coolly, "and we'll take you back with us."

Cam tightened his grip. A warm bed, food and shelter—*survival.*

It attacked me, he justified to himself, grinding his teeth together and taking aim.

Kara, unwanted in the moment, popped in his mind. He didn't want to remember any of her lessons right then, her benevolence and empathy, or imagine what she'd do in that situation.

("It's going to be okay, sweet boy.")

No, to save Kara would take something more than what he was. He couldn't be merciful, not when the same pack of dogs could come back for him later. The whispering man was right. *Kill the enemy before he's got a chance to kill you.*

Cam shot once. Then, after the shock of the kick wore off, he shot a second, third, and fourth time, until he was hitting the trigger, and no more rounds came out.

The thought echoed up from somewhere inside him: *(It's not going to be okay. Not for me.)*

As the soldiers muttered amongst themselves, the man with the unlit cigarette stood tall, analyzing his shots. Cam hit the dog only once out of the four times, but right in the head. Not much of the dog's skull remained but a sizzling hole.

"You taking the Dominion entrance exam?" the man asked, looking him up and down.

Cam, still holding the gun in his hand, stared at the dead dog, wondering if its companions knew.

"You hear me, boy?"

"He's just a rub, Sarge."

"Nah. Not rubbish. This one's a fighter. Boy—you'd kill a leech just the same?"

Cam accidentally put weight on his mangled foot and fell over, eliciting a round of laughter from the soldiers.

"What you say, boy?" the man said, grabbing him by the collar and pushing his scarred forehead against his own. "You want to go kill them leech bastards and win this war?"

Cam, swallowing the lump of semi-coagulated blood in his mouth, tasted something new, something terrible; something that would allow him to become what he couldn't otherwise, what would help him save his sister.

Baring his bloodied teeth, he answered in a voice he didn't recognize. "I'll kill them all."

Chapter 3

Fever set his mind ablaze. At some point, after the soldiers lifted him into the truck bed and drove him away, Cam remembered looking down at his mauled arm, not believing the green and yellow pus already oozing from the bite marks. *I don't want to lose my arm.*

The thought came and went as he fought to keep his eyes open, shivering in the exposed back of the truck, as the soldiers drove him somewhere deep underground, into a maze of dugout shelters and subbasements. Hugging his injured arm close to his chest, trying to will the toxins out of his body, someone lifted him off the truck bed, and gruff voices discussed his fate.

"He's goin' lose that arm. Maybe that foot, too."

Chuckling, followed by the sound of someone spitting. "*Chakking* dogs. I'd rather get shot than bit."

"Last kid didn't make it more than three hours."

"You sayin' we shouldn't bother?"

Silence. Then, an answer that sounded flat and uninterested. "Nothing we can do about it."

Kara appeared at some point, standing behind the woman in a dirty surgical mask that tended to his wounds under a bright dome light. As much as he tried to speak, to call out to his sister, the words burned up in the back of his mouth, consumed by the flames of sickness.

Please, Kara—don't leave.

"I've done what I can," the woman said, removing her dirty surgical mask and bloodied rubber gloves. She stood next to the whispering man. Both regarded him with grave expressions. "But with his human genetics, and his injuries, he'll make a good martyr at best, Sarge."

"Ah, but a boy dying for a cause will make great headlines. That'll get the Sovereign's attention."

"He's dead one way or the other."

No, Kara—wait—

"Well, then use the derms on him. Make him cute, adorable; whatever will grab hearts."

"We're almost out."

"Then, just on his face."

No—please—Kara—

His body, scorched from the inside out, provided an uninhabitable residence, and he sought his only means of escape.

Sleep, dreams of yesterday, gave him comfort. He remembered his father's baritone laughter and his mother's embrace; the giggling fits of the twins, Kara dancing around the house, showing off her latest moves. Happy times, before the war—before the skies turned black, and all he loved was taken away.

When the flames died down, he woke up in his underwear on a cot, drenched in sweat. The room, carved from the ground, smelled like damp mud and wood. Medical posters adorned the wall, warning of potential diseases and infections on Cerka in bright orange letters. In contrast, someone had stacked up biohazard-labeled boxes and empty medicine vials against the opposite wall. Cam remembered the room in some vague recollection, knowing that he had been placed here as a last resort.

If I don't wake up, I'm dead. If I wake up, I'm dead.

Cam looked down at the limbs that had been mauled. Ugly lumps of grafted, mismatching flesh and zig-zagging sutures marred his arm. The grafted flesh looked older, dotted with black hair, as if it had come off of a middle-aged man. Before, he might have been squicked out. Now, as he flexed and extended his fingers, feeling their stiffness and the numbness along the palm, he didn't care. He didn't lose his arm.

Or my foot, he thought, rotating the swollen ankle. It felt just as strange and numb, but it didn't hurt, and seemed to function well enough.

With shaking hands, he brought up his fingers to his face. No lumps, no sutures, no loss of sensation. Even the bites on his skull had been repaired. *"Make him cute, adorable; whatever will grab hearts."*

Anger percolated through relief.

I'm not dead. I'm not dying. Not yet.

Standing on his good leg first, Cam tested his opposite foot on the ground, slowly adding pressure until it bore half of his weight. Pins and needles prickled the bottom of his heel, as if it had fallen asleep. Deciding it was good enough, Cam limped around the room searching for his boots, sweater, and pants amongst the piles of medical junk, instead finding a storage locker with a cache of old clothing: A woman's floral blouse, a red scarf with *brother* in old Cerkan stitched on the end, pairs of stained pants, a faded hoodie, and a beat-up pair of sneakers. Perhaps artifacts of others that had come before him, or a lost and found. Either way, he didn't hesitate, pulling on the pants, sneakers, and hoodie, ignoring the unusual body odors still clinging to their fabric, or the dark stains that stiffened areas of the cloth.

Wrapping the scarf around his face, he tried the only door to the room. A simple three-button lock kept the door closed. Kara taught him how to crack a lock before he could spell his name. Two minutes later, he picked about the keypad and panel, and crossed the wires. The door mechanism clicked, and the lock released.

Too easy.

He pushed it open, eliciting a loud creak, making him cringe.

He stuck his head out into an empty hallway. Overhead lights illuminated several other doors and a larger, open, lit chamber at the end. Hammering, electric saws, and the sound of men shouting at each other floated down to him. It smelled like tar vats, burning plastic and freshly-stamped iron; like the old mechanical factory his father worked at. Squinting, he made out the large wheels of a land rover, and the jagged face of a weaponized crawler. Modern war vehicles, not the antiquated vessels he'd seen at demonstrations months earlier.

This must be the CCWF base.

His father talked very little about his involvement in the group, only that the Dominion loyalists had acquired weapons and machines outside their planetary government to fight back against the USC. Cam just never expected them to be so well armed.

At the other end of the hall, Cam spotted stairs to a steel-plated door, and movement behind a barred window. Hoping that the stairs lead back up to the surface, he slunk down the hall, using the wall as balance.

Crouching below the window, he listened for movement, voices. *Are those... kids?*

Without thinking, Cam popped his head up to reconcile the laughter, the sound of excited chatter. Dozens of kids ranging from his younger sisters' age to late teens crowded inside a windowless place about the size and look of his old classroom. Holo-desks, arranged in five long rows, filled up the entire room. Most of the younger kids played games on the desks, giggling as animated creatures pranced across projected landscapes. The older kids flipped through military simulations or pulled up lewd material, teasing the quieter ones that had faded to the back of the room.

Cam didn't understand it at first. Not until one of the bigger kids slapped a boy with dark hair and overalls.

Colin.

"You dumb *assino*. You'll never get into the Core," the bigger kid laughed.

This is the secret Dominion Academy entrance exam testing site!

A few others joined in, mocking him, pointing at Colin's disheveled appearance, his dirty clothes. Not that their clothes looked much cleaner.

Cam almost didn't recognize him. His neighbor looked gaunt, on the verge of starvation. That didn't shock him as much as the deadness to Colin's expression, the light that vanished from his eyes. As if all the world had abandoned him.

Cam swallowed the lump building in his throat. *I have to find my sister.*

Yes, Kara. How could he find her, especially with the CCWF planning to use him as a martyr for their cause? He had to get out of the city, off of Cerka—out to the stars. But even then, how could he fight the USC on his own? He'd need a fleet.

The most powerful fleet in the galaxy.

Chewing on his thumbnail, he thought through his options, his stomach twisting and turning as he counted the kids and the desks.

Fifty and fifty. No chance to just sneak in.

A gray-haired adult in a fresh-pressed Dominion Core uniform entered the room through the door on the opposite side of the room. Cam bit down hard on his thumb as the man started writing on the interface board at the front of the room.

Only one way.

His stomach tightened, nausea clenching his throat.

(No tomorrows.)

Cam tested the door: locked and bolted, but from his side, as if to prevent the kids from getting in his area. As quietly as he could, he opened it up and slipped inside, angling himself to the back of the room. Most of the other kids were too distracted by their games and sims to pay him any attention, allowing him to walk over to the corner where Colin had taken refuge away from his tormentors.

Pulling down his scarf from his face, Cam whispered: "Colin."

"Cam!" The boy flung his arms around him, pulling him in close. Cam stiffened and pulled away.

"Don't do that."

"Sorry," Colin said, blushing.

"Follow me."

Without giving Colin a chance to ask questions, he slipped back to the door, waiting for Colin to exit before leading him to the room where he woke up.

"What's going on?" Colin asked, "why are you here? Are you taking the test too or something? I thought it was all full up."

"Did you sign in already?" Cam asked.

Colin shook his head. "No. They haven't assigned us a test yet," he said, scanning the room full of junk and medical equipment. "It's just starting."

The next moment happened in dreamlike separation. Cam saw himself unraveling the scarf as Colin turned away from him, and flinging it around the boy's neck. Twisting it tight, he yanked back, until Colin fell to the ground, his face turning red as he fought the noose around his neck.

"Don't fight it," Cam said as Colin clawed at his hands and arms, leaving red streaks on his newly-grafted tissue. "Don't fight it!" he repeated as Colin kicked the ground.

I don't want to—

"Finish the job, kid."

32

Cam lifted up as Colin jerked to the right. He heard a snap.

"No...No—no—no!" he cried, releasing the tension on the scarf and easing the gray-faced boy to the ground.

It wasn't supposed to be like this!

He was just supposed to go to sleep. Not—

Tears stung his eyes as he felt Colin's face. Still warm, no indication that—

(What have I done?)

Colin, the kind boy who only tried to help him. "Why did you fight it?" he whispered, clenching his shaking hands.

I'm so stupid. I didn't mean it; I'm so, so sorry.

(I'm a—)

He stopped himself.

Kara. Think of Kara.

He knew better. He had to be stronger, braver.

For her, he thought, turning over the cot to make it look like an accident. *No tomorrows.*

"No tomorrows," he repeated to himself. He took a handful of his hair in his hand and yanked hard enough to elicit a grunt. *(I can't be weak.)*

Running back down the hall, he snuck into the classroom just as the adult finished marking the interface board and turned.

"Find your seats and sign into your desks."

A few kids threw him a strange look, but none of them really cared enough to say anything or bring attention to the new kid sliding into the desk at the far back of the class.

With shaking hands, Cam typed in his name. CAMZEN FERROS, age 10.

His hand hovered over the delete key. *Colin Feller. It should read, Colin Feller, age 10.*

He chided himself. *NO TOMORROWS.*

"Testing will be by age only," the Core proctor announced as the words ENTRANCE EXAM popped up on Cam's screen. "No special consideration will be made for your species or education level."

The proctor changed the tone of his voice, as if he were reciting a line from a movie, exaggerating his emphasis: "The hour of battle is upon us. Will you take up arms against evil and injustice? Will you defend your family, your people, against the Dissembler threat? Do you have the courage to raise your right hand and take the military oath to become the heroes and the leaders of this galaxy?"

Dissemblers. Cam remembered the propaganda against the subspecies of telepaths. They were the reason for the Dominion's call to register and restrain all persons with psionic abilities, why the Cerkan government had decided to imprison its telepathic population. He remembered his father's words: *"Those bastards will rip you apart with their mind! Burn them all!"*

"Good luck, candidates," the proctor said as test questions populated on his desk. "Only the best and brightest will be selected for the Dominion Academy."

Cam stared at the first question, reading it over and over before his mind finally steadied enough for him to comprehend it.

"You and a civilian are trapped in a building. There is only one meal ration left. If you eat a full meal ration, you will survive long enough for a rescue. If you split the ration, you may not. Do you:

A. Give the meal ration to the civilian.
B. Split the meal ration.
C. Kill the civilian and keep the meal ration for yourself."

Cam resisted the urge to look at the back door, worried he'd see Colin's sheet-white face pressed against the barred glass.

Survival means sacrifice.

As he typed in his answer, he remembered the blue mint, the pieces of dried fruit that got him through the first rough days scavenging on his own. A sacrifice that kept him alive.

Cam fought back the tears, biting on his tongue until the feeling melted into pain. If nothing else, even if he didn't pass the intelligence exam, he'd show them what he was capable of, what monstrous deeds he'd do in the name of survival, of the fight.

For you, Kara, he thought as the next series of questions populated on his desk. He flexed his damaged arm, his fingers and palms tingling, remembering the sound of the gunshot, the snap of a neck. *For you, Kara, I'll blacken the skies.*

Chapter 4

Four hours later, as soon as Cam finished the test, he realized his error.

The CCWF must have found Colin by now.

Worry wrung his intestines into a knot. He stuck his thumbnail in his mouth and bit down hard, enough to split the skin. *They'll take me away for murder—I'll never find Kara—*

STUPID. It's all for nothing.

He stayed at his desk, frozen in his seat, waiting for the rest of the students to finish their test. Some of the smaller kids had been taken away by CCWF soldiers after wandering away from their desks, not to return.

"Attention!" the proctor barked after the last student closed out his exam. Two Dominion soldiers, dressed in battle armor, appeared at the front door and moved to a position behind the proctor. "Tomia Nosik, Iggie Prys, please report to my desk. The rest of you are dismissed."

"Dismissed?" The bully that had tormented Colin earlier slammed his fist on his desk. "I wanna blow up leeches!"

"Dismissed. Or you'll feel the end of my shockwand."

The bully gave the proctor the double-finger, but picked up his pace as soon as the proctor's hand moved to the electrified wand at his hip.

The rest of the kids shuffled out, some crying, others keeping their grief tied up inside them. Most, he guessed, were orphans like him, now stuck with the terrible choice of joining the dangerous ranks of the CCWF or returning to the streets.

What am I going to do?

Cam, too shocked to comprehend his own failure, kept his head down as he followed behind the last kid. He didn't bother looking at the two girls, Iggie and Tomia, who had passed, who at least now

35

had a chance to get off Cerka and find another home amongst the stars.

"Ferros. Wait."

Cam stopped at the door as the soldiers escorted Iggie and Tomia out. He exchanged a brief glance with them, unsure of what their cool gazes meant, or their willingness to follow the armored soldiers out of the classroom.

"Come here, candidate."

Cam approached the desk. Stuck at the far back of the room, he hadn't been able to distinguish the proctor's finer features. He didn't like the way his angular face bore no hints of joy or gaiety, or how his eyes looked over him with a vicious cunning that made him feel naked and weak.

"Your test scores are an issue for your acceptance into the program," the proctor said, typing something with his left hand while keeping watch of Cam's reaction. After a moment he diverted his eyes to the results that projected in holographics from his desk. Cam didn't understand the cryptic language and numbers that raced across the projections, but he recognized his face and the squiggly vital signs that appeared at their side. "We don't accept stupid children into the Academy."

The words *stupid children* punched him in the gut. He'd never been the brightest in his class, but stupid? He blushed and grit his teeth, unsure if he would cry or smash his fists into the projector.

The proctor's eyes widened, as if delighted by something he saw. "However, in some cases, eagerness and willingness can overcome such things. Are you disposed, young cadet, to become soldier of the Sovereign, to follow orders, to fight, to give your life for the Dominion?"

"Yes."

"Yes?"

"Yes, Sir," he corrected, keeping his eyes level with the proctor's.

"Are you willing to kill, to defy your peers, and do as your superiors ask?"

Cam's mouth went dry. "Yes."

"Are you willing to follow Commandant Rogman's *every* command?"

He didn't know who Commandant Rogman was, or what that meant. Surely, it could be no worse than what he'd already done, or been through. Still, his injured ankle throbbed, and he shifted his weight onto his good leg.

Something in his gut pulled down on his throat, as if to steal the answer he prepared to give the proctor. He didn't understand the feelings roiling through his stomach, or squelching the blood from his extremities. Still, he sensed one thing: *This is dangerous.*

This man, this military position, was nothing like he'd experienced.

And there was no turning back. Not if he wanted to find Kara. "Yes, Sir."

The proctor sat back, something like a smile pinching up the corners of his mouth, distorting his militant face. "Then congratulations, Cadet Ferros. Welcome to the Dominion Military Academy."

Chapter 5

"You're sure?"

Cold and naked except for the flimsy disposable cloth covering his crotch, Cam gripped the edge of the exam table, avoiding the eyes of the Dominion nurse holding the dermawand.

"You don't have to carry these scars…" she said, fixating on the bite wounds to his arm. "The other cadets, well, they might say something about them."

Her awkward phrasing, overglazed in false sincerity, made him angrier than the suggestion to get rid of his scars. No, they were his protection, the only thing that would keep the other kids away.

"Alright then," she sighed, interfacing with the holographic projection of his health report on her tablet. Trading out the dermawand for a hypo full of red solution from the nearby tray table, she grabbed his upper arm. "Kids can be mean."

Yeah, right, he thought, stiffening to her touch but not pulling away, *what are a bunch of rich kids from the Homeworlds gonna do?*

He doubted there'd be many kids like him – well, except for Iggie and Tomia; street kids, orphans, who understood real pain, the cost of war. What survival meant.

"You're a tough one, aren't you?" she said, depressing the solution into what little shoulder muscle clung to bone.

He chanced looking her in the eye. She flinched, then diverted her attention to her tablet, making notes and appearing immersed in whatever documentation the Dominion required of his health status.

Why'd she jerk away?

"You're cleared for transport, Cadet Ferros."

Curious and upset, he didn't move, not understanding why she would no longer look at him. After an uncomfortable few seconds, she pointed at the bright yellow and blue uniform sealed in plastic on the tray table, and a pair of black boots. "Get dressed and follow the lighted signs to the transport."

Without another word, she left, the automatic door shutting behind her.

Cam slid off the exam table, his bare feet touching on the icy tiles. For a second, he missed his own clothes, the awkward hand-me-downs from Kara and whatever his mom could adjust of his father's old garments. But after ripping open the plastic packaging, the new-fabric smell wafting up to his nose as he ran his fingers along the tightly-woven synthetics, his longing turned to dread. The Dominion insignia, printed in reflective colors onto the yellow fibers, glinted in the light.

I don't deserve this.

But the proctor saw something in him—something worth shipping him directly to a temporary Dominion camp on the outskirts of the city and performing a full medical workup and vaccinations. And now, giving him a jumpsuit, and sending him into deep space to the highly competitive Dominion Military Academy.

I can't compete with those other kids.

No, not with their genetic enhancements and their overpriced educations on elite homeworld boarding schools. At least that's what the schoolyard rumors informed him long ago. The kids sent to the Dominion were bred for the military, and their ruthless hearts only understood rankings, grades, and, most importantly, the games.

"...eagerness and willingness can overcome such things."

No, that didn't matter. *I'm not here to be the best soldier,* he thought, sliding his legs into the jumpsuit. It seemed too big for him, at least until the smart-weave constricted down to a snug fit.

I'll climb the ranks, he determined. However possible. At least enough to hold some kind of station, a position that would allow him to search for his sister.

Once suited, his left sleeve lit up and provided him with an interface. Directions to the transport and instructions for his conduct scrolled across in blue-light images hovering a few centimeters above his arm.

Do not deviate from the path, flashed over the three-dimensional map of the interior of the base camp.

Cam followed the green blips and arrows on his arm, passing by medical staff, patients, soldiers, and other adults that gave him no more than a cursory glance.

"Move!" shouted a team of soldiers with medical armbands as they carted an injured pilot down the hall. Cam flattened against the wall as they passed by, averting his gaze as the bloodied man screamed in a foreign tongue, and flailed as they pushed him inside a set of double-doors marked *RESTRICTED*.

The sight of his injuries didn't upset him, not like it used to. But the smell did. Decay and rot touched his nose, much too pungent to be coming from just that man.

His wounds were fresh.

No, it wasn't from that man. *It's from that room,* he realized, staring at the doors marked *RESTRICTED*. Inside, though muffled, he heard the man's screams silence, and the sound of—

Gears?

Rusted gears, metal, something grinding across the floor. Like the sounds he heard in his father's old factory. All those big, heavy machines clanging and grating—

His sleeve flashed and buzzed. *Keep moving or a soldier will be sent to your location.*

Cam pinched his nostrils and kept going.

Once outside the medical operations unit, Cam walked across the open swathe of bulldozed land teeming with Dominion personnel and vehicles. A congestion of brown clouds hid the midday sun and swallowed the gigantic transport ships that blazed into the sky. Groups of soldiers and pilots ran this way and that, making him stutter and stumble.

"Watch it, kid!"

"Out of the way!"

Cam thought to run, to head back to the darkened city in the distance, to the only place he'd ever known. Back to—

Nothing.

"Hey!" A girl in a yellow and blue jumpsuit like his waved at him from across one of the transport pads. *Is that Tomia, or Iggie?* A handful of other kids, dressed in the same jumpsuit, lined up outside a black starship. He recognized only the two girls he'd seen earlier.

"Tomia," the first girl said, offering her name, but no other gesture of welcome. Tall, red-haired and freckled, she reminded Cam of the Czeks, the indigenous people that preferred the long winters and icefields of the northern continents. She looked at least twelve, or at least acted confident enough for him to believe she was older, crossing her arms over her chest and shifting her weight onto one foot. Still, she was skinny—too skinny—another victim of the war.

"Cam," he said, waiting for the second girl to introduce herself.

Smaller, though just as confident, the frizzy blonde-haired girl glanced at Tomia before introducing herself with a head nod. "Iggie."

He couldn't place her accent. The weird way she pronounced *Iggie* sounded more like *Ig-gay*.

She's not from the city, he determined. Probably neither of them was. Not that his family wasn't a bunch of immigrants, either. Just they didn't look as human as him, not with their studded ears and stronger jawlines. They probably came from pure Cerkan bloodlines, untainted by the human refugees that came centuries ago to their planet.

They have faster reflexes. They're probably better at math. Cam dug his toes into his boots, trying not to weigh his inadequacies against their strengths.

"You from Calenthia?" Tomia asked.

His answer came out rushed, defensive, and he didn't know why. "Yeah. So?"

Tomia sized him up with cool, cerulean eyes. "Tough. I thought Midra was bad."

Midra. A small, northern city. He remembered hearing about it from his father. *"Those* chakking *leeches think they can hide out in Midra? We'll find every last one of 'em."*

Two months later, only ashes remained, and a new wave of displaced people crowding Calenthia's refugee camps.

"Brehn is worse," Iggie chimed in. Cam didn't know the place, but recognized the pain she masked with a frown.

He didn't want to say any more, to make any more connections that might somehow hinder him later. But an older boy, about fourteen, in front of Iggie nosed his way in the conversation.

41

"*Chak* the leeches, right?" he said, making a fist and expecting them to knock theirs against his. "Burn 'em all."

Cam expected the two girls to feed into the boy's sentiment, to add their own stories of hardship and hatred of telepaths, and the violent reasons they joined the Dominion. Instead, Tomia shrugged her shoulders and offered a flat, "whatever, mate."

Iggie hocked up something thick from her throat and spat it near the boy's feet. "Mind your own business, right?"

Red-cheeked, the boy turned back in line, striking up a conversation with the kids ahead of him.

Cam didn't understand their protocol. Everyone on Cerka hated leeches. They caused the civil unrest, blackened the skies with warships, divided families and friends. Why not damn them with the other kid, celebrate their demise under the Dominion banner?

Tomia must have seen it in his eyes. "We're not telepathic."

Cam didn't know what to say. He'd never addressed his own feelings on the matter, only reacted to his ever-changing environment. In the moment, he didn't care about leeches necessarily, only about his sole objective. "That doesn't really matter."

"Don't it?" Iggie said, her gaze piercing right through him.

He didn't want to tell them about Kara. Instead, he offered the obvious answer: "The Dominion would take you down if you were."

"Truth. Those military bastards have a way of finding out *everything*."

Colin's face flashed through his mind. "Y-yeah?"

Tomia combed her fingers through her long red hair and looked to the horizon. "Yeah. But I don't have any secrets. My family's dead. This world is dead. There's nothing left for me here. This is my only way out."

Iggie stared down at her boots and grunted.

"I suppose that's everyone story here," he mumbled, looking down the line. A total of seven kids, ranging from about eight to fourteen made the cut.

"Just don't get iced," Tomia chuckled as a guard and the proctor for their test stepped down off the starship ramp and reviewed a roster.

"Huh?" Cam said, fiddling with the tabs at the hips of his jumpsuit. He didn't like seeing the proctor. It felt as if the whole world could see his secret.

"They didn't tell you?" she said, flipping over her arm and calling up the interface on her sleeve. Her stats and ranking, grayed out and not yet activated, showed in the top right corner of the holographic display. "Once the games start, you gotta maintain at least a 3.5 ranking, or they'll boot you to the frontlines."

"Or worse. Back to Cerka," Iggie muttered as some of the kids up front laughed and teased each other in some spontaneous competition.

I've got to win half my battles. The thought twisted his stomach into a knot. *I couldn't pass the entrance exam—how can I beat these qualified kids?*

The kid that interjected into their conversation earlier turned around and directed his insult at Cam, bending over and making a knife motion across his neck. "Don't unpack your bags, sweetheart."

"*Chak* off, Marten" Tomia said.

The other kids at front of the line stopped and tuned into the rising tension.

"What? You defending that rub?" Marten laughed. "What'd you score, mate? You even in the 50th percentile? How'd you hack your way in? You're just gonna ice out up there."

Cam reacted before he could think, swinging his leg up, into the boy's chin. The toe of his boot hit him squarely in the jaw. Teeth splintered against teeth. The boy dropped to the ground, screaming, holding his mouth in his hands, blood spilling through his fingers.

"I'm not going back," Cam whispered, frozen in place as the guard from the ramp ran over, gun in hand. After glancing at Cam, he spoke into his shoulder com and then grabbed the injured boy by the armpit and dragged him out of line.

"Cadets! On board now!" the proctor barked. The rest of them hurried aboard, not looking back as the boy continued to cry.

As Cam passed the proctor, the gray-haired man whispered to him, a glimmer in his eye. "Well done, cadet."

Chapter 6

Cam had never been out of the Calenthia, let alone off the planet.
And after the first jump, he discovered how much he didn't like
space travel. The jumps, folding space-time and punching through to
another side of the galaxy, upset his stomach, frazzled his nerves.

I can't cut this, he thought, emptying the last of his watery
stomach contents into the emesis bag as the ship lurched and
resettled somewhere in a dark ocean of unfamiliar stars. Seated at the
end of a row, he tried to hide his sickness, but the other kids couldn't
have missed his retching. Or the smell.

Iggie, seated next to him, didn't acknowledge his sickness.
Neither did Tomia. He appreciated that. To do otherwise would have
made him look feebler than he already did.

"Attention, cadets. We will be docking in five minutes. Check
your sleeves for your assignments."

Wiping his mouth off and stuffing the bag under the seat in
front of him, Cam called up the assignment on his sleeve. Big letters
flashed in red: REPORT TO A-BARRACKS.

"What'd you get?" Iggie said, leaning over her seat to check out
his assignment. "'A' barrack?" she whistled and sat back down.
"Careful with those *assinos*. Can't be fighting everyone."

Bracing his stomach, Cam glanced at the empty seat in front of
him. Marten never made the flight. And now, even sick, the other
kids left him alone. Still, he didn't like her implication.

"Why? Who's in 'A'?"

"Usually the older kids, some of the best-ranked cadets."

Cam's heart sunk. *Why'd they have to put me with the best?*
The proctor.

Cam tensed his entire body, trying to keep from screaming.
Why is he doing this to me?

Kara. He reminded himself of her, of his only purpose. *I've survived worse than this,* he convinced himself.

"*Chak* it," Iggie said with a wave of her hand. "Those snobby kids just know games. We know how things really work."

Cam took a deep breath, but didn't answer, trying to keep himself from another round of vomiting as the ship quaked under the starbase's tractor guidance system.

Once de-boarded from the starship, the other kids dispersed without a single goodbye, leaving Cam to follow the instructions on his sleeve to A-barrack. The Academy, a sleek, hulking Dominion starbase with curving walkways and fast-moving lifts cruising down the corridors, made him uneasy. Even the most modern buildings and schools on Calenthia didn't have the same amenities and features as the starbase. As he passed by classrooms, he caught glimpses of both live and holographic teachers lecturing on everything from advanced gaming theory to astrophysics. Bright-eyed kids in crisp blue and black uniforms, sitting at interfaced desks, took notes on datapads or removable optical readers. Before his school got bombed-out, the best he could hope for in his over-crowded classroom was a good view of the teacher—assuming a teacher showed up to class.

After passing by a set of guards, Cam found the barracks near the mess hall. Kids ranging from age six to early teens milled in the hallway and between barracks, some chatting, others rough-housing, some exchanging homework questions and notes on datapads. A few threw glances his way, snickering under their breath. Cam kept his eyes forward or on his sleeve, navigating his way to the barrack designated "A."

"Where do you think you're going?"

A hand shot out and grabbed him by the collar as he tried to step inside, pulling him back into the hallway.

Cam turned toward his assailant. A boy with red hair and freckles grinned at him, his mustard-colored eyes searching his face. "No *rubes* allowed."

Cam bristled.

"What's a *rube*?" one of the other boys chuckled.

Cam kept his eyes on the red-haired boy, but alerted to the small crowd of kids his age and older drawing up around him.

Please help me, he thought, pleading to the guards positioned near the entrance to the barracks. *Stop this before it gets worse.*

"A poor little Cerkan orphan. Diseased and dumber than dumb."

"It's *rub,* Stempton," an older girl said, rolling her eyes in front of her own circle of friends and looking perturbed. "Like street rubbish."

"Stay out of this, Shiggla," Stempton said. The other girl flipped him off and continued on another conversation with her entourage.

The bully got in his face. "We don't want your kind."

Cam said nothing, terrified, not knowing what to do. The soldiers didn't move, nor did they give notice to the rising argument. Stempton, taller and stockier than him, and probably trained in hand-to-hand combat by the looks of all of the award ribbons decorating his uniform, would crush him if he chanced a fight. Not that the rest of his cronies, about the same size, wouldn't join in and help him demolish the skinny street kid from Cerka.

Cam thought of Kara, how she could calmly talk anyone down from their alcoholic mother to violent neighbors and vigilante thugs, but he wasn't Kara. And Kara wasn't here. Not smart enough, not good enough, he had to do something.

He bit down on his tongue, hard. Blood gushed from the bite, but he didn't swallow it, letting it build in his mouth.

"Did you hear me, rub?" Stempton said, pronouncing the insult correctly as he slapped Cam's shoulder. "We don't want your kind!"

Cam stayed firm, slowly rolling up the sleeves of his jumpsuit. Stempton's eyes, as did the rest of the group's, fell to the grafted skin and crisscrossing scars on his arms.

Horrified, Stempton muttered, "What the—?"

Cam spit out the contents of his mouth right into the bully's face.

"*Chak!*" Stempton cried, pawing the blood from his eyes. Grabbing him by collar, Cam pulled the bully forward and tripping him with his right foot. He fell with him, on top of him, straddling Stempton and seizing him by the neck.

"No fighting!" shouted two of the Dominion guards from down the hall. The rest of the kids immediately dispersed, but Cam leaned into Stempton's face. Wide-eyed, Stempton froze as Cam revealed his blood-stained teeth.

"Stay away from me," he whispered.

Rough hands ripped him off of Stempton and shoved him against the wall. Cam didn't resist the soldiers, or react to the shockwands aimed at him, their tips sparking and sizzling.

"This goes on your record, cadet!" one of the soldiers threatened.

Cam didn't care. He got the reaction he wanted as Stempton scrambled to his feet and hurried off in the opposite direction.

All of you, stay away from me, he thought as the other kids stared and pointed at him.

After the commotion died down and he was sent to his barrack with a warning, Cam found the top bunk furthest away from the rest of the kids, at the end of one of the rows. With only fifteen minutes to check in to and key his storage locker, change uniforms, and report to mess hall, he climbed up on his bed and faced the wall. Tongue throbbing, and mouth tasting like the inside of his mother's cast-iron stew pot, he let the tears fall onto the starched sheets, promising himself they would be his last.

Chapter 7

No one bothered him after the incident with Stempton. Any time he entered the showers, or training gym, the area around him cleared out. The same happened in the mess hall. No one sat with him, but no one paid him any attention either. At least until Iggie and Tomia showed up.

"Hey," Tomia said, dropping her tray down across from him. Iggie threw her leg over the seat next to Tomia and plopped down. "Thanks for the rep."

Cam, poking one of the umber cubes of pressed meat with his fork, shrugged his shoulders.

"No, I mean it," Tomia said, opening her pre-packaged meal and organizing the contents. "One week, and no one talks to us. Stempton's let everyone know that 'all Cerkans are psychos.' It's great."

Iggie laughed, and then slammed her milk drink in one gulp. "Saved us having to kick some rich-*assino* butt."

Keeping his head down, Cam stabbed at a cube of meat.

"I mean, I get playing the part of a psycho, but don't *be* psycho," Tomia said, placing her hand on Cam's. He froze.

I'm not. I just… He couldn't finish the sentence, let alone speak, stunned by her touch.

"It's like on Calenthia, always a battle. But it's better not to go at it alone."

Colin.

His gut squeezed down and his heart beat against his rib cage as he tried to shut out the memories of the boy he betrayed.

(Murdered—)

"A *rat-chakker* like Stempton is bound to come back at you for embarrassing him. It's better to keep a few friends, yeah?"

Remembering the three pieces of dried fruit, he called out silently, *you don't want to be my friend.*

When she finally lifted her hand, Tomia changed topics. "What class schedule you guys get?" she asked, taking a bite out of her bread roll.

Iggie replied with a mouth full of green gelatin. "Calculus with that crabby ol' professor Vosh, chemistry, biotechnics, and intro to combat."

Tomia whistled. "You got off easy. I tested into that advanced astrophysics class. There's so much *chakking* homework."

Both girls looked at Cam, expecting his reply.

Cam cleared his throat, preparing himself for their negative response. "Basic training."

A glob of green jello dropped from Iggie's open mouth. "That's it?"

Cam stabbed his fork into the imitation meat. "Yeah."

Tomia and Iggie fell silent, studying him. Turning red, his mind conjured their judgment, their deduction of his wrongful placement in the Academy, of the imposter he was.

"What the hell do they have planned for you?" Tomia finally asked, spreading butter onto the remainder of her roll.

Cam hated the question, too afraid to even consider an answer.

"Are you willing to follow Commandant Rogman's every command?"

He shoved the memory aside and took a bite of his meal. "Don't know," he finally said. "Don't care."

Other kids might have questioned him, prodded him for a better explanation, but neither girl did. On some level, he guessed they understood him, or at least the driving force for getting off of Cerka.

"*Chak*, this stuff tastes weird," Tomia said, pushing aside her half-eaten tray full of food.

Cam didn't understand how she could pass up free food, even if it did taste artificial and carried a lingering chemical aftertaste. For the first time in years, his stomach didn't gurgle and ache from hunger, and he could eat something that he didn't have to scrape the mold off or fish out of garbage.

"They'll just make you eat more next time," he said.

49

Tomia considered his point, twirling her spoon around her fingers. The Dominion kept strict watch of their intake, recording their every meal when they turned their trays. If she didn't finish her food, they'd just double the next meal.

"Hey, look." Iggie nodded her head at the peculiar new kids that had arrived a couple days after them. Painfully skinny and young, the pair of girls and one boy looked lost and out-of-place. "It's those weird kids from Fiorah."

Fiorah, Cam thought, dredging up what little he knew about the black-market planet located in the backwash of unregulated space. *Nobody survives Fiorah.*

Especially not young kids. *How'd they not get sold off?*
Or worse.

He hadn't yet crossed paths with them, but had heard rumors of the new arrivals. Words like *freak. Diseased. Launnie.* Names he understood all too well, even in foreign slang. But there had to be something special about them—something valuable to the Dominion—or else they wouldn't be here.

Or did you make a terrible promise too?

"They're not that weird," Tomia commented. "Just…human. And really young. Five, maybe? I bet they're the youngest here."

Leaning forward, he tried to catch a better glimpse of the trio.

"They're twins," Iggie said, regarding the two girls. Identical in appearance, at least from a distance, the two girls walked up to a food administrator and waited for a tray to pop out. The boy, tray already in hand, floated his eyes over the sea of children in the mess hall, brows pinched up by concern.

"Triplets," Cam said. Tomia and Iggie gave him a side-eye. He would have added, *they're close, like my little sisters,* but he didn't think they needed, or wanted, to know about his former family.

"This won't be good," Tomia muttered, watching the trio try and find a spot to sit next to Stempton and his cronies.

"Gross—launnies!" Stempton turned around in his chair and stuck out his foot to trip one of the girls.

"Be careful, Stempton," one of his buddies at the table laughed. "They're probably diseased!"

The girl caught herself before spilling her tray full of food, but instead of walking away and finding a different table, she stood her ground, shoulders hiked, eyes ablaze.

"That kid's got balls," Iggie snorted.

The chatter in the mess hall died down to an exchange of mutterings and whispers. Cam's chest tensed, as if it were him, not the triplets, in the bully's headlights.

"Move your foot," the girl said, tone defiant, confident, as if she could possibly stand up to a bully twice her size.

"A launnie doesn't talk to a Crexan like that." Stempton spat something her direction, inciting her further.

"Crexan?" The girl rolled her eyes.

Cam couldn't believe her moxie. Questioning his descent—anyone's descent—guaranteed a fight. No one wanted to admit a mixed bloodline, especially one muddied by unfavorable human genetics.

"You got something to say to me, launnie?" Stempton said, rising from his seat.

The boy grabbed his sister by the arm and pulled her in the opposite direction before she could respond. But as they turned away, Stempton shouted, "that's right, just walk away, rat!"

The girl slammed her tray down at the nearest table where Shiggla and her band of loyal followers sat.

"Move, kid," Tomia muttered.

Shiggla sneered and pointed her finger away from their table. "There's no room for little *launnies* here."

The boy tried to get his sister to change seats again. "Come on, let's find another table."

"The only thing you should find is the ejection hatch," Shiggla hissed. "Since when did they let launnies from Fiorah into the Core? This is an *elite* academy, not a *chakking* shelter. I don't want some slum disease because I had to share the bunks with a Fiorahian."

"What *assinos,*" Tomia said, tightening her grips on her milk drink, deforming the carton.

"Yeah, you rotten street rats!" one of Shiggla's cronies said.

Other kids at their table joined in:

"Scabs!"

"Lurchins!"

"Deadskins!"

"Jeez…" Iggie said. "Now that's getting real personal."

Deadskins. Lurchins. Scabs. All terrible names for fourth-class humans, the lowest class of Sentients in the galaxy. Cam didn't know how he'd handle such insults, especially in front of the entire mess hall. Fourth-class humans were laborers, meat stock for flesh farms—not Academy material. And to be labeled as such meant that every cadet—even the older ones with nothing to gain from beating up a fresh recruit—would target them for destruction.

You've got to end this now, before it gets worse, Cam thought, drawing from his own experiences.

"I'll take on any one of you *passyes* right now," the girl said, pushing her meal aside and stepping into the aisle.

"What's a *passyes*?" Iggie chuckled.

Tomia shrugged. "Probably Fiorahian."

She's too upset. She's forgetting her Common, Cam thought. He caught something—a coolness in her brother's gaze, and the strange posture her sister assumed; as if both of her siblings trained their attention on the vocal sister, not the mounting tension amongst the other kids.

"Whoa!" Stempton laughed from the next table over. "Please, don't hurt me little rat! If you bite me, I'll get the plague!"

Cam watched as Stempton made gurgling sounds and pretended to keel over. While his cronies laughed, the triplets stayed put, the brother and second sister keeping their attention on the angry one as she tensed her whole body for the fight.

The boy whispered something. The irate sister's shoulders relaxed, her fists unclenched.

No way, Cam thought. What did he whisper for her to back down like that? Anger like that couldn't be reasoned with, couldn't just evaporate under spoken sensibility.

"Go sit back down, launnie, before you mess your pants," Shiggla sniggered.

The triplets picked up their trays and moved to a table near Cam, Iggie, and Tomia, toward the farthest corner in the mess hall. A few of Shiggla's and Stempton's lackeys threw half-eaten pieces of food their direction, but the trio didn't react.

Cam continued to watch them, even as the general interest in their presence died down and the rest of the kids in the mess hall resumed their previous conversations.

"Looks like Stempton found someone new to pick on for a while," Tomia remarked as Iggie finished off the last of her tray. "It'll keep him off our backs."

"Sucks for them," Iggie said, licking off the food bits on her fingers. "That guy's a real *assino*."

"They're too young." Tomia straightened up, lips pursed. "They shouldn't be here."

"I dunno. I like that mouthy one," Iggie said, angling her fork at the triplet girl who gave lip to Stempton. "Bet she'll handle herself."

Tomia hugged her arms to her chest, staring at her tray full of half-eaten food. "This place will kill them."

Cam dropped his fork, but quickly picked it back up.

"Huh?" Iggie said, just as shocked.

Tomia leaned forward, eyes darting back and forth as she whispered her secret. "I heard that some kids die in the Academy. Training accidents, bad battle sims." She nodded her head in Stempton's direction. "Psycho competition."

Mouth dry, heart thumping in his chest, Cam reached for his drink, but retracted his arm as soon as he realized his shaking hand.

Iggie sighed. "They won't last a week."

"They'll need friends," Tomia said.

Something his sister would say, something she would do. Thinking of Kara's sacrifice, of his last moments seeing her before her abduction, Cam blurted out, "What good will that do?"

Both Iggie and Tomia both cocked their heads at him. Flicking his eyes away from them, he mumbled the rest of his thought. "I mean, we don't know them is all."

"He's right," Iggie said. "We don't know them. They could be psychos, too, just like Stempton."

Tomia took a hard look at the triplets as they quietly consumed their meals, then returned to their private conversation. "Or maybe they'll be the bloody bastards to save the universe."

Iggie laughed and raised her drink. "Hell yeah. To the street rubs and rats, saviors of the Starways!"

As his two companions changed subjects, talking about their upcoming classes and other Academy gossip, Cam hung on Tomia's observation. *"Or maybe they'll be the bloody bastards to save the universe."*

Yeah right—a street kid saving the universe? What a joke. Even Tomia and Iggie, who rightly qualified for the Academy, would never rise into any leadership position. Not with their background. And even if they did, they'd be sent into the worst battles, to the front lines against the USC. That's how it always went for Cerkans.

Cam dug his fingernails into his uniform pants, wanting to break through the tough fabric. *None of us could ever make that kind of difference.*

(Especially a cheat like me.)

The boy turned his head in Cam's direction, blue eyes connecting. Cam gasped, surprised by something in his gaze, contrasted against the emaciated frame of a poor kid plucked from a black-market world.

A calm sentiment, wound into single word, slipped through his chest. *Always.*

Frightened, but not knowing why, he looked away, pretending to pick at the last few morsels of food left on his tray.

"See ya, Cam," Tomia said, taking her tray and walking over to a disposal with Iggie.

He gave a quick nod and then chanced another look at the boy. Him and his sisters had vacated the table.

As he threw away his tray and headed back to his barrack to change into his training uniform, he couldn't shake the strange feeling. Once at his bunk, he rifled through his storage locker until he unearthed his practice gun. Holding it in his hand, even with the safety mechanisms overriding any kind of real protection, his nerves steadied.

Play it safe, he promised himself, taking a deep breath. *Stay clear of everyone. No friends, no enemies. Can't die now.*

He would find a way to survive, then find his way to Kara.

Alone.

It's all the mattered.

Cam changed his uniform, holstered the gun, and left for training, avoiding his reflection in the chrome finish of the transport lift that would take him to the arena.

It's all I'm worth.

Chapter 8

The next six weeks went by faster than any he could remember.
With back-to-back basic training courses, only broken up by meals,
Cam didn't have time for anything other than sleep.

No more, he thought, hunched over on his knees, struggling to
catch his breath as the obstacle course reset into a new pattern. The
teacher, positioned by the one-way mirror looking into the training
arena, signaled him to ready for another run by lighting the sleeve of
Cam's training uniform yellow. *Not again…*

Other kids, at least the ones above age eight, only trained once a
day with other students. He trained alone most sessions, up to seven,
sometimes up to nine, times a day. And with minimal instruction,
only the red, yellow, green lights to signal him to stop, ready, and
start, and a thirty-second holographic tutorial on how to use his
training gun when he first arrived, he didn't know what he needed to
do better or change each run, only that the enemies, and the obstacles
proved more challenging each time.

Why are they doing this to me?

Cam put his hands on his head and straightened up, trying to
allow more air into his lungs as the landscape, previously resembling
a pitted moon, smoothed out into a gray-sand desert with a glowing
horizon. Pale aliens with fast-moving tentacles populated the last
simulation, whipping him into the rocks, leaving him with fresh cuts
and bruises. Looking down at his battered hands and the bloody rip
in his uniform along the leg, Cam didn't see how he'd complete
another sim. Especially if they kept upping the difficulty.

No place to run, he realized, not seeing hiding spots in any
direction in the infinite gray landscape.

His sleeve flashed yellow. The sim would start any second now.

Cam tried to unholster the gun strapped to his right thigh, to
ready himself for whatever monsters would soon appear, but the gun

wouldn't move, striped interface glowing. He tried again and again, using two hands, but the gun stayed fixed, as if it had locked in place.

"*Chak,*" he muttered, slamming down on the grip with his fist.

His sleeve blipped. Turning over his forearm, he read the instructions highlighted in red: DESTROY THE ENEMY.

Huh?

Something slammed into him. Cam fell hard to the ground, catching glimpses of red hair and bared teeth as he tried to regain his bearings. The gray sand flew in every direction as his attacker struck him again and again with his fists, landing each blow on recent bruises and fresh cuts.

Cam shrimped to his side and kicked himself away, allowing him enough time to realize his attacker.

Stempton.

As the red-haired boy lunged for another assault, Cam took a fistful of sand and threw it at his face. Stempton grunted and tripped, falling just short Cam's position.

Cam slammed the boy's head into the ground, then threw himself on his back. Exhausted, he hit Stempton in the back of the neck, hoping to end the simulation as quickly as possible. As soon as he heard the *crunch,* and the boy's body went flaccid, he backed off and stumbled away.

What…why did they want me to do that?

An even harder thought chased after the first. *How could I do that?*

(Colin.)

Standing a few meters back from the body, he looked to where he thought the observation room sat, disguised by the holographics of a dusky sky, and pointed to his arm. No red to stop, to indicate he'd completed the simulation.

"Come on!" he shouted, voice cracking.

No more. I don't want to do this anymore.

Killing aliens and USC soldiers in simulation was one things. But other cadets—

I'm not like that!

As he waved his arms, trying to trigger the exit to appear, he heard a grunt. Turning on his heels, Cam saw the boy jerk and twitch until he placed two hands in the sand and pushed himself up.

But it wasn't Stempton. Not anymore.

A boy with black hair and pale blue eyes stared back at him. *That strange Fiorahian boy I saw in the mess hall weeks ago—*

Cam froze, even as a locking mechanism on his holster clicked.

No—why him? he thought, backing up. The boy followed him with his eyes, posture relaxed, looking just as pale and skinny and helpless as before. *He's just standing there!*

A message popped up on his sleeve. DESTROY THE ENEMY. The gun in his holster buzzed.

No, he thought, backing up faster. But the boy stayed fixed, even as Cam turned and quickened his stride, only to look back and see him the same distance away.

A shriek filled the air, piercing Cam's ears. Cam fell on his knees, bracing his head, unable to escape the terrible cry. The boy stood in front of him, mouth shut, eyes plastered wide open in a crazed expression.

DESTROY THE ENEMY flashed on his arm.

Writhing on the sand, Cam felt something warm trickle out of his ears.

Make it stop—MAKE IT STOP!

Screaming, he reached for his gun and squeezed off six shots in the direction of the sound. The shrieking ceased.

Cam, disoriented and nauseated, wobbled and swayed until he collected enough of himself to assume a crouched position. Ears ringing, he searched his surroundings.

No...

The boy lay on his back, blood pooling around his head.

Dropping his gun, Cam looked away.

"Well done, cadet."

Cam turned his head toward the sound of a speaker as the landscape disappeared, but the hologram of the dead boy remained. A man with a thick mustache and dark eyes approached from the illuminated exit. He wore an officer's uniform, and had more service decorations than any teacher, officer, or soldier he'd seen.

"I am Commandant Rogman. Proctor Garrisen informed me of your special status. I've been watching your progress for past few weeks." He shifted his gaze to the hologram of the dead Fiorahian boy, his stern tone punctuated by thrill. "I am pleased with your performance."

Cam got to his feet and stood at attention, knees shaking. He didn't look at the Commandant, afraid of the intention in his midnight eyes.

"Keep this up, and I'll make you into something more than any of these other cadets."

What? Cam didn't understand. How could I? I'm not taking any classes, I'm not doing anything but train.

"S-sir," he said, barely squeaking out the words as the Commandant walked away. Rogman stopped and turned around, black eyes cutting straight through him. "Might I take classes as well?"

The Commandant raised an eyebrow. "You want to take classes?"

"Yes," he said, still averting his eyes. He didn't want Rogman to look into to him, to see why he needed to take regular classes in order to have access to computers and interfaces.

"Why? The other cadets here are the best of the best. The competition will annihilate you. Here," he said, waving his hand at the training arena, "is where your talents are best invested."

Cam rubbed the scars on his arm. *I don't have any talents.*

Or maybe he did. He glanced at the dead boy.

"...just hold out, my love...."

"Please, sir," he whispered.

Rogman twitched his mustache, regarding him before supplying his answer. "Three conditions: it cannot disrupt your training, and you must pass your classes, or else you will be terminated from the program."

Cam gulped. *I shouldn't have—*

"Finally," Rogman said, black eyes glistening, "I want monthly reports on the cadets in your classes and group training sessions. Observe them. Tell me their strengths, their weaknesses. Tell me how you'll beat them."

Cam didn't understand. "Beat them?"

59

Rogman sneered. "Yes. This Academy isn't just a school. It's a battlefield. Each cadet is your enemy, your competition for survival to the next level. What will you do to ensure your survival, Cadet Ferros?"

Kara, he thought, hands tightening into fists, chest muscles tensing. Ears still ringing, body aching, he steeled his gaze to the Commandant's, and poured all of his confidence into his words: "Anything."

The Commandant smirked, his mustache twitching. "Well then, Cadet, let us begin."

Chapter 9

As Cam opened his storage locker next to his bunk that night, he noticed a flashing message on his sleeve.

SCHEDULE UPDATE: REPORT AT/TO
0730 Biochemistry – 104
0730 Gaming Strategy – 102

Two classes, scheduled on different days, between his hours of physical training. Cam closed down the message, excitement and terror lighting up his exhausted muscles. He hadn't gone to a formal class in months. Years, if he didn't count all the times Kara tutored him, or he squeezed into an overcrowded classroom with kids both above and below his grade.

What grade would I be in? he thought, pulling off his uniform top and kicking off the bottoms.

Fifth, maybe, on the Starways standard track. Biochemistry wouldn't be an option, not until high school, and definitely not to a student of his caliber.

His hands shook as he folded his uniform, placed it in the locker, and put on his sleep shorts. *How am I going to even pass those classes?*

"You're smart," Kara once told him, showing him a paper of his he marked up with a red pen, *"but you're not the type of smart that people recognize right away."*

"What kind of smart am I?" he asked her, upset that he'd missed so many questions.

Kara smiled, returning his paper and prompting him try again. *"The one who always figures it out in the end."*

"Ferros."

Cam turned around. Stempton and three other kids about his size stood between him and the aisle, blocking him against the bunk lockers. Cam's bunkmate, a squirrely kid who kept to himself, scampered off with his datapad, not wanting to find himself a part of whatever was about to go down.

Cam stared at all four of them, not moving, letting them see his bare chest and arms. He wouldn't let the medical staff treat any of the old scars, or even the new wounds. Most kids couldn't stand the sight of his disfigurements, turning away, just as Stempton's cronies did.

But not Stempton. Grinning, he turned his hand into a gun and fired it off at Cam.

"What's up, killer?"

Cam didn't know if he meant it literally, not that it made a difference.

"What do you want?" he replied, confused by his own shame and anger at the sight of the red-haired boy.

"Just talk," he said, shooing off his mates. Alone at the end of a row of bunks, Stempton took one more look around before lowering his voice. "I hear you're tearing up the basics program. Killing 'bots, soldiers, aliens—whatever they throw at you."

Yeah, whatever, he thought, remembering how the red-haired boy's neck crunched. ...*Or whomever.*

Frustrated and unable to look him in the eye, Cam shut his locker and tossed his datapad onto his top bunk. *I just want to sleep.*

"You're in group training sessions C and D, yeah?"

Cam's gut kicked in, sensing the edge of some kind of manipulation. "So?"

"I also saw your name added to my classes in 104 and 102."

Cam's stomach dropped.

"Look, Cerkans are stupid, especially half-breed humans like you. And you're already a month behind; you'll never pass those classes."

As he squared to Stempton, the bully laughed and casually shoved his hands in his pockets. "Relax, psycho, I'm not trying to start something; I'm just speaking truths."

"You don't know what I'm capable of," Cam said through gritted teeth. In the last six weeks he'd put on 10 kilos, mostly muscle, gone up a shoe size, and outgrew the length of his first jumpsuit by centimeters. He'd never grown so fast or seen himself with muscle before. The fears he had matching up against the kids

62

from the Homeworlds faded. Now, he sized up to most anybody his age, or even a few years older.

"I think you're capable of the best kind of thing in a soldier," Stempton said, the violence in his eyes offsetting his grin. "So, here's my offer—I'll help you pass your classes. In return, I'll give you some names of some kids in C and D that need a *break* from curriculum."

It took him a moment to process what the bully proposed. *He wants me to hurt his rivals in basic training...*

Why couldn't he just take care of it himself? *That jerk has plenty of followers.*

Dread tore at his gut. *I'm missing something; he's got an angle on me.*

But what? He cracked his knuckles and ground his teeth together. *I'm not smart enough to see it.*

"Just leave me alone," Cam said, sounding just as unsure as he felt.

Stempton shrugged. "It's your dumb *assino*, not mine, that'll get iced."

With his followers watching from a few bunks over, Stempton, chin up and still smirking, walked away.

What just happened?

Too tired to give any more thought to it, Cam crawled into bed.

I'll figure it out, he told himself, shutting his eyes and imagining Kara's reaffirming hug. Stempton's freckled face, and Rogman's menacing grin, infiltrated the image of his sister. Discomfited, he pushed it all away, until the only thing that remained was his anger, and the acid burn in his throat. *I have to.*

***

With his first training session ending at 0720, Cam rushed to his class on the other side of the starbase, jumping lifts and running down the halls until he reached room 104.

"Ah, Cadet Ferros, welcome," the teacher said, looking up from the holographic image labeled *macromolecule* rotating over his desk. The entire class, already seated with their datapads out and interfaces launched, stared at him. "You must be quite the genius for

Commandant Rogman to allow you to join my class so far into the curriculum."

Stempton and his group of followers, sitting toward the middle of the classroom, whispered amongst themselves and pointed his direction.

"Go on, take your seat," the teacher said, inputting commands into his sleeve.

Still catching his breath, Cam wanted to shrivel up and run back the other way. He felt the entire classes' gaze on him as he searched for the only open seat in the far back of the class, his cheeks burning red.

"Today we continue our studies of the structure and functions of proteins," the teacher said, waving his hand at the classroom entrance. As the door slid shut, the lights dimmed, and the holographic image on the teacher's desk changed to show coiled structures that Cam didn't recognize. "Let's first look at this chain of amino acids…"

Cam produced his datapad from his backpack and clicked it into the desk, downloading the day's lesson and all that he'd missed.

"*Chak*," he whispered, despondent at the volume of reading alone he'd have to catch up on. And the study questions—more than he'd ever done in his lifetime—how could he fit any of that in with his training schedule?

Cam looked to his left, to the boy staring at him. He didn't recognize him at first, not with how much he'd grown and filled out. *It's that weird boy from Fiorah,* he realized, recognizing his dark hair and cherubic features. The air squeezed out of his lungs. *The boy I killed—*

"What?" he whispered, not intending to sound as harsh as it came out.

The boy didn't respond right away, studying him with intention. Even in the low light, Cam couldn't help but stare back, taken by the calming blues of his eyes.

"I'm Jahx," he said, offering his hand, palm up.

Cam jerked back in his seat, muscles tensed. But Jahx kept his hand out, a faint smile upon his lips.

A Fiorahian greeting? Cam didn't know how to respond. Unsure of himself, or the protocol, he offered a grunt and an uncomfortable glance at the boy's hand.

Jahx took his hand back, unperturbed by his discourtesy, and focused on the teacher as he continued the lesson.

Cam shifted in his seat, unable to sit still. *What's a polysaccharide?* By the time he looked it up, the teacher had moved on, discussing a new term he didn't understand. *Nucleic what?*

The other kids took notes with the one-handed input system on their datapads, their eyes on their teacher. Still struggling with the basics on the datapad, Cam recorded the lecture and resigned himself to figuring it out later.

I hope Gaming Strategy isn't this hard, he thought, chewing on his thumbnail until he tasted metal. Looking down, he saw the blood trickling from the deformed nail.

Discouraged and lost, Cam fiddled with his datapad, pulling up everything he could about the teacher, professor Rotu, the course, and his classmates, from previous session rosters, to ratings and profiles. The class ranking surprised him: Stempton sat high at the top, outscoring the second-place student by a large margin. Most of his cronies filled the subsequent rankings.

Curious, Cam looked for where Jahx stood. *Right in the middle. Average.*

He fought the urge to look back over at the kid. As young and human as he looked—and being from Fiorah, where no educational system existed—how could he have managed an average score?

Out of the corner of his eye, Cam noticed that Jahx didn't even take notes. Instead, he sat forward in his chair, listening intently to every word the teacher spouted.

Thinking of Rogman's secret assignment, to report on the students and how he'd beat them, he created a new document and wrote down his first observation.

Jahx: average student. Doesn't take notes. Friendly.

His hand hovered over his last word. A feeling he couldn't name pulled at his heart until he amended the observation and swallowed hard. *Too friendly.*

The teacher changed the tone of his voice, projecting his question into the classroom. "Amino acids with side groups carry a what kind of charge at physiologic pH?"

When Rotu fixed his gaze on Cam, he slid down in his seat, hoping that the professor would somehow pass him over. No luck. The teacher pointed at him. All eyes turned to him.

It's my first day, I don't know anything, he panicked, seeing Stempton elbow one of his buddies and laugh. *I'm just—*

Jahx, covering his mouth with his hand, whispered: "negative."

"Negative," Cam repeated.

"Correct. You're a fast learner, cadet Ferros."

He didn't let out his breath until the teacher resumed his lecture. Shaking, he added a note to his observation on Jahx: *Kind.*

He stared at the word, remembering the taste of dried fruit, then erased it. *Kindness gets you killed.*

"Your study paper is due on the 30th," the teacher announced. A collective groan followed. "Ah, now, this counts as half of your grade. Remember, you may do this as a partnership if you incorporate a research component in your results. Class dismissed."

Partnership. The word churned in his stomach as he dared a look around the room. Other kids, already engaged in negotiations, grouped together in the front, with a several of the older cadets pining to get Stempton's attention. The red-haired Crexan looked up at him, one of his eyebrows perked in the question he didn't have to ask aloud.

There's no other way, he thought, squeezing the end of his desk. But at what cost? How many kids would he have to sideline to meet Stempton's demands?

Colin's face flashed through his mind, his dimpled smile lighting his face as he shared one of his mints.

(I can't do it.)

For Kara. I have to.

"Hey, you need a partner?"

"Huh?" Cam looked to his left. Jahx, with the same calm, sweet expression, pointed at his datapad.

"We could do the study paper together. I can send you what I've started tonight."

Cam looked back to Stempton. The red-haired boy marched up the stairs between the rows of desks, scowling.

"Uh, I don't know," Cam mumbled, shoving his datapad into his backpack. "I'm not..."

...*good*. He thought of Jahx, lying on his back, blood pooling around his head. *You don't want to be my partner.*

"Ferros," Stempton said, standing a row below him, arms crossed over his chest. "What are you doing talking to that launnie?"

Cam stood up too fast, toppling over his chair. Before anyone could say anything else, he blew past Stempton, making sure to hit his shoulder on the way out.

"Psycho..."

Stempton said the insult loud enough for him to hear it as he exited, but not enough for him to want to turn around and chance fighting him in front of a teacher.

Furious, he grabbed the next lift as it whizzed down the hallway.

"Get off!" he shouted at the smaller kid already on the lift. The cadet ducked under the railing and leapt off, crashing into another student as Cam took the controls and directed the transport back to the training arena.

"*Chak,*" he muttered, gripping the railing. *I'm screwed. I can't do this.*

Cam checked his sleeve: twenty-five minutes to get back to the training arena. Not enough time for a real break, but enough not to rush like he did that morning.

He slowed the lift as passed the lower-level barracks, hoping to see Tomia or Iggie. When he spotted Tomia in the corridor talking to another cadet, he stopped the lift and hopped off.

Tomia stopped her conversation as soon as she saw his face. "What's wrong?"

When he wouldn't answer, she excused herself from the conversation and pulled Cam inside her barrack, to her bunk toward the front.

"What's wrong?" she repeated, looking over her shoulder to make sure no one could hear.

All of the questions brewing inside him, every confession and stupid sentiment, clawed at the back of his throat and pulled at his tongue. Losing his family, Kara. Being afraid all the time. Stempton, Rogman—the strange last training session. *Colin.*

But as he noticed the other kids around them watching, some looking to Tomia, he clenched his jaw and swallowed them back down.

"You're acting weird, Cam, even for you," she said.

"Sorry," he muttered, rubbing the numb parts on his right arm. "Just... Just class. Pressure."

"Yeah, jeez," she said, plopping down on her bottom bunk. "Who the hell joins over a month into a course? Maybe you are crazy."

Seeing that the statement aggravated him, Tomia scooted over and leaned against one of the bedposts, allowing him enough space to sit across from her. "Talk. Or get back to smooshing bugs, or whatever it is you do in your training sessions."

Cam sat at the very edge of her bed, waiting until the other cadets walking between the aisles passed by.

"Look, real talk, rub to rub."

"Real talk," he said, picking at the remnants of his right thumbnail. Without so much as a grimace, he peeled off a chunk of nail and waited until the blood beaded in the raw bed. "You and Iggie should stay away from me."

Tomia scoffed. "This place eats up street kids. You can't do this alone."

"I have to," he said, raising his voice.

Tomia eyed the other cadets as they tuned into their conversation, then returned her gaze to Cam. "Don't do this, Cam. Don't isolate yourself. That just makes you an easier target."

For reasons he couldn't explain to her—let alone himself—he got up and, without looking at her, whispered, "no tomorrows."

"Huh? Cam—wait!" she shouted as he exited the barracks.

I can't drag her or Iggie down with me, he thought, grabbing a new lift. Not now. Not when the girls had a chance, and he all he had were drastic measures and deals that would kill every last part of him that ever mattered.

As the lift dropped him off at the training arena, he pushed aside the memories of his older sister, of Cerka, and a life already lost, and readied for the next battle.

Chapter 10

After his final training session that day, Cam hauled himself onto a lift and leaned against the railing as it zipped him down the corridors toward the mess hall.

I'm beat, he thought, the ache of fatigue reaching into his bones. Usually he'd shovel enough food in his mouth reach satiety, then retreat to his barrack for a quick shower before crashing on his bunk. *I just want to sleep…*

The thought dragged on his body. But it would have to wait. *Gotta figure out how I'm going to pass chemistry.* He thought of Stempton, of his offer. And Jahx.

No, I'll do it alone, he thought, banging his fist against the guardrail. But what about gaming strategy?

He pulled up the class roster on his sleeve. Most of the faces he only recognized from rumor, group training sessions, or from the mess hall. Two, however, stuck out: Shiggla – and Jahx.

Shiggla, a popular older girl that ruled the game rooms and the rivaled most of the top students in any competition, would probably ignore a weaker opponent like him. *At least I won't have to deal with her,* he hoped.

And Jahx. The sweet younger kid who offered to help him. He shuddered, then stopped himself. *Why do I even care?*

Maybe because I killed him, he reasoned, thinking of the bizarre training simulation with Rogman. *Or because he's a street kid like me. Or maybe—*

He stopped himself.

Can't get caught up in anything.

Or anyone.

No attachments, no feelings. *No tomorrows.*

He ate his dinner alone, believing it better that Tomia and Iggie didn't show up to add to his stress. As he dumped his empty tray, he noticed an unopened package of noodles sticking out the receptacle, as if someone hastily got rid of their tray without putting it all the way in the disposal system. A quick check in his peripheries confirmed none of the other kids looking his direction.

After swiping the package and sticking it in his pants pocket, he hurried out of the mess hall and grabbed another lift. Once past the barracks, the training arenas, and the restricted medical labs, he jumped off the lift and walked the rest of the way to his secret place.

The lavatories in the c-wing corridor had been taken out of use some time ago, before he had arrived on the starbase. From the looks of all the mechanical equipment and tools gumming up the entrance and clogging the walkway, the Dominion heads intended for the lavatories to be converted into something else, but for whatever the reason, the project had gotten sidelined. A thin layer of dust covered the sinks and the fixtures, undisturbed for months.

Cam tiptoed inside, following his usual path foraged amongst the equipment and rodent traps to the last stall. Familiar voices made him pause, as did the three sets of boots he saw shuffling around under the divider.

"What are you doing back here, Drachsi?"

"Yeah, launnie boy—what kind of sick games you playin' by yourself?"

A body slammed up against the stall in the ensuing scuffle; one of the pairs of boots went upward, disappearing behind the divider.

The movement, the vibrations—the three other kids in his secret area; violence, the stronger preying on the weak. Something snapped. Without thinking, Cam kicked open the stall door, teeth bared, hands in tight fists, ready to take down whomever stood in his path.

"*Chak*—" Walli, one of the older cadets Cam recognized from A-barrack, cradled his nose as he got out from behind the swinging door.

"Ferros, jeez," Hoch said. An outerworlder with snake-nostrils and flinty eyes, Hoch held Jahx by the collar against the stall divider.

Cam said nothing, chest heaving, staring down the imposters, fists turning white.

"Alright, everything's cool, mate," Walli said, grabbing Hoch and pulling him out of the stall.

As the two other cadets hurried out, Jahx slid down the divider to a sitting position, catching his breath and readjusting his uniform top. "Thanks."

Cam, still tensed for a fight, couldn't unclench his fists just yet. "For what?"

Jahx studied his face. "Good timing."

Why aren't you afraid of me? he thought as the black-haired boy crawled over to the toilet and reached for something through the crack in the wall. Without a reaction, his fists unclenched.

"What are you doing here?" Cam said, eyes slipping for a split second from the boy's face to his hiding spot in the removable panel above the toilet.

With a grunt, Jahx pulled out his hand and whatever prize he captured. "You caught me," he said, a sheepish half-smile upon his face. He offered up the evidence: a half-eaten bread roll.

What? Him too? Cam felt the weight of the noodle package in his pants pocket. "How much you got in there?"

He didn't mean to sound so aggressive, but he couldn't help it; he had to know.

Jahx scrunched up in the corner. "Enough to get me a week in detention."

Anger struck free the words he meant to keep to himself. "Why food, right? I mean, the teachers track everything—but why can't we just eat whenever the hell we want to?"

Jahx shrugged. "There's always a reason."

"Like a test?" Cam frowned, then produced the noodle package from his pocket. "Why do they care if I have another 300 calories?"

Jahx looked at the package, then at Cam, caution in his voice. "Full-blooded Cerkans don't have the digestive enzymes to be able to process those noodles. You could get sick."

"Maybe," he said. "Maybe not."

Jahx regarded him for a long moment, seeming to take in more than his rigid posture. "My sisters don't know about this."

"What? This bunk lavatory, those *assinos*, or the food hoarding?"

"The third," Jahx said, picking at one of the ribbed knee guards on his pants. "Jaeia might understand. But Jetta... She'd be embarrassed. Angry. She'd tell me we aren't starving, that we're not launnies. It's just…"

Cam recognized the mournful look in his eyes, the way he clammed up, unable to finish the thought. "…just a hard habit to break."

Reaching over the boy, Cam loosened another panel higher up, revealing his stock of food he'd stolen out of the garbage or snuck off other kids' trays. He added the package of noodles to the stash and then replaced the panel.

"Don't tell anyone."

Jahx looked at his hiding spot. "I won't. But we should probably switch up locations just in case Hoch and Walli come snooping back."

"Just moving all this one stall over would probably fool those two," Cam said.

Jahx stifled a grin. "You're right about that."

As he thought to leave, a question slipped: "Hey—what's a *launnie*?"

The boy averted his eyes.

"Is it like a rub? Street rubbish? That's the Cerkan insult for homeless orphans."

Jahx looked back up at him, blue eyes bespeaking much more than his words. "There's no real translation in Common. 'Rat' is the closest."

Cam thought on it a moment. "How'd you get off Fiorah? Didn't think even the Dominion went there."

"There's a new occupation."

"On Fiorah?" Cam couldn't believe it. "There's nothing there but those red rocks."

"Yeah, the mines," Jahx said, rubbing his knee even harder, eyes losing focus. "The Dominion want something."

Memories of his family surfaced. "Fiorah have a leech problem?"

"W-what?"

"Leeches. Telepaths," he said, thinking of his mother and father, his three sisters, of vacant eyes and lost laughter. His hands curled into fists. "They killed my family. The Dominion's gonna rid the Starways of every last one of 'em."

Jahx's gaze drifted away from him. "I-I don't know. The Dominion just offered the entrance exam to some of us kids." His voice trailed off. "It was better than staying."

"Yeah," he whispered, "I get that."

Cam kicked his boot tip against one of the rat traps, poison capsules spilling out, lost in thoughts of his old life until he remembered Rogman's threat: *"...you must pass your classes, or else you will be terminated from the program."*

"I gotta go," he said, turning to leave.

"Wait." Jahx sprung up and caught Cam before he could wiggle through the obstacle course of machinery and parts. The boy's hand brushed his fingertips, surprising him with their warmth. Whipping around, Cam didn't mean to scare Jahx, but he didn't expect the touch.

"What?"

"Here," Jahx said, highlighting his sleeve where his direct contact link floated above his arm in blue light. He wanted Cam to receive the image by touching forearms. "Just in case."

"In case what?"

Jahx responded with a faint smile and a steadfast gaze.

Who are you? he thought, confused by the confidence, the kindness, the dark-haired boy continued to show. He touched forearms, transferring his own private link.

Uncomfortable, but not knowing why, Cam cleared his throat. "I gotta go study."

As he turned away, Jahx called after him, hope in his voice. "See you tomorrow."

Cam hurried back to his barrack, afraid of what he might say back.

***

After thirty minutes of going through the chemistry class lessons on his bunk, eyelids growing heavier and heavier, Cam wanted to throw his datapad across the barracks.

"Chak," he muttered, rubbing his forehead and staring at the forty-two opens tabs. *I can't learn all this.* Not if he had to look up

every other word or cross-reference with something else he understood.

"Be patient with yourself," Kara would have told him. *"You'll get it."*

I can't. I'm not smart enough. Looking around at the other kids uploading their homework or playing games on their datapads, he couldn't imagine them struggling half as much as he was just to grasp basic concepts, let alone answer the study questions.

"There's always a way," Kara once told him as she tried to pick the front lock to an apartment of a neighbor they hadn't seen in over three weeks. When it wouldn't open, he followed her to the rooftop as she scaled down the broken fire escape and tried the window. He ran downstairs, catching her opening the front door just as he arrived, a grave look upon her face. The foul smell hit him before her bad news about Mr. Etterman. "I'm sorry, Cam," she whispered, tears in her eyes as she covered up her nose.

Cam pushed aside the memory and the emotion, and latched onto the lesson. "There's always a way…"

A fire escape. A backdoor. Something he could use to circumvent his weakness.

Or maybe someone.

"Ferros."

Cam turned over onto his other side facing the rest of the barracks. Stempton had stepped on the bottom bunk and pulled himself partway up so that he could rest his elbows on Cam's mattress. Below, his bunkmate muttered a protest, but otherwise kept quiet. Hoch and Walli, hanging farther back, scowled and tried to look intimidating.

"What?"

"What business you have with that launnie?"

Cam scoffed and turned his attention back to his datapad. "Nothing."

"Why were you in c-corridor?"

Cam leveled his eyes with Stempton's. "Why do you care?"

"Keep lippin' off, rub. See where it gets you."

The thought crossed his mind to slam Stempton's head against the bed frame, but a fight now, especially in front of so many witnesses, would land him in the brig. Besides, if Stempton wanted to beat a *psycho*, he'd figure out a way to do it so that he wouldn't be kicked out of the Academy, but guarantee a victory that would kill Cam's reputation.

Or me. The thought quickened his heart as he stared into the boy's mustard-colored eyes. He knew that look. He'd seen that kind of hatred in his father's face when he came home after losing his job to a leech. *I humiliated you, and now you want me dead.*

But something kept him from doing it right away. Stempton wanted something—needed something—from him.

I need you, too, he thought. Rolling up his right sleeve of his pajama shirt to reveal his scars, he cut all emotion out of his voice. "Yeah, let's see."

Stempton grunted, and faded back for a second. Cheeks turning red, he grabbed a dataclip out of his pocket and held it in front of Cam's face. "We have a deal?"

Cam looked at the red chip, insides burning.

"Come on, killer. It's not like you're going to be the one saving the galaxy. Take it."

Rogman's admonition resurfaced: *"The other cadets here are the best of the best. The competition will annihilate you."*

He swiped the chip from Stempton's hand.

The red-haired boy smirked. "We'll talk later, killer."

Stempton, Walli, and Hoch returned to their bunks, laughing and elbowing each other.

Alone again, Cam held on to the red chip in his left hand, feeling cheap and dirty.

It doesn't matter, he tried to tell himself. *It's a means to an end.*

With this chip he'd pass chemistry, and get one step closer to finding his sister, even if he did have to rough up a few of Stempton's enemies.

Opening his secret document, he wrote a note on Stempton: *Manipulative. Cunning. Don't trust him.*

Chewing other his thumbnail, he added: *Afraid of me.*

Fear. His one advantage. Thinking of Colin, he realized his second: *need.*

Still, he didn't download the answers. Not yet. Something, a hot feeling pooling in his stomach, kept him fitting the chip into a port.

Lying back down on his bed, he turned onto his side and checked his sleeve. No messages, no alerts. He thought of Jahx's private link, typing it in twice, but deleting it both times.

I don't need anyone, he told himself, closing his eyes. He tried to imagine himself curled up on the sofa, his big sister's feet propped on top of him as she read her ancient literature presentation on her datapad. The twins, playing by the fireplace, babbled in their secret language as their father cursed the losing rumbee team on the television. Off in the kitchen, their mother yelled for someone to come help her with the roast.

Kara, he thought as his grip loosened on his datapad and the chip, his body sinking into the mattress. In the distance, he saw her limp body carried off by USC soldiers. *Don't give up on me.*

Chapter 11

"Just take a seat," the professor said, waving Cam toward the back of the class.

Cam trudged up the stairs to the only empty desk, trying not to lose his footing in the dark. The lighted walkway gave him some idea where to place his feet, and glowing interface ports outlined the desks. The other students, whispering to each other in anxious tones, paid no attention to the new addition.

"Alright, class," the professor announced, "today's match – Cadet Walli against cadet Teahvo."

Anxiety turned into excited chatter, at least amongst the students not pitted against each other. Two dark figures walked down to the front of the class where a large, circular console projected a spherical playing field.

Walli stepped into the projected light first and took his seat in one of the two chairs. His opponent, a hulking, muli-limbed hominid with amphibian feet, banged his knees against the console as he tried to fit his oversized body into the smaller seat.

The other kids laughed. All except one.

Jahx.

The dark-hair boy watched with concern from two rows down.

What's his problem?

A second thought came at the heels of the first as the teacher ran down the rules of the match. *What's he looking for?*

"…Walli will take the ground force, Teahvo the air strike. Each player will be evenly matched in playing pieces. However, the air strike will have a 60% fuel loss, and ground force will have only phase missiles and disruptors. The match will start in thirty seconds. Ready yourselves, players."

Cam leaned forward, fascinated as the spherical playing field lit up with a variety of different game pieces. Teahvo and Walli changed the angle of their viewpoints on their personal interfaces close to their keyboards and controllers as the holographic timer ticked down above the sphere.

"Walli's gonna crush that freak," he heard someone whisper.

Cam gripped the edge of his desk. Nothing Kara ever played with him—from the trick-taking card competitions to the challenging strategy game they played in their heads—compared to this.

The timer buzzed. Teahvo swarmed Walli's base, coming in hot with his entire fleet of battleships. Responding with tanks and crawlers, Walli kept his ground forces tight and controlled, but couldn't keep up with Teahvo's multi-faceted attack. The battle lasted two minutes.

"*Chak*," Walli said, slamming his fists against his console as his base of operations blipped out.

Teahvo pointed one of his limbs and jeered through a translator fixed below his mouth. "You talk big, but you play like a girl!"

Cam quirked an eyebrow. Females made up forty percent of the Academy students and professors. Such an insult didn't make sense. *Unless he feels threatened by feminine qualities.* He got out his secret document and wrote down his observation.

"What did we learn class?" the professor asked as the two opponents returned to their seats.

Students shouted out various answers. "Take the enemy by surprise."

"Don't crowd your base."

"That's right," the professor said, resetting the playing field with a swipe of her hand. "You can't always afford to be conservative, not when time and supplies are a factor. Next up: Cadet Drachsi and Zhow."

Jahx and Shiggla. He watched the two rise and walk to the console. Jahx quietly took his seat, making no adjustments to the keyboards and controllers, his demeanor even, calm.

Too calm, Cam thought. He pulled up the class roster on his sleeve and reviewed the rankings. *Shiggla's the top student in this class. He's going to get smashed.*

But then he looked at Jahx's standings. Dead center. But instead of an even win/loss ratio, his stats held him close to zero. *How is that possible?*

Shiggla whispered something from across the way as the teacher announced the game's restrictions. Cam couldn't quite tell, but it looked like, *you're dead, launnie.*

"In this simulation, we will explore one-sided advantages," she explained, typing something on her datapad as the playing field populated with new game pieces. "Tough decisions must be made in battle. Loss and death are inevitable. How will you deal with these challenges? What is more important—the objective, or the life you preserve?"

Heart thudding in his chest, Cam watched as the playing field appeared. On one side of the open space, thousands of red playing pieces populated, from dreadnaughts to warships, and on the other, a radioactive fuel transport and a battleship at 20% power.

That's not fair! Cam couldn't believe the odds. Jahx, in control of the two starships, didn't stand a chance against Shiggla's massive fleet.

"Cadet Zhow," the professor said, addressing Shiggla, "to win this match, you must destroy the enemy with zero loss. Drachsi – to win, you must last five minutes."

Five minutes? He's not going to last five seconds, he thought as the other kids laughed and cheered on Shiggla to obliterate Jahx.

Cam gripped the edge of his desk, biting his lip as the time ticked down about the sphere. Other kids stood up, clapping their hands and chanting Shiggla's name.

Standing, Cam held his breath as the timer approached zero. He wanted to do something—not that he knew what—as Shiggla changed the angle of her game to focus on the warships. A smug smile upon her face, she gave a thumb's down to her opponent as the timer read *10, 9, 8...*

Jahx, what are you doing? Cam thought as the blue-eyed boy stared at Shiggla, his focus beyond her conceited expression, somewhere that didn't make sense to him, as the slaughter approached.

But as the timer hit *3, 2, 1,* Jahx's hands shot up to the controls.

Cam held his breath. The entirety of Shiggla's fleet locked on to Jahx's two ships. But not before Jahx, overcharging his engines, turned his own battleship on his fuel transport.

What are you—

80

He fired, targeting the fuel tankers on the ship as his engaged his battleship's jump drives, the engines that folded space-time. The entire playing sphere exploded in a flash of light.

"No!" Shiggla shouted as her playing pieces vanished.

The simulation ended, scoreboard remaining 0-0. The entire classroom went silent.

"Another draw. Congratulations, cadet Drachsi; I've never met a student more determined to sacrifice everything to avoid a fight. Return to your seats," the professor said.

That's why his class ranking is so weird, Cam realized. *He must tie a lot of his matches.*

But why? Why would a human from Fiorah want to tie his matches instead of winning?

Or losing.

Cam didn't understand it, but as he sat back down, he made note of it in his profile on Jahx. *Doesn't want to win. Or lose. Class ranking is average – again.*

Cam watched as some of the other students whispered insults to Jahx.

"Cheater."

"Wimp."

"Launnie."

But the black-haired boy remained lost in his own thoughts, returning to his seat and facing the front of the class as the teacher called two new students down for another match.

There's something more to you, isn't there? he thought, studying Jahx as the boy watched the other players taking centerstage. *Tying can be harder than winning or losing.*

Cam decided to find out what. After all, Jahx was a street kid, like him. And street kids knew how to survive, how to beat all the odds.

Or at least that's how he justified planning their next encounter.

Jahx Drachsi, he thought, as if the human boy could somehow hear him. *Can you help me find my sister?*

Chapter 12

Cam looked for Iggie and Tomia at breakfast the next day in the mess hall, but didn't see them anywhere.

Where are they?

As much as he hated to admit it, just seeing them, even at a distance, gave him some kind of reassurance.

It's early, he thought, checking his sleeve. 0530. *No, Tomia would be here. She eats early.*

As he dumped his tray, he did one last visual scan of the half-full mess hall, hoping to see their familiar faces. *I'll just go check on them later, in the barracks,* he decided.

Stempton's red chip in his pants pocket, Cam hurried to 102, trying to keep the anxiety from his face. With only a couple hours left until class, he needed to upload his answers to the study questions or else he'd lose points in his class score, as well as ranking. *Not that I need to do anything but pass.*

Still, everything counted. Hopping off the lift, he used his student code to gain access to 102 and entered the dark classroom.

The center gaming console, lit and projecting a rotating spherical battlefield, cast restless shadows across the room. He wound his way around the console to the gaming terminals at the far side of the room. Four stations, all with glowing keyboards and flat screen monitors, waited for the next player.

Crouching underneath the terminal, he pried off the protective panel and studied the internal wiring. At four, Kara taught him how to rig arcades to give them a free game. By seven, he'd figured out how to open most door and vault locks, with only a few burns and gashes to show for his mistakes. But he didn't need to play games or steal food. Now, he needed information.

Pulling out a bundle of yellow wires, he clamped off two of the lines to isolate a free port.

"Let's see what you're up to, *ratchakker*," he said, fitting the chip inside the port.

Standing back up, he watched as the data streamed across the flat screen. Research papers, study questions, and test answers from former students as far back as ten years ago, zoomed across the screen.

He hacked the system, Cam thought. *Or he stole this from someone who did.*

As smart as Stempton was, something like this required a level of hacking genius he didn't think the red-headed Crexan possessed.

Everything seemed legit until he saw the code at the very bottom right of the safe view, appearing as blips of zeros and ones. *Chak.*

"Hey."

Cam reared back, fists up, ready for an attack.

"Sorry," Jahx said, stepping out from behind the second row of desks and holding up his hands. "I didn't mean to scare you."

"What are you doing here?" Cam said, trying to shield the download with his body.

Jahx descended the stairs until he stood across from Cam, hands at his side, looking anything but threatening. "Just needed the quiet."

Cam slowed his breathing, but stayed in front of the terminal. "Why here?"

Looking at his feet, Jahx answered in a less confident tone. "I don't like games like this... but I feel like I have to be here."

Cam looked over his shoulder, at the desk Jahx popped out from. *Shiggla's desk.* "Are you rigging the games? Is that why you tie all the time?"

"I know why you say that," Jahx said, pointing to the terminal Cam tried to cover up. "You just found out Stempton gave you a hot chip. Yeah, some kids cheat and lie to get ahead, but I don't. Players like you and me don't have to."

Cam's mouth hung open before he regained enough of himself from the shock to clamp it back shut. "W-what?"

As Jahx walked toward him, Cam got out of the way, surprised and weirded out by his actions. He watched as the black-haired boy used the keyboard alt functions to display the code hidden in the chip's programming. "See, right here," he said, pointing to the

83

highlighted areas, "Stempton wanted you to download this to your personal datapad so he could access all your files. Then he could have watched you, framed you for anything... you know."

Cam swallowed hard. He gathered Stempton wanted to screw him, and the chip had been rigged, but not to this extent. Still, it made sense as he looked at the code. "That *assino.*"

"He's a six," Jahx said as he tapped the keyboard and edited the code, "meaning he thinks about six moves ahead in any scenario, game or not. He's smart, but he's got a weakness."

"He thinks everyone else is dumb," Cam replied.

"Yep," Jahx replied, wiping the terminal record of their interaction.

"So, what's your game then?"

Jahx pulled out the red chip and handed it back to Cam, blue eyes bespeaking of a troubled past. "Survival."

He's... like me. Cam took the chip and held it in his fist, unsure of what to say next. "How am I going to pass chemistry? Or even gaming? I'm not... I didn't go to school like everyone else. I'm not... I'm just not like the other kids."

Jahx sounded as if he chose his words with care. "Right, but kids like us have had the cruelest—and best—teacher of all growing up. They don't get what you and I know."

Desperation, he thought, but didn't answer aloud.

To his surprise, Jahx closed his hand around his fist. His heart fluttered at his touch. "I got rid of the malware. If you want, you can have all the answers in an instant. Or, I can help you get started, show you a few tricks how to figure this stuff out faster, and you can do it without cheating."

An old memory, from when Kara first taught him how to pick a lock, came to mind. He remembered the feel of her strong grips underneath his armpits as she held him up so he could reach the exposed door keypad, the confidence in her voice as she waited patiently for him to select the correct wires to cross. *"You're smart, Cam-cam. You've got this."*

"Ok."

"Ok," Jahx said with a hint of a smile.

Withdrawing his fist, Cam asked again: "What were you doing at Shiggla's desk?"

Jahx waved at him to follow as he made his way back to her desk.

"Student information, other than rank, is private," he explained, calling up the video files recorded from the desk. "But how a student watches the battle matches are accessible by anyone because it's considered 'battle footage.'"

Cam watched as Jahx flipped through the last several battles Shiggla both witnessed and participated in during class.

"Wait," Cam said as Jahx came to the battle between Walli and Teahvo. He watched as the two older kids went head-to-head in the match he witnessed. But from the angle of the game she chose, and the way she zoomed in on certain game pieces and the scoreboard, he suspected something more than just interest in how the players strategized. "Show me the others matches again."

As Jahx flipped through some of the matches, he saw the pattern. "She studies the players' strategies, but she's more concerned about the scoreboard," he observed. "She checks back to it every fifteen seconds."

"Right," Jahx said, freezing the holographic projection the image of point totals after one of the matches. "She doesn't just want to win…"

"…She wants to win with the most points possible," Cam deduced. "She plans her game around point totals."

But as Jahx clicked off the desk, Cam realized his next question. "Why do you care? You're just tying all your matches. What's your angle?"

Jahx smiled. "Maybe if you watch my footage…"

Cam shook his head. "I saw you; you just watch the players. You don't manipulate the camera angles on your desk. The footage is garbage."

With the same smile on his face, Jahx shrugged his shoulders. "Maybe I'm not that good of a player."

"Maybe you're better than everyone, but you just don't want to get found out. Not yet."

Smile faltering, he diverted his gaze to the door.

"You're a strange one, Fiorahian," Cam said, checking his sleeve. Time to get back to the arena. He'd have to figure out the study questions after his training session. "But I don't hold anything against you. None of these kids know what real war is like."

As he turned to leave, a meek voice arose in song:

"Little launnie in the gutter,
No one loves a rat,
Your momma's smoking jihja
And your daddy's getting whacked."

He slowed his pace as Jahx recited the Fiorahian slum-song, chills running down his spine.

Little launnie in the gutter,
Broke and full of woe,
Float downstream away from me
To the Block where you will show.

Four and twelve you might have gotten
If your face was not so rotten,
Hurry up and die already
So this all can be forgotten."

I've never heard anything like that… he thought, horrified by the compassionless tune. *How could anyone survive a world like that?*

The answer stirred deep within his chest, in the feeling of the red scarf in his hands, the sound of a snapping spine.

Almost to the door, Cam turned enough to talk over his shoulder, clearing his airway to make sure he didn't sound jolted. "Like I said, Fiorahian, I don't judge you. We all do what we have to do for our own needs."

"What's your need, Cam?"

Cam paused at the door, his heart in his throat. "See you, Jahx."

"See you, Cam."

***

As Cam checked and holstered his gun, the regular few cadets trickled in to the morning open training session. Most kids, exhausted by the previous day of classes, chose to study, get an extra hour of rest, or hit the gaming rooms to blow off steam—not physical training.

Not these bastards, he thought. Vorri, Wexlen, Sanders, Criele. All older cadets in impressive shape, especially for their age. He didn't remember twelve-year-olds with such massive muscle development like Wexlen, or speed like Sanders – at least not Cerkans.

Not any kid, he realized, thinking of all the intergalactic species he'd encountered in the city.

He wished he could talk to them, but he feared more than a perfunctory acknowledgement and an occasional nod during cooperative training. And besides, with the way the Academy shuffled cadets around, they'd be gone in a month or two anyway.

I hope this isn't another massive attack, he thought, massaging his sore arms and stretching his back. The idea of a fourth day of an endless barrage of enemy soldiers sounded impossible, especially since he still had to resolve his study question dilemma after training.

"Cam."

He turned toward the entrance. "Tomia—Iggie—"

Jetta, Jahx's more outspoken sister, trailed behind the two. He'd seen her in the hallways, but only with her brother and sister, never alone. *What's she doing here?*

As he thought to ask them where they'd been, his eyes fell to the training guns strapped to their thighs, and their unblemished training uniforms. "You guys are training now?"

"Iggie and I registered for next session," Tomia said. "Thought we'd check it out."

"And you?" he said, addressing Jetta.

The Fiorahian girl gave him a slanted once-over. "It's an open session, isn't it?"

Cam shrugged his shoulders, seeing their lighted sleeves. "Hope you're all warmed up."

"Any advice?" Tomia asked, touching her holster. "I've never fired a gun before."

"Me neither," Iggie said.

Jetta stayed silent, watching the other three.

Cam scoffed. "Come on, you think I got any training?"

"Seriously?" Iggie said, eyeing the playing field. The arena spanned at least half a kilometer, with highly sensitized interface modules and holographic projectors lining the ceiling grid in ten-meter intervals.

Cam drew his weapon and showed them the basics. "Point, aim, fire. Don't hold your breath when you hit the trigger."

"How much ammo is in here?" Iggie asked, flipping over her gun and inspecting the design.

"You get twelve shots. Reload by tapping the gun to your holster. You all have your ear pieces in?"

"Yeah," they each mumbled, touching their ears.

"Good. Stay on your com. It's easy to get divided in a sim."

"What's this?" Iggie ran her finger along the reflective stripe on her holster.

Cam pointed to the hashes. "Your player interface. It allows the teachers to turn off your gun or whatever, registers your ID."

"What... what happens when you get shot?" Tomia asked.

"It hurts."

"What?" Iggie said. "Why'd they do that?"

"To make it real, I guess," Cam said, pointing to the silver nodes tracking the length of the arms, legs, chest, and back on his uniform. "These send pain signals to wherever you get hit."

"What about the part that's not covered?" Tomia said, referring to their hands and head.

Cam turned up his head to show them the neckline, and then offered up the ends of his sleeves. Silver bands and node clusters wrapped around the edges of the uniform. "Signals get sent out to your hands, paralyzing them, if you get hit there. And your face... you don't want to know."

Iggie and Tomia looked frightened, but Jetta dared to ask. "Tell us."

"You go blind, mute, deaf. Just depends on where you get hit."

"How long does it last?"

Cam shrugged, trying not to sound as uncomfortable as it made him feel. "It wears off after the game is over. Sucks if it happens straight out. But I guess there are some perks."

"Like what?" Iggie guffawed. "You don't hear when you're about to get blasted?"

"If you're blinded, you're as good as dead."

"But you're not dead," Jetta interjected.

"No. But the enemy doesn't come after you. You're considered a downed target."

Jetta took the information with interest, inspecting her gear as the other two eyed the exit.

"How'd you figure all this out?" Tomia asked.

Cam felt his sleeve buzz. Turning over his arm, he saw the yellow ready light and game instructions: *ALL PLAYERS MUST PASS THROUGH ENEMY PORTAL.*

"*Godich,*" Cam muttered. Passing through an enemy portal meant crossing the battlefield lines, usually into a trap. Sneaking one player through to the other side could be managed with experienced players – but all eight of them?

Cam clustered together with the other four players as they awaited the simulation to unfold. Tomia, Iggie, and Jetta followed him, mimicking his crouch.

"What the hell?" Sanders exclaimed as he scrolled through the sim stats on his sleeve. "Why does this count toward 50% of our training sim grade?"

"What?!" the others exclaimed, all checking their sleeves. At least for the other students, open training sessions were treated as practice sessions, not counting toward any grade.

"But we haven't even officially started—" Tomia exclaimed, checking her readout.

Cam brought up his cumulative training session grade. As it stood, he would pass, and with a good battle sim rating. But not if they failed to complete this assignment.

Panic threaded through his heart, quickening his breath, tensing his muscles. *Rogman.* He turned to the observation window, the last strange session, Jahx's dead body, on the edge of his mind. *Why are you doing this?*

"This isn't fair," Wexlen said, looking to the exit.

Criele grabbed Iggie by the arm. "Did you rubs do this?"

Wrenching herself free, Iggie got in his face. "I didn't have nothing to do with this."

"Quiet," Cam said, watching the simulation unfold. A dark, mountainous region, with two outposts and a foreboding stronghold materialized in front of them. From a quick visual sweep, Cam guessed they'd have to cut across half a kilometer of enemy territory to reach the circular blue portal on the other end. *At least it's dark,* he thought, glancing at the pale stars stretching out along the horizon. *The enemy won't be able to see us very well.*

Addressing Tomia, but speaking loud enough for all to hear, he said, "you asked how I figured out all this training *gorsh-shit*?" He slid up his training uniform sleeves, revealing his old battle wounds, and new. The other cadets, except for Jetta, gasped and murmured. The Fiorahian met his gaze, undeterred by his display. Cam paused, his stomach knotting. *She's just a little girl.*

Rolling his sleeves back down, he punched up his 4.85/5.0 rating. "Because I had to."

Their sleeves turned green. The exit, and all other signs of the Academy, disappeared.

Taking a slow breath, Cam reassessed their situation. The simulation placed them behind the protection of a boulder, out of the enemy line of sight. But given his past experiences, they couldn't stay there for long.

Vorri stuck her head out from behind the boulder for more than a second, drawing an enemy shot. The blaster fire took a chunk out of the boulder, spraying them with rocks bits.

"Careful," Wexlan said, pulling her back.

"What did you see?" Cam asked.

"A dozen soldiers positioned near the first outpost," she said in her thick Hexronian accent. "Can't see much else."

"We're pinned down," Sanders said, rubbing his forehead with his gun. "Someone's going to have to make a break."

"And what, get iced from the start?" Criele said.

The arguments continued, but only between the other six. Cam stayed out of it, as did Jetta.

"We can't do this."

"It's impossible."

"No way we can get past all those soldiers with these rubs."

"Hey! Watch your mouth," Iggie said, shoving Sanders.

Shots fired, chunks of boulder sprayed over them.

"*Chak,* we can't stay here," Vorri said.

As the older cadets discussed formations and strategies, Cam thought about the game objective.

How do we get all eight across the playing field?

Jetta's actions caught his attention. The young girl picked at the reflective strip on the holster, her brow in a stitch, then relaxing.

"You guys want to win this?"

The conversation stopped. All eyes turned to the Fiorahian girl unstrapping her holster and tossing it in the middle of their group. Then, more surprisingly, she offered her gun to Vorri.

"Tomia, Iggie – give your guns to the others. Cam, you too. There's only one way we can do this."

"What?" Sanders laughed as another blast took out a sizeable portion of their cover. "You suicidal, rat?"

"No. I want to win," she said.

Cam crouched down lower as the blasts continued, increasing in frequency. *We've got to make a decision. Now.*

"What's your plan?" Tomia asked.

"Each player is identified by the interface on the holster strip. All we need to do is have one player carry the holsters through the portal and we win."

"Why do we have to give up our guns?" Iggie asked.

"We can't fire as well as these guys can," Jetta explained, "and we can fool the enemy into thinking there's two of us in one spot when there's really just one."

"Why make Cam gives his up?" Tomia said.

Jetta locked eyes with Cam. "Because he doesn't need a gun to take an enemy down."

How did you...? Cam swallowed hard, fists flexing, trying to keep from thinking of Colin.

"What kind of dumb *assino* plan is that?" Criele said.

"A brilliant one," Tomia whispered.

Cam silently agreed. *How did you see that?* he wondered, impressed and ashamed at the same time. Jetta, at only five or six years old, and no training, figured it out before any of them could.

"So, who's going to make that suicidal run?" Wexlan asked, firing a quick shot around the boulder.

"Someone who's not afraid to get hit," Jetta said, glancing again at Cam.

The rest of the group fell silent.

But as Cam tried to process what she suggested, Tomia volunteered herself. "I'll do it."

"Wait—she hasn't told us how," Iggie said.

Jetta lowered her voice. "We'll blind you. Then we'll guide you through the terrain on the coms. If what Cam says is true, the enemy won't care about you, and you can reach the portal without drawing attention."

Tomia looked to Cam. He nodded absently, still shocked that she would volunteer for such a task. It involved more trust than he'd be willing to give any other soldier, especially older cadets who didn't care for street kids, even ones with good rankings or brilliant, though unorthodox, strategies.

"You'll need a strong assault to off-balance their forces, draw their sight away from the valleys so you can cut through to the scree field."

How did you see all that? Cam wondered. The Fiorahian girl must have an eidetic memory to have such a detailed picture of their training simulation.

"We'd need a good position to be able to guide her," Iggie said. "We'd have to take over one of the outposts."

"Right. Wexlan, Criele, Sanders, and Vorri, take the extra guns and attack the second outpost. Firing the extra guns, they'll think it's our entire squad, so they'll draw from the first outpost. Cam will lead Iggie and me in the attack against the first outpost. From there, the three of us will guide you from that vantage point."

"It'll have to be fast; they'll wisen up quickly," Vorri said.

"*Chak.* Does anyone have a better plan?" Wexlan remarked.

Shouts from the enemy soldiers, and another series of blasts, answered.

"Ok," Tomia said, shaking out her hands.

A blast tore off a huge chunk of the boulder, hitting Sanders on the shoulder. He screamed, clutching his shoulder.

"We've got to do this now. Come on," Cam said, pulling Sanders out of the debris and tossing his holster in the middle. "Now!"

The others hurriedly removed their holsters and handed them to Tomia. After tying them together and slinging them over her shoulder, she approached Cam.

"You do it," she said, cerulean eyes tearing as she handed him her gun.

No, he thought, taking her gun in his opposite hand. He couldn't look at her, not with her trust gathered in her gaze, in the lingering touch of her hand on his forearm.

But he had to. He had to win at any cost. He couldn't think about the consequences of his action, only the victory that Jetta assured them. As the others called out for help, trying to return fire as the enemy neared, he raised his gun to her face.

"Hurry up, Ferros!"

"Come on, we're getting killed out here."

I'm sorry. His insides screamed and protested, his hands shaking as his first finger tapped the trigger.

"Do it," she whispered.

Kara, I—

"Just hold out, my love..."

He fired, the light flash from his training gun hitting her in the face.

"*Chak!*" Tomia stumbled backward, hands over her eyes.

"Tomi!" Iggie said, grabbing her wrist and pulling her to safety before she stepped out of their shelter and into enemy fire. "I got you. Jeez, Cam."

She told me to! Swallowing his anger, he gave up both guns to Wexlan and Sanders.

"Don't hesitate at the outpost, or we're all *chakked*," Wexlan said, punching Cam in the shoulder.

With Wexlan in the lead, the four older kids kept low the ground, staying behind the craggy rocks jutting up from the uneven terrain. Sanders, nursing his injury, brought up the rear.

"Tomia, can you hear me on the com?" Jetta said, touching her earpiece.

"Yes," Tomia said, eyes wide and unseeing as she crouched low to the ground, afraid to move.

"Hold Iggie's hand. She'll guide you down to the valley before we go up to the outpost."

Whispering assurances in her ear, Iggie took Tomia's hand in hers and led her around the boulder, and down the steep slope leading to the valley.

Alone with Jetta, Cam watched the progress of the armed four. Wexlan, Vorri, and Criele kept up on the fire, but Sanders, injured and lagging behind, attacked sporadically.

"There's still two left up in the first outpost," Jetta said, noting the black-armored enemy soldiers concentrating fire on Sanders' position.

"We have to go now," Cam said, grabbing her arm.

Jetta jerked free. "It's too soon. We need to wait for Iggie."

"Wait for Iggie, then," Cam said, "I've got to take them out now, before they take out Sanders."

"No, Cam—that's not what—"

He didn't wait to hear her explanation. Something about her, about the entire simulation, frightened him. *I've got to end this.*

As he climbed up over the rocks and scaled the back of the towering outpost, his concentration sharpened, his fingers slipping into cracks and hauling him up to the next handhold. He didn't care about the fatigue of his muscles, or the vituperations Jetta shouted into his earpiece. As he climbed over the top of the tower, he flung himself on one of the soldiers, tackling him from behind. In the ensuing scuffle, an elbow caught his nose. Though a simulation, he felt bones crunching, and part of his left eye went dark. Shots fired from behind. His back and leg seized with pain, making him buck and roll off the first soldier.

The soldier pointed his gun at Cam's head. Without thinking, Cam launched himself from his sitting position and double-leg tackled him to the ground. Grasping the soldier by the helmet, he slammed him repeatedly onto the floor until his limbs went flaccid.

Cam took the second soldier's gun and aimed it at the first. Still crumpled in a ball, the soldier raised his hands up in the air as Cam shot him in the neck.

Limping over to the edge, his leg and lower back shrieking with pain, he assessed the battle between the four other cadets and the second outpost. *They're pinned down.* He raised his gun, taking aim at the second outpost.

A loud thump, followed by a cry, caught his attention, and he spun around. Jetta spilled over the edge of the back wall and shot her hand out, as if she could stop him from a distance. "Don't!"

But as Cam returned to his position, taking aim once again, Colin's face ghosted across his sight.

He backed off, dropping the gun. "What the—"

Old panic sluiced through. *(I killed him—I KILLED HIM—)*

He braced his head in his hands. *Stop! No—I didn't mean to—*

Iggie popped over the wall, breathing hard as she dropped herself next to Jetta. "Tomia's off. We gotta help her."

"What... I need to..." But Cam couldn't finish the sentence. Confused, he picked up his gun again and looked back to the second outpost. All the anger and fear that spurred him up the tower and fueled his attack dissipated.

Jetta gathered herself up and caught him by the arm before he could take aim again. "Fire at the other four—but don't hit them. We can't let the other outpost know we've taken over. Not yet."

Cam nodded, still shaken by what he thought he saw. *No way... I couldn't have seen him.*

"Cam," Jetta said more sharply.

I'm losing it. Shaking his head, he got back to the notch in the wall and took aim. From the zoom on the gun sight, he saw the four cadets spread out in a line, firing at the second outpost. Soldiers fired back, from both the tower lookout, and from behind rocky barriers on the ground.

He fired off a few rounds near the four cadets, hitting the tops of the rocky crags and sending plumes of dust into the air. *That will buy them some time.*

He looked back at Jetta and Iggie. Both girls stood on their tip-toes, looking over the wall to the valley below.

"You give her the instructions," Jetta said to Iggie, pushing off from the wall and grabbing the rifle from the other downed soldier.

"But I—"

"You can do it!" Jetta said, joining Cam's side.

"Nice," she said, noticing the dust he had kicked up.

Cam eyed her, waiting for sarcasm or an insult; things that would have come out of any other cadet's mouth when he made a good move. But none came. Instead, the green-eyed girl took aim, firing off into the air, in the general direction of their team, but missing by a large margin.

"*Skucheka,*" Jetta muttered in her native tongue as the gunfire slowed from the ground team, and the enemy soldiers advanced, coming within twenty meters.

"Sanders is out," Cam guessed. "They won't hold."

Jetta ran over to Iggie, looking out into the valley. Concerned by the intensity of their conversation, Cam shot off a few more rounds, then joined them.

"She needs more time."

"We don't have time," Jetta said, looking to Cam, then looking back out.

Cam squinted, his Cerkan eyes not accustomed to such low light. Out in the distance, Tomia stumbled through the uneven terrain, her hands reaching out before her, keeping balance and searching for obstructions. Spotlights from the stronghold, previously trained on the ground team, fanned out, scanning the scree fields, ridges, and valley.

"Tomia – crouch down, now!" Jetta shouted.

The Cerkan did so, flopping down as a spotlight swept over her area. Covered by a rock outcropping, she stayed hidden, but trapped. By the timing of the spotlight sweeps, and with her blindness and communications delay, she couldn't move more than four or five meters at a time.

Cam ran back over to check on the ground team. Only four guns flashed from inside the protection of the dust plume. Enemy soldiers now surrounded whomever remained active, firing relentlessly, pinning them down.

"She can't make it," he heard Iggie say.

"She has to."

Cam looked back, seeing Jetta climbing over the wall. He knew what she would do, the sacrifice she intended. But it wasn't hers to make.

Jamming his weapon into his waistband, he ran over to Jetta and grabbed her by the arm, pulling her back over. As she crashed down on the tower floor, he flipped over and scaled back down, half skidding down the stone wall. He landed on an angle, twisting his ankle, eliciting a sharp pain that traveled up his leg and caught his

96

breath. Forcing himself onward, he put most of the weight on his opposite leg, running as fast as he could toward Tomia.

"Cam, what the hell?!" Jetta shouted into the com.

He didn't know how to explain it to her, let alone himself. With every step he took, with every crunch of his ankle and aching pleas from his back, he closed in on Tomia, ducking and dodging the sweeping spotlights, his need an iron wall against all pain.

"What—"

"It's me," Cam said, crouching down and holding down Tomia as she fought his grip. "I got you."

"You can't, Cam—"

"I'll shield you. We have to run."

"Cam, I—"

"No time," he said, slinging her arm over his shoulder. He looked at rocky incline fifty meters ahead, where the blue portal glowed underneath a ledge. Part of the stronghold stretched out over the cliff. He spotted three gun turrets, all lit, but none firing. Not yet.

He tried to time his run, but by the frequency of the spotlight sweeps, he knew it wouldn't be long until all sights turned on them.

(I can't do this).

I have to.

"No tomorrows," he whispered.

As the yellow light grazed the top of their cover, he lurched forward with Tomia. "Come on!"

Tomia gripped his sides, nails digging into his suit. He grimaced, pushing forward, hauling her when she couldn't see the step.

"Stop, Cam, I can't go this fast," Tomia pleaded, tears streaming down her face.

"Cam, you're spotted," Iggie said as the spotlights froze, then converged on his location.

He didn't reply, not as the gun turrets zeroed in on him and Tomia.

"Get on my back," he said, stepping in front of her and allowing her to climb up. "Don't cross your legs – squeeze my sides and hold yourself up; grip under my arms, on my shoulders. Hide your head!"

"Cam!" she screamed as the turrets crackled to life.

97

Gritting his teeth, Cam pushed himself faster, harder. Tomia's weight against his body, the feel of her tension, her vulnerability, of the pain that crashed over him with every step, stripped away all thought, all of his cares except one.

"Cam, fall back," Jetta cried. "You won't make it—"

Twenty meters.

The first shot hit him in the chest, shooting fire across his torso and into his heart and lungs. Suit constricting, his breath squeezed down into desperate gasps.

Thirty meters, he told himself.

The second shot hit him in the hip. White fire cut across his pelvis, blazing into his intestines, singing his bowels. Nausea rippled through his belly, and he gagged and coughed, struggling to breath, to stay upright, as another shot grazed his right thigh.

Pain was one thing, but the suit constricting, making it harder for him to move, was another.

"Cam, please," Tomia begged, pressing her head behind his. "You're hurt, I can't hold on—"

You have to. I have to.

"Ah!" she screamed, another shot grazing the top of her knee and splashing his abdomen. She yanked back, off-balancing him as another shot clipped his ear. Right side of his face blazing with heat, he tried to tell her to hold tight, but his stiffened jaw wouldn't respond.

Ten meters.

The final shot got him in the face, blinding him in an instant. The whole world went dark as he crashed down on the terrain, striking his face on the rock. His nose, already throbbing from the enemy's attack, exploded open. Blood gushed down into his mouth, and neck, but he didn't stop to tend to the injury. Instead, he rolled over, on top of Tomia, shielding her as best she could as the shots continued, pummeling his back and legs, setting every nerve fiber ablaze.

"Cam… Cam…" Jetta's words buzzed in the distance. "We're coming. Just hold out."

Just hold out…

("…For blue sky tomorrows.")

Suit rigid, his breath constricted and face bloodied, he laid on top of Tomia, arms wrapped tight. He could tell by the feel of her hip and shoulder that she faced up to him.

"Tomia..." he eked out.

No response.

"Tomia..." He shook her shoulder, then touched her face. Smooth cheeks, breath on his fingers near her nose. He patted her around the neck, then felt something warm and sticky near the base of her skull.

She's out.

His heart squeezed down. This was his fault. He acted irrationally, put her in danger.

What if she's hurt, bad? No, the teachers would stop the sim, wouldn't they?

"I heard that some kids die in the Academy," he remembered Tomia saying. *"Training accidents, bad battle sims..."*

Chak—

I have to do something, he thought, his body trapped in the hardened suit. *But what can I do? I'm already dead.*

He thought of Rogman, of his black eyes, the way his smile portended a lust for violence and war. *"What will you do to ensure your survival, Cadet Ferros?"*

A cry boiled up from his stomach, leaking out in a high-pitched howl through his constricted throat. Every muscle in his body screamed, every cell bursting with rage. His suit cracked and bent like weakened plastic. Face and body buzzing, he grabbed onto Tomia's uniform top with one hand, and, crawling on his hands and knees, his suit zapping him with pain signals, he shuffled them forward. Sharp rocks cut into his suit, sliced through his palm.

"Cam!"

Off in the distance, he heard the scuffing of feet. The gun turrets overhead fired in rapid succession.

Blinded, in the darkness, he pushed forward, lungs on fire, entire body burning inside electric flames. He didn't know where the blue portal lay, only that the sound of the turrets, the sound of death, meant only one thing.

"Left, Cam, go left!"

Words and sound meshed into the rapid pulse in his ears, his breath sucked inward as he gave everything he had to haul Tomia forward, into darkness, into the promise of blue sanctuary.

Hold out…

Hold out…

Please…

"Cam-cam, don't make me sing it."

(Kara—I'm so sorry I couldn't—)

Something chimed. The gunfire ceased. In the background, he heard the whine of the holographics as they powered done.

"You did it!"

Kara?!

No. Not her.

He collapsed, his body finished.

(I'm so sorry…)

Hands turned him over, onto his back. Voices cried out, sounding shocked, horrified.

"Did we…?"

"Yeah, Cam." Iggie's voice, giddy and thankful. "You *chakking* killed it. How'd you do that? I thought they got you…"

As the suit relaxed, letting him breathe again, he opened his eyes. Shadows and light circled in front of him. He made out faces, and a glowing blue sky.

He wanted to smile, to feel relief, to believe that it meant something. All of his body throbbed and ached. He allowed the others to sit him up, and watched as they tended to Tomia as she revived. The other four, with Wexlan and Vorri assisting Sanders, ran over to their position, cheering and whooping.

"Aw, *chak*, here comes the teachers," Iggie muttered as the doors to the arena opened, and two teachers and a team of medics raced inside.

Jetta turned to Cam, face grim, perturbed. "You didn't have to do that, you know. I would have figured something else out. You can't just sacrifice yourself like that."

Cam didn't have the strength to fight her, to tell her the truth.

"Is that your idea of 'thanks?'" Tomia muttered, shaking out her head. "I'm pretty sure he just cheated simulated death to save us."

100

Jetta frowned, but nudged his boot with her knuckles, muttering, "yeah thanks, Cam. I don't know how you did that."

"We couldn't have done it without you," Tomia added softly.

Cam let his head drop down, his strength failing. Still, his heart felt lighter, steadied. As the medics hauled him off, he thought of Rogman.

You're watching, aren't you? he thought, tasting the dried blood on his teeth. The simulations would only get harder, worse, putting more at stake than his academics or physical health. Rogman was up to something, testing him, testing all of them. *I have to figure out why, for what,* he thought, as the medics shone a light into his eyes, making them sting. Gloved hands lifted from his face, smeared with his blood. *Before it's too late.*

Chapter 13

Cam didn't think they'd keep him for more than an hour or two in the infirmary – and certainly not more than a day. He'd shown up with broken bones, lacerations, and abrasions before, discharged after treatment, and expected by his teachers to show up to his next training session. But whatever he'd done this time—whatever damage he'd caused his body or the expensive training uniform—was enough to necessitate more than one doctor reviewing his chart, and medication line to be threaded into his upper arm.

Cam turned over on his side, trying to relieve the pins and needles running the length of his nervous system. White, over-starched sheets and the thin blue patient gown felt like sandpaper against his bare skin. Grimacing, he adjusted his shoulders and neck to better rest his head against the flattened pillow, trying to find some angle of relief. Flashing monitors, positioned in a ring around him in the isolation bay, shone on his face, making it impossible to find darkness, even closing his eyes.

Not that it really mattered. Whatever white medication dripped down from the intravenous bag and into his veins made all his problems distant. Even when masked attendants applied cooling gel to his skin, he didn't stir for more than a few seconds, settling back into a place somewhere in between reality and dream.

"He'll need another few weeks at least, Commandant," someone said, their voice floating in a baritone tremble above his head. "I've never seen someone override the neuro-stims in the training suits."

A cold, familiar voice hissed back. "I want him back in service as soon as possible."

"I'm worried about neuropathy, some of the long-term effects— "

"Then dose him with bioenhancers."

"I can't keep doing that to these kids, sir. We just don't know the consequences—"

"I know someone who will."

Feet shifted, a chill settled over the conversation.

"No... No, not that, uh—" Disgust, a fumbling of words. *Thing?* "I'll take care of it."

"You have your orders, Verdebear."

Swallowing felt like crushing glass in the back of this throat. But he felt no thirst, no hunger, only the fires of his nerves, and the teasing flames of old haunts.

"Wake up, Cam..." someone whispered. A frightened voice. Young, female. "Please, wake up. Something's happening. I'm scared."

When he tried to peel open his eyes to catch a glimpse of her face, a hand touched the back of his arm, sending a shock up into his shoulder.

"Sorry, Cam!" The hand withdrew as he moaned. "I'm so sorry..."

Time ticked by again in a confusing blur. At one point his mother visited him at the bedside, her dead eyes staring through him, clutching a bottle to her chest, whispering accusations. *"It's those* chakking *leeches—they've done this! Murderers! Killers!"*

Veins turning white, he heard Iggie's snorting laugh, saw a glimpse of Tomia's red hair.

(Kara. I have to find Kara.)

Flash forward. The triplets appeared at his bedside, the girls holding hands, Jahx standing far off the right. Their eyes burned like embers, their mouths sucked inwards. *"Run, Cam."*

What is—

Machine noise, a grating of gears. Something heavy and terrible creaked over him.

What is that?

A putrid, earthy odor, punctuated the air, making his nostrils flare, his shoulders hike. Terrified, he forced his eyelids back, vision swimming as a red eye, burning in gray flesh, hovered over his face.

He shut his eyes, scream caught in his throat. *What is that?!*

Iggie and Tomia, their disembodied voices squeezed by fright, answered: *Monster.*

103

No—

He tried to lift his head off the pillow, but it felt impossibly heavy, pinned to the foam. When he opened his eyes again, there was no monster, only beeping machines, and the steady white drip.

What is happening to me?

Then, as the fires died, and his skin no longer seethed like an open canker, he had enough. Reaching over with his right arm, he pulled out the white line threading into his arm. Blood oozed out of the attachment site, but he sat up and staunched it with the white sheets.

"Hey, you're awake."

Cam drew up the sheets as if to shield himself. When he saw Jahx standing by the doorway, he relaxed a little.

"What are you doing here?" he croaked, his throat scratchy and dry.

Jahx looked over his shoulder, as if he was breaking a rule. "Thought you'd like a visitor."

Shaking his head, he tried to regain some sense of time and orientation. "What day is it?"

Jahx walked over to the cabinets until he found a sterile specimen cup and filled it with water from the sink. "The seventh."

He did the math twice, to make sure it wasn't just his clouded mind as Jahx handed him cup.

"It's been two weeks," Jahx confirmed as Cam took a sip, then gulped the rest down.

Two weeks?! It couldn't have been that long. When he looked down at his body, at the thin frame beneath the sheets and the fading pink spider-marks interconnecting across his arms and legs, the weight of the reality sunk in. *Two weeks…*

"I made you something," Jahx said, pulling up a work stool next to the bed and taking a seat. He pulled out a dataclip from his jacket pocket and handed it to Cam.

"What is it?"

"My notes from both classes. Stuff you missed, homework help, research for our study paper…" He trailed off, shying away for a moment as he wiggled in his seat.

Cam held the dataclip between his first three fingers. Even touching the cool plastic made his skin tingle. He tightened his hand around the clip, making his hand and arm buzz.

"I'll never catch up," he whispered. Tears stung his eyes, but he blinked them back. "I can't…"

(Kara. I'm so, so sorry.)

Jahx regarded him, soft blue eyes assessing what to say. "Let me help."

Guilt tightened down like a vice around his heart. "Why would you do that?" He thought of Colin, of kindness and sacrifice. "Why…?"

I don't deserve that.

Jahx twirled the black hair at the nape of his neck, sending waves of déjà vu rippling through his stomach.

"You helped me. You helped my sister, Jetta, in that sim."

"But you don't have to help me," he replied. "I'm not anything. I'm just a…nobody."

Jahx tilted his head. "Who made you believe that?"

Cam looked away from him, discomfited by his innocence.

"Look, I'll go through my notes with you between classes."

"You really believe you can help me?"

"You need to trust yourself more," Jahx said, pulling himself closer with the side rail to the bed. "I've seen your 4.85 rating."

"Just because I'm good at killing—"

"No," Jahx said, touching his fingertips. Prickling sensations shivered up Cam's arm. "You're good at figuring things out, even with everything stacked against you, like the teachers not explaining how the battle sims work. You're good, Cam. You just don't see it."

A lump forming in his throat, Cam covered up his embarrassment with a chuckle, withdrawing his hand. "You sound like my sister."

"You have a sister?"

"Well, three. Younger twins and an older sister. The twins were really close. Annoyingly so."

Jahx grinned. "I can relate."

"But you're triplets. I figured you'd all be close."

"We are," he said, voice dropping to a whisper.

Jahx didn't have to say it. *He's still the odd one out.* Cam wasn't sure what that meant, or why Jahx felt that way, only that he seemed pained by it beyond what his blue eyes showed.

The words blurted out of his mouth before he could stop them. "They're dead."

"Your family?"

"Except…except for my older sister, Kara. She was taken by the USC."

Jahx thought for a moment before speaking. "Is that why you're here?"

"She's all I have."

Jahx didn't say anything, studying him with a long gaze, his hands resting on the siderail.

Bending his knees up, Cam allowed himself to be pulled back into memory, into his final moments with his sister. "She used to always sing this stupid song, *Blue Sky Tomorrows.* It was like her promise that things would somehow get better, even when things were the worst. I guess I used to believe in it because *she* believed it." He closed her eyes, imaging her face, the soft, melodic hum of her voice. "She was always fighting, always doing the right thing for us, me, everyone around her. She always believed things would somehow be okay because of the good people of the world. Good people like her."

"Would you…" Jahx stopped, his voice cracking.

"What?" Cam didn't believe the pain he saw in Jahx's face.

"…could you sing that song?"

Cam scoffed, but when Jahx's eyes, now misted, met his, he cleared his throat. "Um… *Rain drops a fallin' today, washin' all our tears away. But the sun will come again, and take away our sorrows. Just hold out, my love—*"

He stopped, blinking back the tears before speaking the last words:

"—for blue sky tomorrows."

A long silence stretched out between them.

"That's beautiful," Jahx finally said, wiping his eyes with the back of his uniform sleeve. "I needed something like that."

Cam frowned. "Come on, really?"

106

"I'm afraid," he said, eyes darting back to the door, "of the future. It's hard to talk to my sisters about it. We don't always agree about things."

Cam bunched up the sheets in his fists. "Kara would know what to tell you. She'd give you hope."

Jahx's response sounded weighted, strange, full of wistful longing. "I wish I could see her memory."

"Yeah, right," Cam said, waving him off, "then you'd be a *chakking* leech."

Silence.

What? Cam looked at Jahx, at the way his blue eyes iced over, his hands slipping off the siderail.

"I'd better get going," Jahx said, walking to the exit. He paused at the door, forcing a smile. "I'm glad you're feeling better."

"Jahx—" He reached out, as if to stop him, though he didn't know what he wanted to say. He didn't want him to go, but he knew he'd hurt him somehow, more terribly than he even knew. *I'm sorry.* He pulled back his hand, hiding it under the sheets. "Um…see you later?"

"Yeah, sure," Jahx said, giving a slight wave before heading out.

Cam laid back, listening to his heart beep on the monitors, reciting the promise he made to himself.

"No tomorrows…"

The words fell against him, hollow and fragile, breaking against whatever sorrow still lingered in the room.

***

One of the doctors came in fifteen minutes later, scolded him for removing the medication line and replaced it with the aid of a nurse.

"When can I get out of here?" Cam asked, trying not to show how much even simple touch pained him as the nurse wrapped the new line around his left upper arm and the doctor restarted the drip with a transparent liquid.

"If you're lucky, in a few weeks," the doctor said, pinching the line below a port as he screwed a syringe. He drew down the medication from the bag and into the syringe, released the line, and then pushed it through. A salty taste spread out across Cam's tongue and touched his nose. *"If you're lucky."*

Cam's heart sank. In a few weeks, the academic semester would come to an end, meaning he'd back into class right in time for finals. And if he failed—

I've got to get out of here.

Cam gripped the siderails to the bed, and with a grunt, swung his legs over the side of the bed. The second his bare feet touched the ground, he screamed. Daggers lanced up toes and exploded into his calves.

"Nurse, get a sedative—"

"No!" Cam said, gritting his teeth as the doctor helped him reposition his legs back on the bed. Where the doctor touched him felt scorched, burnt to a crisp, even though his skin appeared intact. Cam hyperventilated, unable to tolerate the movement or the stimulus.

The nurse, returning from medicine cabinet from across the room, handed the doctor a hypo as the monitors alarmed of his rapid heart rate.

"No!" he screamed as the doctor accessed his medication line.

"We're just trying to help you, Cadet."

"He said no, doctor."

Cam's breath hitched in his chest at the sound of Rogman's voice. All eyes turned to the darkened man standing in the doorway, his hands clasped behind his back.

"But, Commandant—"

"Leave us."

The doctor and the nurse scurried out, leaving Cam alone with the Commadant.

As he tried to slow his breathing, Rogman walked over, taking his time, cold indifference in his face as he watched Cam struggle.

"Quite the feat you pulled off in the arena, Cadet."

Cam couldn't tell if he meant it as a compliment, or an insult. Unnerved by his dark gaze, Cam rushed to fill the silence. "I did it for the win, sir."

"And at cost," Rogman said, nodding to spider-like irritations covering his skin. "I'm impressed."

Still sitting up, Cam scooted back in the bed on his knuckles, too terrified to mind the pain.

"Pathetic, though, that a soldier like you would take orders from a launnie."

The change in his tone, the sharpness to his pronunciation of the word *launnie*, shocked any response right out of him. Cam stared at the Commandant, unable to comprehend his sudden shift.

"The Drachsi triplets are a disease," Rogman said, emphasizing his disgust with a twitch of his mustache, "their marginal performances and ill-effect on other students jeopardize the entire academy."

"B-but sir, it was Jetta's strategy that won that match."

"Jetta's strategy?" he said, eyes narrowing.

"Yes sir," he said, stomach twisting as the Commandant studied him.

"Are you saying that they're underperforming in class?"

The heart rate monitor ticked upward. Cam clutched the bedsheets in his hands, sending electric needles into his palms and wrists.

"I-I don't know, sir. I'm only in class with Jahx."

"And what have you observed?"

Cam's heart fluttered in his chest. Gut screaming at him, he didn't want to share what he knew, not when he didn't know the stakes. But Rogman, his dark eyes cutting through him, dissecting his silence, threatened him with authoritative power that promised swift punishment for any defiance.

"He's avoiding fights," he blurted.

"Avoiding fights?"

Stupid. His cheeks heated with anger. *Why did I say that?*

"Uh… I mean, he's figuring out ways to stay out of trouble."

Rogman straightened up a moment. "I'm aware of your report."

"But I haven't submitted it—"

Rogman's lips compressed into a strange smile. "You don't think I'm always watching?"

Cam gulped, his hands extending out, releasing the sheets.

"You're a true soldier, cadet; hardened, brutal. I suggest you display those skills outside the arena as well – unless you're planning on being sent to the front lines, too."

The Commandant bent down, mustache tickling Cam's ear. "Show me what you're really capable of, cadet."

As the Commandant left, hands clasped behind him as he marched out the door, Cam didn't relax. Instead, he stayed upright in his bed, breath caught in his chest, unsure of what he just witnessed.

Rogman knows more than he's telling me.

The observation felt oversimplified, and did nothing to quell the dread burrowing into his stomach.

Looking at his hands, at the inflamed tracks that branched across his palms and down his arm, he realized a more terrifying truth. *I am a monster.*

Ready and willing to do anything for the kill, for the win. For his sister.

But Rogman didn't know everything. He never filled out his observations after the training simulation about the other cadets. Or Tomia and Iggie.

Or Jetta.

Squeezing his eyes shut, he tried to keep the Colin's face from flashing across his mind as it had when he defied Jetta and took aim at the second outpost.

His chest tightened. *Rogman doesn't know what I saw...*

Should he?

He considered Jahx's strange reaction not an hour ago when he made a racist remark.

No, he decided, lying back down on his bed, allowing his weakened muscles to relax. *Rogman is the enemy.*

Quietly, as he stared up to the ceiling, skin buzzing, he decided he couldn't afford to trust anyone. Not now, not when he sensed Rogman about to change the rules again to shake out the dead weight.

Everyone here is my enemy.

He thought of Tomia, Iggie. And Jahx, the boy with the kindest smile and bluest of blue eyes. His heart aching, he reaffirmed his intentions out loud, fingers digging into the specialized mattress. "Everyone."

***

As soon as he saw the second shift nurse coming down the hall toward his bay, intravenous medication bag in hand, Cam feigned sleep, letting his head loll off to his left.

Heavy boots thumped against the tile, but paused at the door, then proceeded inside lighter, softer.

Breathe... he thought, relaxing his muscles as best as possible, trying to keep himself steady. The medication pump to his left chimed, then popped. Cam opened his eyelids a crack, stealing a glance of the nurse changing out the medication drip. He shut them again, waiting what he paced out in his mind as fifteen seconds, then ventured another look. He caught her as she fiddled with the settings, and the pump chirped.

"Identification, please."

Even from the side, unable to see the actual keypad, he deciphered the numbers from the sound and the angle from which she entered the passcode.

113775, he thought, closing his eyes again. She fiddled with the monitor above his head and checked the vital signs scanner arcing over the bed, but he didn't care about those things. As soon as he heard the soft *click-click* of her typing away on her datapad, he dared peek open an eye again. Sitting at his bedside, her head down as she worked, she charted away, blue and yellow light reflecting off her face.

And her glasses...

It took him a moment to adjust to the image mirrored on the lenses. Words like *neuroregeneration* and *doperidenimium 50mg* stumped him at first, but as she flew through her charting, he grafted more and more from the reflection.

The nurse checked her sleeve, noting the time, and glanced at the door. Cam shut his eyes, sensing trouble. A moment passed, then he heard her typing again.

He peeked only one eye open. The images reflecting off her glasses changed into pictures of people in uniform, news breaks, social media feeds, and videos. At first the idea of her taking a break in his room irked him, but a headline captured his attention.

"Sightings of Deadwalkers Near Homeworlds Raises Concern."

Deadwalkers.

111

He'd heard the name before, long ago, when his sister got involved with one of her many political protest groups. Even Kara's most liberal friends spoke of the unusual biomechanical species in whispers, as if too afraid to share their fears out loud. Something about them being reanimated corpses. *Something about their suffering,* he thought, trying to remember the details.

"Bloody filth," the nurse muttered under her breath as she scrolled through the article. When she stopped on the picture of a man twisted by machine, half of his face punctuated by wires, his heart rate spiked.

That face—

Not that one, but something similar. Something he just saw—

(A red eye, burning in gray flesh.)

No, he shut his eyes, not wanting to see more, *just a dream!*

The nurse clicked her tongue, then whispered: "If you know what's good for you, cadet, get out. Now."

Confused and already terrified, his heart rate doubled.

The nurse's voice rose in pitch. "F-ferros?"

"Nurse!" a sharp voice said, cutting through the steady beep of the monitors. Cam jumped a little, but kept his eyes closed, hoping his movement didn't get noticed. "This is not your assigned break time."

Something tipped over, smacking against the hard tiles. "S-sorry, doctor."

Holding his breath, Cam opened his eyes just enough to see the nurse, head bowed as she righted the upturned chair, drop the datapad on the opposite counter and scuttle out of the bay. The doctor wavered a moment, hands on his hips, looking back and forth at the nurse and Cam. Finally, hands jammed in his white lab coat, he hurried after her.

After a few calming breaths, Cam sat up with a groan. The medication dripping into his arm made him sleepy, his head spin with even the slightest movement.

Not anymore.

Leaning over the siderail, angering the left side of his ribcage, he caught the edge of the medication pump with his fingers and dragged it toward him. Turning the face of the device toward him, he brought up the keypad and typed in 113775. The device menu opened up, giving him access to everything from the drip rate to the bolus amount.

What are you giving me? He scrolled down to the concentration and obtained the name. *Cryoxotin.*

After pausing the pump, he talked himself into a terrible – but his only – idea.

Only a minute left.

This is going to suck.

He swung his legs over the bed again. As his bare feet and legs, atrophied and covered in spidery streaks, poked out from his patient gown, he prepared himself for the worst.

This is going to really *suck.*

He touched his right foot down on the floor first, then his left. The pads of his feet lit on fire, shooting flames into his calves and burning up his thighs.

No—I can't—too bad—

Grinding his teeth together, he envisioned his sister's face just a meter away, near the counter, where the datapad lay, and put more weight on his feet. The monitors alarmed of his high heart rate.

"*Chak,*" he muttered. He couldn't alert the medical staff.

Gotta slow my heart rate.

Against the pain, against the rapidly approaching deadline of the datapad shutting off, he took a breath and held it, forcing his heart to slow. He'd seen the trick before, when his mother evaded the social service lie-detector tests, holding her breath to slow down her heartrate during the most painful questions about her caretaking competence.

It'll pass, he told himself, letting the pain wash over and pass through him, until the over-sensitized nerves in his feet calmed to a pulsating throb. Using the siderail, he got himself on his feet, his legs wobbling. Once steadied, he took his first step, then another, his weakened muscles protesting the expenditure.

My heartrate—

Alarms sang.

After grabbing the datapad off the counter, he took a stumbling step and caught himself on the IV pole.

Boots clacked against the tile, heading toward him.

Chak—

He threw himself on the bed. The crash drove fresh spikes through his hips and shoulder, but he held his breath as he wiggled back to the head of the bed, wedging the datapad under his pillow.

"Cadet!" one of the medics barked at him, rounding into his bay, "what are you doing?"

The pump—

Stupid. He shouldn't have messed with the settings just yet. *Can't let him think I'm with it!*

Flopping over on his side, he slurred his words and let his eyes drift shut. "Don't go, Mom…"

He moaned a few times, then stilled, pretending to fall back asleep.

The medic took a few steps inside.

He's not buying it.

The thought of being tied down—or worse—chemical restraints—

What if they tell Rogman?

"Sir."

A young voice called from not too far away.

"What are you doing here, cadet?"

Jahx?

Cam opened an eye, not able to see more than the medic's blue scrubs, and the back of his head tipped down to speak to the much smaller young boy.

He came back—

"I came to visit my friend."

Friend. The word didn't seem right. Reflexively, he curled his toes and flexed his arms against his side.

Someone adjusted the sheet over his lower body. "Your *friend* is sleeping."

"That's okay. I'll just sit with him."

Pause. "Don't you have something better to do, cadet?"

Jahx responded, a quiet assurance in his voice. "I'd like to be here, sir."

The IV pump chirped once. *It's back on; it must have been on preprogramed minute pause…*

Maybe the medic didn't hear it. Either way, Jahx bought him some time, enough to evade immediate capture.

The medic rounded over to the pump and the vital signs monitors, checked whatever he needed to, and then left. Cam waited until Jahx had pulled up one of the stools on the opposite side of his bed before scooting up on his elbow and re-pausing the pump.

"You're not surprised," Cam said after resetting the pump to pause for ninety minutes instead of one.

Hiding his grin, Jahx pulled out his datapad and called up the lessons from their chemistry class. "Not at all."

Cam raised the head of the bed with the side rail controls and shifted his weight back. The pressure aggravated the sensitized skin on his tailbone and buttocks, but he didn't show his discomfort, hoping that Jahx wouldn't pick up on how weakened he'd become.

Not that he'd say anything, Cam thought. No, Jahx was too polite.

"Okay, let's start with covalent bonding and isomerism," Jahx said, projecting a holographic image with his datapad.

Cam listened closely, unaware of the time that passed. Without meds, his skin burned, but he cared less and less, drawn into Jahx's words, by the excitement in his voice, and the knowledge he shared with such ease.

"…So, depending on the number of electrons shared, the bond energy and length vary."

"I get it," Cam said as Jahx projected an electron. "When the number of shared electrons increases, the bond length between the atoms is decreased, and the energy increased."

"Like…?"

"Um, Silicon…" Cam squeezed his eyes shut, trying to remember the others. "Oh! Diamonds, germanium."

Jahx beamed. "Yep."

"Let's go over ionic bonding—and metallic bonding—and—"

Jahx chuckled as he shut off the projection. "Later. I've got to get back."

"No," Cam said, looking to the door, knowing that a nurse or tech was bound to come back soon anyway. "Stay."

The black-haired boy blushed. "My sisters are expecting me at dinner."

"Can't you be late?"

"You've met Jetta," Jahx said, raising an eyebrow.

"Yeah…she is kinda bossy."

"Kind of?"

Cam couldn't help but laugh. "Okay, she's very bossy."

"She's just overprotective. My other sister, Jaeia, isn't as bad, but she's a worrier."

"Sounds like they smother you."

Jahx shrugged. "We watch over each other. We've always had to."

The lilt in the boy's voice, the way his gaze shifted, his fingers twitched. "What happened… on Fiorah…?"

He didn't know how to ask it, nor did he even know how to continue as the boy shrunk into himself.

"S-Sorry."

Jahx shook his head. "Don't be."

"I just—God—sorry," he said, pulling at his sheets, trying to do something with his hands.

"Really, it's okay." Jahx rest his right arm on the side rail, blue eyes meeting his for a second before looking down at the floor. "Nobody's ever asked before."

Cam picked at the hem of the draw sheet. "Forget it. It's not my business."

Jahx stared at him with such intensity that Cam looked away. *Is he mad at me?* Chak. *I shouldn't have said anything. Why would he tell me anything? I'm not his—*

(Friend? But he said—)

"We were adopted," he started, voice low, trembling, "by a kind man and his wife, Galm and Lohien. But Galm had some kind of debt to his brother, Yahmen, who owns the Fiorahian mines. Yahmen took Lohien away and put the rest of us to labor in those mines."

Cam held his breath, sensing something far more terrible on the tip of Jahx's tongue.

"My sisters and I did our best, but it was never good enough. We were starving, stealing food and water, doing desperate things to survive. And Galm—Lohien—our parents, we couldn't help them, and they couldn't help us."

116

He trailed off, his focus going beyond the room they occupied. "He always came at night. He'd choose one of us to beat and torment the rest with whatever game he'd concoct."

Violent images of a hulking humanoid barging in on his home ghosted his mind. Without wanting to, he imagined Jahx and his sisters huddled together, and a brittle older man trying to shield them.

"…And sometimes our parents weren't there. That's when he was the meanest. He liked to target me, because I was so small and sick, but Jetta would provoke him so he'd come after her," Jahx said, blue eyes misting. "I couldn't stand it—any of it—the violence, the cruelty—the way my sisters did everything they could to save me."

Jahx gripped the siderail, knuckles turning white. "But I couldn't stop him. I wasn't strong enough."

"Stop him?" Cam guffawed. "A full-grown man? What were you, like three years old?"

Something sparked in his blue eyes, a light Cam didn't expect. "I'm not strong like my sisters. Like you, Cam."

Cam swallowed hard. "Don't say that."

Jahx said nothing, his blue eyes steeled to his.

"You don't know what that means," he whispered, remembering the feel of the red scarf in his hands, and the snapping of bones.

Tears spilled onto Jahx's cheeks. With a quick wipe, he dashed them. "Sorry."

Body throbbing, Cam allowed whatever answer dwelled deep in his bones to surface. "I don't know what I can offer you, Jahx. I'm the last person that should ever give anyone advice."

He remembered the bittersweet taste of dried fruit, of the kindness etched in a dimpled smile. "But I do know one thing— you're good, Jahx. And this place—this galaxy—needs you more than it needs another *chakking* soldier."

Jahx sucked in his breath. From the knot in the boy's forehead, Cam couldn't tell if he provided relief, or caused more tension.

I shouldn't have said anything. What the hell do I know?

Then, blue eyes holding back all the words he couldn't speak, Jahx breathed a sigh of relief and grinned. "Thanks, Cam."

"Get going," Cam said, waving him off. "Last thing I want are your sisters pissed at me."

"Don't worry, it's our secret," Jahx said, gathering his things and standing.

"Our secret?"

Is he ashamed of me?

Jahx seemed to read his worry. "Maybe it's selfish," he said, reaching over the siderail, and touching the bedsheet near Cam's hand, careful not to cause him discomfort. "But I'd like to have one experience—one friend—that's mine."

As he turned and walked to the exit, he paused at the door, a lighted smile upon his face. "Thanks again, Cam. See you later."

Why is he thanking me? Cam said, waving as the boy left. *He just tutored me and—*

Cam stopped, realizing the tension in his muscles. *Jahx trusts me.*

He shouldn't, not after what he vowed.

Not after what I've done.

Hearing footsteps coming down the hallway, Cam reached over to the pump and restarted it. Later, he'd access the datapad stashed under his pillow, figure out more of what was happening, what they infused into his body, and the truth about his chances of recovery.

Now, he stared up at the ceiling, his pain growing distant as the medication flowed into his veins, he felt something ache in his heart, a longing he couldn't name, as he tried to forget the word that could undo all that he'd vowed.

***

"That's weird," someone said. Beeps and boops followed. "It says here that the only 250mls were infused over the last few hours. Must be an error."

A second voice, deeper, responded. "Clear and reset the pump. If it acts up again, we'll but a remote monitor on it. We can't take any chances. Hey—has Reppen found that missing datapad?"

"No. She probably left it in the mess hall again…"

Cam stirred, seeing a doctor and nurse exit. Fuzzy from the medication, but aware enough to realize his error, he chided himself. *Of course there's an infusion record. I've got to be more careful!*

Head spinning and body aching, he inched his way over to the edge of the bed and reached over the siderail for the pump. The keypad shifted and swung side to side, but he took a deep breath and inputted the nurse's code.

The hell is this stuff? he wondered, stopping the infusion and lying back down. After several minutes, his head cleared and the pains of his body returned in full force.

Not wasting any time, he reached under his pillow and retrieved the stolen datapad. Fiddling with the controls awakened the screen, and a prompt to enter an ID and code. Cam tried to remember the nurse's ID badge, but even on a good day he didn't think he could have retained such detail.

Screw it, he thought, ready to chuck it under the bed to make it look like it accidentally got dropped, but his eye caught several icons on the bottom of the screen: a mortar and pestle, a blue cross, and a calendar.

I've seen that blue cross before. Looking around the room, he spotted a button jutting out of the wall with a blue cross stamped on its face near the vital signs machines, *core zero* written in bold letters across the top. *An emergency call button,* he guessed. *Don't need that now.*

The mortar and pestle reminded him of the apothecary shop he'd seen in the old marketplace on Cerka. Biting his lower lip, he tapped on the icon. A simple grey screen with a search bar and alphabetized list of medications popped up.

A drug lookup? He didn't hesitate, typing in the word he remembered seeing on the pump: *Cryoxotin.*

He skipped over the words he didn't know like *GABA neurotransmitter, trehalose, nucleating agents, analgesia, amnesia,* absorbing everything else he could: *for nutritional support, nerve-repair and protection, dose at 3 mg/kg per hour. For induction of cryostasis, bolus dose to 10mg/kg, then maintain at 5mg/kg per hour.*

Cryostasis. Freezing people, turning them into popsicles. Old memories stirred. He heard his mother, her venom punctuating her words as she slammed close the empty refrigerator: *"Freeze all those* chakking *leeches. Shoot them out into space; let them die."*

Into space. Cam recalled his sister talking about it with some of her friends. *No, that blonde guy.* The one that she left with right

119

before her abduction. But the conversation happened weeks before as Cam dug and crawled through trash cans in the break between apartment buildings. His sister and the blonde man rounded into the alley and continued a private conversation, unaware of his presence.

"They're freezing telepaths?"

"Yes, for relocation into deep space."

"Why?"

"That's classified, Kara."

"James, please—"

"Be patient. Help is coming."

The conversation didn't make sense to him then, hungry and exhausted, but now, sober enough to realize the deeper implications, he tensed.

Classified? Why would one of her friends say that?

(Why did she care?)

Other thoughts bubbled deep beneath the surface, but he shoved them aside.

Gotta figure the rest of this out.

He tapped on the calendar. Last names and times appeared. *This must be the shift assignments.* He didn't see much he could garner from the schedule. *Except...*

The shift change, a thirty-minute overlap that guaranteed a lull, or potential oversight. And Reppen; she'd be returning in twenty minutes for her regular shift. The words she whispered to him recycled through his mind: *"If you know what's good for you, cadet, get out. Now."*

What does she know?

Cam looked at the infusion pump and the line running into his arm, remembering the doctor using a syringe to draw up medication from the bag. *I need to stay awake, but I have to trick the pump.*

After stashing the datapad underneath his pillow, he looked around the room. A supply cart with labeled drawers stood near the vital signs machine. Squinting, he made out *hypos* and *syringes* on the third drawer down. With a clenched jaw, he swung his legs over and prepared for the worst.

Just three steps.

The same fires came roaring up the soles of his feet as he touched down and hobbled his way over. He rifled through the drawer until he found the biggest syringe.

I need something to pinch the line... Legs aching, he leaned on the supply cart, struggling to catch his breath against the pain driving at his nerves. He opened the first, second and forth drawer. Finally, a silver pair of scissors—

Not scissors—what are these? He grabbed the tool in his hand and tried to open it, but the interlocking teeth at the end wouldn't budge. *Oh, there—*

The locking mechanism on the pivoting tool. He disengaged it, and it opened. *Like a clamp.*

Perfect.

With a grunt, he eased back into bed and repositioned himself on his back. After screwing in the syringe to the port nearest to his arm, he clamped the line right where it attached to the hub.

Is this going to work? He restarted the pump and laid back down, pulling up the sheets over his arm and the syringe. The pump whirred and the medication chamber dripped. Without realizing it, he held his breath until the oxygen saturation monitor chirped that his sats dipped below 93%.

Breathe. He took a few gulps, still too anxious to find any relief until he saw the syringe back filling. Now, no discrepancies in drug-dose delivery. *And I'll just dump it in the sink later.*

As he lay in bed, pain a rising pulse throughout his body, he regained more of himself, his senses, and thought of what he'd say to nurse Reppen. Intimidation wouldn't work, especially coming from a sick, scrawny kid with no leverage, and he didn't have innocent charm like Jahx.

There has to be something.

Footsteps padded down the hall. Closing his eyes, Cam rolled onto his side with the medication line and pulled up the sheet over his shoulder to hide his contraption. *What do I have?*

A dimpled smile and trusting eyes ghosted his thoughts. *(...or take away?)*

He scrunched his hands together, into tight fists, making his fingers and palms tingle. *Don't think of that—don't—*

121

"Cam…" A tentative touch on his shoulder followed. "Wake up."

Cam didn't expect to see Iggie, nor the tears in her eyes. "Iggie?"

"You need to get out of here, Cam."

Propping himself up on his elbow, he tried to make sense of her distress. "What's wrong? What's happened?"

His gaze fell to the blue patient gown she wore, and the red track marks up her arms. Everything about her had changed. He couldn't reconcile her greater height, or the broadness to her shoulders. But his attention drew to her eyes, wide and sunken into her skull, that no longer held the assured attitude, only fear.

"The monster. The machine man. He's here. He's watching you. He's watching all of us."

"What?" He watched as she rubbed her forearms and lost focus. "Iggie, what's going on?"

"Cadet Prys." A tall figure appeared in the doorway, casting a shadow across his bed. A second figure, also obscured by the light, stood behind them. "You're not to be in here."

When she didn't budge, the tall figure entered. Cam recognized the man as one of the doctors that had been treating him, but didn't know his name.

"Increase the dosing rate on Ferros to 4mg/kg," the doctor said, grabbing Iggie by the arm and yanking her up. She cried out, but he half carried her out with urgency, only looking back to scold the nurse still lingering by the doorway. "I want him out!"

Cam didn't know what to say, or to do as Reppen stepped inside and headed toward the pump.

"Wait—what's happening?" he asked, sitting up too quickly. The sheet covering his arm and the syringe fell down, but he snatched it up and curled up on his side.

Reppen didn't look at him, keeping her eyes trained on the pump. "Stay calm, cadet."

"What happened to Iggie?" he insisted. "What is that doctor doing to her? Is she in trouble?"

Bending over, Reppen fiddled with the keypad, then eyed the door before answering. "Asking questions will get you in trouble."

"Just like checking social media and newsfeeds on duty?"

The nurse paused, her breath catching. "What?"

Cam watched her tense, her expression hardening as her hands retracted from the pump. *She's afraid.* But why?

That news feed— "Sightings of Deadwalkers Near Homeworlds Raises Concern"—*she didn't want me to see that.*

And Iggie, her ramblings about a machine monster; his nightmares of a red eye burning in gray flesh. The connection, just out of his reach, nagged at his gut.

"I need to get out of here," Cam whispered.

"You do," Reppen said, straightening up. "I'm trying to help you."

Cam eyed the pump. "This stuff keeps me asleep. I don't want to sleep anymore. I need to get back to training."

"This medication is repairing your nerve damage."

"But I don't like my dreams," Cam said. He watched her closely, playing his only card. "I've seen monsters."

"Monsters?"

"A machine monster," he whispered.

The nurse stiffened. "It's just a dream."

"Help me," Cam said, sensing something more to her discomfort as she glanced at the doorway. "I don't know what's happening."

Cam watched her response. Reppen, a young nurse with a pretty face and the pinched-up ears of some kind of human-hybrid, should sedate him right then until she could bring the doctor in and discuss his behavior, and file a report to their academy superiors. Instead, she looked at him with familiarity and consideration, something the Academy, especially the Dominion Core, should have eradicated in her training days.

"It's this war," she said, voice pitched just above a whisper. "Hatred, fear, violence—that's nothing new. But what this conflict has driven people to do, how it's being fought..."

She drifted off, her line of sight dropping to her feet.

What? In space? On the ground? Cam didn't understand what made this stupid war different from any of the other ones fought over the last million years, aside from the advances in weaponry and technology.

123

"It's not right," she whispered, voice quavering. "Some prices should never be paid, even in the name of freedom or justice."

"Is it the telepaths?" he asked.

"Not exactly," she muttered. Realizing herself, she ran her hand through her dark hair and cleared her throat, regaining her composure. "Look, I have a nephew your age. He's not a soldier, and neither are you. You're a kid, you should be a kid. This place shouldn't have you."

"It doesn't have me," he affirmed.

Reppen sported a humoring smile. "You don't have any family, do you?"

It took everything he had to keep from shouting. "What's that got to do with anything?"

"Everything, at least to the ones that make decisions around here."

Reppen got up and pressed the start button on the pump. "Heal fast, cadet."

"Wait—I thought you wanted to help me," he said, grabbing her arm as she turned to leave. The skin-to-skin contact lit his nerves afire, but he held fast until she gently removed his hand from her arm.

"I do. Sleep, recover. And whatever you do, stay out of the east wing."

As she walked out, Cam pretended to rest his head on his pillow and drift off, in case she looked back to ensure the efficacy of the new dosing. But even as he feigned sleep, his mind latched on to the last six words she spoke: *"...stay out of the east wing."*

Why would she say that? It made no sense; not when he couldn't walk more than a few feet in sheer agony, and she'd just upped his dosing, expecting for him to—

She knows.

He looked down, seeing the end of the syringe poking out of the sheet. When he grabbed her, it must have slipped.

But she didn't do anything about it.

Cam didn't adjust the sheet, allowing his secret to remain exposed. *Then I have to do something about it.*

But what?

I have to get stronger, fast.

He looked at the pump. Reppen upped the dose. *"This medication is repairing your nerve damage."*

This is the only chance I have.

Cam unscrewed the semi-full syringe and limped over to the sink, dumping and rinsing out the contents. Before getting back into bed, he unclamped the silver tool and placed both devices back where he found them.

Chak. *The datapad.* He hesitated as he removed it from under his pillow, noting to the 5% remaining battery life. In the end, it wouldn't serve him to have a dead datapad, but he could figure out something else with it. Leaning over the siderail, ribs screaming, he dropped the device under the bed to make it look like an accident. *So at least I won't get in trouble.*

As the medication flowed back into his veins, Cam stared up at the ceiling, at the light-controlled panels on the dimmest setting. Thirty seconds later, his vision wobbled, and he couldn't stay focused on any particular fixture.

Get stronger, he vowed, allowing the medication to take hold, mitigating the fires raging across his body. As he drifted off, he thought of the machine man, of Iggie's terror, and the battles still ahead.

Rogman, he thought, unsure if he imagined the shadowed figure standing in his doorway, *what horrible secrets do you keep?*

125

Chapter 14

When Jahx came back the next day, he stirred to the boy's touch.

"You okay, or should I come back tomorrow?" Jahx whispered, resting his hand on Cam's shoulder.

"No," Cam said, sliding himself up with a grunt. Head spinning, he motioned to the supply cart. Somehow, without explaining himself, Jahx figured out what he wanted and brought him back the syringe and clamp.

With fuzzy fingers he rigged the medication diversion and waited until his head cleared.

"How'd you come up with that?"

"Just got lucky," Cam remarked, rubbing his eyes and stretching out his legs. Then, as he scratched an itch on his neck, he realized that he didn't hurt. At least not as much. His nerves still tingled and burned, but the fierceness to the fires had dissipated.

Jahx pulled up the work stool next to Cam's bed and dropped an armload of datapads on the adjacent tray table. "You look better."

Cam regarded his skin. Faded pink and red spidery splotches still covered his arms and legs, but the optimism in Jahx's eyes challenged the ugliness he still felt. "Thanks. I feel…"

He didn't know what to say. *Weak* and *useless* came to mind.

"…like you need to get out of here?"

"Yeah, for sure," Cam said, shying away from Jahx's smile. "You… you look different."

"I know," Jahx said, tugging on the front of his uniform jacket. It strained at the shoulders and arms, as if he'd grown a few centimeters in width and height overnight. "I know me and my sisters are eating all the time now, but I never expected to grow out so fast."

Cam tilted his head, trying to remember Jahx's age and race. *Human…and five? That can't be right.* Now with how big he looked

126

now. If he didn't know any better, he'd guess Jahx closer to his age. *Especially the way he talks and thinks.*

Something didn't add up, but Cam didn't know what any of it meant.

"I don't like it," Jahx said, squirming in his seat, "but at least the bullies have lost interest."

"Stempton and those other *assinos* leaving you guys alone?"

"For now."

"Hey, that's worth something."

"Yeah."

"*Chak*...I don't think I've tasted food in weeks," Cam said, poking at his flattened belly. Not that he felt any hunger. Whatever else the cryo drug did, it certainly killed his appetite.

"Maybe it won't be too much longer. You do look better."

"Not soon enough," Cam said, running his fingers along his protruding ribs.

"Well, if you're up for it," Jahx said, picking out one of the datapads, "I thought we'd go over both chemistry and gaming strategy."

"Both?"

"Yeah..." Jahx diverted his gaze. "Everybody's so bent about the games around here."

Cam frowned. "What do you mean?"

"Like all the kids get hung up about scores in the gaming rooms, or in gaming class. And older kids keep talking about academy competitions."

"Competitions?"

"Yeah, something called the Endgame. The older kids make it sound like it's more important than grades."

Intrigued, Cam pointed to Jahx's datapad. "Show me."

"Here," Jahx said, holding up it up as he played a series of video files.

It's just like from class, he thought, watching as two cadets maneuvered their opposing fleets through an asteroid belt. Except this time the spherical playing field spanned ten meters and included hundreds of game pieces in more complex scenarios. *More like a real battle bridge.*

127

Cam considered what he said. "So maybe being good at games is better than acing chemistry?"

Jahx shrugged. "I guess."

"But it's not like you're trying to win at anything."

Jahx stiffened, holding onto the siderail with whitened knuckles. "I don't want to win; I just don't want to get iced out."

"So, you're saying you could?"

Anger flashed across his eyes, but then cooled as soon as he released his grips. "I'm saying that I don't want to play."

"It's not like you're killing real people, Jahx; it's just sims."

A troubled expression pinched up his brows. "For how long?"

The question surprised him. Cam pulled up his legs, mulling over his response as he eased himself into a cross-legged position. "You'd have to be the best, Jahx. You'd have to beat every last student in this academy and then some, just to get Rogman's attention. Orphaned humans and hybrids like you and me are just soldiers—just killers—to him. We'll be on the front lines before we're in charge of a real fleet."

Jahx studied Cam's face before responding. "Don't underestimate Rogman."

The seriousness to his voice, the shiver that escaped up Jahx's spine.

Jahx is afraid of Rogman.

What did Rogman say—or do—to Jahx?

"Come on," Jahx said, punching up the datapad in his hand. "We've gotta study."

Jahx moved on with the lesson, squelching the possibility of whatever questions Cam might have wanted to ask in that moment.

After thirty minutes of drilling two weeks' worth of lessons, Jahx paused. "Hey, the nurse is coming back."

Cam wormed his way back down in the bed, pulled the sheets over his shoulders, and closed his eyes. Without missing a beat, Jahx continued on, reading the lesson.

Soft footsteps entered. "Cadet."

"Nurse Reppen," Jahx acknowledged.

Cam kept his eyes shut, trying to steady his breathing, slow the ticking of his heartbeat on the monitors.

"Reading to him while he's in a medicated sleep won't do much."

"I have to try."

"Why, cadet? You should be studying yourself, or resting."

A pause. Cam tensed, fearing and anticipating Jahx's response. "I'll stay with him."

Why? he screamed in his head. *Not me—you don't know me, the awful things I've done—you shouldn't even be here—*

"That's commendable, cadet, but you should be worrying about your own academics and performance."

"Yes, ma'am," Jahx said, his tone automated, neutral, as if to defer any further conversation.

Monitors clicked and toned. Whatever Reppen adjusted or checked didn't stop Jahx from continuing the chemistry lesson, going on about carbon and nitrogen until she left.

"She's gone," Jahx said after another minute had passed.

Cam, not yet ready to open his eyes, stayed curled up as he whispered, "You shouldn't be here."

Jahx set down the datapad. "I'll go if you want me to."

Cam didn't know what to say, why his chest hurt, or an aching lump formed in his throat. "No, I just... I'm..."

(Scared.)

Opening his eyes and clearing his throat, he tried to regain some kind of self-control. "The teachers—Rogman—the other kids—this place isn't safe, Jahx, for either of us."

"Then we should help each other."

Cam's hands flinched, the feel of the red scarf ghosting his palms and fingers. "Why are you doing this?" he said, anger tinging his words. "What could I ever offer you back? I'm not smart like you, and I'm no *chakking* strategist."

He flung off the covers, sat up and turned out his arms, scarred and covered in inflammatory tracts, to Jahx. "Is this what you want?"

Jahx faded back, watching him closely, not belying any distress at his outburst. With a coolness he'd only known his older sister to possess, he replied: "You're more than your scars, Cam."

129

A forgotten memory, awakened by Jahx's words, trailed behind. *"I love you; there is love in your heart. Don't let anybody—anything—take that away, make you forget who you really are."*

Kara...

(You wouldn't recognize me anymore.)

Cam crumpled up the sheets in his fists and repeated himself just above a whisper: "What could I ever offer you back?"

Jahx pulled over the tray table with the datapads within Cam's reach. "I programmed some learning modules for you. This is everything you'll need to catch up for both classes in case you want to study while I'm away, or work on our research paper. It's all in there, okay?"

"Where are you going?"

"I'll be around," he said, rising.

"Wait," Cam said, trying to think of anything to keep him from going. *The datapad—*

"What?"

"Look under the bed."

Jahx bent down and picked up the Reppen's datapad.

"I couldn't get much out of it, but maybe you can."

Jahx flipped it over in his hands, running his fingers along the top.

"I mean, it's got military security systems, but maybe you can get something out of the other open access aps."

"Huh," Jahx said. But the way his eyes scanned the blackened screen, how his brow scrunched together—

He's going to try and hack that. But how? He's just a little kid—

Cam stopped himself. *Jahx is smarter than I even know.*

"That's the best I can do," Cam said as Jahx hid the datapad in his jacket.

"For now," Jahx said, blue eyes gleaming.

"Alright, well, if you do crack that thing—and don't get your *assino* caught—try and get me an early discharge."

"Haha, okay." Jahx reached out and closed his hand over Cam's, lingering for a moment. "Thanks, Cam."

Cam didn't immediately pull away; not until he realized how much he needed the touch. "And Iggie... Find out if she's okay. I saw her in here—"

Yesterday? He wasn't sure how much time had passed.

"Iggie? I saw her this morning on a lift with Tomia."

Cam shook his head. *Maybe it was just a nightmare.* "Okay, yeah, sorry; I thought... I don't know."

"Don't stress. You're on some heavy meds. Hey, I gotta go," Jahx said, checking his sleeve for the time.

"You know how to wake me up when you get back."

"Do you need help with that?" Jahx asked, pointing to the syringe backfilling with the cryotoxin as Cam fiddled with the line.

"Nah, I got it figured out."

"You sure?"

"Yeah. Bye, Jahx... and thanks."

The boy smiled, his face lighting up the room. "See you soon, Cam."

***

Dreamlike voices discussed his fate as he drifted in and out of chemical slumber.

"He's progressing better than I anticipated. I could have him discharged in a week."

"Keep him here until I say."

"Commandant, forgive me, but I thought you wanted him back in service as soon as possible—"

"This is a critical observation period."

"Sir?

"You have your orders, doctor."

Time passed, sliding him into the next dream. Machines, rusted and clunky, lumbered away somewhere distant. The sound pulled up a memory, one from long ago, before the skies turned black.

"Careful, Camzen," his father said, grabbing him by the hand and helping him up the factory steps. The feel of his rough callouses, the warmth, the comfort of a hand so much larger than his made him feel safe and secure, even as his father lead him inside the gigantic building with iron framing, towering smoke stacks, and slanted, sheet-metal roofing.

"This is where I work, son," his father explained, leading him down the aisles full of pumps and piping, rotating gears and open-

faced machines. He didn't understand most of it, only the sounds it made, the terrible grinding and grating, and the sparks that flew out from the conveyor belts as shiny raw materials got stamped into usable parts. He stayed close to his father, even as he proudly introduced Cam to his co-workers.

"This is my son, Camzen," his father shouted above the din, pushing him forward into a crowd of men and women in overalls and hard-hats, their faces covered in black grime. "Say hello, boy."

He couldn't, terrified by the machine noise, and the crowd of over-enthusiastic adults all wanting to tease and torment him for the sake of their own amusement.

"How you doin', sport?" a large man laughed. "You as tough-skinned as your Daddy?"

"How old are you, sweetie?" someone else asked. "Gosh, he's small for a Cerkan, isn't he?"

"Half-breed," someone chided.

"Watch your mouth," his father said, pointing to another oversized worker in the crowd.

Leave me alone.

Other folks chimed in:

"You're not going to keep him in school, are you?"

"Yeah, sign him up next year!"

But as the adults continued their badgering, the machine noise increased, drowning out their words.

Cam covered his ears. He didn't remember it playing out like this. No, his father should hoist him on his shoulders and lead him down another aisle, to let him marvel at the steaming vats of molten steel.

This isn't right, he thought, turning to his father and tugging on his jacket sleeve.

But his father didn't move. No one did.

What's happening?

The adults froze in place, caught in the middle of sentences or gestures, others in awkward poses.

Overhead lights flickered, dimmed.

Still covering his ears, Cam curled into a tight ball on the dirty factory floor.

Make it stop, make it—

"Camzen."

Cam looked up. His father, hands clasped behind his back and standing perfectly erect, stared back. None of the other adults moved. All the machine noise ceased. "Follow me."

Confused, but not knowing what else to do, Cam brushed himself off and followed his father, down the long aisles where both machine and person stood fixed in time.

But the environment didn't. The work overalls and hard-hats worn by the men and women turned into scrubs and surgical masks. Stamping machines transformed into scanners projecting images of wires and rods, and other metallic pieces screwed into bone.

As he trailed his father, he spotted a small-bodied person with frizzy blonde hair lying prone on a table, under surgical lamps. Her back, opened at the spine and retracted back with bloodied instruments, drew the interest of a half-circle of masked men. Iggie? No—!

Somewhere, beyond whatever boundaries he imagined, the steady tone of heart monitor flatlined.

When he stopped to investigate, a firm hand slapped down on his shoulder. "Keep up."

"Wait," Cam said, trying to understand the changing world as his father wrenched him forward. The machine noise picked up again, this time higher-pitched, unlike anything he'd ever heard from one of his father's factory machines. "Please, stop—"

His father led him down another aisle, then to the left, where the last hint of the factory disappeared, and white walls covered in orange biohazard signs gave warning of something terrible and hideous behind secured doors.

A voice, filled with terror, echoed down the hall. "Cam, run!"

Tomia? He looked all around. Where are you?

"Stay focused," his father said, coming up to a set of double doors. The sight of ISOLATION: EAST WING, painted across the frame, made Cam's knees lock and his stomach drop away.

"Father—" he said, trying to be heard above the sound of tortured metal.

Something bad is in there.

Something that grated and shrieked, like a mechanical scream.

133

His father waved his hand in front of the scanner affixed to the right of the double-doors and walked inside the darkened hallway. With a slight turn of his face, revealing the thick mustache that now adorned his upper lip, he whispered. "It's time, cadet."

At the far end of the east wing hallway, Cam made out the outline of some enormous object; something hunkered down with gray skin that gleamed in the emergency lights. A thing that bellowed like a blast furnace and screeched like a rusted gear as it unfurled, multiple legs stretching out, reaching—

Like a spider—

With a glowing red eye.

Cam screamed, trying to turn and run as the darkened hallway—and the machine monster—telescoped toward him.

"Camzen..." it wheezed, rearing back on its back legs. Colin's grey face prolapsed out of the reddened gash in its underbelly, his tongue rolling out of his mouth. "We've been waiting for you."

"Ferros, wake up—wake up!"

Strong hands shook him by the shoulders, shaking the nightmare's hold. The glowing red eye and Colin's dead face retracted in the flurry of small lights flashed into his eyes.

"Give him another amp of buridol," someone said.

As he became more aware of himself, of the tingling feel of his patient gown and bedsheets against his over-sensitized skin, the monitors alarming, and the five masked people crowding over him, he screamed.

"Stop, no!" He went for the medication line feeding into his arm, trying to yank it out, but the masked people pinned him back down on the bed. "Let me go—get me out of here!"

"Calm down, cadet."

Cam recognized the man's baritone voice, but, still frazzled, couldn't make the connection.

"You're safe. Calm down," he repeated, typing in in something to the medication pump.

Coolness followed into his forearm, branching up and out across his body. The trembling adrenaline reaction waned, then dissipated. Cam took a deep breath, then another.

134

"Good," the man said, waving off all but one of the other masked assistants. "Keep breathing. You're fine."

"W-what happened?" he asked, bewildered by the fear still lingering in his belly.

"We're tapering you off medications. It can give you very vivid dreams."

No, nightmares, Colin thought, wiping the cold sweat from his forehead. He looked again at the deep-voiced man. *Doctor...*

He couldn't remember the rest of his name until he snuck a glance at his name badge. *Verdebear.*

The doctor he'd heard in his dreams, discussing his fate with— *Rogman.*

Butterflies fluttered inside his ribcage, drawing up his shoulders and tightening his breath. *That was real?*

His words came out halted, unsure, anxiety drawing them halfway in before he could rush them out. "G-get me o-out of h-here."

"Soon, cadet. Very soon."

"B-but how much longer? And why does my skin still feel—"

He didn't want to say *hurt*, not when it could intimate some weakness. "...d-different."

"Let's maintain this dose, augment with selective wave suppressants," the doctor said to the assistant, using more medical terminology he didn't understand. "Also, let's start him on clears, then advance as tolerated. We'll test his stimulus response tomorrow."

Test my what?

"Rogman will want a full report," the doctor continued. "Patch him to the monitors; make sure he has full observation access."

No—I don't want him watching me!

The doctor and his assistant adjusted a few more things on the monitors and medication pump, then walked out, ignoring any of his other questions, even as he sat back up and shouted after them. "How much longer? Wait—stop—I—"

(Don't leave me here.)

Not with the monster lurking in the shadows, and whatever secrets Reppen feared in the East Wing. And especially not with Rogman watching, waiting—

135

Planning. Cam braced his head in his hands. *I have to do something.*

But what?

Stop the medication—

No. Not if Rogman was watching. And not if he wanted to recover.

Figure it out, he told himself, slapping the heel of his hand against his forehead. *Come on. There's got to be some way...*

As his mind shot out one stupid idea after another, his own feelings drew back to the last game he played with his sister, where he ran away:

"I'm not smart enough to beat you on the board. All I could do was stall and hope you got annoyed enough to quit."

"But you are smart," Kara said. *"You identified the real threat—me, not the game pieces. And you figured out your opponent's weakness."*

"Pesky little brothers?"

"You got that right."

"Identify the real threat... figure out my opponent's weakness..." He repeated the phrase over and over to himself until he relaxed enough to lay back down and draw the sheets back up to his chest.

As he stared at the ceiling, his thoughts floating away on the cloud of medication, terror wound its way down inside his chest, chilling his heart. Eyes drifting shut, he whispered, "help me, Jahx."

Chapter 15

A pinch on his left thumb's nailbed shot Cam awake.

"Ow," Cam said, pulling his hand away from the grips of a beak-faced nurse. Burn grafts, not fully integrated, covered most of her face and what he could see of her neck and arms. He couldn't tell her mixed humanoid species, only that she only seemed to anger at his returned eye contact.

With a scowl, she pointed to the bowl and cup she left on his tray table and said, "time to eat."

She left without saying anything else, leaving him more confused than anything.

Still groggy but feeling more awake than he normally did after emerging from the medicated sleep, he scooted over to the edge of the bed.

Are you watching me? Cam thought, panning around the room, looking for hidden cameras or recording devices. He'd already committed defiance and no one stopped him. But what Verdebear said about patching Rogman through the monitors for some kind of observation—

I can't risk it.

Pretending to stretch, he glanced at the medication pump and the settings.

The dose of cryoxotin is down to 1.5 mgs, he read. *And it's not on a continuous cycle.*

He noted the breaks in delivery, and how the medical staff tapered the dosing. *Maybe I'll be able to stay awake on my own.*

At least for an hour or so, according to the pump.

Sitting up, he pulled the tray table over the siderail and inspected his meal. From the salty odors wafting up from the soup bowl, he guessed they'd concocted him some kind of imitation meat broth. The clear color made him frown.

Meat broth doesn't look like that, he thought, reaching far back to the days when his mother took time to cook their meals. He recalled her brining pink and gold game birds while Kara stirred the gravy on the stove.

He checked the contents of the cup, finding a yellow-tinged liquid with a sweet odor. *What the hell is that?*

He took a tentative sip, his dry lips and tongue singing at the first taste.

Juice. Or something close enough to juice that he didn't care. It tasted wet, cold, and deliciously sweet. *So good—*

Hunger and thirst, however chemically managed before, steam-rolled to the forefront of his mind, and before he could even think to pace himself, he chugged the entire thing, spilling some of it down his patient gown. He slurped down the warm broth just as quickly, letting out a belch as he set it back down.

Even after years of privation and delighting in even the smallest of edible treasures, he'd never tasted anything so good, so needed.

"Satisfied?"

Cam whipped his head toward the speaker standing in the door frame. The same beak-faced nurse that brought him his food guided a hoverchair to his bedside. After disengaging him from the infusion pump and capping his medication line, she snapped her fingers at him. "Get on."

"I can walk—"

"That's an order, cadet," she squawked.

Avoiding her heated gaze, Cam scooted over to the edge of the bed and used the siderail to hoist himself up. Pins and needles pricked his feet, but he stifled any kind of reaction, sensing that this nurse—*Kull,* he read, catching a glance of her name badge—would prey upon, if not delight, in his pain.

Without another word, the nurse drove him down the hallway, winding down long corridors with large windows observing other patient bays and surgical suites. The sharp odor of disinfectants and cleansing agents stirred feelings of unease, but the muffled cries and monitor alarms made grip the ends of the armrest.

Who's that? Why are they here? he wondered as they passed by pediatric patients restrained to their beds by blue-tinted forcefields or stuffed with tubes and lines, their eyes taped shut.

138

Isn't that...? Every kid looked familiar, but he couldn't quite place them, as if he'd passed them in the hallway, or took a lift with them to a part of the Academy, but never actually interacted with them. *What happened to them?*

The nurse rolled him up to a set of double-doors and held up her ID badge to the adjacent scanner. Cam shrunk into his chair at the sight of the orange biohazard signs.

Not the East Wing—no—

He looked for anything—a wall map, a number, any kind of designation as to where she was taking him. Finally, as she took them around a corner, he caught sight of *Neuroscience Dept* written across the nurse's station.

Phew, God...

Cam knew better than to ask nurse Kull why she wheeled him into a private room with an exam table, strange equipment, and high-definition monitors, but made sure to take in as much as he could as she directed him to transfer to the table.

Without explanation, or any further instruction, she left, leaving him sitting on the edge of the exam table, under the glare of four surgical lamps.

"Cadet Ferros." A tall, lean man in a red surgical gown entered the room, trailed by two assistants. Hidden behind a surgical mask, Cam could only make out his flinty eyes, and a few strands of dark hair poking out from underneath his surgical cap. "Lie down."

Squinting, Cam made out something else. *Burns—*

Scars similar to nurse Kull's marred his forehead and part of his cheekbone. *Were they in the same accident?*

Cam couldn't put any more thought to it as the assistants surrounded him on both sides and helped him down when he didn't move fast enough. Their firm grasp on his upper arms made him grimace, but he took a calming breath as they freed him.

"Who are you?" he asked.

"Your doctor," the masked-man replied, unaffected by his disquiet. With black-gloved hands, he motioned for something outside of Cam's field of vision.

"What are you doing?" Cam said, trying to sit up, but the assistants brought him back down.

"Testing your nerve-response."

"Why?" Cam asked as they set the paddled arm of a scanner above his body.

The pause, the chill hanging in the air, made him even more nervous than before.

"You are unique, cadet," the doctor said, initiating a force field over her body.

"Let me go!" Cam shouted. Struggling did nothing. Only his hands, feet and head could move under the force field, enraging his already sensitive skin.

"Quiet now," the masked-man said, reaching behind him and grabbing something off a silver tray. Cam strained his neck to see the hypoinjector pressed into his shoulder. Seconds later, all the fight left his muscles, and his vision sunk down and away, as if he had been pulled down into a dark well.

Distant voices discussed his condition as twitches and twinges ran up and down his legs and arms. Above him, far and away, he saw the four surgical lamps, and heads bob in and out, obstructing their light.

"Remarkable," one of them said, "he has almost complete neurogenesis."

Someone emitted a low whistle. "Have you seen his training gear? Totally fried. The kid should be a vegetable."

"Something in his mixed bloodline?"

Electricity zapped his stomach, made all his muscles seize. Cam wanted to scream, but he had no breath, not until his muscles unclenched. Even then, whatever they'd injected him with disconnected his voice and his voluntary response.

"I wanted his blood and tissue samples sent to my lab. If we can replicate this phenomenon, we can begin the final phase."

"Yes, Dr. Naum."

Naum.

He needed to hold on to that name, to remember it for later.

"Inform Rogman that I want this subject reassigned to me."

"Sir, he's part of the beta trials."

"He's too valuable to be their fodder."

Fodder? What does that mean? He didn't know the word but sensed its implication: disposable. Some kind of test subject. *And for who?*

And final phase of what?

He thought of Iggie, of Reppen's warning. *I have to get out of here.*

Someone snapped gloves off their hand. "Notify me when you're through."

"Yes, doctor."

The heads disappeared. Lights shined down, into his eyes, making them burn. With what little control he had, he closed them, waiting, listening, for any clue as to what they would do next.

Something whirred and whined. *A drill?*

Fingers palpated his sternum, as if someone tried to locate the perfect spot for—

(no no NO—)

He wanted to cry out, to scream for his sister, for Jahx—for anyone to come to his rescue—but the undeniable reality, his awful truth, gouged his hope.

Do something, he thought, his hands clenching and unclenching in a disordered response. *Anything—*

He opened his eyes, catching the light glinting off the spiral drill bit as it angled toward his chest.

"Wait, is he still awake?"

"Gods, this kid's tough."

The fear in their voices, the way they couldn't bear witness to his pain.

That's right, you assinos, he thought, doing everything he could to shake his hands and feet, to let them see his anger, his fight. *You can't beat me like this.*

A shuffling of feet, items clinking on the silver tray table in some kind of scramble. The whooshing sound of a hypoinjector refill preceded another exclamation from one of the assistants: "Rogman and Naum are really going to fight over this one."

"Well, and—"

Something terribly cold plunged into his right shoulder and spread throughout his body like a wave crashing over a shore.

"—don't say it. That *thing* shouldn't have a name."

Wait—what thing—what are you…? Cam's eyes grew heavier and heavier, his mind swirling in and away from the conversation, from himself. *No, stay awake—*

"Besides, *it* won't want this one. Ferros is just a brute; he's got no talent."

As the last of the light faded away, the other assistant forced a mirthless laugh. "That doesn't mean he won't help end the world."

***

Cam woke lying flat on his back, attached to the infusion pump, sheets drawn up to his chest. Sitting up, he flung off the sheets before realizing himself back in his medical bay.

Naum, he thought, breathing heavily, *don't drill my—*

He touched his sternum with the tips of his fingers, too afraid to apply any real pressure until he sensed nothing more than a mild ache. Lifting up his patient gown, he saw the usual pink, spidery branches of inflammation on his belly, but other marks—neat, three-centimeter lines covered by transparent dermal patches, scored the area around his hip bones and thighs.

He inspected his chest, where a red circle covered by another dermal patch sat in the lower third of his sternum.

What did they do to me?

Cam dropped his gown back down, uncomfortable by the look—the feel—of his own body.

"Knock, knock." Reppen stood at the doorway, a tray full of food steaming in her hand. "Can I come in?"

Unsure of her intent, he twisted up one of the sheets in his fist and readied for—

—Anything—I'll do anything—don't take me away again, I'll—

"Hey, it's okay," she whispered, approaching slowly. She set down the food on the tray table and stood at a distance. "I'm not going to hurt you."

Before he could even think of a response, she walked over to the monitors, but angled her face away so he could see her bring first finger up to her lips and hear her whisper: "Shhh."

"Huh. There's some kind of feedback delay. I'd better reboot," she declared, sounding as if she read the line off a script. He watched as she hit a squiggly-marked button on the primary monitor. It chimed three times, then powered down. "We've got three minutes."

Cam flinched when she tried to touch his shoulder.

142

"Please—I just want to help you."

The lilt of her voice, the familial glint in her eye.

Cam didn't believe her, but something inside him—whatever part of him that survived so far—needed to. Releasing the sheets in his hands, he held his breath until the sting of his sinuses, the prick in the inner corners of his eyes, passed, and he could trust his own voice.

"What is happening to me? Who is Naum? I—" His voice cracked as the thought of Naum, the drill—the terrible dreams of the East Wing, of Rogman and the machine monster, Iggie's terror—came crashing down all at once. "...I don't know who my enemy is."

Reppen's mouth opened and shut several times until she gave up and plopped down on the work stool near his bed. With a quaver to her words, she tried again. "You're from Cerka, right?"

He nodded.

"You know who the Sovereign is?"

Cam frowned. "I'm not an idiot."

"Then you know he's just another dictator trying to take over the Starways."

"No, he's different," Cam snapped back. "He's not going to let leeches silently rule over the rest of us for any longer. He's going to clean up the galaxy, make things fair."

Reppen sat back in her chair. "Fair? Do you even know what that means?"

"Fair is getting a chance to go to school or having something to eat that isn't filled with sawdust or dirt," he said, rage undamming his words. "Fair is my father not losing his job to some *ratchakker* leech, and my mother not choosing booze over me and my siblings. Fair is my father not blowing himself up to save our infested city!"

Reppen raised her hand to quell his rising voice, but he didn't—couldn't—stop.

"Fair is not losing your entire family to a stupid war or watching your sister get taken away. Fair is not—"

(Hurting someone just to survive.)

A sob clenched the last bit of his sentence, and he stopped himself before he lost what little control he still possessed.

With one hand covering her lower lip and chin, Reppen whispered: "I'm sorry, Cam."

143

Calming himself, he finished: "You're right. I don't know what fair is."

Reppen reached out and took his hand, even when he tried to shy away. "Listen to me—what they're doing to you—to all you kids—isn't fair, either."

"What do you mean?" he said, still trying to take his hand back, but she held fast.

"Kids aren't war machines."

War machines.

MACHINES.

His mind conjured the monster with the burning red eye scurrying down the hallway its mechanical spider-legs, rusted gears grinding, screeching with a carnal hunger.

(Why did she say it like that?)

"And more importantly, these telepaths—without them, my mother would have died in the civil wars on Thamosin. Doctors gave her a terminal diagnosis from all the pollutants she inhaled from the bioweapons. But my relatives took her to Algar, the Prodgy homeworld, where Healers saved her life."

Cam thought to argue her, but the relief in her eyes, the indefatigable hope upheld by a miracle, stole his anger.

"Fear, hatred, and ignorance are your enemies," she said, squeezing his hand. "Everything else is a deception."

Reppen eyed the monitor as red lights flashed and the startup menu scrolled down the screen. "I've got to go. Listen, Cam—you're smarter than they've let you believe," she said, standing up and fiddling with the infusion pump. "Don't give up hope. In the meantime, I'll do everything I can to help you, okay?"

The monitor flickered back on. Reppen's demeanor changed, her expression hardened.

"Rehab is in one hour, cadet. Eat what you can, leave the rest on the tray."

He said nothing, watching as she made adjustments to the pump, and checked the monitors. When she bent down again to finalize the medication dosing, he whispered: "What's in the East Wing?"

144

She didn't react, her countenance closed off and stern. After locking the pump, she made her way to the door, pausing before she exited.

"Rest up, cadet. Things are only going to get tougher."

Chapter 16

Reppen never returned. Not after he finished his bowl of fruitsauce and protein shake, and hid the packet of crackers between his sheets, or to check on him before an attendant picked him up for transport.

"Where's nurse Reppen?" he asked, but the stone-faced attendant grunted and pointed to the hoverchair.

"Mind yourself, cadet."

Cam paid better attention this time as he rolled down the hallway, noting everything from the scuff marks on the floor to the names and numbers posted on the signs and doorways. The medical ward maze would confuse anyone—

No, he thought. *Gotta remember.*

Biting his lip, he started a game in his head, associating the numbers of the bays with the Cerkan city shops, overlaying a map he could understand.

Bay 71, Varnee's Thrift Store. Bay 72, Used Goods. Bay 73, Corner Market.

The attendant turned the corner, bringing him back to another set of double doors with warning symbols on it. With a flash of his keycard, the doors parted, letting them into the separate wing.

Rehab Dept Cam read off the sign hanging over the nurse's station.

No sign of Naum, or red-suited assistants. Instead, the attendant guided him inside a huge open room with white-paneled walls and floors, reminding him of the training simulations arena. Kids around his age, some dressed in patient gowns, others in their regular academy uniform, interacted with the holographic programs, exercise equipment, or the staff at various stations.

"Over here." A pale-faced woman dressed in a stark-white suit motioned to them with one hand while clutching a datapad in the other.

As the attendant directed them to her station, Cam caught sight of red hair and a long, lean stature on the opposite end of the room. *Tomia?*

He leaned forward, trying to get a better view around the other activity. It looked like her, but she was so much taller, broader—*just like Iggie and Jahx.* And her left arm looked as if it had suffered some kind of trauma. A lighted, regenerative casing ran from her wrist to her elbow, and the immediate tissue surrounding the casing, including the entirety of her hand, appeared red, almost purple, as if infected.

"Tomia!" he shouted, rising out of the hoverchair.

She turned, baffled, on the border of terrified, until she spotted him. A broad smile countered the disbelief that pinched up her brows. "Cam!"

"Settle down," the attendant said, clamping a strong hand down on his shoulder.

"Get him on the table." The pale-faced woman pointed at the therapy table to her left. On an adjacent tray lay several four-centimeter, rectangular objects with flashing red lights.

Cam jerked back, remembering Naum, the drill—

"Calm yourself," the woman said, showing him one of the devices off the table. The gray housing and tiny script written in a foreign tongue meant nothing to him. "These are motor assist modules, designed to help your muscle control and minimize your pain."

Cam scoffed. *Why would anyone care about my pain?*

"Just get him on the table," she said, snapping her fingers at the assistant.

Without any warning, the assistant hoisted Cam up by the arm, half-flinging him onto the table. Cam stifled a cry but couldn't help the pain that kept him hunched over on the edge of the table, or the veins that popped out on his forehead as he held his breath and waited for the rain of electric fire to pass.

After the assistant left, the pale woman introduced herself. "I am Jao, your physical therapist. Do as I say, and we won't have any problems."

As terrible and strict as she tried to sound, Cam didn't sense the imminent threat he grafted from Naum, or even the beaked nurse

Kull. The wrinkles etched into her brow came equally from scowling and worrying, and the faded lines around her mouth meant that at one time she laughed. Instinct told him she vented her frustrations on her patients but didn't possess the sadistic streak he'd seen in other staff members.

Jao attached the rectangular devices to his arms, legs, and one that strapped around his chest, and ordered him to walk. Still recovering from the rough handling, he didn't move as fast as she liked, and incurred a swift slap to the shoulder.

"Come on, we haven't got all day."

Cam stumbled-stepped forward, shocked by the hit and unable to compensate for the rapid change in posture. However, after catching himself on the tray table, he noticed something that made his heart sing: *My feet—it doesn't hurt to walk!*

And his shoulder—which should have been set afire by such a blow, only stung.

"Walk up and down the room four times," Jao ordered.

Cam did so, eager to touch each wall and return back. Some of the kids murmured and pointed, stopping their exercises to stare.

Yeah, look at me, he thought.

He wanted everyone—Jao, Tomia, all the cadets, teachers—Rogman—to see his strength return, to know that he wasn't some waste of a patient rotting in a bed.

When he returned to the cross-armed Jao, he didn't surprise to her sour expression, or her inability to compliment him on his achievement. "Well?"

"Ma'am?"

"Any unusual sensations?"

He didn't know how to answer that question. Nothing felt right, not since the training incident. "I don't know what you mean."

Jao huffed. "Any delayed responses, numbness?"

Cam rocked back and forth on his heels and wiggled his fingers. "Yeah, my feet and hands are pretty numb."

Exasperated, she pointed to the table. "Sit while I make adjustments."

Cam did so, trying to stay quiet as she took off the arm and leg modules and fussed over the settings, going back and forth between her datapad and the devices.

As she fiddled, Cam looked again for Tomia, to see if she witnessed his feat. *Where'd you go?*

He didn't see her at the same station he'd see her at before, or anywhere in the open therapy room. *But she was right there.*

Doubt crept down into his gut, unsettling his stomach. *(Wasn't she?)*

The question bothered him enough to elicit a shiver. Maybe he'd imagined seeing her. After all, Jahx just saw her and Iggie—totally fine, without a busted arm—riding on a lift not too long ago—

Wait—how long ago?

He rubbed the bridge of his nose. Time was so hard to keep track of. *Maybe I'm just imagining—?*

No. I saw her. She's hurt, just like Iggie.

He touched the tender point on his chest.

I've got to get out of here.

"*Io'deka,*" Jao said in her native tongue. It sounded like a swear, and the glower in her face confirmed his suspicions. "Wait here. I need to make manual adjustments."

Cam did so, holding himself on the edge of the table by his arms as Jao exited the therapy room and walked around to the nurse's station. As he waited, he looked for other familiar faces, hoping to find someone—anyone—

"*Chak,*" he said, his arms giving out. *Don't fall—don't fall!*

Not in front of the other cadets.

Or Rogman.

Despite his will, he pitched forward, catching himself on the tray, but sliding off the table, his legs not ready to catch his weight. Knees buckling, he tensed, anticipating the fall when a gentle arm slipped around his waist.

"I've got you."

"Jetta?"

No, not Jetta. This girl looked identical, except for her eyes. Gray, not green, reminding him of spring clouds bursting with fresh rain.

"Jaeia," she corrected, as she helped him back to the table.

Red-faced, he looked around, but no one seemed to notice his near-fall. "Sorry, and, you know, thanks."

149

"You're welcome," she said, brushing back the loose hair that fell in her face.

She watched him as he shifted back farther on the table, putting most of his weight on his bottom this time. It hurt, especially without the modules, but at least he wouldn't embarrass himself again.

Cam looked around, discomfited by her continued presence. "Uh, why are you here?"

Jaeia showed him her left wrist fitted with a similar regenerative casing he thought he saw on Tomia. "Sprained it in training."

"Basic or sims?"

"Basic."

Cam looked her over. She seemed bigger than Jetta, but then again, he hadn't seen her sister since the incident. Either way, the human-looking Fiorahian didn't look as wimpy as she did when he first saw them in the mess hall. In fact, from what little he could see outlined by her jacket bespoke of muscle tone, fitness.

"Did you get the kid back that hurt you?"

Jaeia twisted around in her boots. "I'm not really much for physical combat."

"Look, you've got to stand up for yourself," he said, surprising her with his insistence. "There's going to come a time when you're alone, and all you've got left is the fight."

Stunned, she stared at him wide-eyed. "Alone?"

"Yeah, I mean, you do stuff apart from your sibs, right?"

Jaeia looked down at her feet. "Sometimes Jetta and Jahx do stuff without me."

Cam noted her reaction, and how, with her good hand, she picked at the end of her jacket sleeve, struggling to keep her facial expression neutral. Her slip, her admission, diaphanous and fragile, projected out like a lone beacon in a night sky.

He tested his theory. "I know what you mean. I had twin sisters. I was always 'the third' with them."

She squeezed both of her hands shut.

"Your name's Cam, right?" she asked, turning around the conversation.

Cam watched as she eyed the nurse's station. He resisted the temptation to also look, studying her, why she cared about Jao's return, or what the therapist would do about their interaction.

"How'd you know?"

She turned her head back to him. "You've got a reputation."

Hearing the negative inflection, he shrugged. "Then you must be pretty brave."

Her gaze fell to his right arm, to the uneven lumps and scars that carved their way up to his elbow. "My sister respects you."

Cam shocked to hear that. Jetta seemed like a hard one to win over.

"And my brother."

His heart skipped, and his stomach fluttered. Embarrassed, he lowered his head to hide his pink cheeks.

"You're still hurting."

The way she said it, with such confidence and assertion in her voice, and an intense gaze that would have convinced anyone of anything, shook him down to the bone. He automatically brought one of his arms across his chest, as if to shield himself, to keep back the truth she sought.

"I'm sorry," she said, softening her voice. She reached out as if to touch his knee but pulled her hand back. "I just... I'm sorry. I just know what it's like to act tough all the time. Well, at least try. I'm not very good at it. But not everyone here is after you, you know."

Cam shuddered. Something about her words, the way she said them, how they quietly unpinned his armor, prying underneath and exposing—

"I don't have friends," he blurted.

Anyone else would have startled. She didn't, studying him, absorbing his every reaction.

"I-I just—" He didn't know how to recuperate, how to smooth out the glaring, awful confession in his exclamation.

"I don't either."

Not detecting any sarcasm, any hurtful intention in her voice, he let out the breath he didn't realize he'd been holding.

"At least you've got your brother and sister," he said.

"Yes, but it'd be nice to have someone else to talk to."

"Isn't Jahx pretty easy to get along with?"

Jaeia focused on something beyond Cam. "Jahx is not always there, even when it seems like he is."

Cam burned that into his memory banks, making sure he'd remember it for later.

"A daydreamer?" he said, trying to bait her into giving him more.

Instead, she glanced again at the nurse's station, as Jao got up and headed toward the two of them. "I've got another half hour in this thing," Jaeia said, raising her arm. "But I'd better go. Jao's one of the mean ones."

"You mean there are nice ones?"

Jaeia smirked. "Well, not really."

Jaeia isn't vicious, he decided, noting her continued relaxed posture, her even temperament. *But there's something more to her.*

Something that he dared not underestimate.

"Nice to meet you, Cam," she said, turning away.

"Wait," he said, not sure what he meant to add. Scratching his head, he came up with: "Uh, how long you gotta wear that thing?"

Jaeia's smirk broadened into a smile. "A few more days. See you tomorrow, then?"

"Yeah," he said. "Sure."

Jao returned with a predictable glare, and an admonishment. "This isn't time for socializing, cadet."

"Yes, ma'am," he said, allowing her to reconnect the modules and start the second trial.

As he went through the next round of physical therapy, he couldn't get Jaeia out of his head, glancing every so often her way as she walked around as played with interactive holograms, waiting out the restoration session.

What's your deal? How do you fit into all of this? he wondered. As he sat back down for Jao to analyze his latest walk, he locked eyes with the Fiorahian for the briefest of seconds. A smile, tentative and wistful, touched her lips.

A memory of Kara jarred awake; he saw her face in the morning sunlight, humming the latest pop tune as she chopped old vegetables on the kitchen counter, trying to fix them all some kind of breakfast.

Cam looked away quickly, realizing the lump in his throat.

"Cadet, are you paying attention?" Jao said, slapping his shoulder.

"Yes, ma'am," he muttered.

152

When he looked up, Jaeia was gone, but the memory of Kara's quiet sacrifices, her sweetness, remained.

Who are you, Jaeia Drachsi?

He thought of Jetta, Jahx, what he knew so far, and the terror that still owned his heart.

Reppen's voice, calm and steady, floated up from recent memory: *"Fear, hatred, and ignorance are your enemies."*

No, he countered, grinding his teeth together, suppressing whatever emotion tried to surface against the anger of his torments, of the injustices he had incurred, and would continue to suffer until he completed his mission.

"Everything else is a deception."

***

Points of light swirled all around him in a nebulous world of sight and sound.

This place—

Not a dream.

But not real, either. Or at least not in a way Cam understood. Somewhere, standing far beyond the rim of consciousness, he reached out, skimming his fingers along the orbiting stars, stirring the iridescent clouds. As he marveled at the sensations—impossible, vibrant hues, perfect harmonic chords shimmering across the astral plane—a voice, steady and calm, whispered to him: "...reaction between a deprotonated alcohol and an alkyl halid that forms an ether..."

Cam listened, captivated, breathless. Neurons and gray matter split apart painlessly, shooting out roots and connecting with parts of himself—and beyond himself—he didn't realize. He touched the world around and within, a complex, fluid sphere once perceived beyond his reach, and shuddered. More. I need more.

The voice continued on, relaying information faster. Concepts, once beyond his grasp, fell into place like jigsaw pieces righting and arranging themselves within the puzzle. Tell me everything.

The world around him changed. Points of light converged and connected, glittering like a dewy spider web among the cosmos.

He could reach out, touch any point in the link, and—

153

No, this isn't right.

Connection beyond himself was a violation of everything he had come to know.

What do you want? *he called out, pulling back and away.* Who are you?

Blue, the color of the clear skies, secrets bound to his heart, skittered across the cosmic vastness. The universe retreated, fell back.

(I'm sorry.)

Cam woke to the black-haired boy sitting at his bedside, reading test questions off the datapad. Whatever impossible dream of vast connection, of knowledge strung together across the cosmos, decomposed under the dim light of the medical bay.

"Hey," Jahx said, putting down the device and swiveling in the work stool to face Cam.

"Hey," Cam replied. Jahx's eyes, his calm demeanor made his stomach flutter.

Was that real?

No. Not possible. How could anything lie beyond the broken mess of his body? *Don't be stupid.*

With a groan, he sat up, his muscles already aching from the morning therapy session.

"How'd you rest?"

Cam stretched out his arms and legs, twisting at the waist, trying to get the kink out of his back. Turning out his left forearm, he considered pinching and dumping off the medication line to give himself more of a break than the thirty-minute window programmed into the machine. *I hate being out of it.*

But he did feel better and getting back—and away from the medical ward—was more important than anything.

"You want the—?"

Cam raised his brows and widened his eyes, hoping Jahx would pick up on his anxiety. With the monitors behind him, he aimed his gaze to the left and right, trying to alert the boy of the unwanted eyes and ears monitoring their conversation.

Jahx, without missing a beat, offered Cam his datapad. "—latest lesson from chemistry?"

154

With a sigh and smile, he accepted the datapad. "Yeah, sure. But I haven't had a chance to review anything."

"That's okay," Jahx said, resting his hand and chin on the siderail. "I'm sure you'll get it."

Cam laughed. "Yeah, right. Somehow I'm all caught up."

But as he scrolled through the lesson, something clicked. Acid-base reactions. Aldehydes and ketones. Esters and amides.

How is this possible?

Excited and terrified at the same time, he switched over to the practice test.

I know which reactions would produce a 2-pentyne in good yield. The hybridization of the central carbon in CH3C=N and the bond angle CCN = sp, 180 degrees...

Cam swallowed hard. *This isn't possible.*

Holding tight to the datapad, he thought of the dream, trying to recall the details of that fully accessible place within the stars. *Did... did something happen to me?*

Cam eyed his medication line, his mind whirling. *Is it the drugs? Did that doctor do something to me?*

(Did Jahx—?)

"Hey," Jahx whispered. "You okay?"

"Yeah, I dunno, I just... I shouldn't know all this."

"You're too hard on yourself," Jahx said, taking back the datapad and typing something into the keyboard. "You pick up stuff pretty quickly."

"But, I mean, we haven't gone over it that much. Unless..." Cam half-laughed as he considered the most absurd possibility. "Have you always read to me while I slept?"

Jahx paused, blushing. "Yes."

"Okay, but still—people don't just wake up being smart."

"No, they don't," Jahx agreed.

Shaking his head, he tried again. "Is... is it the meds?"

"Well, they do promote neurogenesis," Jahx said, as if trying to believe it himself.

Digging his fingers into his forehead, Cam fought against the anxiety tangling up his belly.

"Hey, relax," Jahx said, touching his arm. "I'm sorry if I did anything to upset you. I'm just trying to help."

155

Cam brushed off the boy's hand, but then caught and held on to it for a few seconds before letting it go again. "No, I'm sorry; I just don't understand this. Everything's always been hard for me."

"But hard because you haven't really had a chance," Jahx countered.

The muscles between his shoulders knotted. *You don't know me.*

"Besides, every kid earned their spot here one way or another."

Cam tasted bile in the back of his throat, clenched his teeth together. "You're right about that."

With a tilt of his head, Jahx lowered his voice and paced out his response, as if he didn't want Cam to miss a single word. "You're here for a reason, Cam."

Rogman's delight, his threat, tightened down like a vice on Cam's ribs. *Not the one you think.*

Then, the dark-haired boy whispered something he would have never expected: "I'm glad you're here, Cam."

Blushing, he tried to play it off. "It's not like I'm going to be a galactic commander or anything; I'm just going to be another bloody soldier. You, Jahx—as smart as you are, you're going to figure out this whole stupid game. Hell, maybe you'll even figure out how to win this war."

Jahx stiffened. "I don't know about that."

"No, really," he chuckled, thinking the boy's reaction a sign of humility. "If you can teach me organic chem and gaming strategy in a matter of a few weeks, you've got to be wicked talented."

Talented. The word resonated between them like a scream from one mountain range to another. Cam didn't realize his loaded remark until he watched Jahx cringe, then try and wipe the expression from his face with the back of his sleeve.

Talented.

Talent.

A word that held a negative connotation to most Starways Common speakers. Talent could mean natural skill or aptitude—or it could mean someone who possessed extrasensory perceptions.

Like telepathy.

No...

Jahx forced a smile, jocularity. "Like you said before—I'd have to be the best. And I'm not really cut out to be a galactic commander."

Cam wavered, still in shock by his reaction. *(Could it be...?)* *(Rogman wouldn't allow a leech in the Academy.)*
Or would he?

No. Cam wouldn't have it. Not Jahx. Not the only person that he—

Cam stopped himself, took a breath.

"But if you were..."

The words trembled off the boy's lips. "Well... I guess even a galactic commander needs a good friend."

Cam didn't know what to say or do. *No. Not possible.*

Not that he even allowed himself to think past the cold weight sinking into his stomach. He braced his arms across himself, against whatever raw understanding iced his gut, as he stared at Jahx, at the boy who sat by his bedside, organic chemistry homework in hand.

"I-I have to go," Jahx said, fumbling with the datapad. After an awkward few seconds, he handed it to Cam. "Here's that research project. I think I've got most of it figured out, but I need help on the final calculations. Well, only if you're interested."

Cam looked it over, seeing the numbers and the formulas, but knowing only the thudding of his heart. Still, he couldn't refuse the boy, not for reasons he could understand. "Okay."

Jahx flashed a shy grin. "Great. I didn't know if you'd still want to be my partner."

So kind, he thought. He shuddered. *No way he's a leech.*

Leeches lied, manipulated, stole. Jahx never did any of those things.

Jahx has only helped me.
(Just like—)
(—don't say his name—)

"Come on—I owe you," Cam said, waving him off. Without thinking, he added: "But you shouldn't stick around here too much."

"Why?"

Jahx diverted his eyes again, as he always seemed to do when Cam struck a nerve. But this time, fear pinched his brows, as if he gleaned Cam's warning before he could say it.

157

"Uh..." Something stopped him from saying anything to Jahx—something more than the potential of Rogman spying on their conversation, or that he had hallucinated the machine monster and Iggie's terror. Another possibility, one more terrifying than he could bring himself to believe as looked back at the blue-eyed boy, pained his heart more than he could bear. "Well, I'll be out of here soon anyway. No sense in you wasting your time on me. And, you know, I've got your learning modules."

"Cam—"

"Play those games," he said, "that's what's so hot now anyway, right? Get really good and then teach me everything when I get back."

Jahx's eyes flitted again to the door, down the quiet hallway. "Okay."

"Wait," he said as Jahx gathered up his things.

With an awkward grab, he pulled Jahx down. Pretending to give him a hug, he reached down with his right hand between the mattress and fished out the crackers. Keeping hold of Jahx, he slipped the package into the boy's pocket.

"Um, okay, get going," Cam muttered, releasing him as soon as he made the transfer.

Jahx stood back up, his cheeks pink, eyes bright. "Thanks, Cam."

For a second, Cam allowed himself a return smile. "Later, Jahx."

Chapter 17

The next day, as he waited again for Jao to recalibrate his motor assist modules during his afternoon therapy session, Cam searched for familiar faces amongst the other patients. Dozens of kids crowded around holographic sims, some of them playing games, others observing as they waited out their therapies. Sitting again at the edge of the table, he hoped to see Tomia, Iggie, or—

"Hey, Cam."

Cam jumped, surprised to see Jaeia pop up behind him.

"Jeez—I didn't see you," he asked as she came around the table.

"Sorry," she mumbled, curling her loose hair behind her ears.

"You're just really quiet; like a mouse or something."

Jaeia sighed, as if she'd heard it before. "Sorry."

Cam checked on Jao's status. Back at the nurse's station, outside the therapy room, she discussed something with big sweeping motions of her hands with one of the doctors. Squinting, Cam couldn't make out if it was Dr. Verdebear or—

Naum? He gripped the edge of the table. *Oh,* chak, *no—*

A gentle hand touched his. "You okay?"

"Y-yeah," Cam said, broken from the thought. When he looked back, the doctor had left, and Jao stood hunched over the station, unaware or uncaring of their conversation.

Jaeia followed his line of sight. "I don't like it here, either."

"You mean the doctors?" he asked as a group of kids laughed at the loser in a fighter-sim match. "Or this entire place?"

Jaeia watched as the loser of the match stormed off, tears in his eyes. "All of it," she whispered.

"Hey, launnie!"

The shout caught both of their attention. Cam zeroed in on the culprit in the crowd of kids surrounding the fighter-sim. *Walli.* One of the kids he caught harassing Jahx in the out-of-order lavatory awhile back. His right lower leg bound in a restorative cast, he leaned on a lighted crutch and stabbed his finger at Jaeia. "Get over here, street rat."

Reflexively, he looked for Stempton, but didn't see the freckle-faced bully.

He's on his own, Cam thought, scanning the room again. Mostly younger kids populated the therapy room—ones that would be intimidated by a lesser thug like Walli.

"Come on, rat, play me," he said, punching up a new game on the fighter sim. "Or are you just a *chakking* Scab?"

The other kids howled with laughter, as if their two-legged, upright postures and four limbs didn't contain mixed human genetics.

Jaeia tapped on the restorative casing on her right wrist. "It's almost done. I should get going—"

"No," Cam said as Walli continued to rile the group of kids around him, pointing and laughing at Jaeia. "Don't back off. Not now."

"But I—"

"Sometimes, all you have is the fight," he said, making a fist with his right hand, the scars on his arm turning white. "And it doesn't even matter if you win. Just show them that you won't back down."

Jaeia balked, brow furrowed, hands twitching. Cam recognized the behavior, remembering his younger sisters, how they reacted when separated, not being able to stand any stressors apart from one another. Part of him softened, understanding her trepidation and anxiety, but survival instincts, driven by pain and terror, caused him to grab her by the jacket sleeve. "Fight."

As she walked over to the jeering crowd, he eyed the nurse's station. Jao, and a few other medical staff, stood with datapads in hand, watching from afar.

Is it because it's a competition? he wondered, watching as Jaeia took the controls at the gaming console.

Or was it something else? Something about the circumstances—
Or the players?

He didn't know anything about Jahx's gray-eyed sister—if she possessed any of her siblings' smarts or strategies, what she'd do in

160

a contentious situation such as this one. But as Walli initiated the game, fighter-class starships taking flight across a blue and yellow projected playing field, Cam regripped the therapy table, his hands burning.

Walli's better than I thought. The older cadet maneuvered his fighter with the deft skill of an accomplished player. With only two equally-matched ships pitted against each other in an all-out dog fight, Cam didn't know how'd Jaeia, with just a few months of academy training, would fair against someone with experience.

Doesn't matter, he thought as Jaeia dodged Walli's fire, *she just needs to fight.*

"I'm going to gun you down," Walli taunted, flicking his wrists left and right, his fighter winding through the geometric obstacles, laying down traps if she dared come around to face him.

Sweat dotted the girl's brow. The onlookers snickered as Walli clipped one of her wings, making her tense her grips on the controls and jerk too hard to the right, sending her fighter into a tailspin.

"Stupid launnie," someone laughed.

Others chimed in as Walli overtook her fighter and prepped his missiles. "Yeah, waste of a space. Go back to your stinkhole."

"Scab!"

Or maybe not...

Although she kept a cool guise, he could see the storm in her eyes, the quiet vexation brewing, mounting, as she righted her fighter and tried to use the environment to buy her some time.

She doesn't want this—doesn't want any of this, he gleaned. But some fights couldn't be avoided. And when she sucked in her lower lip as Walli launched his missiles, his audience cheering, Cam saw the flicker of an inner flame, one that couldn't possibly originate from a meek young girl.

Oh, chak—

"Die, launnie!" Walli shouted as his missiles collided with her ship. Electric colors exploded, leaving behind images so bright and sharp that Cam covered his eyes until it subsided.

"Haha, loser," the thug said, refitting his crutch back under his armpit. "Go back to the gutters."

Someone shoved Jaeia from behind and echoed Walli's sentiment. "Yeah, get out of here!"

161

And then, as Cam launched himself off the therapy table, struggling to reach her before the next kid joined in on the attack, Jaeia pulled the arm of the boy closest to her. With him bent over, his ear by her mouth, she whispered something. A terrible something; a secret that bugged out the boy's eyes and peeled back his lips from white teeth as a kick from behind sent her sprawling. He made a guttural choking sound, like a laugh caught up in a sob, before jolting back upright.

"You're next!" the boy cried, pointing at the kid standing over Jaeia and cocking back his fist. In a panic, he grabbed Jaeia's attacker, shaking him until he screamed and fought his way out of the boy's grips. "You're next!"

"Quit it, Dav," Walli said, crutching a few steps back as the crazed boy screamed and shouted, kicking and shoving anyone in his path. Some of the kids fled, running out to the nurse's station or to their therapists, pleading like frightened children for their intervention.

But none of the adults came to their rescue, some even moving to better positions to observe the escalating situation.

"Dav—no—what are you—?"

Walli screamed as Dav tackled him to the ground. The crazed boy pounded him on the chest with his fists, screaming: "YOU'RE NEXT. YOU'RE NEXT!"

Legs and feet on fire, Cam reached Jaeia as two of the other kids took to the same panic, grabbing at each other and screaming the same nonsense.

"Come on," Cam said, batting away the attackers as he pulled her to the safety of a far therapy table. None of the other kids followed, blinded by whatever hysteria afflicted Dav, pushing and shoving each other.

"You okay?" Cam asked, chest heaving as he tried to calm himself down.

Jaeia, white as a ghost, looked seconds away from bursting into tears. Still, she kept whatever grip she needed, but afforded him only a terse nod as they crouched behind the table.

"What the hell is wrong with everyone?" he asked, peeking over the table.

Jao and a few other therapists, trailed by shockwand-wielding soldiers, clapped their hands and shouted, "order. Order!"

Cam couldn't stand the tension, the heat in the air that frayed his nerves, pumped iron-hot blood through his veins. It took everything he had to steady his breathing, to blow the steam out of his lungs and remind himself to stay calm. *What's happening to me?*

(What's happening to all of us?)

"It's going to be all right," he said, putting his hand on her shoulder. He gripped her hard, his fingers digging into his muscle. He didn't mean it, but he couldn't let up. "Jaeia…" he said, unable to control the way he sounded, the pleading tone to his words. "Really, it's okay. You did it."

"I did?" she whispered, chin quivering.

"Yeah, you did. You made a good fight," he said, slapping the tiled floor with his free hand in a Cerkan sign of respect.

Tears brimmed her eyelids. "I didn't want to."

"But you did what you had to do. Not many people can do that."

Something inside him loosened; the fires within abated, all except the frazzled pain of his nerves.

"Thanks, Cam."

Cam reached his arm around her, giving her a hug he didn't think he had in him. But something about her, whatever quiet, sweet quality juxtaposed the unnamable thing he'd just witnessed, elicited such a radical gesture.

"Ferros! Drachsi! Fall in line!" Jao shouted.

Cam looked over the therapy table, seeing the two rows of injured kids sobbing and trembling at attention.

"Hey," Cam said, catching her before they would be parted. She hesitated, looking at him with uncertainty, like a young kid about to be outed for whatever shameful misbehavior they'd committed. Tongue caught in his mouth, he teetered on the edge of two extremes. One, terrified of what he already knew but could not face, and the other, remembering the girl who'd saved him from a fall. *(Ask her what she said—*

Ask her if she's—)

"Ferros—Drachsi—*now,* or a day in isolation!"

With a deep breath, Cam squeezed her arm. "You're okay. You're brave, Jaeia Drachsi. I won't forget this."

163

Jaeia put her hand over his and squeezed back. "Neither will I."

***

Reppen returned late that night, but something about her had changed. As she made adjustments to his medication pump, Cam scooted up in bed and tried to reconcile the difference between the caring nurse and the woman before him that brought a chill to the air.

"N-nurse?"

Reppen acted as if she didn't hear him, turning to the vital signs monitors. As she reached over him, he caught a closer glimpse of her face. Darkened circles ringed her eyes, as if she hadn't slept in days, and her cheeks, anemic and gaunt, belonged to a starved prisoner, not the nurse he'd talked to not that long ago.

"Are... are you okay?" Cam asked, confused and scared.

Her lips moved, but no sound came. Finally, as she checked off her finally task on her datapad, she looked at him, familiar eyes covered by an icy-sheen. "Did you kill that boy?"

All of the air left the room. Cam clutched the neckline of his gown, struggling against whatever constricted his throat. *How does she know?!*

"It's not fair what'll they do... Just a child... I can't..."

"W-what?" he squeaked.

Finally, glassy-eyed, she whispered: "Rest well, cadet."

She turned back to the pump and hit start, then hurried out of the medical bay.

A 1,000mg/kg?

An overdose.

No—

He tried to stop the machine, change the dose, override the system—anything—but the lockout screen flashed red, keeping him from stopping the medication delivery.

She changed her password—

I'm chakked—

Do something!

Cam yanked hard on the medication line attached to his upper arm. Pain tore up into his shoulder and down his chest, but he flung the bloodied line across the room.

Bracing his arm to occlude the bleed, he kicked off the bedsheets and stumbled to his feet.

Why did she try to kill me? Anger and fear dulled the pain shooting up into his legs, and the ache of his muscles trying to keep up with his pace. *(How does she know about Colin?)*

Cam followed her down the hallway, ducking and hiding in the other adjacent medical bays when the few night-shift medical staff appeared. Most of them, heads down into their datapads, wouldn't have noticed him even if he stood in the middle of the hall flailing his arms.

Slowed by his sluggish muscles, Cam lost Reppen around the nurse's station.

Chak—*I'm still bleeding,* he thought, noticing the dots of blood that had dripped from his arm and splashed the white tiles. Squatting next to a supply cart, he opened a few of the drawers and searched for something useful. Finding a brown-colored bandage, he used his teeth to unravel the material and then wrapped his arm the best he could. After managing an uneven but effective bandage, he continued his search. He listened down the dim hallways for footsteps, hearing only the steady beeps of heart monitors, and the hum of the ventilation systems. One of the nurses, still buried in her charting, sat at the desk, chewing on something that made her lips smack together.

Where would she be going? he thought, trying to reason out her direction. Not that any of this made any real sense. But whatever he'd seen in her dead eyes, something about her manner and wooden posture, triggered the vague horror he'd witnessed—

—*dreamed*—

—and he had to see for himself what spawned her transformation.

And what might be hungering to take him next.

Movement down the to his right caught his eye. A feminine figure leaned against the wall, shaking. With jerky movements, she pushed herself off, and staggered further down, toward a red-lit door marked *AUTHORIZED PERSONNEL ONLY.*

Reppen?

In her left hand, she gripped a sharp, silver object that glinted in the low light. *What is she doing?*

Keeping low to the ground, Cam hurried after her. His weakened muscles and over-sensitized nerves throbbed with every step, but he pushed on, spurred by the same need that made him run out of his apartment door when the Cerkan skies turned black.

Unlocking the door with her keycard, Reppen slipped inside. Cam lunged forward, trying to catch the door, but it slammed shut.

"*Chak*," he muttered, tapping his fist on the door.

He checked the map to his left. *Isolation: East Wing.*

What if...?

Heart pounding, he stood on his tip-toes, and dared a glance through the oval window.

No Reppen, no machine monsters; just another low-lit hallway leading to a transparent surgical suite.

Wait—is that...?

Inside the surgical suite, bright overhead lights shone down on an unmoving figure strapped to an angled table.

... a person?

Cam tried to raise himself higher, digging the tips of his fingers into the oval sill.

A petite frame, frizzy hair.

Iggie?

But he couldn't make out their coloring or face, not at a distance. However, he could distinguish the figure, stripped down and naked, wires and tubes thrust into their mouth, shoulder and arm, like some kind of cybernetic experiment put on pause.

Horrified, he slipped, stumbling backward and falling onto his hands and tailbone. Aggravated nerves shot daggers into his wrists, hips and through his spine, roiling up through his windpipe in a scream. He held the cry back with a grimace, counting the seconds as the fires raged.

10

9

(just breathe!)

8

7

166

(it will pass—IT WILL PASS)

...

Thinking of Iggie, he pulled one foot underneath himself, then the other, grunting and muffling the groans until he hoisted himself up and limped back over to the door.

When he looked again, Reppen obstructed his view, standing in front of the patient, her back to him. Slowly, she raised her arm. The blade gleamed in the light just before she whipped her arm back down.

"No!" he screamed, pounding on the door.

"Hello?" someone shouted from behind him. Then, panic. "Call for backup."

The footsteps rushing toward him didn't stop him from beating his fists against the glass, kicking the base of the door, or smashing his knuckles into the keycard reader. "Stop it! Don't hurt her! STOP!"

A flash of red, a metal screech. Cam didn't know what he saw or heard as something sharp pierced the back of his neck, only that Reppen turned on her heels and screamed, raising her arms to ward off whatever stormed toward her.

What's happening?!

Muscles failing, Cam collapsed backward, into strong arms that gripped him, held him to the ground as lights shone in his eyes.

"Give him another 10mls!" someone shouted.

As Cam struggled to free himself from the grips of the medical staff, someone—or something—gigantic bashed into the walls, sent vibrations through the floor.

The monster—THE MONSTER—

(Iggie, please—I'm coming—I won't let them hurt you—)

"Put him under."

"Stop it—let me go!" he mumbled through numb lips. Time fractured, the past pouring into the present as his pupils dilated and his heart rate slowed. The darkened ceiling above him transformed into black skies, the smell of disinfectant and sterilizers turned to gun smoke. "Kara..."

(I failed you—)

But any fight, any terrified thought, washed away in whatever cocktail dulled his system.

(I'm so sorry…)

Aggressive hands turned out his left arm, inspecting the discontinued medication line. "We've got a problem."

Other voices made exasperated sighs, swore.

"Call Rogman."

"No, Naum."

"I don't want that madman coming back here—"

"Just get the kid sedated before he has a chance of retention."

Hands lifted his body, but he floated above them in the swirling dark, pulling farther and farther away from himself.

"Do you think he saw…?"

Someone huffed and squeezed his arm. "For his sake, I hope he didn't."

Chapter 18

A steady thumping, like a heartbeat, pulsed in the distance. Cam couldn't open his eyes, nor did he want to. Something terrible—old, rotten, like a gutted fish roasting in the sun—hunkered down above him, breathing hot air into his face.

Don't look don't look DON'T LOOK—

Mechanical clicking; skittering tiny, pointed feet. Cam tried again to move, but his arms and legs wouldn't budge. Whatever restraint paralyzed his muscles, pinning him to a cold, hard surface, left his senses untouched. Save his sight, he could sense everything, right down to the prickling fingers dancing up his left arm to the electric whirring of machines.

"This is Rogman's little pet project," someone said, sounding both annoyed and scared.

Screeching, grating; like a blender grinding up metal flecks.

"Well, don't chak *it up."*

The whirring increased to a steady whine. Pain exploded up his arm. Cam wanted to scream, to thrash about, but he couldn't, not even as flesh tore and bone splintered.

Alarms screamed, a commotion of feet and nervous hands.

"That heartrate—"

"Get him under!"

Cam shot upright, swinging his arms.

"Compose yourself, cadet."

Rogman. The Commandant stood next to his bed, holding a datapad in his gloved hand, lips pressed together in a tight line. Dr. Verdebear, bloodshot eyes cast down to the floor, cowered behind him.

Wait—what's going on? No medical staff held him down, Reppen, machine monster—*Where am I?*

169

It took a moment for his surroundings to sink in. Back in the medical bay, Cam sat up in his bed, sheets in a tangled clump by his feet. His skull thrummed with pain, and his throat ached, as if rubbed raw by sandpaper.

My arm!

He inspected his left arm. A tightly wrapped, neat bandage lay over the medication access point where the line once threaded into his body.

Was it real? He picked at the bandage, but the Commandant clicked his tongue, and he retracted his right hand.

"Where's nurse Reppen?" he croaked, dry tongue sticking to the back of his mouth. Holding his neck with one hand, he searched for his tray table, for a cup with water—anything—to soothe his sore throat.

Rogman didn't move to help him, not when Cam struggled to pull the tray table closer and fumbled with the water cup.

"There are a few matters to be settled, cadet. First, you've been taken off cryoxotin. These reports state that you've been found wandering the hallways, hallucinating—"

"But I—"

The Commandant slammed his hand on the siderail, making him jump. "*Hallucinations.* Do you understand?"

"Y-yes."

"Second, you're to be discharged today and put back into class."

Cam picked up on his omission. "No sim training?"

Clasping his hands behind his back, Rogman eyed Verdebear. "Per your medical team, the training suits will no longer be *effective.*"

Verdebear muttered something under his breath, then resumed his demurred posture.

I wouldn't feel pain? He thought about Jao, how she constantly had to adjust his motor assist modules. *Or the shock would kill me?*

Too afraid to ask, he kept his mouth and waited for the Commandant to continue.

Rogman lowered his voice. "Finally, in order for you to stay enrolled in the Academy, I require a different demonstration of your skill."

"W-what…what do you want?" he asked, goosebumps breaking out across his skin.

Tapping the datapad on his open hand, Rogman inhaled sharply. "You've become quite close with cadet Jahx Drachsi, yes?"

Cam gulped. "He's helped me keep up with my classes."

"I warned you that the triplets are a disease. I don't want a motivated cadet like you adopting their lackadaisical attitude."

"Sir?"

"You yourself observed that they're underperforming, especially Jahx."

What's he getting at? Cam ground his fingernails into his palms.

"As unimpressive as they've turned out to be, all three will be axed from the program at semester's close and sent back to their homeworld."

Fiorah—no. Cam remembered Jahx's fear, the abuse he suffered at home. *He's older—stronger—maybe he could defend himself—*

No. Not against Yahmen. Jahx was terrified of his owner, as if he held even more power over the small boy than Cam could ever understand.

I shouldn't care, he thought, stomach knotting. *Gotta think of Kara.*

"Unless," Rogman said, twitching his mustache, "you think they're worthy of a second consideration."

Cam didn't like how he emphasized *consideration,* or how Verdebear shuddered.

"I… I think all three are really smart. I think they belong here." The last few words filled his gut with ice, as if he committed some kind of grievous betrayal.

"Really? As future commanders of the Sovereign's great fleet?"

"Y-yeah," Cam said, unsure why he phrased it in such a way. "Why?"

Cam thought of Jahx, his unusual feat of avoiding wins and losses, of Jetta's tactical prowess in the training arena, of Jaeia's highly attuned observational skills. "There's something more to them, sir."

"Something more to them?"

Verdebear flinched. Sensing himself in dangerous territory, Cam backtracked. "Yeah, um, it's not something that regular academics shows."

"Then how, cadet, would you suggest eliciting these yet unseen skills?"

Cam bit his lip and averted his eyes, trying to get away from Rogman's dark gaze.

"Come now, cadet," Rogman said, punctuating each word with an air of disdain, "show me how well you understand your enemy."

But Jahx isn't—

(You know what he is!)

"Or," Rogman said, revealing a sickle of stark-white teeth, "are you unfit for your duty?"

(Kara!)

"The Endgame," he said, the words rushing out of his mouth. He tipped forward, holding on to the edge of the mattress with all his strength. "That game the older kids compete in. Make it open to the entire Academy."

"And?"

Cam sucked in his breath, remembering Jahx's fear: *"I don't want to win; I just don't want to get iced out."*

"It has to be their ticket—up the ranks or out."

With another twitch of his mustache, the sickle-smile vanished. "So shall it be, then."

(What did I just do?)

Cam glanced at Verdebear. The doctor, still cowering behind Rogman, locked eyes with him for just a moment. In that fraction of a second, stresses that whittled deep furrows into his brow came to light, as did the strains that creased the corners of his lips.

Why is he so afraid?

(WHAT DID I JUST DO?)

"Dr. Verdebear will take care of your discharge arrangements," Rogman said, nodding to the doctor. "I will expect your continued reports on the other students as you participate."

Cam's stomach dropped. *I can't compete in the Endgame.*

He hadn't had the training, let alone the time to figure out the controls.

172

Chak, who am I kidding? I'm not even smart enough even if I did. Cam flexed his left hand, eliciting a sharp twinge in his forearm, underneath the bandaging.

That dream—

(Or was it real?)

No, the cryoxotin causes hallucinations—

—But the excruciating pain, the look on Reppen's face, the machine man—

"What's... What in the East Wing?" he blurted.

Rogman scoffed. "The East Wing?"

"I need to see," Cam whispered. If Rogman wouldn't show him, it would confirm his fears, but if he did and he saw that *thing—*

(Kara—what have I done?)

"Alright, cadet." Rogman walked to the door and then turned around, an expectant look upon his face. "Well?"

Verdebear offered him a hand as Cam got out of bed, the usual electric zaps from his aggravated nerves charging up his feet and legs. Keeping the pain out of his face, he followed behind Rogman, heart beating against his sternum. *Nothing. It's going to be nothing, and I'll feel like a fool.*

Only a kid would believe anything so dumb, he thought, continuing to admonish himself as the nurses and techs they passed by in the hallway gave their trio side-long glances. *They're just nightmares. I need to focus on getting out of here, passing class, the Endgame—finding Kara—*

"Here you are, cadet," Rogman said, opening the isolation doors with his keycard.

Cam stood in the middle of the parted double-doors of the east wing, staring down the hallway he remembered so vividly from his—

(nightmare?)

This isn't the same.

A hallway and transparent surgical suite stood before him, well-lit and smelling of cleansers. No Reppen, no patient strapped to the table, no sign of machine monsters or foul play. Just a lone housekeeper bot mopping and drying the floors, green lights flashing across its spherical body as it hummed down the sparkling hallway.

173

Rogman clicked his tongue, his mustache twitching. "Satisfied?"

I'm a fool.

"Yes, sir."

"Doctor," Rogman said, addressing the silent Verdebear before parting ways. "You have your orders."

"Yes, Commandant."

As Cam turned to follow the doctor back to his room, he caught sight of a blemish in the floor near a corner. A dark streak, something the automated bot could easily miss near a tight angle. Cam paused and squinted. Not blemish, more like a—

Gouge. As if something very large and heavy cut into the floor. *It could have been a cart, or some other machine—*

(MACHINE)

"Please, Cam," Doctor Verdebear said, voice halting, feeble. He motioned for him to hurry, his eyes darting back and forth from down the East Wing hallway to Cam's face. "It's time to go."

Cam followed him back to his room, a pitting feeling in his stomach. Still, as the doctor went over his discharge protocol, and what to expect, he could only think of the gouge mark.

"Take it easy—and if you're hurting, take these pills," the doctor said, setting down a reddish bottle on the tray table.

Sitting on the edge of the bed, Cam picked up the bottle and inspected the contents, then pushed it aside. "No, thanks; I don't want to hallucinate."

The doctor looked up from his datapad. "About that…" His eyes flicked to the doorway, then the monitors. "…these won't to do that. But I can understand keeping your wits. You'll need that for what's next."

"Huh?"

"The Endgame. You're very smart picking that as an evaluation tool. It's the toughest challenge in the Academy."

For whatever reason, the doctor's comment rankled him. "I didn't want to do that," he muttered. *How the hell will I ever compete? I'll get kicked out within a week.*

"Rogman is very interested in you because of how you see problems. I hope you take that to heart."

Cam frowned. "What do you mean?"

"I mean…" Again, the doctor checked the doorway, then the monitors. "I mean just take it easy, cadet. Don't push yourself."

Cam flexed his feet and his toes, the burn traveling up his legs. Thinking of Jahx, of his sister—the Endgame—

(it's all my fault)

—he ground his fists into the mattress and steeled his voice. "I don't have a choice."

Chapter 19

"Cam!"

Before Cam could take more than a few steps inside the barracks, a lanky figure with long, wiry arms wrapped around him and squeezed.

"I was so worried."

Blowing away the mess of red hair in his face, Cam gave Tomia a stiff pat on the back, then removed himself from her hug. His skin ached where she'd squeezed, but he didn't dare show any signs of discomfort. *She's okay—*

(Maybe it was all a hallucination.)

"I'm fine," Cam said, not wanting to draw the attention of the kids milling around their bunks. Dressed in a fresh-pressed school uniform, he was hoping he would blend in, but the whispers and the stares indicated otherwise.

Stepping back from her, Tomia surveyed him from head to toe, worry and relief in her eyes. "You were gone for so long."

"Sorry," he said, heat climbing up his cheeks.

Tomia followed him to his bunk but waited to say anything else until he got to his locker and checked on his things.

"Are you okay?" she whispered as he rifled through his datapads and alternate training uniform.

Exhausted, but not wanting to show her how much effort it took just to keep up the conversation, he leaned against his locker. "Yeah, I'm fine."

"I… I wanted to visit you," Tomia said. Wringing her hands, she looked at her feet. "I don't know where the time went."

Cam shrugged his shoulders, then realized her phrasing: *"I don't know where the time went."*

"What do you mean?"

Tomia shook her head. "I don't know," she whispered. "I feel like one minute, I'd be in class, the next, back in my bunk, fully dressed, on top of my sheets."

Under any other circumstances, Cam would have dismissed her, chalking her complaint up to stress. But not with what he remembered—

Hallucinated—that's what the Commandant said—

Cam pressed his knuckles into his eyes, not wanting to take in Tomia's pale complexion, or the fatigue etched in her face. "Don't worry about it."

"Did you see Iggie?" she asked.

Cam sucked in his breath. "In the infirmary?"

"Yes—she's been gone for days now. I don't know where she is," Tomia said, pointing to the undisturbed bottom bunk across from them.

"What do the teachers say?" Cam asked, keeping his voice low.

"Nothing," she whispered back.

Cam's sleeve beeped. Turning over his arm, he read the alert: *You are now eligible for Endgame matches.*

Misreading his frown as confusion, Tomia explained: "You missed the Commandant's speech in mess hall today. They're opening up the Endgame competition to all levels. It's going to be a blood bath."

Cam closed out the message and tried to act unaffected. "Whatever."

She guffawed as he crawled up to his bed and laid down. Climbing up part way, she nudged his shoulder as he closed his eyes. "How can you be so casual about any of this?"

"Any of what?"

Tomia leaned in. "Iggie's gone. My memory gaps. They kept you for weeks, Cam. That isn't normal. Didn't you see—or experience—anything weird?"

The paranoia in her voice alerted other students. A few stared, others quieted their own conversations to listen in.

"Check yourself," Cam muttered under his breath.

"No," she said, slapping him on the forearm. For a split second, as her wrist popped out of her sleeve, he spotted a horizontal scar he hadn't noticed before.

177

Catching her arm, took a closer look. "Where did you get this?"

Tomia blushed and yanked it back. "That's what I'm trying to tell you. I don't know. I've got several more marks like that, and I have no clue how they got there."

Cam pushed up the sleeve on his left forearm. A similar scar laid over where the medication line used to be. When he touched it, he felt a rectangular mass just beneath the surface, as if attached to his bone. *What did they do to me?*

"I'm scared, Cam," she whispered. "All the time, now. I'm scared to sleep. There's a monster in my dreams."

A chill ran up his spine and he turned over onto his side to face her. "What kind of monster?"

"Hey, loser—you're back."

Cam looked over Tomia's shoulder. *Stempton.* The freckle-faced boy approached with Walli and Hoch in tow, violence in his eyes.

"Go," he whispered to Tomia.

"No, I can't leave you—"

Cam put his hand on her shoulder, applying gentle pressure to get her off of the bunk ladder. "I said, go."

Tomia shot him a hurt expression before sliding down and heading the opposite way, toward the lavatories.

"They finally fix your broken *pusa*?" he laughed, substituting his native slang for a Common derogative.

Cam ignored the insult, tracking the way the three moved together, and how the other kids in the bunks dispersed. By Stempton's rigid posture, Cam guessed he wasn't coming in to just talk, especially when he had such a distinct advantage over Cam to leverage out whatever he wanted.

"What the hell is with his skin?" Walli muttered, upturning his nose.

Hoch chimed in: "Yeah—you stick your tongue in an electrical socket?"

"I don't have time for any of your *gorsh-shit*," Cam said, sitting up on his top bunk and crossing his legs. "Get on with it."

"I thought we were partners for the chemistry research project," Stempton said, standing at the bottom of the double-bunk. "Then I hear that you're helping that dumb launnie. Thought you were smarter than the average rat, Ferros, but apparently not."

Instead of their usual braying, Walli and Hoch stayed close to Stempton, their gazes flicking back and forth, checking the peripheries.

"Well, here's your deal, rub," he said flashing a red chip Cam's way. "Once I put this in any console, the teachers are going to trace it back to your profile and find a lot of stolen homework and assignments in your folders."

Is that possible? He couldn't be certain, not with his limited computer skills. *Maybe Stempton cracked my profile while I was gone.*

Not that it really mattered as much as the reason behind it. *Stempton is desperate to make me his grunt,* he thought, *but why me?*

Cam said nothing, waiting for the rest of the deal.

Unable to get a rise out of him, Stempton continued, angrier than before: "But if you're smart, you'll do a favor for me, and you won't get iced."

"Don't you have enough scrubs to do your dirty work?"

Walli and Hoch zeroed in on him with heated glares.

"Certain wimps keep avoiding us. You can get close to them."

Certain wimps. Cam curled his toes, not wanting to guess at his targets. "I'm not your *goddich* thug."

"Well then what the hell are you? Cannon fodder?"

The others laughed.

"We all know you're going to fail the Endgame competition, and your grades are smashed."

"Then what's the point of helping you if I'm going to ice out anyway?"

Stempton grinned, as if he'd been waiting for the moment. Holding up a blue-colored chip he said, "this is the stat hack. You can get yourself ranked as an average student with passing grades. A *chakking* phenomenal feat for a street rub. And, me, Walli and Hoch will make sure you win a few of your Endgame matches."

Stempton tossed the chip on Cam's bed. "Figure it this way, rub: you're not smart enough for any of this. Just do what I ask you, when I ask, and you won't ice out. Yet."

179

After the trio left, Cam took the chip and inspected it. *They had me three-to-one and they still didn't attack,* he thought, running his fingertip along the corrugated edges. He didn't expect that, not with how they postured, or his weakened state.

Then they're still afraid of me. Cam stuffed the chip down his front pocket and laid back down with a heavy sigh. *At least I still have that.*

Tomia popped back up on the ladder, her face close to his ear. "Cam."

"Look, Tomia—I don't know what to say," he said, closing his eyes as if he could escape the moment. "Nothing really makes sense to me right now."

"Are you still enrolled in gaming strategy?"

He turned and faced her. "Yeah, so?"

"Get me in the classroom. We can access the terminals."

Cam perked to her suggestion. Before, he didn't have the resources or knowledge to circumvent the network firewalls and do an extensive search for his sister. And now he needed to know why Stempton wanted him to do his dirty work—and whom he intended for Cam to target.

"What are you going to do?" he asked. "And how?"

"I'm going to find out what's going on here," she said, eyes plastered open in a half-crazed stare, "by any means necessary. *Any.*"

Thinking of the gouge in the east wing floor, of the ache in his forearm, he couldn't deny her that need.

Cam checked his sleeve. 2015. If he had any choice in the matter, he would have gone to sleep right then, and maybe for the next week. But not now. *Not when I can finally get some answers.*

"Alright," he said, ditching his jacket so he wouldn't be live-traced. Tomia did the same, tossing hers on her nearby bunk. "Let's go."

After crawling out of bed, he followed her to the front of the barracks to catch a lift.

"I don't recognize half these kids," he remarked as they passed by rows of new faces. Dressed only in his pants and t-shirt, the scars and blemishes that scored his skin snagged the eyes of the recent recruits. If he caught them staring, he met their eyes until they turned away.

"Lots of changes happened while you were gone."

"Bunk reassignments?"

She tightened her jaw. "That. And a lot of kids graduated or, I don't know—just disappeared."

This is not the Tomia I remembered, he thought as she signaled for a lift and they got aboard. No longer cool and calm, she jumped at the slightest provocation, from a stray laugh or even a bump in the ride.

"What about Jahx?" he said. Quickly, he tacked on, "and his sisters?"

"They got transferred the same time as me and Iggie. I'm sharing a bunk with Jetta, and Iggie with Jaeia."

"That's a risk," he said.

"Why?"

"All the street rubbish stinking up the back of the barracks? You don't see how you've made yourselves a target?"

"Hey," Tomia said, a hint of fire in her eye, "they're not so bad. Not at least as bad as some of the *assinos* around here."

"That's true. What about Jahx?" he asked as the lift took a sharp corner, nearly pitching the two of them off.

"Didn't you notice?" she chortled.

"What?"

"He's your bunkmate. He even specifically asked to be your bunkmate for your return."

Butterflies tickled the inside of his stomach. Still, he didn't disclose any hint of the excitement he felt. "Sure. Whatever."

"I don't know why you're so uptight," Tomia said. "You've got a reputation. I don't think anyone will be *chakking* with you or anyone in your immediate radius."

Cam blushed. "If they only knew…" he muttered.

"Huh?" Tomia said.

"Nothing."

As soon as the lift dropped them off in front of the gaming strategy classroom and Cam unlocked the doors with a wave of his hand, Tomia rushed inside.

"Jeez, wait," Cam said, navigating around the consoles to the back row of computer access terminals.

"Um, you know what you're doing?" he asked as she pried off the cover panel of one of the units.

"Come on, didn't you ever cross a few wires to get an extra game in the arcades?" she asked, vetting out the bundles of cables from the other mechanical innards.

Cam didn't see how the two could ever compare. "That's just a cheap trick."

"Not really," she said, swapping chips and testing the keyboard.

"Who's that?" Cam asked as a student profile popped up on the screen. Stats and summaries scrolled by, but Cam stopped the feed at the photo. A black-haired boy with yellow eyes and freckles stared back at him, familiar and yet foreign at the same time.

"Slick, huh? I made it during combinatorial analysis when the teacher opened up the class's access to student projects."

Cam squinted, his mind hitching on the juxtaposition of the yellow eyes against a cherubic face. "But this isn't a real student..."

He stopped himself, glancing at Tomia. With a proud smirk, she crossed her arms. "I couldn't create a totally new student profile, not without getting flagged."

Touching the picture, he traced the curve of the boy's cheekbones. "So you mish-mashed existing ones?"

Tomia nodded. "It's a copy and cut of about five students. It flies totally under the radar."

"You used Jahx. And Stempton," he said, stepping back.

"Good eye," she said, typing some commands on the keyboard.

Cam watched in silence as she tried for access outside of the intra-school network under the falsified profile. Finally, he asked: "Who taught you this?"

"There's wasn't a lot to do in the icefields of Midra," she said. Then, with a detached coolness, she added: "one of my brothers was a data hustler."

Cam knew what that meant. "Arrested or killed?"

"Arrested," she said, still typing away. "He didn't really take sides in the telepath war, but he did like money. Telepaths were paying ten times the normal prices for transport info to get off Cerka..."

She stopped mid-sentence to input a set of commands into the opened search. "*Chak.* I can't get us access."

Cam came up beside her, opening a second screen so he could view the fake profile. "You named him 'Jim Walker?'" he chuckled.

"It's from an Old Earth short story I read years ago. The kid was conflicted, weird. This fake kid is just as weird."

"Yeah, I can see that. Enrolled in five classes, rated highly in three, just passing one, and miserably failing stats. And he's listed on gaming probation for failure to show up to challenge matches?"

"Well, it's tough to have him physically show up to game," she said with an irritated breath.

Reflexively, he brought his thumb to his teeth, but chewing the nail made his entire hand ache.

"*Chak,*" he muttered, shaking out his hand. "Okay, so what can we do with this profile?"

"Jim's got normal student access."

"No external network access?" he said, glancing at the door. At this hour he didn't expect any other students or teachers to interrupt their secret operation, but that didn't mean a guard wouldn't sweep the area, or some late-night wanderer would come strolling in.

"No; that's only for students in officer training corps since they run real operations."

"That doesn't really help us." Snapping his fingers, he nudged Tomia aside to take the keyboard.

"What are you doing?"

"We can find Iggie," he said, typing in a search for her signature.

"I've already tried that," she said. "She's not listed on the premises."

Cam encountered the same frustration as the map of the entire school lit up in the holographic projection, but none of the hundreds of blinkers moving around the map registered as Iggie.

"These are all students wearing their uniforms, right? So they're being live-tracked?"

"Yeah, why?"

"Well Jim is a student, and he isn't on here. But he exists?"

"Yeah, I guess. Look, I've already tried that," she said as he typed in a filter to highlight all the last-known locations of students not wearing their uniforms. "See—Jim and Iggie show up the same—inactive."

Giving it another try, Cam applied a new filter, showing how many times a student logged into their profiles.

"I tried that too," Tomia said, exasperated. "Iggie logged into her personal datapad two days ago, and no activity since. No log-ins, no live-tracking."

"There's got to be some way to find her," he muttered, hitting the keyboard harder and harder as his frustration mounted.

Tomia crossed her arms. "Seriously, Cam, I already tried all of this. I even tried tracing her through her private signature."

She's right; how could I possibly figure something out that she already hasn't?

After all, Tomia earned her way into the Academy by merit, unlike him.

Ashamed, Stempton's criticism resurfaced: *"Figure it this way, rub: you're not smart enough for any of this."*

Then, the freckle-faced boy tossing him the blue chip.

The stat hack...

"Wait—Iggie's listed as inactive because she hasn't logged in for two days, right? What if we forced her profile into activity?"

"How?"

"Jim challenges Iggie to an Endgame match."

"Not if he's on probation," she countered.

"Not with this," he said, pulling the chip from his pocket.

"What?"

Cam ran his other hand through his hair, over-excited by his idea, unsure if it would work. "Stempton's gift to jack me up. He said it was some kind of stat boost, but I'm sure it's a setup."

Tomia took it from him, inspecting the chip. "But if it worked..."

"We could boost Jim's stats, and he can challenge anyone."

Wagging her finger, Tomia followed his line of thought. "And then the gaming system would find the nearest location for the two of them to meet."

"At least we can figure out what part of the Academy she's in without exposing our *assinos*," Cam said.

"Yes...but you'd lose this chip. For whatever it's worth."

184

He hated the pity in her voice, the way she diverted her gaze. "I'll manage."

After slotting in the chip, Cam stood back as Tomia worked Stempton's cheat.

"So why is Stempton after you so hard?" she asked, her fingers flying across the keyboard.

"He wants me to go after other cadets."

"Isn't that what Hoch and Walli are for?"

"Apparently they can't get close enough to some of his targets."

Tomia paused, tilting her head to the side. "That sounds fishy."

"I know," Cam said, glancing at the empty desks, and the inert gaming station. "I think some of the competition is making him nervous."

"Yeah, well, with the Endgame open to all students, I'm sure he's crapping his pants that some little punk is going to make a fool out of him."

Who are you so afraid of? Cam thought, heading over to the desks as Tomia continued to work.

Remembering the conversation with Jahx about battle footage, he called up the files from Stempton's desk. Nothing remarkable caught his eye; as he would suspect, the Crexan prioritized the highest-ranked student battles at the top of his desk and shuffled all the other lesser battles below.

I don't have time to go through all the footage, he thought, blowing a breath through his teeth. Body aching, he plopped down in the seat and knotted his fingers in his hair. Staring at the long list of battle files, anxiety and inadequacy crept up his spine like icicles. *(How am I ever going to catch up, let alone compete with kids like this?)*

He'd have to study every student for hours.

That's it.

The number of views. A kid with an ego as big as Stempton's wouldn't rank his files with anything but the biggest, most epic battles. But what he watched and returned to the most would reveal the true nature of what he prioritized.

And what he fears.

Cam filtered out Stempton's battle footage records by the number of user views.

185

Stempton's got his eye on Shiggla, he noticed as her top twenty battles against other students populated near the top of this list. His eye caught the same last name higher in the list.

She's got a sibling? As he matched the surnames and compared the profile pics, he saw the familial resemblance. A stronger player, Shiggla's brother Soling proved to be a top contender in the games. *I bet that makes her crazy...*

But it wasn't Shiggla's, or any other older cadet's battles, that were Stempton's most-viewed files.

Stomach turning to ice, Cam stared at the name highlighted in electric blue on the desktop.

Jahx Drachsi.

Why? Cam thought. The boy still held a neutral rating.

I wonder... Typing in a new set of commands, he searched the desk for any other stored battle footage in the Academy. A long list of battles showed up, mostly between senior students and final competitions. Applying the same filter, a short list of names turned up amongst the top battles.

Jetta. Jaeia. Jahx.

Stempton viewed everything from their solo gaming sessions to their individual stats just as must as he did the final Endgame competition from several years ago featuring the famed Drakken Varkanian.

Drakken Varkanian is a legend, Cam thought, reading down the list of all the boy's accomplishments. Sent off to officer training corps as a preteen, he held an impeccable rating throughout his Academy days, as well as several unbeaten school records. *Why the hell does Stempton care about three little street kids as much as he does a military prodigy?*

He leaned back in the chair, letting out the air in his lungs as he stared at the triplet's names. *Why is he so afraid of you three?*

Stempton watched as a video of Jetta struggling against a newbie cadet in a fighter sim, but then, after watching a match between two older students, beating her next opponent, a sophomore student, in less than two minutes.

Her eyes, he said, rewinding the video of her watching the older students' game and zooming in on her, arms crossed, gaze intense, as if she meant to bore through their skulls. *What is she looking it?*

Beads of sweat formed on his palms and forehead, his breath quickened. Whatever nerves he felt, maybe Stempton felt it too.

That's why you want me to hurt them, he thought, watching the video of Jahx tying up another game with a formidable opponent.

(...you're afraid of them, too.)

"Hey, Cam—I've got something."

Returning to Tomia, he looked over her shoulder at the map with a yellow marker hovering over a smaller gaming area near the operations and command center of the Academy.

"She's by the infirmary."

Cam zoomed in on the map, noting the greyed-out areas inaccessible by students.

"And the isolation units."

Silence captured the moment as they both took in what that could mean.

"What do you think... what do you think happens there?"

Thinking of the East Wing, of his dream of the machine monster, he shuddered. "I don't know."

Cam checked the door again. "How long before this profile gets noticed?"

"Not long. A few days? Stempton's cheat was designed to fail," she said, pulling up lines of code that meant nothing to him.

Before he could catch himself, he whispered, "Stempton just needed me to hurt the triplets."

"The triplets? Why?" she chuckled. "I mean, Jetta can be a sour turd, but Jaeia and Jahx are sweet and innocent. I mean, Jaeia still can't go to the restroom without her sister, and Jahx cries in his sleep. They're just frightened little kids."

"Frightened little kids that don't want to get noticed," he mumbled, thinking of his last interaction with Rogman.

"Huh?"

"Look, we can't wait; we need to risk it all," he said running his right hand along the abnormal contours beneath the surface of his left forearm.

"Risk what?"

"We both want external network access, right?"

"Well, open access, yeah."

"We gotta bump Jim into officer's training corps."

Tomia pursed her lips, her brow knotting. "That will get the profile shut down in hours. Maybe minutes. And besides, who the hell am I going to mesh in with this profile to give Jim that kind of boost? We can't just hack his stats."

"Drakken Varkanian."

Tomia whistled. "Yeah, I heard about him. The older kids talk about him like he's a god." After doing a quick search, Tomia's jaw dropped. "Holy *chak*. I guess they're right."

Cam watched as she scrolled through his impressive list of credentials. "Undefeated, top scores in every Endgame category... He's flawless."

"Wait, stop," he said, seeing a gap in his service and training history. "Why is there a six-month gap?"

Tomia shook her head. "It could be anything."

Cam looked at the explanation noted in the gap. "He was shipped off training grounds? And right after a live battle? Something must have happened."

"Oh wow, I didn't know he was the Fleet Commander's son."

"Second son. He had a brother, Xercius," Cam read, noting that the young man only lived to seventeen. Clicking on the file for Xercius, he scrolled down to the date of death. *Right before Drakken's service gap.*

Biting his lip, he fit together the pieces as he noticed the two brothers had been in the same battle. *Maybe he witnessed his brother's death and freaked.*

"Come on, Cam, if we're going to do this, I'd say let's steal from Drakken."

"Okay," Cam said, standing back as she hacked into his file.

Unable to aid Tomia, Cam walked over to the rectangular window in the classroom door and checked for any activity. Lifts whizzed by, crammed to the rails with kids, but none stopped at any of the classrooms.

Where are they going this late at night? Not that he couldn't guess. *The Endgame...*

Turning around, he leaned against the door, his body aching, his stomach aflutter. *What the hell did I do?*

Tomia motioned for him to join her. "Okay."

"Jeez," Cam said, coming up beside her. "That didn't take long."

"You said to risk it all…" she said, punching in another set of commands into the keyboard as she used the profile to gain access to the wider network. "We don't have much time."

"Can you patch me through?" he said, starting up the adjacent workstation.

"Yeah. Hey, Cam—do you think they're watching us?"

Cam paused, resisting the urge to look over his shoulder and to the ceiling and walls, where he imagined cameras—*Rogman*—recording their every move. Avoiding her eyes, he tried to sound unaffected by the question. "No."

As soon as Tomia connected Jim Walker's profile to his station, he dove into the search he'd been waiting to make since he first arrived: *United Starways Coalition, list of survivors and prisoners of war, Kara Jhean Ferros.*

When the search produced no hits, he specified his home planet and her date of abduction. A list of Dominion prisoners of war populated on the list, but none from the USC.

"*Chak,*" he swore through gritted teeth.

"What's up?" Tomia said.

Too frustrated to answer, he typed in a new search: *United Starways Coalition, prisoners of war.*

Several articles, written by Dominion analysts, populated on the screen. He clicked on the first, then the second, third, and fourth. The same words popped up as he skimmed the articles: *telepath, demonstration, law of retaliation, death.*

"The USC doesn't keep prisoners of war," Tomia said, glancing over at his search. "They kill all prisoners in demonstrations, under their laws of retaliation, for the deaths of the telepaths. Didn't they teach you that in your intros course?"

"I didn't get an intros course, remember?" Cam grinding his knuckles into the keyboard, confusing the search engine. Heat burned through his chest and up his throat, tensing his shoulders and his jaw. *If they murdered my sister over a* chakking *leech—*

He couldn't finish he thought, his mind frenzied by the possibility. Without her, without Kara, then—

No, she's still alive, he told himself. *She has to be.*

189

"Cam…"

Shaken by the frailty in her voice, Cam looked over at what Tomia had unearthed in her own search. Under Jim Walker's profile, she'd infiltrated the Academy network, and pulled up the personal files of all the students.

When he didn't realize what she intended fast enough, she pointed at her own profile, highlighting the notes and flags at the bottom of a row of candid pictures.

"What is this?" she said, her finger shaking as she highlighted the date of her arrival—and her termination from the program. "That's next month… Are they planning to ice me out? Why?"

Cam couldn't make sense of it. Per her teacher reviews, Tomia maintained good grades, performed well, and got along with other students. But the yellow and red flags tagged to her name bespoke of something else—something that even open access couldn't unlock.

"Iggie is the same," she said, pulling up Iggie's profile beside her. "Same termination date. I don't understand this—"

Before Cam could look over Iggie's profile, she brought up his. "And you—your entire profile is locked," she said, tapping on the greyed-out areas under his picture.

Except for one line at the very bottom of the screen: *pending beta trials review.*

Beta trials. With a flinch and a retraction of his left arm to his chest, he remembered the words spoken over him as he lay trapped:

"Inform Rogman that I want this subject reassigned to me."

"Sir, he's part of the beta trials."

"He's too valuable to be their fodder."

A name resurfaced. *Naum. Dr. Naum.*

And pain.

Sweat breaking out across his forehead, Cam pushed Tomia out of the way.

"Hey!" Tomia said, catching herself on the adjacent workstation.

Ignoring her distress, he typed in a cross-search on all the students. Seven popped up with the words "beta trials" in their file. Iggie, Tomia, himself, and a few other kids he didn't recognize.

"What's the deal?" she said, irritated that he wouldn't divulge any of his intent.

I don't know—but there's something. I know there is, he said, looking over each kid's stats and figures. All of them from war-torn worlds, flagged and highlighted, all—except Cam—listed with termination dates. None of them particularly stood out as poor or outstanding students. *There has to be a reason...*

Then, as he compared family status, Reppen's words sunk into the back of his mind: *"You don't have any family, do you?"*

"What's that got to do with anything?" he replied.

"Everything, at least to the ones that make decisions around here."

"We're all orphans..." He stood up straight, his heart thudding in his chest. All the air left his lungs as he added: "no one would notice if we disappeared."

Tomia gasped and froze in place.

Before she could ask, before he lost the nerve to check, he tapped on the word *beta trials.* A limited result came up:

Commandant L. Rogman, head of operations
*Consultant: **redacted – level 1 security access required***
Dr. Charl Naum, assistant director, MD, Biotech MPA
Maio Kull, acquisitions coordinator, RN-IV, DvN
Bioenhancers and implanted modifiers, phase II
Isolation: East Wing, 001-101.

"What... what are they planning?" Tomia squeaked. Grasping the scar on her wrist with her opposite hand, she whispered. "I can't stay—gotta leave—gotta get out of here."

"Tomia," he said, taking her by the shoulders, trying to stop her shaking.

"I can't, Cam," she said, tears streaming down her cheeks, "I can't—the machine monster—"

"I know," he said, holding her tight. His chest burned as she buried her face in his chest. Voice cracking, he whispered: "I've seen him too."

Tomia pulled away a little bit. "What do we do, Cam? We can't stay here."

Cam glanced at the door, then back at the opened profiles. Instinct told him to leave, now, while they had a chance, but something—a need that pulled stronger than his primitive fears, tied

191

to the bleak discovery about his sister—drew him back to the console.

I have to know.

Calling up the triplet's profiles, he stacked them three across, with Jahx's in the center. As he guessed, numerous flags and alerts colored the text and stats, but nothing that allayed or confirmed his deepest suspicions. However, teacher reviews, scornful and unimpressed with the Fiorahian children, marred their reports. All except one.

Mine.

Although disguised under the name "student observer," he read his own words describing Jahx, and his notations on the boy's weaknesses—and unappreciated strengths. *Kind, quiet; doesn't want to be noticed. Avoids fights at all costs. Humble. Age six? seven? — but understands advanced chemistry. Maintains average grades. Has secrets. How can a human kid survive Fiorah? Maybe he isn't really human?*

And then the final damming note: *Too passive; would have to be forced into real battle.*

Heart aching, he realized how Rogman played him. "He already knew," he whispered. *Then why did he make me decide to use the Endgame?*

"Oh, *chak*—them too?"

Cam looked to where she pointed on the screen on Jahx's profile. In the same bottom corner, a notation flashed in red. Instead of "beta trials," though, it read something else. Something he reread three times.

Priority status: Alpha
Awaiting final results: beta trials
Forced acquisition approved
RE: Volkor

Alpha-priority status? Final results? Forced acquisition? What the hell does any of that mean? He tried to click on the file, but it wouldn't open. *And what—or who—is 'Volkor?'*

Then, in red at the very end, a notation from Naum: *Subject unpredictable; inappropriate candidate re: Volkor. Recommend vivisection to acquire critical data for Med Oculus II program, destroy specimen.*

Vivisection. Cam's stomach turned on itself. Blood draining from his face, he took a few short gasps, trying to keep himself from throwing up.

"Cam, come on," Tomia said, tugging his arm. "We have to go."

Why would anyone do this? His mind couldn't wrap around such cruelty, or any kind of reason.

Reading down further, Cam's eyes snagged on Rogman's response: *Pending results of Volkor.*

Volkor. Jahx's life hinged on the success of whatever or whomever that was. If not, Naum would flay him alive.

I need to know what Volkor is.

When he tried to click on the file again, the console went black. One by one, the adjacent consoles also blipped out.

"*Chak,* Jim's been traced." Tomia yanked hard on his arm, pulling him to the door. "We've got about thirty seconds before—"

Cam didn't see the shockwands, only a streak of blue as the doors parted and Tomia lost her grip on his arm. Tomia's scream strained at his eardrums, but his arms and legs went flaccid as electricity zapped through his body.

"*Chak,* not that one—he won't survive—"

A scrambling of feet and arms, shouting.

"Call a medic!"

Gasping for breath, all the blood left Cam's face and his limbs, his heart quivering uselessly in his chest.

I'm going to die.

The thought brought a stillness to his mind, to the feverish scene around him. Thinking of Kara, of the madness of the world, of all that he had done in the hopes that she was still alive, he let go.

Chapter 20

"Cam, are you paying attention?"

Sitting cross-legged next to the fireplace, Cam nudged one of the red and black game pieces on the checkered board with his knuckles. The fire felt good against his face, and through the holes in his sweater and his pants. But as he realized the hunger in his belly, and the gloom of the dilapidated old apartment, the teenage girl sitting across from him addressed him again: "Cam? What's wrong?"

Am I dead? *The thought stirred within him as he relived the memory of Kara trying to help him learn the latest board game.* The guards came—I got shocked—

No guards in sight, no Tomia, no Rogman, no Academy. Just this place, like a memory caught up in a dream, ethereal and transitory. How is this possible?

Cam looked around, trying to reconnect the missing pieces. Mom should be passed out on the couch—

And the twins, barely two years old, should have been laid out next to Kara on a blanket, jabbering to each other in their made-up language.

But not here. Not in this place where the windows looked out into pitch blackness, and the walls and ceilings flexed back and forth, as if trying to hold their shape.

"Come on, it's your turn," Kara said, pointing to his red knight.

"You aren't real," he whispered, bringing up his knees to his chest. "This isn't real."

Kara mirrored his posture. "You have to decide what is real, Cam."

"What?"

"Now, play."

He looked back to the playing board. His knight faced an army stretched out beyond the playing board, beyond what his eye should have been able to see. Mechanoid creatures, crawling over each other, bucked and hissed, ready to destroy his lone player.

"I—I can't," he said, shoving backward. "It's impossible."

"Trust yourself," Kara said. But this time, as she got to her knees, her voice changed, softening, growing younger with each spoken word. "It's your move."

Bending over the checkered board, Kara reached down and placed her hand in the middle of the mechanoid fray. Creatures shrieked and howled, digging into her with their claws, pulling her down. Cam screamed as his sister's eyes turned from brown to pale blue, her face draining of all color as she was drawn further and further into the board. Wires and tubes spun up her arm and split apart her shoulder, her skin hardening into metal plating. "You have to play."

Cam looked down to the board, to the knight that could do nothing against such an army, against an indomitable force more powerful than the greatest galactic fleets.

I can't do anything—

I can't win this—

"Cam," Kara whispered, her voice frail, pierced by pain.

"No!" he screamed, lunging over the board and wrapping his arms around her. He held her tight, against the machine monsters that pulled her down, her body cold and rigid. "Please, Kara—stop—I can't lose you."

He buried his face into her neck, his arms shaking as he tried to pull her up and out, the last of her sinking into the burgeoning maw. "Don't go."

Squeezing his eyes shut, he fell to the ground, still holding on to her as his own arms sunk beneath the board, into a sea of molten pain. "I love you."

Everything stopped. The fire no longer crackled, the pain in his arms ceased, the room stilled. Kara's moved her lips to his ears and whispered in a young boy's voice, "thank you."

"Finally."

Cam groaned, his neck stiff and aching as he lifted his head. Sitting upright, strong hands held him to the back of a chair facing a long desk. A hardened face with dark-set eyes and a thick mustache came into focus. "Can you hear me, cadet?"

Where am I?

His hands gripped the faux wooden armrests to the chair. When he tried to move, the hands that held him back dug into his chest.

"Leave us."

Cam looked again to the speaker, room still spinning as he tried to grasp his place. The hands left his chest, and he pitched forward, catching himself on the lip of the desk. Behind him, footsteps walked away, followed by the sound of a door swishing open and shut.

"You surprised me yet again, cadet," the man behind the desk said, interacting with a holographic projection of a student profile. "That shock should have killed you."

Cam looked down, seeing the fresh, pink and purple inflammatory streaks that branched out across his hands and up his arms. As his awareness grew, he realized the pain in his chest, and touched the scorched mark on his shirt.

God— he immediately retracted his hand, jarred by the slightest touch. Terrified, he pulled at the collar of his shirt and looked down to the burned skin on his chest. *I'm not dead?*

"Only a soldier with a true purpose can survive as much as you have," the man said, dark eyes connecting with his.

Rogman— he thought, shedding the last of the dream webs that caught up his mind.

"Now, explain this," the Commandant said, turning the student profile around so Cam could read the name: *Jim Walker.*

Tomia! He looked around the sterile office, trying to find some sign of her in the empty chair to his right. "Where's Tomia?"

"Dealt with, as all students who break Academy rules are dealt with," he said, his voice sending chills up Cam's spine. "Your explanation, cadet."

Cam didn't know what to say. *Rogman already knows everything,* he thought, digging his fingernails into the armrest. *What the hell is left?*

The words came rushing out of his mouth: "I need to find my sister."

"Your sister?"

"Kara. She was taken by the USC. I needed external network access."

"To do what?"

Cam hesitated. What could he tell Rogman? That he intended to hack into the USC database? That he would infiltrate their command center? That he, a lowly Academy cadet who probably couldn't pass an intro class, would somehow command a legion of soldiers on a rescue ops? No, none of it was ever possible, and if he had ever been honest with himself—

No, she's alive. She has to be alive. And I will find her.

Eyes and cheeks heating, he wanted to lunge across the desk and rip the mustache right off of the Commandant's ugly face as Rogman pulled up another hologram adjacent to the fake profile.

"Kara Jhean Ferros, Cerkan, age 20," he said, showing Cam the three-dimensional image that looked like his sister. But instead of bright eyes and a kind smile, the woman rotating on the projectors appeared gaunt, hollowed-out, vacant, dressed in grey-striped prison jumpsuit. "Killed in a USC demonstration eight weeks ago."

Cam froze. *No, not possible.*

"Just hold out my love—"

"The USC kills all prisoners," the Commandant said evenly. "Law of retaliation."

"...for blue sky tomorrows..."

No. Light motes dotted his vision as he held his breath, lungs ready to burst. *No no no no—*

"This incident has made me question your loyalty, cadet," the Commandant said, enunciating each word. "A half-breed imbecile like you has no place here in the academy, not unless you have a purpose. What is your purpose, cadet?"

Head spinning, Cam could not hold on to any real thought, anything other than the pain that carved into his chest, and the despair that pitted his stomach.

(Just hold out—)

The law of retaliation—

No more blue skies.

No tomorrows.

Kara's gone. KARA'S GONE.

And all because of the leeches, the war that had taken everything from him.

What's left? He flexed his left forearm, feeling the implant grate against his tendons. *Not this place.* Not with cadets disappearing, countless violations, and machine monsters lurking in the shadows. Not when enemies were sheltered, and every game, every test, was rigged.

"What is your purpose, cadet?" the Commandant barked, slapping his hand on the desk.

A cool wave splashed over him, spreading an unexpected calmness throughout his body. A playing board appeared before him, his lone game piece lined up against his endless enemies. In this game, without the need for win, he would play for the only thing that mattered anymore.

"Revenge," he whispered.

"Revenge?"

"There are leeches here, at the academy," he said, clearing his throat to mask the quaver.

"Is that so?"

"Yes. I'll expose them."

Rogman twitched his mustache, his eyes narrowing. "Do so, cadet, and I'll reconsider your termination."

Cam didn't care what else the Commandant had to say, or his terms. What he had planned, what he wanted to do, didn't require his enrollment or his safety.

"How do you intend to accomplish this?" Rogman asked, freezing the hologram of his sister so that her dead eyes cast down on him.

"Let me arrange some of the Endgame matches. I'll force them to use their powers. Then you can take them away."

Something like a smile nipped at the corner of Rogman's mouth. "Now you are beginning to understand your enemy, the true purpose of this war."

Cam didn't falter, holding Rogman's cold gaze. "I do."

***

After spending the night in the infirmary's observation ward, Cam returned to the barracks, dressed in his pants and burnt shirt. Curious stares turned into gasps and averted gazes as he walked down the aisle to the last bunk on the right. He kept his gaze fixed, not caring whom he ran into, ignoring the questions as well as the insults.

Whispers, shock: "What's wrong with him?"

"Look at his skin—"

"Is he hurt?"

"His shirt got burned—"

"Jeez, Ferros—you look like a zombie," Stempton said, hanging off the rungs of a bunk ladder. Hoch and Walli, sitting together on the opposite bunk, snickered and shook their heads, but did nothing more to aggress him.

After gathering his datapad out of his locker, he couldn't help but glance over at Tomia's top bunk. Perfectly made and undisturbed, it looked like it had been unoccupied for the night. As did Iggie's.

As he passed by her bunk, a stain on the end panel caught his eye. A red smear, the size of three small fingers, colored the top of grey metal.

Blood. He didn't stare for too long, not wanting to draw attention to his discovery. *What happened last night?*

Stomach in knots, he didn't want to think of the possibilities, but another quick glance didn't yield any clues. Besides, Jetta's bed below appeared otherwise intact and made, as per protocol.

It doesn't matter, he reminded himself. *None of this matters anymore.*

Still, he had to know. Pretending to forget something, he made his way back to his locker, using the opportunity to get another look at Jaeia's, then Jahx's bed. No disturbances, no stains, no cause for concern.

Get to class, he told himself after rummaging around his locker to give the appearance of his deliberate return.

But as he turned to leave, he found Stempton, Walli and Hoch blocking his only way out. Stempton, eyes burning with contempt, grinned from ear to ear.

This time, Cam didn't give him the opportunity to state his terms. Dropping his datapad, he grabbed the Crexan boy by the neck and slammed his knee up into his groin. The boy howled and doubled over onto the floor. Hoch and Walli, shocked by the sudden onset of violence, backed away, but Cam didn't let them get far. Shoving both at the same time, he back them into the lavatory door.

"Stay away from me!" he screamed, punching in between both of their heads, leaving a dent in the metal plating.

"It's cool, Ferros," Walli pleaded, bringing his hands up. "Everyone's cool."

Rearing around, Cam readied for more assailants, only to find the other twenty or thirty kids staring down the aisle, watching the fight unfold. Something inside him, born in the darkened streets of Cerka, stitched together by hunger and defined by pain, wanted the rest of them to rush him, to try and strike him down. But they did not. Only Stempton's moans and the sound of Hoch and Walli hyperventilating filled the elongating silence.

"You're dead, Ferros," Stempton said, still tucked in the fetal position.

Cam shook out his throbbing fist, sensing the breaks in the bones but not giving it a second thought. Calmer now, he remembered his plan, what he needed to do with Stempton.

Crouching down to grab his datapad off the floor, Cam whispered to the freckle-faced boy, "you'll wish I finished you."

As he walked out of the barracks, the other kids ran out of his way, avoiding him at all costs. In the back of his mind, an old memory tried to form, one that would have challenged his anger and the hatred that numbed his pain.

For you, Kara, he thought, signaling a lift with the curled fingers of his broken hand. *Because there are no tomorrows.*

Chapter 21

Skipping breakfast, Cam sat alone at his desk in his empty chemistry class, going through the list of lectures he'd missed while recovering.

I don't remember any of this, Cam thought, pulling up one of the lessons on polymers. And yet, as he scrolled through the talking points, everything read as a review, stirring up knowledge he didn't know he possessed.

What the hell?

He pulled a second lecture, a third; all of them made sense to him, bringing to light concepts and information he shouldn't know.

I couldn't have picked all of this up while... he paused, eyes falling to the desk not far from his. *...while asleep?*

(While Jahx read to me—)

—On more occasions than he probably remembered.

Something heavy and hot crawled into his belly. Closing out the lectures, he called up the research project Jahx had all but completed aside from the final calculations. Due that day, he didn't think Jahx would have waited for him to turn it in, but as the project unfolded across his desk on the holographic projectors, he sat back in his chair as the empty slots of the final calculations flashed in red.

He waited. Even if it meant failing the project. *Why, Jahx?*

Cam looked at his uniform sleeve. Twenty minutes until class started.

No way I could figure this out, he thought, knotting his fingers in his hair. And yet, as his eyes darted back and forth across the numbers and letters, his mind snagged on one point, then another.

Well, this can't be here, he thought, rearranging the reaction coordinate energy diagram. By the time he finished the last calculation, the first few students trickled in.

"Hey!"

Cam looked up. Jahx, blue eyes lit by his smile, greeted him with unexpected cheer as he climbed the stairs. "I'm so glad you made it."

Blushing, Cam hid his broken hand under the desk as he fumbled with holographics.

"Oh, nice—you finished the project."

Jahx studied the calculations for a moment, face unreadable; serious. Nervous that he did something wrong, Cam blurted: "I shouldn't have even tried. It's probably all wrong—"

"It's right. It's all correct," Jahx said, smile returning to his face.

"But how…?" Again, Cam couldn't explain his own turnaround. Baffled, relieved and upset, he couldn't decide what to say, or what to do next as Jahx hit save and pulled up the same project on his datapad.

"With two minutes to spare," he chuckled, sending off their project to the teacher's inbox. "Great job."

"I don't understand this," Cam said as Jahx took his seat and faced the front of the class.

"You don't have enough faith in yourself," Jahx said, turning on his desk and fiddling with his interfaces. "You're here for a reason, remember?"

Cam said nothing, words failing him as conflicting emotions he couldn't name churned inside him. He didn't show up to class to finish the project or take the test with any hopes of passing. He just needed to buy some time, to go through the motions—

(And see him)

—before he set the final parts of his plan in motion.

"Good morning, class," the professor Rotu said, standing behind the teacher's desk in the front of the class. The rest of the students hurried to their seats. Cam caught sight of Stempton walking up the stairs, red-eyed and furious. "Ah, cadet Ferros. I'm glad to see you could make it for the final."

The entire class turned to him. Stempton, a wild grin upon his face as he took his seat, whispered up to him: "You're finished, rub."

"You'll have one hour to complete the test," Rotu said, typing in a set of commands to his desk to send out the exam to the students.

As Cam selected the test icon on his desk, a private message from an anonymous sender flashed in the bottom corner. When he

202

swiped it open, the image of a red chip popped up along with a note: *Don't even bother.*

Cam ground his teeth together. In the end, he figured the biochem test would be a moot point anyway, but some part of him, however stupid and ridiculous, wanted to at least try.

No point now. Not if Stempton uploaded the chip and ruined his profile like he threatened.

Cradling his broken hand, he edged toward panic, his breaths shorter and quicker as reprimanded himself. *I shouldn't have hit him.*

Or threatened him after he was down.

Stupid. I'm not good at these kinds of things—

(No tomorrows).

No tomorrows. He reminded himself of his own endgame, of the ultimate objective. In the end, it didn't matter if Stempton ruined him, only that he kept the Crexan from doing so for just a little bit longer.

Cam got up and walked down the stairs, pausing by Stempton's desk long enough to say in a dry and even tone, "I'll do it," before walking toward the door.

"Cadet Ferros—leaving so soon?"

"It's broken," he said, raising his deformed right hand for the professor, and all the class, to see.

"How did you—?"

"Accident," he said, cutting off the professor before he could question him too much further.

"Go to the infirmary," Rotu said, sighing as he waved him away. "But you're taking this exam today, or you'll fail the class."

Before he turned, he caught Stempton's eye. Still angered, but caught up in his own satisfaction, the Crexan stared back. He wouldn't attack him—not yet—only after he'd finished the freckle-faced boy's dirty work.

As he walked out the door, he couldn't help but feel another pair of eyes on his back. An ache swelled inside his chest, snagging at his breath and making him pause as he signaled for a lift.

(What am I doing?)

Righting himself, he made a fist with his broken hand, letting the pain quell his nerves. He felt the coarse fibers of a red scarf against his palm, the weight of a limp body against his own.

Whatever I have to.

***

As much as he didn't want to return to the infirmary, Cam didn't see any way out of it, not with Rotu able to keeps tabs on his compliance. Behind every closed patient door, he imagined Iggie tied to a bed, tubes and wires draped from her body, and a machine monster hiding in the shadows.

Stop it, he told himself, walking up to the triage station at the end of the long white hallway. *Keep it together.*

"You again?" The beak-faced nurse popped up behind the desk.

Maio!

As she sized him up from across the counter, yellow eyes looking him up and down, he thought of nothing but the exit. "What is it this time, cadet?"

Chak. *Not her.* He looked around for Reppen, but he hadn't seen the kind nurse since—

(That nightmare?)

"Well?" she said, rapping her knuckles on the counter.

His gut screamed out at him: *(Her name was on the list for the "beta trials!")*

Screw it—

"Sorry—nothing," he muttered, protecting his swollen hand behind his other arm and turning on his heels to walk right back out.

"Stop right there, cadet," she barked. With a scowl, she circled around, the other staff dodging out of her way.

Cam could nothing as she pulled out his arm and zeroed in on his swollen hand. Waving a scanner over his injury, her eyes widened, then resumed their usual glower. "Get to bay five," she said, pointing to an isolated bay at the end of the ward as she typed something into her sleeve communicator.

It'll be okay, he told himself. *It just needs casting. She can't do anything else.*

Cam did as she instructed, sitting on the edge of the stretcher until she returned. Staring straight ahead, he tried not to offer her any clues of how much her presence unnerved him, or the sight of any medical equipment, as she turned on the monitors.

"Cadet Ferros."

Cam jerked at the sound of his voice. A dour-faced doctor entered the medical bay, blue scrubs darkened by wet splotches around the chest and thighs, tugging off his black gloves and throwing them at the trash. Cam didn't recognize him at first, not until he saw his flinty eyes, and connected them to the sound of his voice.

Naum!

Cam diverted his gaze, staring at the floor, gripping the end of the bed with this good hand.

"What is the problem?" he asked, standing in front of Cam, hands behind his back.

Cam couldn't think of a response, only the sound of a drill, and the ghosted ache of his sternum and forearm.

Maio handed him her bioscanner.

"Metacarpal fractures, heterotopic ossification," he said, reading off the results. Excitement crept into his voice. "Interesting; accelerated growth at 135%. Prep him for surgery, nurse Kull."

"What?!" Cam shot out of the bed, but Maio caught him by the chest and slammed him back down.

I don't need surgery—

Maio dug her clawed fingers into his shoulders, pinning him down.

(He's going to vivisect me—)

He pushed against her neck as she let go of one side and reached for something in his pocket, but Naum aided her, holding down Cam's legs.

"Stop right there."

Taking advantage of the distraction, Cam elbowed Maio in the face, enough that she squawked and let go of him.

"He's not a surgical candidate."

Verdebear. The young doctor grabbed on to Naum and pulled him away.

"You're out of line, Verdebear," Naum hissed, stumbling back and catching himself on a med cart. "This is my patient."

205

"You won't touch that boy," Verdebear said, putting himself between Naum, Maio and Cam.

A chill settled over the room as Naum stood tall, slicking back his hair under his surgical cap. "Under who's authority? Yours?"

Cam tried to get a better look, but every time he moved, Verdebear stepped back in front of him, obstructing his view. "He'll recover with a restorative cast."

Naum chortled. "Nurse Kull, take the cadet."

"Ferros is under the Commandant's personal protection," Verdebear countered, holding out his hand to keep the nurse at bay.

"The Commandant? Since when did you suddenly become his supporter? His dictates are far crueler than mine. This boy is just a plaything to him, where to me—to us—he could be the final solution to this war."

"This boy is just a child," Verdebear said. "As are all the others."

What the hell do either of them mean?

Naum scoffed. "You're merely delaying the inevitable, doctor. My solution is far better than anything that—" He stopped himself, then restarted, ire marring his pronunciation. "—that *beast* has to offer."

Beast?!

Verdebear reached in his labcoat and withdrew a cautery wand. The electric blue tip buzzed and sparked as he waved it at Kull when she tried to take a step closer. "This is all going to end."

"You're right, doctor," Naum said. Cam jumped at the chill to his voice. Scooting back to the headboard, he enabled himself a view of all three of them. "Rogman's faith is misplaced in this whole operation. And so is yours."

Kull struck first, grabbing an IV pole and slamming it down against Verdebear's head and shoulder. The young doctor screamed but managed to slice the cautery wand across the nurse's abdomen as she charged him. Wet, pink intestines flopped out of the charred and opened wound.

Grabbing a hypoinjector from a drawer, Naum readied to attack as Kull clutched her spilt intestines and stumbled into the stunned Verdebear. But he didn't set his sights on the other doctor.

He's going to kill me—

206

Cam looked around the room in panic as the surgeon approached him, hypo in front of him, poised like a weapon. Monitors, tray tables, gauze—nothing would help—

Except—

Core zero. The blue button; the one he remembered in his own room, affixed just above his bed by the monitors. It would bring others—

Naum moved faster than he anticipated, latching onto his leg as Cam lunged for the button. Kicking and fighting, Cam rolled onto his back on the bed, as Naum wrenched him back.

"Ferros—" Verderbear, head bleeding from Kull's blow, fell against Naum as the surgeon depressed the hypo into Cam's leg, taking him to the ground.

"*Chak*," Cam said. Despite the barrier of his pants, coolness dispersed around his calf and up into his thigh.

He got me. Or at least partially. Cam's head swam in circles as he tried to crawl back up to the bed, to the emergency call button. The world seesawed back and forth as he batted at the button, unable to get a firm fix on its shifting location.

Come on—

His hand bashed against the button. Overhead lights came on in full, illuminating the entire room. Sirens sounded. He slumped back down in the bed. *Others will come.*

They'd save him.

Then, as he looked over at Kull, crumpled in a heap, trying to scoop her bloodied intestines back into her body, and Naum, hands wrapped around Verdebear's neck, an old haunt whispered in his ear: *"Kill the enemy before he's got a chance to kill you."*

Nobody's coming to save me.

And nobody ever would.

Launching himself off the bed, Cam slammed into Naum. In the confusion of the scuffle, he couldn't tell his own legs and arms from Naum's, or Verdebear's, flailing and punching at anything he could connect with.

"You little bastard," Naum hissed, grabbing him by the neck. Cam bucked his hips, sending the surgeon forward. Grabbing Naum's arm and rolling out, Cam ended up on top, but not for long as the surgeon cocked back a leg and kicked at his face.

207

Cam ducked, but misjudged the angle, and the surgeon clipped his ear. Knocked onto his side, Cam lay dazed, facing the bed, unable to tell which direction to push himself up.

The cautery wand. It lay under the bed, blue tip still ignited. As Naum attacked his neck again, Cam snatched it up and brought it up to the surgeon's face.

"Recommend vivisection—"

"No!" he screamed. Mind spinning, he sliced wildly, garbled screams and the stench of burning flesh filling the air.

Naum let go of him, slumping to the ground.

Shouts and the anti-grav carts approached. In the confusing swirl of sights and sounds, Cam thought enough to find Verdebear amongst the wounded medical staff. The doctor, passed out alongside the dead nurse, head wound bleeding out onto the white tiles, saved him. The realization cut into him as he placed the cautery wand into the palm of the doctor's hand and stumbled back into the bed.

"We've got four down," someone shouted. Splayed out on his side, Cam didn't look to see the rescue team that rushed inside and assessed the grisly scene. Hands turned him over, lights shined in his eyes.

"Cadet—can you hear me? Cadet, wake up. What happened here?"

He didn't respond to any of their questions, allowing himself to sink lower into the swirl of whatever Naum had injected him with. Instead, he listened to the commotion of the medical team tending to the bloodbath next to him.

"Massive head trauma—"

"I can't get a pulse."

"—cut straight through his trachea and carotids—"

"Active bleeder—"

"Prep her for surgery—"

"—she won't make it—"

"—alert the Commandant—"

Cam closed his eyes, drifting even lower. As the other staff drew off his blood and shouted about his abnormal chemistries, he tried not to think of anything but his own endgame. Curling up his broken hand into a throbbing fist and steeling himself to the young doctor's fate, he whispered, "don't wake up."

Chapter 22

The rough feel of starched sheets against his skin made no sense. Neither did the snoring sounds and steady drone of the air ventilation system. As his eyes came into focus, he recognized the drab, gray walls and the metal beams.

My bunk—

Groaning, Cam turned over from his left to his right shoulder. Everything ached, liked he'd been stuck in the same position for hours. *How'd I get here?*

Nighttime. Or at least lights-out. Only the floor strips lit up the dark barracks, with the overhead light illuminating the lavatories next to his bunk, and the hooded light at the opposite end to the entrance.

Cam looked to Tomia and Iggie's bunks first. Squinting in the dark, he saw only two made, unoccupied beds.

No...

Memories trickled back in as he recognized Jetta and Jaeia sleeping in their bunks, and below him, Jahx curled into a fetal position, facing the wall.

The infirmary.

That nurse.

Naum.

(Verdebear!)

"*Chak,*" he muttered. Shucking off the sheets, he noticed the deformity to his right hand. A knob of bone jutted from the backside, and his last two fingers didn't extend or flex all the way. Still, it didn't hurt—not as much as when he'd first injured it. *It didn't get fixed.*

But Rogman wouldn't allow him to be thrown back into his bunk not after—

(what I did).

210

Unless he got away with it. *But there should be questions—*

He shouldn't have been just dumped back in his bunk without interrogation.

Doubt crept in as he found himself in his usual white sleep shirt and pants. *Either it wasn't real,* he thought, remembering the smell of burnt flesh, *or this is another one of Rogman's games.*

Not knowing what else to do, he grabbed his datapad from the storage slot at the end of the bed and checked the time. 2315. A message alerted at the top in white lettering: *Due by 2359: Biochem final, Professor Rotu.*

Cam huffed. *Yeah, screw it,* he thought, finger hovering over the close button.

But he couldn't. Not if he wanted to finish what he started.

At least take it, he reasoned. Besides, he could easily take one of Jahx's datapads out of his locker and search for answers. But as he reached for the ladder, his affected fingers brushed the open button.

"*Chak,*" he muttered again as a red light came on near the camera. With Rotu enabling the pupil tracking feature, his eyes couldn't stray for too long outside the datapad field. But as he cursed his broken hand, he read the first question on hydrogen.

Well, at least I know this one.

The rest proved less easy. Still, he plugged in whatever answer came to him first, blazing through as the timer ticked down.

I'm so chakked.

It doesn't matter, he told himself. *Just finish the thing. Rotu won't announce anything until the end of the semester, after the projects are graded.*

The end of the semester. Three weeks. He could finish his plan by then, he decided.

Cam exhaled as he typed in the answer to the last question and the test closed, red light blinking out.

Three weeks. He repeated the idea over and over to himself as he accepted his failure on the test, and the inevitable shaming that would follow.

I'm icing out anyway.

Another voice whispered an even darker truth: *(If I even make it out alive.)*

Returning the datapad to the slot at the end of his bed, he resigned himself to his fate when he heard a sob. He waited several seconds, listening closely amongst the sleep sounds and ticking ventilation system. The sob came again, this time with a rustling of sheets, and a vibration of the beams as a knee or elbow struck the side of the bunk.

Holding onto the metal frame, Cam leaned himself over and looked at the boy below. Curled up in tight ball, he shook and twitched, as if something—or someone—terrible was about to strike.

"Stop… please don't…" Jahx mumbled. A sob escaped his lips as his hands flew up above his head.

(Just leave him be) bade the harsh voice inside him.

No—he can't wake up the others. I don't want any trouble tonight.

(It will only make things harder.)

"*Chak*," Cam muttered, lowering himself down the ladder and putting a knee on Jahx's mattress.

"Hey, Jahx," he whispered, gently patting him on the side. "Wake up. Come on, man—wake up."

The boy woke with start, flipping over to face Cam, arms out in front of him. "C-Cam?"

"Yeah," he said, ducking under the bed and bringing a finger to his own lips. "Keep it down, alright? Don't want to wake any of these *assinos*."

Jahx rubbed his eyes with his knuckles, long eyelashes sticking together with his tears. "Sorry."

"Don't worry about it. Nightmare?"

He nodded, scooting up to a sitting position. Sweat slicked the front of his sleep shirt and matted his hair.

He's really afraid, Cam thought, unsettled by the boy's appearance.

Forgetting himself for a moment, Cam asked, "what about?"

Jahx looked away. "Home stuff."

"That Yahmen guy?"

Jahx nodded, scrunching up the bedsheets in his hands.

"Jeez," Cam muttered, not knowing what to say. Stupidly, he added: "he must have been really bad."

Jahx said nothing, his eyes still averted.

212

"Your sisters sleep okay," he said, still keeping his voice low as he pointed his thumb at the opposite bunks.

Picking at the sheets, Jahx shrugged his shoulders. "Jetta's more concerned about the future, and Jaeia just worries about other people..."

Without realizing it, Cam slid down onto his hip, sitting at the head of the bunk. "It ain't worth it."

"Huh?"

"Worrying about a *ratchakker* like that. He's gone. You're here. One day you'll be leading a gigantic fleet. You could crush him like a bug. He's nothing, Jahx."

Somehow, even though he meant his words to make the boy feel better, he sensed he'd missed his mark. Jahx brought his knees up to his chest, looking more isolated and alone than before, even as Cam sat close by.

"You don't understand," the boy said, sounding fragile, about to break. "I don't want to hurt anyone. Not even him."

Cam swallowed hard, cheeks heating up as he sat there not knowing what to say. The reality of what he was doing, and what he intended to not long from now, wrung his stomach. "You shouldn't be here," he whispered.

Jahx shook his head. "I have to be. For my sisters. For..." He trailed off, eyes misting over.

For what?

Anger rising, Cam tried to keep his voice in check. "No, you don't. You can be better than this stupid war. You can get out. Run away. Get to the farthest parts of this galaxy and keep going."

Jahx inhaled sharply. "I can't."

"Why?" Cam said, throwing up his hands.

Blue eyes met his, radiating an intensity that took Cam's breath away. "Because I'm supposed to be here."

"What, like some fortune teller told you?"

Jahx didn't refute his assumption. Instead, he looked away again, indicating the truth went much farther than he initially thought.

"Wait... like a... a telepath?"

Jahx gave a quick nod, eyes flitting back and forth, as if he feared Cam's reaction.

"Come on, really?"

"Really."

"What was he? A hustler?"

"She. No, a nun."

"A nun?" he snorted, irritated by the idea that a telepath could pose as an agent of God. "What'd she say?"

Jahx stared ahead, his mouth falling open for a second, then clamping shut, as if he fought with himself about revealing his secret.

"Look, you don't have to tell me," Cam said, not wanting to upset the boy any further. "Just figure that she, or any vision or prophecy, can't own you. Nothing can."

Jahx studied him a moment, then replied: "You believe that?"

"Everything I've ever believed in is..."

"Just hold out my love—"

"—For blue sky tomorrows—"

He stopped himself before emotions robbed his voice. Clearing his throat, he whispered: "No tomorrows. That's what I believe in."

Jahx tilted his head to the side. "Be in the moment; you can't fear the future. I like that."

Cam wanted to counter his take on his doomed outlook, but didn't have the heart, not as the boy smiled at him, light once again present in his blue eyes.

Go; stop talking to him, he thought, forcing himself to divert his gaze. *It'll just make things harder.*

"You're something else, Jahx Drachsi," Cam said, shaking his head as he pushed himself off the bed and readied to climb back up the ladder.

Jahx lunged, wrapping his arms around his waist, catching Cam in a hug so warm and tight that he held his breath, afraid of what it would do to him. Quietly, the boy whispered back: "So are you, Camzen Ferros."

As soon as Jahx loosened his hold, Cam muttered something between a thank you and a lame excuse and wiggled away. Crawling back into his bed, he tried not to think of anything, especially the tingling warmth that still flowed through his body.

(Kara would have loved Jahx—)

"Goodnight, Cam," Jahx whispered from the bottom bunk.

Cam lay on top of his sheets, cool air from the ventilation grate blowing across his skin. He shivered, staring up at the ceiling, remembering his tenth birthday, the day the skies turned black. The day he lost everything that ever mattered to him, and the vow he made to even the score.

"Goodnight, Jahx."

***

Rising before lights on, Cam slipped out of bed and quietly dressed, keeping an eye on the surrounding bunks.

I need all the practice I can get in the gaming arena, he rationalized to himself, even as he glanced at Jahx's bunk for the fifth time. The boy lay on his side, facing the wall, chest rising and falling in a steady sleep pattern. Not that he was afraid to interact with the Jahx again.

I'm not, he reminded himself, grabbing his datapad out of his locker and heading to the arena. *(It would just make things harder.)*

To his surprise, more than two dozen other students occupied the gigantic gaming arena, spread out between stations, testing and refining their skills in training matches in the early morning hours.

Jeez, this competition is worse than I imagined, he thought, noticing a kid with sleepless, red-ringed eyes mumbling to himself as he ran himself through the same training simulation over and over again.

Cam took a seat in one of the many empty rows of benches that formed a circle around the battle sims and opened his datapad. Using the live feed, he watched all the games at the same time, changing the angles when he couldn't get a good unaided view.

These kids are all so good, he thought, heart sinking. Even the youngest, a first year like him, cut his fleet across the spherical playing field with deft mechanics, leveling his AI opponent in less than twenty-eight minutes. It wasn't just the gaming mechanics—operating the keyboards and controls at the console or understanding how the different starcraft maneuvered in the various environments—it was the totality of it, controlling a fleet and facing a live opponent.

I'm not going to be able to stand up to any of them, he thought, looking back to the nervous, overworked kid still running through the same sim. *Even the bad ones have some sense of strategy.*

Not that he cared about winning. He just couldn't ice out. Not yet, at least.

I'll figure it out, he told himself, cracking his knuckles on his bad hand. He thought of his combat training, of the skills he did possess, gnawing on his lower lip. *Any way I have to.*

He checked the standings and the upcoming matches. All three triplets, still ranked in bottom pool of the Academy students, didn't have any set matches against veterans or upper-ranked students.

Time to change that, he said, looking up as the first wave of students entered the gaming arena after breakfast. Official matches started at 0600, with a mix of newbies and moderately-experienced students pitted against each other. He watched groups clump together as opponents weeded each other out and sought support from their friends. After the usual banter and teasing, cadets took their seats on opposite sides of the holographic globes as the overhead lights dimmed, and the games initiated.

Cam shifted forward in his seat, forgetting about his datapad, or his analysis. The thunder-clash of sound, the dazzling colors blasting from the spheres, the heated tension that cut through the air—he'd never experienced anything like it. Juggernaut warships scraped across digital skylines while electric-blue fighters zipped across enemy lines, engaging weaker frigates and corvettes. He couldn't keep himself focused on any one battle, especially as various groups cheered their friends on, or taunted the losing opponent.

It wasn't until the freckle-faced boy walked in the arena that he was able to pry himself from the excitement and focus back on his objective.

Stempton didn't notice him, not at first. Surrounded by his usual thug entourage, the Crexan made his way around the arena, watching games for a minute or two, making comments to Hoch and Walli, before moving on. Predictably, he stopped at a game between two cadets at his level, making sure to stand next to the yellow-haired boy ranked the closest to his own standing.

You ratchakker, Cam thought as the boy tensed at Stempton's encroaching presence, trying to concentrate but fumbling with the controls.

In some way, Cam respected Stempton; he took the time to identify his opponents and employed any means to defeat or disable them. But at the same time, the same behavior served as his ultimate weakness—something that Cam readied himself to exploit.

As the yellow-haired boy resigned in defeat to his opponent, Stempton laughed and moved on, but not before catching Cam's eye. His entire demeanor changed, shifting from smug satisfaction to shock, then a rising boil. Slapping Walli on the chest and elbowing Hoch to draw their attention away from another match, Stempton pointed his chin toward Cam, alerting his thugs to his presence.

Come on, you bastards, he thought, remaining calm as the trio approached him, hackles raised.

"What are you doing here, rub?" Stempton said, popping up one of his feet onto the bench in front of Cam. Walli and Hoch came up on opposite sides of him, assuming similar relaxed, though threatening postures. "This competition is for qualified cadets—not street trash."

"I have information," he said, pulling up a file on his datapad and giving it to Stempton.

"What the hell is this crap?" Stempton said. "A nursery rhyme?"

"The Fiorahian slum song," Cam corrected. "Something that *certain wimps* hate."

Stempton lifted a brow, then looked over the three-part tune. "Why the hell would I want this?"

"Because they're competing, too," he said, nodding toward the scoreboard affixed on the far wall. Even though the triplets hadn't broken into the top 100, he knew even the threat of them competing would unnerve the Crexan.

The freckle-faced boy held the datapad in his hands, lips moving as he read the words. "This is *gorsh-shit.*"

"Jetta," he said calmly, even as Hoch leaned in on him enough so that his knee knocked into Cam's shoulder. "She's your target."

Stempton scoffed, tossing the datapad back to Cam. "No launnie is worth my time."

"Snuff her out," Cam said. With one quick motion, he yanked Hoch's propped-up leg out from underneath him, causing him to pitch forward into the aisle. Cam picked up his feet as the boy fell, so that when he crashed onto the ground, he rested his boots on his back. "Before you have a real rat problem."

"Ferros, you *chakking* bastard," Hoch said, fighting his way up. Cam kicked him in the face as he rose. Dazed, he tipped backward, catching himself on a chair. As he regained himself, bringing his hand up to check the blood trickling from his nose, Stempton laughed and stuck out his arm to keep him and Walli from retaliation.

"You're one vicious *assino*," the freckle-faced boy said, still holding back Hoch. "I'm impressed."

Cam leaned to the side, catching sight of the triplets entering the arena. "I just want this to end," he said, pointing them out to Stempton and his thugs. "Beat her, and she'll get kicked out. Her siblings will go down with her."

Stempton looked over his shoulder, then returned to Cam, fires blazing in his eyes. "How do you know that, rub?"

"All us rats are in the same trap," he said coolly. Then, to drive in the final thorn, he added: "Besides, what does a player like you gotta worry about anyway?"

Grinding his jaw together, Stempton raised his fists, but Cam didn't react, not when he knew how hard that hit the boy's ego.

"Don't think this is over," Stempton said, motioning for his thugs.

Cam let out the breath he didn't realize he'd been holding in as Stempton walked away and targeted the triplets, calling them out as they stepped into the main arena.

Here goes…

"No way," Stempton said, approaching the triplets with a slow swagger. "I can't believe you'd even show your faces in here, *ratchakkers*."

Other kids, deeply entrenched in their games, alerted to the ire in Stempton's voice. Some broke off their games to join his side, others paused, watching from a distance as the situation heated.

Cam couldn't hear much more, not from the stands. Using his datapad, he picked up the sound from the gaming station nearest the triplets and tuned in to the exchange.

"We came to play," Jetta said, folding her arms across her chest.

Stempton rolled his eyes. "Yeah, I heard you three have been stinkin' the place up. Didn't anybody tell you? No rats allowed."

Jaeia and Jahx, standing behind Jetta, wavered in place, as if they meant to say something, but didn't. Cam watched their faces, how Jetta's anger never faltered, but her siblings' expression grew increasingly concerned.

You won't back down, Cam thought, seeing the fight in Jetta's eyes. *Stempton is a bully, and street kids know what to do about bullies.*

Strike hard and fast—and send a warning to all the other bullies—and everyone else.

Something in Jetta's demeanor relaxed, as did her siblings', as Stempton laughed with Walli and Hoch, and all his other supporters that gathered to see the fight. *As if they've reached some kind of silent agreement…*

Even as he fought to entertain the idea, Cam countered himself: *Jahx is a pacifist,* he thought as Jetta stepped forward and, despite her smaller stature, got in Stempton's face. *How is he allowing any of this?*

"I'll take you, and everyone else in this Academy down," she said.

"Whoa!" Stempton guffawed. "You're even dumber than you look."

"Burn her, Stempton," Walli said.

"Stupid rat," Hoch laughed.

"Alright," Stempton said. "And after I beat you in the Endgame, I'm going to make sure you and your *ratchak* siblings pay for your lip."

A dark shadow crossed her face. *She wants to hurt him,* he thought, shocked at her confidence, and the breadth of her anger.

"After I beat you," she said. "You'll wish you'd never crossed me."

The other kids yipped and howled, thrilled at the prospect of the fight.

219

With a smug grin, Stempton pointed his hand toward an Endgame console. "It's on, little launnie."

Cam couldn't help but glance at the half-domed, blacked-out cameras spying from the walls and ceiling, imagining Rogman keying in on the action from behind his desk.

As Jetta took a seat opposite of Stempton at one of the Endgame consoles, Cam realized how small she was. Dwarfed by the swirling holographic globe, she looked more like a lost child than a cadet training to be the next great fleet commander.

Doubt crept into the back of his mind as her siblings took positions behind her, looking equally as tiny and insignificant, especially against Stempton and his entourage. *What if I'm wrong about them? What if they're just little kids?*

"This is going to be a slaughter," Hoch snickered.

Using his datapad, Cam split up the camera angles so he could see the game and both Jetta and Stempton's faces as the match unfolded.

She's nervous, he observed, watching as she worked the console with shaky hands. *She's still new at this.*

He looked up her stats again. With a dozen or so games under her belt, she wasn't a complete novice, but she hadn't played any cadets with real battle experience or ranking, enough to test any reasonable skill.

She's going to have to really step up.

As the game initiated, a score of battleships, fighters, ground units, a warship and base of operations materialized in blue on Jetta's side, facing off against Stempton's red fleet within the globe.

"Little launnie in the gutter,
No one loves a rat,
Your momma's smoking jihja
And your daddy's getting whacked."

He's going for it, Cam thought, kneading the deformity on his right hand as Stempton sang the Fiorahian slum song just loud enough for Jetta to hear.

Fuming, Jetta tensed her grips on the controls, paying less and less attention to the game, and more to Stempton's taunts as he continued singing:

220

"Little launnie in the gutter,
Broke and full of woe,
Float downstream away from me
To the Block where you will show."

She's going to kill him. Cam had never seen such anger, especially from a tiny young girl. Rage lit her green eyes and pinched her brow as Stempton went into the third verse:

"Four and twelve you might have gotten
If your face was not so rotten,
Hurry up and die already
So this all can be forgotten."

He's sweeping her, Cam thought, looking at the scoreboard. Now up by seventy-five points, Jetta would have a hard time catching up, let alone beating Stempton—unless she pulled something drastic.

As Stempton's forces cut into her fighters, speakers booming with explosions, Cam changed the camera angles on his datapad so that he could watch all three siblings at once. Gnawing on his lower lip, Cam watched their faces, the intensity shifting, as if another battle—one that couldn't be as easily observed—was being fought amongst the three.

"This is a joke," Hoch said.

"*Chakking* launnies. Worthless," Walli chimed in.

Do it, Jetta. Cam zoomed in on her face, watching as her eyes flitted back and forth between the game and Stempton. *Don't hold back.*

The corners of her mouth ticked upward. The subtle change in her composure didn't register for Cam all at once, not until he saw her grips relax on the controls, and the smile settle across her face.

"Come on, Stempton," she whispered. "Make this easy for me and maybe they'll ice you out so you can go back to Mummy and Daddy. Don't you miss them? Or do you think they forgot about you?"

Stempton tensed. In a miscalculated move, he sent two of his ground units into her line of fire.

"*Chak,*" Walli muttered.

221

Jetta's smile broadened as a group of observers massed around their game and Stempton's cronies fell silent.

"Jeez, Stempton—it's not like a Crexan with a Deadskin Mummy is going to get very far anyway. You're human. You're weak. You've polluted the Crexan bloodline."

And there it is. Cam sat back in his chair, watching from afar as the rest of the game unfolded. Where he thought he should feel satisfaction came only chills as Jetta tore Stempton to pieces, capitalizing on his missteps, using his own weakness against him. In less than thirty minutes, the unknown girl from Fiorah, the street rat who shouldn't have survived her own world, let alone found her way into an elite military academy, beat an older, and far better reputed, cadet.

And Cam knew that she shouldn't. Not the way she fumbled at first, or the way she could barely keep her squadrons together at the beginning of the game. Not unless she somehow gained years of experience in a flash. Not unless—

"Good game," Jahx offered as Stempton's face flushed with rage and embarrassment. Without a word, he left, Hoch, Walli, and his other cronies following behind him, trying to console their fallen leader.

Don't do that, Jahx, Cam huffed. *You can't always make peace with these* assinos.

Cam tried to zoom in on Jetta, to continue to observe her reaction, but as the crowd dispersed and the other kids went back to their games, she didn't stay long—not with her siblings dragging her away from the gaming area.

Cam watched from a distance as the trio moved to the stadium seating to his right, keeping to themselves as the rest of the room continued their wars.

What are you saying? He tried to pick up them up again on a different audio feed, but the triplets had moved out of range of any of the public devices he could tap into. Squinting, he tried to make out their conversation as the shifting colors of azure, gold, and crimson lit their faces.

"I know what you're going to say," he gleaned Jetta speaking to her siblings. But they didn't respond. At least not out loud. Instead,

Jaeia and Jahx sat beside her, seemingly watching the battles on the main floor, concern pinching up their brows.

If he'd seen them talking, their changing expressions would have made more sense to him, but he couldn't rationalize their visible mood changes as Jetta's cheeks reddened with frustration, and the other two, particularly Jaeia, looked increasingly troubled, as if she wanted to reach some kind of peace.

A nearly impossible game won, a wordless conversation afterward. Not enough evidence, not yet—but something that couldn't be ignored.

Did you see that? Cam wondered, glancing up again at the domed cameras.

As Jetta stormed out of the gaming arena, Jaeia rushing to catch up to her, their brother lagged behind. When Jahx attempted to talk to a few of the other kids hanging out in the stands, they moved away, laughing at the launnie who tried to engage them.

Those assinos, he thought.

Cam wanted to hide, to pretend like he didn't meet eyes with Jahx from across the benches, but he couldn't—not when his face lit up, and he walked over to his bench.

"Hey," Jahx said, coming around and sitting next to him. "Did you see the game?"

"Yeah. Wow," Cam said. Clumsily, he shut off his datapad while trying not to sound as awkward and exposed as he felt. "Can't believe Jetta pulled that off."

Jahx sighed, rubbing his forehead with his hands. "She's tougher than she looks."

"She looks tough enough," Cam said, half-laughing. "She looks like she wants to take this entire Academy down."

Jahx didn't make any arguments against his statement. Instead, he rested his elbows on his knees, and his chin in his hands. "She does what she has to do."

I understand that, Cam thought. As a long silence passed between them, his mind wandered back to Cerka, to old school days in over-crowded classrooms and family dinners of canned beans and whatever vegetable or meat their mother could get at a bargain. Caught in the moment, he asked: "What do you think you'd be doing right now, if things were different?"

223

Jahx quirked an eyebrow. "Like, if there wasn't a war?"

Despite knowing the risks of asking such questions, some part of him persisted. "Yeah."

The black-haired boy twirled a curl of hair at the nape of his neck and looked off in the distance. "Playing rock dice with Jetta in our pretend fort."

"Rock dice?"

"Yeah, it's a game we made up. It's really fun."

The rest of the gaming arena fading from his attention, Cam whispered: "What else?"

"Reading books with Jaeia and Aunt Lohien. Helping Galm fix stuff around the apartment. Maybe try to find an air conditioner in the dump, repair that."

"Yeah, I heard Fiorah's hot."

Jahx laughed. "Like a furnace. What about you?"

Cam looked out across the arena, at the other children, trying to remember what it felt like back home. "I don't know. I can't remember what it's like to be a kid anymore."

He jumped as Jahx placed a hand on his forearm. "I know."

The warmth of his fingers, even through the fabric of his uniform jacket, made him relax again, and his thoughts loosened. "I'd be with my family," he said, voice just above a whisper as his mind projected himself into better times. "I'd play hide and seek with the twins. I'd try and convince my dad to let me take a drag off his pipe. I'd help my mom hang up the wash out the window and listen to her gossip about the neighbors. I'd…"

He couldn't stop himself, even as he sensed himself in dangerous territory. "…I'd play games with Kara. I'd pester her as she tried to talk to her boyfriend on the phone. I'd make up stories in my head and tell her them by the fireplace. I'd be happy."

"Happy," Jahx repeated, letting the word sit between them a moment. Blue eyes filled with tears. "Those sound like very happy things."

Cam straightened up in his seat, cracking his knuckles on both hands. "Impossible things. At least now."

Jahx, still turned away, replied just above a whisper. "What's there to hope for, if those things are gone?"

Cam didn't understand. "But you still have your sisters."

A shadow crossed his face. "You just saw what this place is doing to Jetta. To all three of us."

Troubled secrets sluiced through his mind, reviving old guilts and dark promises. "I know. But you do what you have to do."

He wanted to add *no tomorrows,* but another memory resurfaced, soothing his jaded response. "Kara would have told you to hold out."

"Huh?"

"My older sister. She was always hopeful something good was right around the corner; that all this *gorsh-shit* was worth it for whatever better days lay ahead."

"Oh, I remember. That song," Jahx said, *"Blue Sky Tomorrows,* right?"

"Yep. She'd be singing it to you right now, whether you wanted her to or not."

Jahx giggled as his face transformed again, and his smile returned. As he started to say something, his sleeve beeped twice, and he sighed. "Alright, gotta go."

"One of your sisters?"

"Both of them," he said, standing up and stretching.

"Double nagging. I can't imagine."

Jahx chuckled. "Yeah, they tend to gang up on me. Hey, how's your hand?"

Cam automatically shielded it under his opposite hand. "Fine."

"I was worried."

Really? He sucked in his lower lip, trying not to sound flustered. "It's fine. No big deal."

"Did you get to take the biochem final?"

Kneading the bony knob on the back of his hand, Cam muttered off a quick, "yeah. It's fine."

"I'm sure you did great," Jahx said. "Well, see you, Cam."

"Bye, Jahx."

After the black-haired boy had gone, Cam sat alone in the stands, unable to reopen his datapad or watch any more of the games. Something unnerved him, something that instilled a restless energy in his bones. Finally, after his first Endgame match appeared on his sleeve and he decided no more could be gained sticking around the arena, he got up and left, glancing up at the ceiling cameras one last time as he left.

Don't worry, Rogman, he thought, imagining the Commandant's mustached face and darkened eyes. *You're about to see what I'm really capable of.*

***

S. Nelson, 1700, console 121-A.

The name looped over and over again in mind as he sat alone in the mess hall with a tray full of food growing cold on the table in front of him. He'd never met the boy, only seen him in passing in the halls or when their meals coincided. Nothing particular stood out about Nelson; average height for a humanoid, light blonde hair, hazel eyes. A handsome face. Per his profile, he'd completed a full year at the Academy, with good grades—

But no combat training.

Not like Cam.

He spotted Nelson dumping the remains of his tray in the garbage, laughing with two other cadets as they exited the mess hall. Leaving his tray at the table, Cam got up and followed them, joining them on the lift as the others inputted their destinations.

"See ya," Nelson waved as the other two cadets got off at one of the gaming rooms.

"Hey, where are you going?" Nelson asked, turning to Cam as the lift picked up again, taking them toward the barracks. The boy's smile vanished the second he gave more than a passing glance at Cam's face.

"What the hell, mate?" he said as Cam bashed his fist against the control panel, stopping the lift midway down the empty corridor. Cam stepped forward on the flat bed of the lift so that the starlight from the slatted windows hit his face.

"Holy *chak…*" Nelson muttered, backing up against the railing.

Cam hadn't looked at himself. Not that he ever really took the time to look himself in the mirror before the training accident. But now he saw the wretchedness of his scars and deformities as Nelson's eyes widened, and the boy brought up his hands in front of him.

226

Good, Cam thought, hardening his gaze. *Be afraid.*

"Come on, mate—I've done you no wrong. What's this about?"

"The match at 1700. Don't show up."

Nelson scoffed. "What? The Endgame?" Disbelief, then anger crossed his face. "You're that psycho, Ferros, aren't you?"

Cam rolled up his sleeves to confirm everything Nelson heard. "Don't show up."

"I'm not going to let a newbie intimidate me," Nelson said, still backed up against the railing.

A whirring caught Cam's attention. At the opposite end of the corridor, a lift approached carrying four or five other cadets. Instead of backing down, to avoid any kind of attention, he intended to capitalize on the moment.

In his mind, he worked out the scenario: Grabbing Nelson by the collar and sleeve and throwing him into the other lift full of kids. That demonstration of brutality, of willingness to defy all authority and rules, to hurt more than just his immediate opponent would be enough to deter future fights. And keep Rogman from icing him just yet.

But as he grabbed Nelson's collar and sleeve, shifting his weight on his toes and preparing for the throw, blue eyes flashed in his line of sight.

(You don't have to.)

The thought, echoing from across a distance he never realized, fixed him in place. In that split second, the internal walls he'd erected, the ones that fortified him from all his pain, all that he feared, vanished, and his sister's favorite song hummed across his mind: *"Just hold out, my love..."*

"Get off me, psycho!"

An elbow smacked him square in the temple. Reacting before his mind could catch up, he switched stances, bringing up his knee into the boy's crotch. Doubled over, Nelson grunted and reached out one arm to defend himself as Cam pulled him to the bed of the lift.

"Whoa!" someone exclaimed as the other lift passed by.

Cam looked up in time to see Jahx and his sisters aboard, the three of them turning to watch with the other kids as they whizzed down the corridor.

I didn't want him to see that, he thought.

"Stay down," Cam said, keeping his foot on Nelson's back as the boy tried to get up. "Don't show to the game tonight, got it?"

"*Chak* you, Ferros."

But as Cam thought to finish the job, two guards appeared at the end of the corridor, shockwands in hand.

Grabbing Nelson by the armpit, he hoisted the boy up and waved to the guards.

"This isn't over," Nelson said.

"It is if you want to wake up tomorrow," Cam replied. "Don't think a little time in detention won't stop me."

The soldiers turned away as Nelson waved them off. Wiping the blood from his nose, Nelson avoided Cam's gaze as he straightened up again. "I'm not losing to a newbie."

"If we don't play, it's no contest. No points lost for either of us."

Nelson eyed him, then looked down again, blood smeared across his upper lip. "You're going to get yours, Ferros."

"Yeah, some day," he said, typing in the barracks as a destination for the lift. The anti-grav transport took off again, down the corridor toward the guards and the kids milling around before the evening gaming sessions.

Nelson jumped off the lift before it stopped in front of the first barrack, stumbling away as fast as possible. Thinking of Jahx, of the fact that he and his sisters witnessed his act, he tried to counter the guilt crawling through his belly with the rationalization that it only furthered his ultimate agenda. "…But not today."

***

Nelson didn't show up to the match. Cam waited in the stands to make sure the boy didn't get any bold ideas, and after a half hour past their scheduled battle, he thought to leave.

But that's when Jaeia made her move.

"Cam," she shouted.

He hadn't seen her in the shadows, sitting behind a mixed group of cadets in the upper level of the benches. Popping up, she hurried down the stairs, skipping the last few to catch up to him as he tried to get up and go.

"Watch it, launnie!" someone shouted as she dodged around another girl walking up the steps.

"Cam, wait," she said, running in the aisle in front of him, stopping him in his tracks.

"What?"

"Can we talk?"

"Why?" he said, half-shouting over the electronic noises from the games.

"Please," she said, putting up both her hands to halt him again. "It's important."

Rolling his eyes, he didn't say no as she dragged him up to the observation booth at the top of the stairs. Normally accessed by teachers and senior-level students to analyze bigger matches, the semi-enclosed box at the top of the stairs stood empty, computer consoles near the gigantic window inert, swiveling chairs unoccupied. As soon as Cam stepped inside the booth, the black-acoustic dampening tiles muffled the game noise from below.

"What?" he said again, confused by her previous urgency, and her current hesitancy as she fiddled with the ends of her jacket sleeve.

"Is everything okay?"

"Huh?"

"You got in that fight with Nelson."

Cam clenched his jaw together, unsure of how to act. He knew better than to answer. *Just leave,* he told himself. *It's not like it's going to matter soon.*

But as he turned to go, her voice stopped him. "Please, Cam— I'm worried."

"You're worried?" Slowly, he turned back around to face her. "Why?"

"Nelson didn't start that fight, did he?"

Cam didn't want to answer her, but something about her question didn't allow him any other choice. "No."

"Then why did you fight him?"

"Because…" The words caught in his throat. *Because I couldn't win the Endgame.* Collecting himself, he took a deep breath and finished: "Because you have to win some fights before they're fought."

Jaeia's answer surprised him. "I can't say I agree with what you did, but it is pretty brilliant."

Brilliant? He wanted to laugh in her face. *I'm anything but that.*

"You don't believe me, do you?" she said.

"No."

Jaeia walked over to the window and watched the activity below before she asked the harder question. "What are you going to do when you have to fight one of us?"

All the blood drained from his face. Fingers twitching, he couldn't tell if he wanted to fight or flee.

"I know you and Jahx are close," she continued, still trained on the battles in the main gaming arena, arms crossed in front of her chest. "I know he trusts you. You're important to him, Cam. What you do has a huge effect on him." She turned to him, eyes the same gray as the pale smoke of a dying fire. "On all three of us."

The words sank into him with the same impact of a stone tossed into water. Shaking his head, he tried to free himself from the immersive sensation as she let her arms fall to her side. "You don't always have to fight."

But her statement sounded more like a question than something she felt with confidence; as if she herself had engaged in the argument more than once, with herself, or with her siblings.

Teeth gnashing through bone, pain tearing through his arm; the taste of blood in his mouth. *"Kill the enemy before he's got a chance to kill you."*

A red scarf in his hands.

"It's all I've ever done," he whispered.

"There's always a choice," she said, a sadness in her voice. "Even if you don't see it right away. Just look for it. Promise me."

"Promise you?"

"Please," she said, reaching out, but pulling back her hand at the last second. "For me. For Jahx."

Cam said nothing, unsure of what he could possibly say to such a thing. Tears in her eyes, the Fiorahian girl left, saying no more.

Cam stood in the observation booth alone, electronic noise rumbling in the distance.

She knows what I'm capable of.

(She's just manipulating you.)

230

(You have no friends; only enemies.)

It doesn't matter, he continued to remind himself. Kara was dead. His entire family was dead. Rogman was playing him for a fool, orchestrating the dark, sick game that stole away his fellow Cerkans and pitted twisted doctors against machine monsters—and who would soon harness the deadliest minds in the galaxy to win a godforsaken war.

She's right, though, he decided, watching the children below battle each other for more than just rank. *I have a choice.*

Tightening both his fists, the scars on his arms and hands blanched. *And I choose to fight.*

Chapter 23

That night, lying his bunk, datapad propped on his stomach, Cam sent a message to Rogman with his Endgame arrangements. Since he'd already seen Jetta face Stempton, he only needed two more matches to prove his theory—

Shiggla, Teahvo

—and the final match, against the greatest Endgame player to date, to weed out the greatest threat of all.

Not that I don't already know.

But he couldn't clue Rogman in. So, he pitted several more cadets against each other in bogus matches, as well as made sure to stack Stempton's schedule so he couldn't do much more than take classes and battle. *That should keep his focus off me.*

And Jetta, especially after losing to her in a public match.

I have to keep Jetta safe, he thought, tapping the keyboard with his fingertips. *(At least for now.)*

If she, or any of her other siblings got beat up or sacked, then it might throw off his gamble.

As he added names to his match list, he realized one more factor: *I can't just throw the triplets into big matches right away.*

Rogman would deconstruct his strategy out, figure out his targets.

Moving around his list, he allowed them each five to six matches against decent older cadets—enough that they'd be challenged but shouldn't lose.

"Where are they?"

"I don't know."

Closing out his email, he looked over his shoulder to see the whispering speakers. Jetta and Jaeia, between their two bunks, looked at their respective bunkmate's empty bed.

Tomia. Iggie. Reflexively, he scratched at the implant in his left forearm, then held it tight. *What happened to them?*

Even though he had some sense, he called up the public student profiles and searched for his fellow Cerkans.

Iggie Prys – transferred; medical.

Tomia Nosik – discharged; disciplinary.

"They're gone," he said, too quiet at first for the girls to hear him. Sitting up and swinging his legs around to sit at the edge of his bunk, he repeated: "They're *gone.*"

Jetta and Jaeia, stepping closer to each other, turned their attention up at him.

"Gone?" Jetta said.

"Discharged. Transferred."

The identical girls looked at each other a moment, exchanging whatever information close siblings did without words.

Jahx poked his head out from the bottom bunk. "I'm sorry, Cam."

Already numbed to the loss, he didn't give Jahx any hint of his feelings. "It's a military academy," he said, sounding more abrasive than he intended. "It happens."

After throwing him a harsh glare, Jetta took her sister's hand and led her to her bunk, away from the conversation. She motioned for Jahx to join them, but he shook his head at her, irritating her further.

"Sorry," Jahx said as Cam laid back down on his own bed.

Hoping the Fiorahian boy would just go back to his own business, Cam didn't respond, opening up a new search on his datapad.

But Jahx didn't, popping up on the ladder, but not ascending farther than to keep his head the same level as Cam's. "Did you see them before they left?"

The question jarred him.

Screech of metal—

Iggie, dressed in a patient gown, transformed, distressed—shattered: "The monster. The machine man. He's here. He's watching you. He's watching all of us."

Blood loss, tubes and wires—

Tomia, tugging on his arm. "Cam, come on—we have to go."

233

"N-no." Then, for whatever reason, he corrected himself, his answer coming out in a trembling whisper. "Yes."

He expected questioning, prodding; an interrogation that would cement his resolve to do the unthinkable. Instead, Jahx gave him something equally disastrous.

Taking two more steps up the ladder, Jahx allowed himself enough reach and balance to lean over and embrace Cam.

No—

The hug surprised him, made his sensitized skin buzz and tingle. But before he allowed himself to feel more than the hurt and comforts it caused, he struggled and resisted, pushing the boy off.

"Get off," he said through gritted teeth, rearing back his fist.

Jahx caught himself on the bars of the ladder. "S-sorry, Cam. I just thought—"

"You can't do that," Cam said, fists still up, chest heaving. "Jahx."

Cam didn't look down. He didn't need to. He knew who stood below the black-haired boy, ready to fight.

"Jetta, I'm fine. It's okay," Jahx said, keeping between Cam and his truculent sister.

Turning back to Cam, Jahx offered another apology, but this time, his eyes, the same calming blues that could still his heart, looked beyond him, into some strange distance that stole him from the moment. "I'm sorry, Cam."

Anger dissolving into an uncomfortable lump in his throat, Cam watched as the boy descended the ladder and followed her sister back to her bunk. Now joined with his siblings, he didn't look back, studying whatever homework or program they ran on one of their datapads.

Cam laid back down, heart thumping in his chest, staring up at the ceiling. Finally, as his breathing and pulse wound down, he grabbed his datapad and pulled up his email to Rogman.

He didn't draw out his request or provide explanation; he didn't want Rogman to understand his motives, but he couldn't allow such an event to occur.

Don't match the triplets against each other.

Such a thing would have devastating consequences. *They're too close.*

234

He sent off the email and shut down his datapad.

Lights out came, but he didn't sleep. He waited, listening for Jahx to return to his bed, and settle in. It wasn't until he heard the boy's snoring that he finally crawled under the sheets and closed his eyes.

Still, he waited, listening in the dark for the inevitable sob and murmur as the boy's nightmares unfolded.

"Please... don't..."

Cam turned onto his side, facing the wall. Pressing his injured hand against the cold metal panel, he imagined himself transmitting through the solid surface, echoing out across the ship, to the stars, and beyond.

Kara, he thought, knowing she couldn't possibly hear him. *You would have done anything to end this war. You were ready to sacrifice everything, weren't you?*

Curling his fingers, the bones popped. *So am I.*

***

A week passed, and though Rogman didn't contact him back, the gaming schedule matched the arrangements he made. The fact that the Commandant enacted his plan made him both excited and nervous.

What if he knows what I'm doing?

What if I missed something?

(I'm not smart enough; I'll never pull it off.)

(What if I'm wrong?!)

He calmed himself with the same raw anger he'd been thriving on since finding out Kara died. *It doesn't matter if he figures it out.*

I can't be wrong.

The war ends here.

Climbing up the stadium seating to one of the middle rows in the gaming arena, Cam found an open bench away from most of the spectators awaiting the next big showdown. Walli versus Hoch caused a big stir, and Stempton fighting one of the juniors would draw a big crowd—but neither of those popular matches interested him. He came for the only one that mattered that day, the one that most other cadets would pass over.

Shiggla arrived first, followed by her usual entourage of admirers and fellow sophomores. As soon as he saw them, he tapped his datapad into the surrounding games, picking up their conversation.

"This is a joke," she laughed to one of the other girls. "I can't believe I have to play a stupid rat."

"It'll be over quick, Shiggla," one of her friends said, looking over his shoulder as the triplets walked through the gaming room entrance.

Cam switched up the angles of the feed, trying to get a good view of the triplets, but they stayed close together, with Jetta in the lead.

What are you doing? he thought. Jetta, with her usual scowl, entered the arena ready to fight. But her siblings, not nearly as aggressive, hung behind her, worried looks on both their faces. *What are you thinking?*

Zooming in on Jaeia's face, he studied her concern, watching as her pupils dilated and constricted, as if she focused back and forth on what was in front of her, and what lay far beyond.

You're worried; you don't know how you're going to fight her, he thought, reading the subtle changes in her expression.

And she was right. Shiggla, a ruthless, skilled Endgame player, outmatched her in experience, and on every stat and tracker.

"She's a jackal," Jetta said as Jaeia sat down at the Endgame console. "She won't go easy on you."

"Great pep talk," Jaeia muttered back.

But she's right, Cam thought.

Jahx put a hand on her shoulder. "Just be patient. Your opportunity will come."

Yes—if you dig a little deeper.

"Thanks, Jahx," she said.

Cam swiped away the old angles on his datapad, changing the feed so he could see the Jaeia and Shiggla at the same time. Standing behind their sister, Jetta and Jahx fit inside the same frame.

The spherical playing field lit up, casting their faces in a blaze of electric colors.

"Kill her, Shiggla!" someone cheered.

The game got off to a fast start, with Shiggla sending her warship and legion of fighters into Jaeia's scrambling fleet. Sweat beaded across the Fiorahian girl's forehead, and ringed the neck of her uniform top.

"You're getting eaten alive," Cam muttered.

Her siblings, though they said nothing, stepped closer to their sister, their eyes trained on the game as Shiggla concentrated her fighters on one of Jaeia's stray battleships.

Do something, Cam thought.

Under heavy fire, Jaeia's battleship exploded, raining digital fire across the sphere.

You're going to lose.

"You got her, Shiggla!"

"Stupid rat."

"Time to send the launnie back to the gutters!"

Cam zoomed in Jaeia's face. Terror, then panic. The threat of deportation to Fiorah sent a shiver down her spine and stole all the color from her skin. Nothing her siblings did—stepping in even closer, swaying, ever so slightly, in unison to some inaudible beat—made any difference.

Jaeia looked again at the game, to the shifting holographics.

What do you see? Cam thought, watching her eyes dilate, as if some terrible monster morphed inside the game.

(She's breaking.)

Cam squeezed the sides of the datapad, waiting—hoping—for her to make the move. *You can beat her. Just look.*

Jaeia's eyes darted to the scoreboard, then back to Shiggla's face.

Look what she's really after, he thought. *It's not just your warship.*

Grips loosening on her controls, Jaeia called out to Shiggla: "You're pretty good," she said, voice sounding heavier, resounding across his datapad speakers, and somehow, over all the booming game noise. "But I hear your brother Soling is the real competitor. Isn't he like fifty spots ahead of you? You'll have to beat me and everyone else by at least two hundred points for the next month to even hope to catch up."

237

Cam dug his fingers into both ear canals, trying to scratch an itch that went deep inside his skull. But as uncomfortable as he felt, he couldn't imagine what Shiggla felt like as the target of Jaeia's attack.

Jetta stepped forward, eyes wide, but saying nothing.

It's too late, Cam thought, rubbing the outside of his ears.

Shiggla's cheeks bloomed red as she moved her ground units too aggressively against Jaeia's base, leaving herself exposed. Locking her fighters on Shiggla's ground units, Jaeia commanded the remainder of her fleet to target the warship.

"It's hard having a sibling who's better than you at everything," Jaeia continued as she set up for the final attack.

Don't stop, Cam thought, especially as Jahx ran a hand through his hair and Jetta shifted back and forth, visibly uncomfortable. *So close…*

"I know how it is," Jaeia said to Shiggla, voice cutting across the room. "You end up as an afterthought. Or just plain forgotten."

Shiggla's lower lip trembled, her face contorting in bewilderment. Distracted and disoriented, she fell for the trap as Jaeia put out her battleship in a seemingly open sector. Springing her hidden forces, Jaeia demolished Shiggla's pieces in seconds.

"How did you do that?" Shiggla asked, watching her own rankings drop on the scoreboard. Humiliation reduced her voice to a whisper. "Do you even know what this does to me?"

Yes, Cam thought, *she knew exactly how to hurt you.*

Members of Shiggla's entourage gathered around her as she sobbed and shouted, muttering to each other.

"Jeez… I've never seen her like this."

"*Chakking* rat."

Wisely, Jetta pulled both of her siblings away as Shiggla, once a cocky and confident leader, descended into full hysterics.

"I can't lose—I can't lose!" she screamed, falling to her knees and pulling at her hair.

"This is *gorsh-shit*," one of her friends said, holding Shiggla in her arms.

Surprise turned to ire for the rest of the entourage. "No launnie can do that!"

"That Fiorahian scum."

Cam got one last look at Jaeia's face as Jetta took her siblings' hands and led them out of the game room. On the verge of tears, the gray-eyed girl looked just as fractured as Shiggla.

She didn't want to do that.

The realization branched out across his chest like wildfire. Still, he ignored the pain, and his own terrible truth. Closing out his datapad, he sat in the shadows of the benches, alone with his secrets. *Now I know what you're capable of.*

***

Ditching his last meal and his classes, Cam waited again in the stands for the last match he needed to see. Jahx arrived first, his sisters following close behind until he took his seat at the Endgame console.

They're more cautious, he surmised, watching as the sisters took a seat on one of the stadium benches not far away from him.

Not that it mattered anymore. But some part of him needed to see Jahx's battle, the one that would force hand, to know just how far the boy would go. To know if—

(He's anything like me.)

Cam didn't care to watch his sisters this time, not that he could with them sitting far away from any hotspot. Instead, he trained the camera angle on his datapad to solely feature Jahx's face.

Worry and frustration wrinkled the boy's brow.

You don't want to fight, Cam thought, watching as Jahx's opponent, Teahvo, took the opposite seat. *But you're going to have to.*

"Jahx—what kind of *ratchak* name is that?" asked Teahvo as he punched into his console.

The black-haired boy didn't react, keeping his eyes trained on the console and the holographics. Whatever thoughts ran through his head, he didn't leak any hints of them outward, at least none that his opponent picked up.

"Let's get this over with," Teahvo muttered, batting at the controls, trying to get the game timer to tick down faster.

Instead of tensing, Jahx closed his eyes and took a deep breath. Cam watched his face, how he tilted his forehead forward, his

239

shoulders and arms relaxing. Just watching him, Cam's own muscles slackened, and he inhaled slowly, filling his lungs, his heart rate dropping.

What are you doing? he thought, watching as the boy blindly typed in his commands.

Jahx didn't open his eyes again, not until after Teahvo moved his battleship above Jahx's base of operations. "Suck it, launnie."

"Good game," Jahx said, his voice calm and sweet as he revealed his hidden corvettes.

"What?" Teahvo exclaimed. "How could you—"

You got him now, Cam thought as Teahvo recalled his starships back to his defensive line. In a matter of seconds, Jahx's force crushed his opponent's, and the scoreboard lit up as it tallied the points.

Jahx hopped out of his seat and ran to Teahvo as he tried to leave. "Want to grab dinner with me?"

"Go *chak* yourself, launnie," Teahvo said, spitting on Jahx's boot.

Jahx extended his hand.

No—you know he's angry—

"*Uk'ep id'p.*"

How do you know his native language?!

Infuriated, Teahvo shoved Jahx out of the way as he stormed out of the game room.

"Why'd you do that?" Jetta said, joining her brother's side.

Jahx said nothing. Instead, the three stood in a tight triangle together, in some wordless conversation that ended with Jetta once again grabbing her siblings' hands and leading them out.

Cam didn't move, his heart heavy as he watched the other matches, mind anywhere but in the gaming arena. Finally, a warning notice from his teachers for missing class popped up on his sleeve. That, and another Endgame match.

"*Chak,*" he muttered, swiping the messages away.

Just survive, he told himself. *It'll all be over soon.*

Jetta, Jaeia, Jahx. Three unknown street rats, a war that ravaged his world, the fate of the universe.

I will end this, he thought, gripping the edge of his datapad hard enough that the screen protector cracked. Rogman's sick games, leeches, machine-man experiments; the reason his family was dead. *All of it.*

I will kill Jahx Drachsi.

"Just hold out my love…"

The arcade noises—high-pitched whines, beeps, and booming explosions—fluctuated, transformed into a living nightmare. Simulated smoke and gunfire made his lungs burn, and the rumble of the bass turned into burning engines and troopers storming the city. He shielded his face, not wanting to see the flashing lights or hear the cry of the emergency warning systems.

Kara—

He looked up to blackened skies. *I'm coming home.*

Chapter 24

After a quick trip to the c-wing lavatories, Cam entered the mess hall with one hand in his jacket pocket. Walking across the aisles, he searched for Tran Su, his next scheduled Endgame opponent. The half human, half reptile-like Cercinian took slack from no one, even the regular school bullies. Knowing that threats would go nowhere, he tried a new approach.

The mess hall, packed for lunch, buzzed with chatter and student activity. After spotting her sitting with her usual set of friends, he studied her tray from afar—meat roll, yellow protein drink, bread knot, vegetable puree—and then went to a meal station and selected his lunch.

"Hey, wait—you're forgetting your tray," a kid behind him in line said as he walked away with only the bread knot and meat strip in hand.

He didn't bother to look back, not caring if another kid picked up the rest of his food, or if he got docked for missing another full meal. After stuffing the meat strip in his mouth and chewing it enough to swallow, he headed toward Tran.

As he came up behind her, bits of conversation caught his ear:

"Did you hear those bastard launnies are killing it in the Endgame?"

"No way."

"You nervous?"

"No."

"You should be."

Inside his right jacket pocket, Cam rolled the single poison capsule around his fingertips, feeling the break between the two halves. Digging his nail into the middle, the capsule broke, and what felt like bits of powder covered his fingers. After withdrawing his hand, he wiped his first finger across the bottom of the bread knot and replaced the food item in his opposite pocket.

Be quick, he coached himself. A girl like Tran would sense something afoul if he at all hesitated.

"Hey—that's mine!" a kid said as Cam grabbed his milk carton and poured it over his right hand, neutralizing the poison on his fingers and then wiping them on his pants. The milk splashed onto the tiles, making the nearby cadets pick up their feet. Still, the kid didn't do much more than whine to his friends as Cam tossed it back. "What a jerk…"

The two other kids sitting opposite of Tran stopped their conversation with her as Cam came up behind her, a mixed looked of horror and disgust in their faces.

"*Chak,* it's Ferros," one of them muttered.

"He looks like *sycha,*" someone else whispered.

Tran twisted around, a prepared smile and gleam in her eyes. "What's up, Ferros? Looking for some pre-game advice?"

Cam said nothing, watching his peripheries, waiting for his moment. Some of the other kids seated to the left and right stopped their conversations to watch, anticipating the fight. Tran didn't seem bothered, as he expected, setting down her fork before swinging her legs around to face him.

"Don't think you're going to scare me off like Nelson," she said, standing up. Her head reached the middle of his chest but that didn't stop her from trying to get in his face. "I'm in it for a fair fight."

From some faraway place he heard an old part of himself cry out, felt guilt tug at his stomach. Tran, with her wild, spiky hair and green scales, would have beaten him, as she deserved to.

But not today.

He didn't attack her. Such a thing would be too obvious, but he did shove her seat mate to her left out of the way and grabbed at the food on his tray.

"Don't be an *assino,*" Tran said, pulling at his sleeve as Cam stuffed his face with the kid's protein cubes and jelly glaze. Pretending to be off-balanced by her grip, he tipped over and hit her tray. The meat roll went flying, as did the bread knot, her drink, and vegetable puree. But he caught the bread knot, and as Tran and the other kids shielded themselves from the splash of yellow protein drink, he swapped out the bread in his pocket for hers and set it back down on the table.

"You *ratchakker*!" Tran said, wiping the protein drink from her eyes.

Cam stood up, not caring that the yellow liquid dripped down his uniform jacket and stared at her one last time.

"I'm not going to forget this," she said as she wrung out her hair.

I'm sure you won't.

Cam walked away but didn't exit the mess hall. Instead, he lingered by one of the trash receptacles, waiting to see what she did as she sat back down. After being consoled by her seat mates, she reached for the one thing that didn't get drenched in the attack.

The bread knot.

He walked out, the sound of laughter and excited voices following him as he hardened himself to his final, and most deadly, deed.

***

Cam meant to ride the lift back to the games, to find Jahx and be done with things. But when the notice of his canceled Endgame match against Tran buzzed on his sleeve, he couldn't help himself. Smacking his fist against the controls, he stopped the lift and hopped off, wanting to get anywhere faster than the anti-grav transport could take him.

Spotting the training arena up ahead, he made a decision before the better parts of himself could intercede. The darkened arena welcomed him, motion-detector lights flicking on as he entered the main staging area.

His sleeve beeped.

Training uniform required for combat simulation.

Cam flicked off the notice. "I know."

Winding back to the storage room near the entrance, he dug through the extra gear in the lockers until he found a uniform close to his size. Stripping right there didn't bother him, nor did the tight, tingling feel of the training uniform against his skin. Nerve-

244

memories revived the terrible pain that disabled him not long ago, buzzing his arms and legs and into his skull, but he pushed on, grabbing one of the used guns on the locker shelf and heading back to the main staging area.

"Run program," he said aloud, checking in through his uniform sleeve. He didn't care what the program chose for him, or the hordes of monsters he might face. Or, the fact that it could kill him.

"Specify hazard level."

Annoyed, he answered, "no restrictions."

"Specify enemy grade."

"I *chakking* don't care. Highest level."

"Custom simulation available."

"Fine, run it."

The black interface modules hummed and whined. A vast winterscape unfolded, with ice formations that reached up to the thick grey storm clouds congesting the skies. He shivered, not because of any chill, but because of the brutal land before him, covered in nothing but snow and rock, tortured by lightning and howling winds, with no signs of life for as far as his eye could see.

A roar in the distance. Something up ahead, hidden in the falling snow, advanced toward him, crunching the snow under its massive feet. Cam readied himself, drawing his gun, preparing for the fight.

What is that?

Silver eyes glinted in the snow, bright red gums rimming sharpened teeth the size of his head. But as it neared, the animal sounds—the grunting and snorting—turned into gears grinding against gears—

No, not possible.

Cam backed up, arms shaking. A rusty engine sputtered, shrieked—

Monster—

"Freeze simulation."

Cam whipped around, gun pointed at the intruder.

"What are you doing?"

Jetta, gun in one hand, stood ten meters away from him.

"What are you doing?" he asked back, not yet lowering his weapon.

"I came to practice," she said, pointing to her training uniform. "Why are you running my program?"

Cam lowered his gun. "You made this?"

Jetta nodded.

Squinting, he couldn't yet make out his attacker in the storm, but sensed its immensity, the untold danger it posed. "Why?"

Jetta reaffirmed her grip on her gun. "I wanted to fight the worst enemy the program could run."

"You have a death wish?"

"No, but apparently you do," she said, pointing to his uniform. "Won't that thing kill you?"

"Maybe. Maybe not. Why do you care?"

Green eyes narrowing, she studied him much the way Jahx and Jaeia did, only what she seemed to glean off his reaction gave her words a vicious edge. "I don't."

Then, as anger lit up his muscles and he tensed for the attack, she added: "not if you're going to throw yourself away like this."

He paused, confused by what she meant.

"You're afraid," she said.

"Right," he laughed, pointing back at the monster hidden in the storm. "I'm playing a non-restrictions game in a suit that could kill me because I'm *afraid*."

Jetta holstered her gun but kept her hand on top of it. "Yeah, you are. Skipping classes, avoiding Endgame matches. Now, this. What are you running away from?"

"Go *chak* yourself, Jetta," he said, whipping out his gun and aiming it at her head.

Jetta didn't flinch, holding his gaze as his finger tapped against the trigger. "Don't stop now," she whispered.

"Cam-Cam—"

No, Kara—

"—don't forget—"

He pulled the trigger.

Jetta took a shuffle step back, then straightened up, raising her own weapon now. "Should have checked your weapon."

Cam turned over the gun, checking the battery life and the virtual chamber.

Chak—*damaged,* he thought, running his finger along the crack in the housing. *Idiot.*

He threw the gun down, into the snow, and raised his fists. "That's not all I got."

Jetta, the aggressor, the one who would tear down an army, an entire world, paused. Eyes blazing, she spoke through gritted teeth: "Jahx was wrong about you."

His sleeve beeped with an urgent message. Cam kept one eye on Jetta as he brought his arm up to his face.

"Endgame rescheduled: 1700 hours."

That's five minutes from now—

"Opponent—"

Cam held his breath as he read the rest:

"Jahx Drachsi."

An additional order, signed by the Commandant himself, flashed at the bottom: *An armed guard has been dispatched to escort you to the game room.*

He exhaled, heart thumping in his chest. A fight he couldn't avoid, the one that would end his career, end his life—and force his final gambit.

"Yes," he said, swiping away the message and lowering his fists. *(I'm sorry, Kara.)* "Everyone is."

Chapter 25

Why did Rogman want us to fight each other?

The question looped in Cam's mind over and over again as the armed guards with silver-sealed eyes and shockwands strapped to their utility belts escorted him into the gaming arena.

Two possibilities surfaced as he avoided the gawking and teasing of the other cadets:

He wants to see how Jahx reacts to facing someone he knows.

And a more troublesome possibility:

He wants to know what I'll do to survive.

The latter made his stomach tighten. Having skipped classes, botched the biochem final, and with a zero-rating in the Endgame—a loss today would spell his immediate termination, especially since he had no intention of making good on his promises to Rogman.

I can't lose, he thought as the guards stopped in front of the central console in the middle of the game arena. Looking up, the gigantic spherical playing field burned with the reds, golds, and blues of the playing pieces, timer already ticking down to the inevitable confrontation. And on the opposite side, flanked by his sisters, sat his enemy. The dark-haired boy gazed at him, blue eyes filled with—

Sorrow? Worry?

(Why—because you know you can beat me?)

Angered, Cam shouldered one of the guards out of the way as he headed to his own seat. "I'm here, alright?"

The guards lingered for a moment, then took up post near the stadium seating.

One-minute left until the game started. Cam refused to look up, staring at the game controls, trying to figure out his plan.

He's going to play you, not the game, he rationalized, *just like he did Teahvo. So, play him back.*

248

Not that he really understood how to do that.

As he wiped the sweat from his forehead, a hand slapped down on his shoulder. "Beat his *assino*," a familiar voice whispered into his ear.

Cam shrugged the hand off, not wanting to acknowledge Stempton with more than a grunt. But the freckle-faced boy grabbed him around the shoulder and pulled in close, digging his fingers into his arm to make it hurt.

"We're all tired of you, Ferros. Beat the rat, or we beat you," he said with a wide-toothed grin.

Somewhere behind their leader, hanging in the shifting shadows of the arcades, Walli and Hoch muttered: "Dumb bastard. Better finish that rat."

Cam twisted out of his grips but said nothing.

As the timer gave its final ten-second warning, Cam couldn't help but look up, across the spherical globe, to his enemy. Blue eyes stared back.

Trust yourself. The words echoed across the sphere, game pieces rippling as if an invisible wave disrupted their pattern.

No, he said, shaking his head. He imagined that.

The timer beeped.

Cam's game pieces materialized behind his defensive line: Two warships, three battleships, and a legion of fighters. A planetary body and two orbiting satellites divided the playing field, with Jahx's forces peeking out from behind the second gray moon.

Cam checked the readout and scans on his personal screen adjacent to his controls. *Jahx has only a single warship, low on fuel, and half a legion of fighters.*

Rogman stacked the game in his favor.

"Jeez, you'd better win, Ferros," Stempton laughed. A group of other cadets, alerted by his taunts, gathered around their game. "Or you're even dumber than you look."

A bitter taste rose in his throat, but he swallowed it back down. *I'm not that big of an idiot.*

Then again, he'd seen each one of the triplets against other opponents, with games clearly rigged against them, and they still triumphed. This wasn't any different.

Jahx sent two fighters out from behind the protection of the moon, skimming past his battleships, firing but doing little damage to their shields. Cam sent out four fighters after them and waited, seeing what Jahx would do.

He's better than this. From what he'd observed in Jahx's previous battles, the boy frequently sent out scout ships to probe the enemy's weakness, even though the rest of the game played out as if he already knew how he would sweep the enemy to begin with.

It's all planned.

But as Jahx evaded his fighters and peeked out his warship, Cam let go of the controls. *There's no point,* he thought, licking his dry lips. *He already knows.*

It didn't matter if he played a conservative game, waiting for Jahx's fuel to run out, or an aggressive one, sacrificing one of his warships to take out his enemy's weaker fleet. Jahx would adjust, he would play out the game to his favor, seeing possibilities in whatever impossible scenario Rogman—or any other enemy—ever threw at him.

Cam looked through the sphere, to the boy playing him from across the electric playing field.

I can't let you win.

Blue eyes turned yellow in the shifting colors, giving them an eerie, otherworldly glow. Everything about Jahx—the innocence of his smile, his warm kindness, the way he saw and understood much more about Cam than he would ever let himself appreciate—dissolved in the blaze of light and arcade noise. His sisters, closer to him now, looked just as inhuman, eyes with the same alien shine, just like—

The wild dogs. The savages that almost killed him on Cerka, ripping his arm up, maiming him; destroying that last bits of him that ever mattered. Bloody beasts that wouldn't have murdered him for their own survival—

Just like everything and everyone in this terrible universe.

Cam tasted blood in his mouth, his right arm curling up to his chest as old haunts whispered in his ear: *"Kill the enemy before he's got a chance to kill you."*

He deployed all his ships, save his warships, straight at Jahx, fanning out in a star formation around the moons, leaving him nowhere to run.

"What the hell are you doing, Ferros?" Stempton said, looking over his shoulder.

Destroying my enemy.

As the rest of his fleet hurtled at Jahx's hidden forces, he programmed the jumps on his warships.

"You're even dumber than I thought," Stempton scoffed. "Don't leave your warships behind."

I'm not.

But just before he hit the punch to engage his warships' jump drives, he looked up. *You can't escape this.*

Glowing eyes stared back, his own words echoing right back: *You can't escape this.*

Terrified, he hit the punch, jumping his biggest starships inside the two moons. The resulting blast seared across the playing field. But what was meant to flush out Jahx's forces straight into his attack did something unexpected.

"What the—" someone in the crowd exclaimed as Jahx's warship jumped a fraction of a second later, deflecting the explosion from his own forces, sending the fatal blast into Cam's oncoming fleet.

"*Chak...*" Walli said as the scoreboard dinged and the match ended.

How did he do that? Cam said as the sphere reset, and a new timer appeared in the upper quadrant.

An impossible victory. A perfectly timed and executed counterattack—one that could only be divined by not just a genius, but a commander with brilliant intuition—

With forethought.

"Jeez, Ferros screwed that up," someone in the crowd muttered.

Others whispered their own insults and explanations: "He's a burnout."

"Stupid half-breed."

"Did you see how bad he lost?"

251

"You gonna take this, rub?" Stempton whispered in his ear as the crowd dispersed and Jetta put a hand on both her siblings to get them to leave.

Cam caught Jahx's eye before he got up. Emotions he could not name swelled within him, boiling through his stomach and chest, and burning through his arms and legs.

Memories assaulted him from not long ago: *"I came to visit my friend."*

A warm smile, a soft hug.

"Thanks, Cam; for everything."

(It's not real.)

All doubt washed away from his mind as steam blasted from his nose and mouth, and his eyes turned into burning coals.

"Yeah, that's right. Get pissed. Take his sorry little *assino* out."

Cam shoved Stempton back. "Get off," he hissed. But the smile never left Stempton's face as he stormed out of the gaming arena.

After scaring a few kids off a lift, he programed it to take him to the c-corridor, to his secret place—their secret place—knowing he would come.

"Come on, you monster," he said through gritted teeth. "No tomorrows."

***

Cam waited less than ten minutes before a sound came at the entrance to the c-corridor lavatory. Crouched on top of one of the door-less stall toilets, he waited until footsteps tip-toed inside, and a timid voice whispered, "Cam?"

He listened for another few seconds, making sure no additional footsteps followed as the boy appeared in front of the sinks. As Jahx turned to face him, Cam leapt out and grabbed him by the collar.

"Cam," Jahx said, putting his hands on top of his as he shoved him backward. "What are you doing?"

"Ending this," he said, driving him hard against the sink.

He anticipated Jahx begging, pleading for his life, fighting back—or worse. But nothing happened, only uncomfortable silence as Cam held him against the sink, breathing hard, teeth grinding against teeth as he willed himself to do what was necessary.

"You don't have to do this," Jahx whispered.

"I know what you are," Cam said, tightening his grip. "I want you to say it."

"Cam, I—"

"SAY IT," he screamed in his face.

Blue eyes, filled with tears, still held his gaze. "I'm your friend."

"Lies!" Cam slammed his fist against the adjacent sink, knocking off a piece of the enamel. The faucet, disturbed by his strike, blasted water into the bowl. "You betrayed me."

"I've never done anything to hurt you," Jahx said, tears falling onto his cheeks. "I only wanted to help."

"Say what you are," Cam continued to scream, letting go of Jahx only to kick one of the stall doors off its hinges and bash down an empty shelf. "Say it!"

"I'm..." Jahx's lower lip quivered. His secret, terrible and damning, rested on the tip of his tongue. Fear and anxiety reddened his cheeks and sucked in his breath. "...I thought you always knew."

Cam cocked back his right fist and struck out. However, his blow landed next to the boy's head, breaking the mirror. The jolt of pain made him retract his hand back. But it was the shock of his image, fractured and bloodied, that stalled his second strike.

He didn't recognize himself. Pale skin, zig-zagging blue marks, sunken cheeks, hollowed eye sockets. *I'm not me...*

No, he had become something else. Something molded by war, pain, and suffering; something reborn in the need for revenge, pitiful and angry, uncontrolled. Someone Kara would not recognize as her brother—the very something Rogman had been trying to procure all along.

(No—end this,) the shadowed parts of him bade. *(There's no other way—)*

Cam shook out the mirror fragments in his right hand and remade his fist, blood squeezing out of the cuts. "You're a leech. You and your sisters."

Jahx did not move, tears sliding off his cheeks and wetting his uniform top.

"Say something," Cam said, kicking over a dusty rat trap and slapping his hand against a sink. Getting in Jahx's face again, he screamed. "Say something!"

"I'm not going to stop you," Jahx said, just above a whisper.

"Yeah, because you could," Cam said. "Twist my mind up, confuse me, fill me with your stupid sentiments. Or better yet, just get your sisters in here, make them do the dirty work."

"I'm not going to stop you," Jahx repeated, this time his voice calm, even.

Cam seethed, punching the mirror again with his left hand, leaving a gigantic crack right down the middle. "Why? Because I'm just some dumb rub? You don't think I could end you? Do you even know what I've done?"

"Yes."

His answered jarred him. Taking a step back, surprise rerouted his rant into a question: "You…do?"

"It was an accident," Jahx said, blue eyes focusing on something in the distance. He made a motion with his hands, as if he gripped the same scarf Cam did months ago. "You didn't mean for Colin to struggle, just go to sleep."

"How did you…?"

"Your dreams," Jahx whispered, bowing his head. "I'm sorry. I didn't mean to look."

"But if you knew, then why…?" He couldn't speak the rest of his question, fearing the answer. *Why would you still want to be my friend?*

Jahx brought up a hand to the base of his neck, tugging at a curl of hair. "Because you're not your past, and you're not this place."

"Then what am I?" he said, glancing again at his fractured image. "And what are you? Rogman's secret weapon?"

"No. Me and my sisters are just trying to survive, just like you."

"No—not like me," he said, revving up again. "I'm a *chakking* street rub. You and your sisters can do *anything.* So ice out, run away—"

"It's not that simple."

"Yes, it is," he said, kicking over another rat trap. "This Academy is lie. I've seen terrible things…" He stopped, afraid of what he might say, of what monsters he might bring to light.

254

(Iggie—)

(—Tomia...)

He clenched his jaw together. "Get out of here."

Jahx shook his head, fresh tears in his eyes. "I can't leave."

"Why?!"

Blue eyes darkened. "There's a bigger war coming; a war to end all wars. I have to be here, at least for now."

"What? Because that nun told you so?"

Jahx didn't correct him.

"That's crazy," Cam said, blood dripping off his knuckles to the floor. "What's your plan then? Take over the Dominion Fleet?"

Jahx shuddered. "I don't want to hurt anyone."

"Then you're a fool," Cam said. But he couldn't hold on to his anger, not as the dark-haired boy looked away, withdrawing into himself.

"You once told me you were afraid of the future," Cam said. Jahx didn't look up, but he continued anyway, "Make it yours. Don't let anybody tell you how's it's going to play out."

"And what does that mean to you? Killing your friend?" Jahx asked, finally looking up. Blue eyes could have bored through steel.

Cam gulped. "You don't understand..."

"No, I don't. Why do you want to kill me?"

"Because I know what you are..."

"What?"

"Limitless," Cam whispered. "And Rogman, that bloody, lying sack of *sycha,* can't have you for his war. Nobody can."

"That's not all, is it?"

Cam's throat tightened. "My family died because of leeches. I— I thought killing you would avenge my sister's death, my family."

"It's not over," Jahx said, plucking a shard of out of the remnants of broken mirror and offering it to Cam. "You can still end this."

Cam took the shard, holding the sharp edge away from himself, pointed at Jahx.

"If you really believe I'm a weapon—if you think that my death will avenge your family—then do it."

Squeezing the shard, the sharp edge bit into his palm and last two fingers, but he didn't let up, not even as fresh blood dripped onto the floor.

"Finish the job, kid," the old officer's gruff voice called out from memory. *"Go on. Before him or his friends come back and finish you."*

Jetta, Jaeia. If they came, he would be done for. And with their interconnectedness, he didn't see how they weren't there already, defending their brother and shredding Cam into pieces.

But as he lifted the mirror shard, blue eyes locking on to his, he remembered Jaeia's words: *"There's always a choice, even if you don't see it right away. Just look for it. Promise me."*

And Jetta's: *"Jahx was wrong about you."*

I'm not the monster, he tried to tell himself, guarding his choice with pain. But as he reared back his hand, his own sister's advice whispered out across his heart: *"This war, this misery; it can bring out the worst in people, Cam-cam… Don't let anybody make you forget who you really are."*

(But I don't know who that is—)

Not anymore. Not after losing everything, and everyone. Not after murdering Colin and destroying the last of his innocence. Not after realizing just how stupid and useless he was compared to the great young minds in the Academy, and abandoning all hope, all care for his own survival.

But looking at Jahx, at the boy who's smile could light a room, who's steady gaze and heartfelt answers warmed the coldest parts of him—

(Was it real?)

—the same boy who visited him in the infirmary, taught him biochem and gaming strategy—

(With his leech tricks!—)

—Who outwitted his teachers, destroyed his opponents in the Endgame—

(He could be the destroyer of worlds—)

—The same boy who understood his need to hoard food, kept his secrets—

"I'm glad you're here, Cam."

256

—who sought him out while everyone else avoided him in fear—

(Who hugged me—)

"Just hold out my love…"

"Go," he whispered, arm trembling, about to shoot forward. Tears pricked his eyes, slid down his face.

"…for blue sky tomorrows…"

"GO!"

Jahx ducked away, running out of the door just as Cam let go. Screaming, he threw the shard against the last of the shattered mirror, tiny bits exploding all around him.

What have I done?

Alone, he gripped the edge of the broken sink, bloody hands oozing into the bowl. He couldn't look at himself, at the monster. *At failure.*

Why he rinsed off his hands, plucking out the glass shards and leaving them in the sink, didn't make sense to him, not when he didn't matter anymore. But he didn't know what else to do, going as far to take off his uniform jacket and ripping up his undershirt to use as a bandage to staunch the bleeding.

He walked back to the barracks, not caring that the other cadets fled as soon as they saw his bloodied, bandaged hands; that Stempton and his gang whispered and chuckled as he passed them by, or that Jahx sat with his sisters in Jetta's bunk, all three of them staring at him with serious expressions, as if their brother had already spilled the horrors of what Cam had done. He didn't look at them, at anyone, as he crawled up into his bed, ripping off his uniform top and throwing it on the ground before curling up to face the wall.

Cold, but not wanting to pull the blanket up over his naked upper body, he shivered and stared into the flat gray paneling. It didn't matter if Stempton finally made his move, or if the triplets decided to end things first. Either way, his fate was certain, and if no one else came at him tonight, Rogman would finish things in the morning.

Mind blank, body throbbing, he tried to remember Kara's favorite song, tried to remember anything of home, of promise.

"Just hold out my love…" he said, pressing his fingers against the chilled metal, trying to remember the feel of her hand in his, the color of her eyes, or the sound of her voice. "For blue sky tomorrows."

Chapter 26

Dreams came in fitful waves of disjointed memories and imagined fears. In one moment, he lay paralyzed in a hospital bed, a machine monster with Naum's face lumbering down the dimmed hallway, pinchers and claws opening and shutting, excited for his vivisection. In the next, he stood at Rogman's side atop a hill made of skulls, surveying a dead world with lightning-streaked skies and ruined buildings.

"I was right about you," Rogman said, turning to him with a bloodied mouth and twitching mustache. "Now, look at all you've done."

But the worst, the one that made him cry out in the night, unfurled from the darkest depths of the unknown:

Cam stood outside his family's old house, looking through the bay window at the scene inside: His mother, carving up the game bird as his siblings and his father passed around the vegetable mix and the steaming pile of red potatoes. A fire crackled in the hearth, and an old-timey tune played over the radio. The laughter, the chatter, filled him with joy and longing, but as he ran to the front door and let himself in, everything—everyone vanished. Instead, he stood in the middle of a red and gray apartment with sagging walls and battered, overturned furniture. The stifling heat crushed down on him, making him pull off his jacket and gasp for breath in the thin atmosphere.

Where am I?

He didn't recognize this place. Light streamed through the boarded-up windows, and the heated air carried an odor of metal and must, like the inside of a mine.

"You should go."

Cam wheeled around to find the speaker. A small boy, frail and painfully thin, stood in the doorway out of the living room. At first

Cam didn't recognize him; the skeletal, bruised-up child before him looked one weakened heartbeat away from death. But his eyes, bluer than the vibrant shallows of the ocean, held the same kindness and compassion that already held his heart.

"Jahx?"

"You should go," he repeated, "before he returns."

I'm on Fiorah. *It took Cam a moment to understand his circumstances, to recall Jahx's fear, and the cruelty he suffered at home.* "You mean Yahmen?"

The boy shriveled up, going to his knees and making himself small inside the doorframe. "Go."

"Where are your sisters?" Cam tore around the doorway to the hallway. Three dirty cots lay in jumble, and pock marks and fresh stains in the dry wall testified of a recent fight. But not with his sisters. No, two little girls could not cause this much damage.

"Where are Jetta and Jaeia?" he asked again. "Where are your parents?"

Jahx stayed curled up in a ball, rocking back and forth.

Cam returned to Jahx, getting down on his knees and taking the boy's tiny hands. "I'll stay."

"You can't—he'll kill us."

"I don't care; I'm not leaving you."

The walls shook, the floor rumbled. Something—someone—was coming.

"Please, go," Jahx said, tears streaming down his face.

Cam put his arm around him and held the boy close. He understood pain, loss, and death, the bleakness of his own existence—but seeing Jahx, so tiny and fragile, all alone in his own insufferable world, pulled down whatever barriers he erected within himself, and muted the dark voice inside him.

"I'll stay," he said, squeezing the boy tight to his chest as someone beat on the front door, rattling it on its hinges. A howl followed, and a sick laugh.

Jahx pressed his head into his chest, tears soaking through Cam's shirt. "I'm sorry," the boy whispered, shaking from fear.

For what? *Cam didn't understand. For being small, helpless, and afraid? Or for Cam seeing the most furtive places in the boy's*

260

life, for the unbearable hurt that shaped his fears and elicited his deepest compassions.

As the plastic cracked and door broke open, Cam closed his eyes and buried his face into the boy's hair. "I'm sorry, too."

I should have believed your trust.

I'm so, so sorry, Jahx.

(I love you.)

A gigantic force barreled toward him, but Cam kept his arms around Jahx, shielding him with what little protection he could offer.

I won't let go. I won't let go—

When gruff hands pulled at the collar of his neck, he dared open his eyes. Death, red-eyed and reeking of booze, stared back.

Cam screamed.

Batting his hands and kicking his legs, Cam tried to ward off his attacker, but the mess of sheets restrained his efforts. He couldn't get away from the clobbering fists or the sharp snap of the belt against his back, but it didn't matter.

"Jahx…" he mumbled, "…run…"

Get away, he thought. *It's not too late—*

A hand rested on his back. The screams and the pain faded, receding back into the nightmarish depths.

"Thank you," a voice whispered.

Still emerging, Cam couldn't decipher reality from dream; if the hand that moved from his back to his shoulder, or the lips that pressed against his cheek in a soft, sweet kiss, originated from the same dark place.

Jahx?

He turned over, his eyes adjusting to the a.m. barrack lights, catching only a glimpse of spiky black hair and a flash of blue.

"Hey, wait—" Rubbing his face, he looked again, but found only the usual crop of kids milling around, some getting ready for class, others playing on their datapads.

"Jahx?" He swung his head and torso over his bunk and looked to the empty bed below.

"He left for the gaming strategy final. Aren't you in that class, too?" one of the kids said as he passed by, toothbrush sticking out of his mouth. When Cam looked at him, he hurried off.

261

Dazed, he didn't realize someone had folded and placed his uniform top at the end of the bed.

"*Chak,*" he muttered, seeing the sleeve flashing in red. At the end of his bed, the datapad, sticking out of its slot, blinked the same warning of a priority message.

Cam took out the datapad and opened the main menu. Forty-seven emails popped up, flagged for immediate notice. Words like *delinquent, failure to appear to class, test results under review,* stood out, but he didn't care to open any of them, even the priority message from the Commandant addressing his enrollment status. But as he thought to toss the datapad and lay back down and wait for his inevitable arrest and removal, he noticed the most recent email, no flags or notifications attached—and without any school tags.

An external email? Something like wasn't supposed to get through the filters. At first, he dismissed it as a prank, but then he saw the title: BLUE SKY TOMORROWS.

Breath caught in his chest, he stared at the email, not believing what he saw.

Not possible—

But he couldn't help himself. Checking left and right, he made sure that no other kid was watching as he lay back on his side facing the wall and clicked on the message. All of his excitement turned to confusion as he opened nothing but a blank page.

What is this? He looked at the sender, but the random numbers and letters didn't make any sense. Still, the email had to come from outside the academy. *But who would send me anything like this?*

"Move aside. Move!"

Cam flipped over as two soldiers, dressed head to toe in full battle gear, tromped down the barrack aisles, guns pressed to their chest. The other cadets stopped whatever they were doing, terrified or captivated. With black-faced helmets, mounted cameras, body armor and weapons strapped to each limb, their intimidating presence could only mean one thing.

Arrest.

The two soldiers stopped at the end of the aisle, by his bed. Speaking through the helmet mic, one of the soldiers addressed him: "Camzen Ferros—come with us."

This is it.

I'm finished.

He followed behind, shirtless, half-dressed in his uniform pants and boots.

"Finally," Stempton snickered as he walked past. He flashed a datachip in his hand and added: "getting rid of the trash."

Cam thought about popping him, about getting one good last lick in, but the idea dissolved as fast as it appeared. No, a bully like Stempton would get his. And violence, as much as it shaped and warped his world, could not save him now.

Rogman waited for him at the barrack entrance, talking with Professor Rotu in hushed tones.

"Please, Commandant—we should reexamine these results—"

But as Cam approached, Rogman raised his arm to silence the professor. "You are dismissed."

Rotu walked away, but not after offering Cam a pained smile.

"Ferros," Rogman said, upturning his lips in a sneer.

When he didn't answer right away, one of the soldiers grabbed him by the upper arm until he stood up straight and addressed the Commandant. "Sir."

"Who are you, if not the vicious killer?" he said, hands clasped behind his back.

Cam looked down, at his boots.

"Have you vetted any leeches? Have you anything to keep me from sending you to Plaly IV?"

The Labor Locks?! He thought he'd just be sent back to Cerka, to some overcrowded orphanage—not thrown into slavery on a desolate planet in the middle of nowhere.

"Yes, now you understand. Cheating on the biochem test is enough to get you expelled—as is putting Tran Su in the ICU. But conspiring with leeches is a criminal offense," Rogman said, mustache twitching. "So—what you have to say for yourself?"

A lifetime of forced labor. A sentence of pain and isolation, worse than death itself.

"I saw you at my side, boy, conquering worlds, slaying savages, bringing order to all that are beneath us," Rogman said, bending down to meet him at eye level. "You are a disappointment to me. Another gutter rat, wretched and disposable. You are nothing."

263

The hand on his upper arm tightened, shook, but Cam didn't give any indication of how much it hurt him. Instead, he looked Rogman in the eye, letting go of whatever anger and pain he'd clung to over the last few months. "No leeches, sir. I was wrong."

"You were wrong?"

He lowered his head again.

"Then you are useless. Take him away."

After cuffing his hands behind his back, the soldier holding his arm redirected him to a lift hovering in the hallway, waiting to take them away.

No one spoke to him, the soldiers staying close as they traveled down one long hallway after the next. Some part of him hoped to see a familiar face—

Iggie. Tomia.

(Jahx—)

—one last time.

"Where are you taking me?" he asked as they exited the student-accessible areas.

"Keep quiet," the soldier holding his arm ordered. Cam didn't suspect anything at first, but as they bypassed into the security zones, the soldiers flashing their passkeys into the scanners, something nettled at his conscious mind. One of the soldiers shifted back and forth between his feet. The other, checking behind them at regular intervals.

Something's not right.

Cam tried to look back, but one of the soldiers pressed his gun into his back. "Mind yourself."

As they approached a security checkpoint station in front of red-painted hangar doors, his stomach knotted.

This is happening so fast—

Flight information ran across digital departure and arrival boards, as engines rumbled in the distance. But as he looked for which ship would carry him to Plaly IV, the checkpoint guard motioned them to his location.

"What are you doing with this one?" the checkpoint guard asked, looking Cam up and down as their lift slowed in front of his station. "Iced out?"

"Immediate transfer."

"Did he go through checkout?" the guard asked, pointing at his bare chest. "He should be in a jumpsuit."

"This is an immediate transfer," the soldier repeated.

The checkpoint guard accessed he terminal embedded in his semi-circular control station. "I don't have any transfers on my list today. What's his name?"

Behind him, the second soldier muttered, "now, Rex."

"I'm going to call this in," the checkpoint guard said, but as he moved his hand over the com, his eyes shot wide open.

What's happening to him?

Eyes bugging out of his head, the guard hunched over, a half-smile propping up one side of his drooping mouth.

"Thanks for your help," the soldier holding his arm said as the other prompted the lift forward.

The guard muttered something unintelligible as the second soldier leaned over and typed in the commands for the hangar doors to part.

What just happened? Cam thought, unable to reconcile why the checkpoint guard giggled and purred, pawing at some imaginary thing in front of him as they passed into the docks without proper clearance.

"We're almost there," the soldier holding him said as the second steered the lift around a docking bay full of mid-sized Dominion starships.

We're almost where? The soldier's tone and inflection sounded less like a command and more like an affirmation.

As they came upon the last starship in the bay, a beat-up transport with a faded Dominion insignia and a rusted com dish, he pulled at the handcuffs, trying to slide them off his wrists.

"Calm down, it's going to be okay," the soldier holding him said, loosening his grip on his arm.

"No—this isn't right," he said, fighting his grip.

"Cam-cam. It's going to be okay," the soldier repeated.

Cam-cam? Only his sister ever called him that. The soldier flipped up his visor. Familiar eyes, blue as glacier lake, stared back, even offering him a wink.

Are these assinos chakking *with me?*

265

But as he thought to fight, he remembered those eyes, attached to a handsome face with a serious expression—

The man standing underneath the rectangular window in the utility room basement of the apartment complex, a canvas backpack slung over his shoulder, holding one of the straps with a fingerless glove—

The one from the alleyway, conversing with his sister—

"…James?" he whispered.

"Go on," the soldier holding him said, thrusting his gun in his back to get him off the lift and onto the weathered transport. Cam stumbled up the ramp, confused and scared, not sure if he should run or—

"Jeez, you didn't have to keep him in cuffs." A dark-haired woman in an old Dominion uniform stood at the top of the ramp, opening her arms in welcome as she admonished the soldiers following right behind him. She also looked familiar, but it was her voice, calm and soothing, that sparked some memory just beyond his grasp.

As soon as the ramp came up and the seal secured, both soldiers removed their helmets.

"Get us out of here," the blonde-haired man said, calling up to the pilot in the front.

"You are James," Cam said as the second soldier released his handcuffs.

"I am."

"You *assino*," he screamed, charging at the Dominion soldier.

"It's not what you think," James said, holding him off with the help from the other two.

"You betrayer! You killed my sister!" he said, clawing at his face.

"He's too strong," the woman shouted as Cam bucked against their hold.

"Gods, I can't hold him—"

Cam wrenched forward, but James ducked his swing. The sudden movement off-balanced the other two holding on to him, and he pitched forward, head-first into the grated floor.

"Cam? Cam? Come on, buddy—stay awake."

266

He tried to push himself up, but the strength left him as he sunk lower, black motes crowding his vision.

"*Chak,* Niks—"

Niks. He'd heard that name before.

But as he tried to keep hold of himself, to stay conscious as someone applied pressure to the fresh split across his forehead, he realized something terrible: *Is there a reason to fight?*

Not anymore.

Not with everything lost, with all hope vanquished.

Still, he couldn't help but hold on to his one truth: *I didn't give you up, Jahx.*

And with a bittersweet smile, he closed his eyes.

Chapter 27

Cam woke in the bottom bunk of a four-person sleeping compartment dressed in gray sleepwear. Lights, dimmed to their minimal setting, illuminated the other empty beds.

Where am I? He remembered being boarded onto an old Dominion transport, and the two strangers that looked and sounded all-too familiar. As he pushed himself up, he noticed his hands, the cuts healed, and even the deformity on his right hand smoothed out into normal bone.

No—

Touching his forehead, his fingers brushed the unblemished skin near his hairline. *How is that possible?* None of his injuries should have healed that quickly—

Unless I've been out for weeks—

Panicked, he rushed to the door and furiously tapped the control panel until it slid open. As he ran into the main chamber of the transport, he came to a halt. The two soldiers, the woman he'd seen in the Dominion uniform, and several others sat around the circular conference table, going over internal schematics. At first, he recognized the schematics—

The Academy—

Incomplete, but showing parts he recognized, including some of the student areas and the teacher's wing.

Then, he realized that none of them wore Dominion uniforms anymore. Instead, they wore a mix of civilian clothing and USC fatigues.

The blonde-haired man cleared his throat and addressed both Cam, and the woman that sat to his right.

"I thought he wasn't going to be up for a while."

"He shouldn't be," she muttered, then got up. "Hello, Cam. I'm sure you have a lot of questions."

"Who the hell are you people?"

She continued, gentle and unrushed. "What's most important is that you're safe. We're friends. We came to rescue you. We got your message."

"My message?" He shook his head. "What are you talking about?"

"Let's start from the beginning. My name is Niks, I'm one of the medical staff on the rescue team," the woman said, introducing herself, and then turning to the others. "This is James, our lead."

The blonde-haired man gave him salute. "I'm a friend of Kara's," he affirmed.

But when Cam tried to argue, Niks continued:

"Rex, part of medical team and support staff," she said, pointing to the tattooed woman sitting in a relaxed fashion in her chair. Her eyes, a striking orange-fire, jolted an old memory.

"You... You were on Cerka," Cam said, touching the old break in his arm. "You helped me when I was hurt."

"Both Niks and I," she answered back coolly.

"Azzi, our pilot," Niks said, nodding to the mammoth, broad-shouldered man peeking out of the cockpit. He gave a friendly wave before resuming his duty.

"And that's Almos, one of our special mission ops members and consultant," she said, pointing to the other man sitting on a flipped-around chair. The craggily-faced soldier gave him a nod, then went back to working a toothpick between the gaps in his teeth.

"Who are you with?" he asked, eyeing for any potential weapons in his reach.

"The United Starways Coalition," Niks replied.

"But this is a Dominion ship—"

"Stolen Dominion ship. Along with everything else," James said, pointing to a row of opened lockers with the battle gear and armor hanging on the hooks at the far end of the main chamber.

"I promise we're USC," Niks said. "Same as your sister."

Cam scoffed. "My sister wasn't part of the..." He stopped, unsure of himself, then shook his head. "No, Kara wouldn't join with the enemy."

"Enemy? Who do you think your enemy is in all this?" Rex said.

Cam didn't know what to say. After his experiences in the Dominion Academy, he understood true terror, violation—but the USC harbored and protected telepaths, his ultimate enemy—

Then it struck him. "What was this message you got?"

"A coded email from inside the Academy net letting us know you'd survived Cerka," James explained. "Not many details. Just these schematics," he said, pointing to the holographic display in the center of the table, "and your student signature so we could track your status."

"Well, and one more thing," Niks added, pulling up the original file.

Cam looked it over, noting the brevity of the alert, but at the very bottom, an attached image of a blue sky and a yellow sun shining in the middle.

"Blue skies…" he whispered.

"Yes, that's how we knew it was real," Niks said.

"What do you mean?"

"Sometimes the Dominion will dispense out false information, but we were able to tie the image to something personal about you."

"You knew about that stupid song?"

The others looked back and forth at each other.

"What? Tell me!"

Finally, James spoke up. "I heard your sister sing it to you in the utility room."

But who else knew—and who else could have had the knowledge base, the resources, and the skill to send that message?

The memory washed over him with fresh meaning: *"Alright, well, if you do crack that thing—and don't get your assino caught— try and get me an early discharge,"* Cam had said.

Blue eyes, a bright smile, shone back at him. "Haha, okay."

He remembered Jahx's warm touch as he reached out and closed his hand over Cam's, lingering for a moment. "Thanks, Cam."

"Jahx…"

He'd given Reppen's datapad to him. With only a 5% charge, Jahx would have had to work fast, with intent—for whatever he deemed most important.

My rescue.

He could have saved himself, his sisters—he could have spared himself the pain of what was to come, of Rogman's vicious intentions, of whatever wicked plans the Dominion Core had for him.

But he saved me.

A nothing kid, a boy who would never command armies or lead worlds. *Why?*

"Who's Jahx?" James asked.

Cam cleared his throat, finding his voice unreliable. But as he dared speak the truth, a feeling, one that he'd all but forgotten, gushed forth, putting a smile on his face. "My friend."

"That's a good friend," James said, pointing to the schematics. "And a smart one. Knew exactly what to send us on a limited file so he wouldn't get caught."

"Yeah, he's pretty smart," Cam said. "But we have to help him—we can't let him stay there. Him and his sisters. Bad things are happening in the Academy."

"Like what?" Niks asked.

As he told them of the disappearing cadets, of the tags on certain kids' profiles, none of them reacted. Not until he mentioned one name.

"...and Dr. Naum—he was the worst. He put this thing inside my forearm," he said, holding up his left arm and tapping on the rectangular implant beneath his skin.

"Naum?" Rex and Niks exclaimed in unison.

James stood up abruptly and walked over to Cam. At first, he thought he did something wrong, but James got down on one knee and took him by the hands. "This Dr. Naum—what did he look like?"

Cam described the surgeon in detail, including the description of his burn scars.

"*Jida'da,*" Rex cursed in her native tongue, running her hand through her blue hair.

"Was a nurse there—beaked nose, stout, named Maio Kull?" Niks asked, joining James' side.

Cam nodded.

"What about an officer named Rogman?" Rex asked.

"The Commandant," Cam nodded. "Yeah."

271

"Jesus—they all survived," James muttered, putting a palm to his forehead.

"No. Naum and nurse Kull are dead," he said, hanging his head.

"Dead? Are you sure?"

"Yes," he whispered. "I… I killed them."

Silence fell over the room.

"In self-defense?" Niks asked, as if she wanted to believe his response before he answered.

"Y-yes."

James regripped his arms and looked him dead in the eye. "Naum and Kull were bad people."

"Naum was *chakking* evil," Rex chimed in.

"I can guarantee that Naum was behind all those terrible things you describe," James said. "What you did probably averted a bigger crisis."

"Yes," Niks added, taking Cam's left arm and running her finger over the implant hiding beneath his skin, "nothing could be worse than what he planned."

No, there's something worse than Naum…

Thinking of the machine monster, Cam's heart raced, his tongue sticking to the roof of his mouth. As much as he wanted to tell them about his nightmares, about the terrible visions in the infirmary, he feared sounding insane, that his truth would be dismissed, that he would be labeled a liar. Worse yet, that he could be right.

And Jahx stayed behind.

"Can we go back?" he asked, trying to run up to the cockpit. James held him fast, not letting him go. "We have to go back. We have to help the others—"

"We can't, Cam," James said. "We used up this ship's ID in that rescue. We can't pull the same trick twice."

"But we have to go back," he begged. "I can't leave Jahx—I can't leave my friend—"

"Shhh," Niks said, holding him with James. "It will be okay. This isn't over. We've still got a lot of fight left in all of us."

Cam wiggled his way out of their hold as he realized something new, something frightening. "If you're with the USC—and my sister was with the USC…" He sucked in his breath, body shaking. "Then…?"

"The Dominion told you about the 'laws of retaliation, didn't they?" James said, discerning his train of thought.

Cam nodded.

"The Dominion lies. I thought you figured that out," Rex interjected.

"Some things are too important to believe are possible," he said, breath hitching.

"Well, Camzen Ferros," James said, standing and leading him to the table. Switching over the holographic projector, he pulled up the nav chart. From what little Cam understood of the lighted projection, one more jump would put them within orbit of a blue and green planet. "It's time for you to go home."

Epilogue

Cam knew. He saw it in the light of each of his rescuers' eyes, in the way they withheld the most wonderful secret so that he would experience the surprise and joy in full. But as Azzi landed their stolen Dominion transport on the Cerkan launch pad, he doubted himself, in the fragile hope that held up his heart, as he stood at the top of the ramp, waiting for it to descend.

She's dead. She's gone. It can't be real. Kara is—

"Cam!"

Early morning light flooded up the ramp, stinging his eyes. But he forced them open, to see her beaming face as she crutched up the ramp and took him in her arms.

"Cam-Cam!" Kara cried, squeezing him tight. He didn't care how much it hurt, how his ribs and shoulders ached, how his skin tingled.

"You're alive?" he said as she backed off for a second to take him in.

"Of course I am," she said, touching his cheek, tears in her eyes.

Will she see my scars? Would she see the monster he'd become?

"You're just as handsome as ever, sweet boy," she said, kissing his forehead. "I love you so much."

"Kara," he said, holding her tight. "I'm so sorry…"

"For what, my love?"

"For not being strong enough," he whispered, not wanting the others, even as they descended the ramp to give them their privacy, to hear his admission. "I couldn't save Mom or the twins—I couldn't help you—I—"

She picked up his chin with her fingers. "You're the bravest, strongest person I know."

"What happened to you?" he said, pointing to her bruised eyes, the cuts on her face, and her injured leg.

"Just a couple scratches from my last mission," she said, standing on one leg and waving her crutch. "Though everyone made a bigger deal out of it than necessary. I should have been able to get you myself."

"But you're here," he said, wrapping his arms around her neck again.

"And so are you."

Kara lead him back down the ramp, to the USC base camp set up in the Cerkan countryside. Temporary housing units constructed of wood, rocks and military supplies, tented command centers, and mobile communications units poked out from the grasslands and swaying oakleaf trees.

"Where are we?" he asked, watching as USC vipers streaked the cloud-studded sky.

"Safe. Halfway around the world," she explained. "We're still fighting to take back our city. But don't worry, we'll win."

Niks, Rex, and a man in a doctor's coat intercepted them, taking Kara aside for a moment.

"He needs to be tested—at the very least screened," the man said, adjusting his spectacles. "Who knows what the Dominion did to him."

"No tests," she said, turning away. Niks and Rex tried to reason with her, but she took Cam by the hand and directed him inside a tent at the end of a long row.

"Kara?" he said, taking a seat on the cot.

"Don't worry," she said, sitting next to him and cupping his cheek. "I won't let anyone harm you ever again."

As they caught up, talking back and forth so fast that Cam would have to start over, or Kara would have to interrupt him to ask for more details, the early morning hours turned to the late afternoon. After the second soldier asked for Kara's presence in the command center for a debriefing, she put a hold on their conversation.

"Look, I gotta go. But I have to know one thing," she said, studying his face. "Why'd you protect him?"

"Jahx?"

275

"Yes. You didn't hurt him in the lavatory—and you lied to Rogman."

Cam nodded.

"…And you really hated telepaths. What changed your mind?"

Embarrassed, but not knowing why, he rubbed his neck with one of his hands and stared at his knees. "He never hurt me. He could have, but he never did, even when I lashed out. I don't think Jahx could ever harm another person, not even when it meant his life. I had to protect him. He's… good."

Kara smiled. "Sounds like it. Especially if he risked everything to save you."

"That's just it," Cam said, fighting for each word. "Why did he do that? I'm nothing. I'm just a rub."

"Just a rub?" Kara exclaimed. "You scored in the top 30% of the academy cadets—most of whom are elitist, privileged brats from the interior. And from what Jahx sent in your profile, you got an 86% on your biochem final. That's pretty *chakking* impressive for a kid with no biochem background *at all*."

"What?"

"What do you mean 'what'?"

"But Rogman told me—I thought I failed—I wasn't good enough—"

"Stop it." Kara grabbed hold of his head with both hands and looked into his eyes. "All of that is crap anyway. You're Cam. Don't you understand that? Your life has meaning, and your every action, however small you may think it is, reaches out across the stars. You must have been very special to Jahx for him to do what he did. I think you have a bigger effect on him than you think."

"Have?" he said, holding on to her arm as she tried to get up.

"Well, this isn't over," she said, pointing out to the tankers rolling across the yellow grasses. "The USC will fight until all telepaths are freed. We can still help Jahx."

We can still help Jahx.

Kara kissed the top of his head. "Stay here—don't leave the tent. I'll be back in an hour."

Half-listening, he muttered an "okay."

"Seriously, Cam. Stay here," she said, wagging a finger as she tucked the crutch underneath her armpit. "For real this time."

276

I can still help Jahx.

Waiting an agonizing five minutes, he peeked outside of the tent flap to make sure his sister was nowhere in sight before sneaking off down one of the hills, to a quiet spot near a cluster of boulders. Climbing to the top of one of the flattened rocks, he laid down, and looked to the sky. He thought of all the times he felt helpless, that his life had no meaning, no impact, realizing how short-sighted he'd been.

Jahx, he said, letting his mind go, reaching out across the stars. Staring out into the open skies, to the infinite beyond, he thought of his favorite memories, of Kara's song, of the love in his life, of all that he treasured, and projected it outward. For his friend. For all the moments Jahx might need something to hold on to, to believe in, in his darkest hours. *For blue sky tomorrows...*

***

The adventure continues in: Triorion: Awakening (Book One)

www.triorion.com

Acknowledgements

This is my ninth novel, and by far the hardest book I've written. From personal health challenges to the dark content of this story, I had a difficult time telling Cam's truths, and exploring his reality in a war-torn universe. Many of my own struggles came out in this work, and even though I feel each book I've written is an extension of my heart and mind, this really exhumed old demons from long past, and revealed the gravity some of my current, more acute trials.

I could not have finished this book if it weren't for my some of my favorite fans: Derek, Ericka, Kellie, Regan, David Christopher, Elle, Cory, Justin, Steve, Steph, Gina, Will, Miya, Kaci—you all are freakin' amazing. And of course, big thanks to my family, my dearest, most patient and supporting wife, my author and artist community, my work family and work wife, my friends from back home, my soccer family, my martial arts family, my music buddies—all the wonderful and lovely people in my life that have held me up and kept me going during this tough 2017-2018 stretch.

But I need to mention two people in particular that made this book possible. Their acts of kindness, though they perceive them as small, meant so much to me, and truly shaped the outcome of more than this book. Noelle—thanks for being there for me no matter what the hour, even when I'm being stubborn and ridiculous. Yuko—I don't know how you are so amazing *all the time*. You have no idea what a wonderful impact you've had both me and my wife. You both have my loyalty and friendship for life.

And finally, to "the real" Cam: Thank you for being brave enough to tell me your story, and to share your secrets.

About the Author

Author L.J Hachmeister writes and fights—though she tries to avoid doing them at the same time. The WEKAF world champion stick-fighter is best known in the literary world for her epic science fiction series, *Triorion*, and her equally epic love of sweets. Connect with her at: www.triorion.com

Made in the USA
Columbia, SC
29 September 2021